Stolen Moments

LESLIE ANN

Editing by: Nina Fiegl
Cover Design by: Echo at Wildheart Graphics
Formatting by: Leslie Ann

Playlist

It's You—Ali Gatie
Crush—Tessa Violet
IDK You Yet—Alexander 23
Fresh Eyes—Andy Grammer
Butterflies (feat. FLETCHER) —MAX
Can I kiss you? —Dahl
Into You—Ariana Grande
Primetime (feat. Miguel) —Janelle Monáe
Fallin' all in you—Shawn Mendes
Heaven—Bazzi
Coast (feat. Anderson.Paak) —Hailee Steinfeld
Feel Like This—Ingrid Andress
I'm In Love With You—The 1975
Be Right There—Fly By Midnight
7 Minutes—Dean Lewis
Thick And Thin—LANY
Come Back...Be Here (Taylor's Version) —Taylor Swift
If I Didn't Love You—Jason Aldean, Carrie Underwood
I Wish You Would (Taylor's Version) —Taylor Swift
When Your Gone—Shawn Mendes
Falling—Harry Styles
Hate My Heart—Carrie Underwood
Back to December (Taylor's Version) —Taylor Swift

After We Broke Up (feat. Frawley) —David J
I Miss You, I'm Sorry—Gracie Abrams
Missing Piece—Vance Joy
Get The Girl—Seaforth
Can't Get Enough Of Your Love, Babe—Jason Morales
My Love will Follow You—Dave Barnes
Tenerife Sea—Ed Sheeran
How You Get The Girl (Taylor's Version) —Taylor Swift
Fall Into Me—Forest Blakk
My Person—Spencer Crandall
That Part—Lauren Spencer Smith
Worth the Wait—Spencer Crandall
Only You—Selena Gomez

Find the full Spotify Playlist here.

Dedication

This one's for you C.

ONE

Mason

OCTOBER

I COLLAPSE ONTO THE empty barstool, the tension in my head incrementally growing with every thought running through my head. Pressing my fingers into the sides of my temples, I attempt to ease the building pain by closing my eyes and taking a deep breath. It does little to dull the throbbing.

"What can I get you?"

My eyes snap open at the near voice.

The bartender, a big dude with graying temples, throws a towel over his shoulder, and places his palms on the bar, waiting for me to give him my order.

"Gin and Tonic with lime. Hendricks if you got it. Please," I add, not forgetting my manners. I might be a grumpy asshole, but I would never treat someone disrespectfully. Especially someone making my drinks or food. My dad taught me better, and he would kick my ass if I was disrespectful.

"Coming right up." The bartender acknowledges my order with a slap at the deep oak countertop before getting to work on my cocktail, leaving me to my thoughts.

My cell phone buzzes in my pocket. Retrieving it, I slide it open and start going through the overwhelming number of messages from my team.

While everything looks to be on track for the TechSec Summit my team and I are attending in Silicon Valley this weekend, there's still a lot to be done. It will be our first speaking presentation since we introduced the new code we'd created in the securities sector. Our latest breakthrough in multi-layered verification helps decrease and prevent identity theft and fraud at a banking level.

Tech security was never something I thought I would go into, but I became interested after my college buddy, Kenzo, became a victim. It took us weeks to track down the hacker who stole his identity and emptied his bank account. After that, the two of us dug deep into the coding world trying to perfect a banking software to prevent this kind of thing from happening to other people.

"Let me know if you need anything else." The bartender places my drink in front of me and walks away, leaving me grateful for his silence.

I'm not in the mood to be chatty.

I place my phone on the distressed wood bar top and take a swig of my drink. Damn, it's perfect. I take a moment to let the alcohol do its job. I'm in desperate need of help to take the edge off.

Work has been hectic since we went freelance and the demand for our software has taken off. It's been great for the team, but lately, work has left me ... unfulfilled. Like something's missing from my life.

I close my eyes, trying to pinpoint when this sense of emptiness began popping up. My mind jumps to Rhys, my nephew.

I shake my head and take another swig of my drink.

Since Rhys entered the picture, my ordinarily work-filled life seems lackluster and incomplete. My oldest brother, Jace, moved up here to Oregon to be with the love of his life, Rylann, and her son Rhys. They reconnected—again—while on vacation, and since, Jace has been the happiest I've ever seen him. Without a glance back, he left his fast-paced city days behind him to become a small-town go-with-the-flow do-gooder.

Okay, he was always a do-gooder, but I'm his little brother. It's my job to give him hell. In all seriousness, though, I'm happy for him. Rylann is beautiful, funny, kind, and an incredible mother. She adores Rhys and worships the ground Jace walks on. This time around, my brother couldn't have found a better person to spend his life with.

I love to come up here and visit them, especially Rhys. He's by far the coolest kid on the planet, and spending time with him is always a great time. He's such a good kid, always up for anything, and goes with the flow—a true testament to Rylann's impeccable parenting. We share a love of soccer and usually end up kicking the ball around, playing his soccer video game, and going on hikes. He's my little dude.

I like to think I'm by far his favorite uncle—something I love to say to mess with Eli and Cameron, my other two brothers. Those two have more demanding jobs that keep them tied up more often than not. Eli works in the entertainment industry and Cameron is a pitcher for the Evaders, one of Los Angeles's Major League Baseball (MLB) teams. Unlike them, I have more flexibility and can work from anywhere, as long as I have my laptop.

I spent the last day and a half driving up from Los Angeles with Jace. He rented a truck to haul the last of his things up here, and I hitched a ride with him for fun. It's going to be strange living in L.A. without him, now that Pine Hills—a small town outside of Portland—is his official residence. I'm going to miss having him close by, but he's been eager to be with his family and start his life with them, and I don't blame him one bit.

An uncomfortable pang hits me in the gut. Is that jealousy?

I hate to admit it, but maybe I am a little envious that my brother has found his person. Jace is planning on proposing tonight. He and Rhys forced me to help decorate their patio with flowers and lights as a surprise for Rylann, while she was out with her best friend, Scarlett.

I look at the clock. I'd bet anything he's on one knee as I sit here alone with my drink, watching the condensation bead and roll down the side of my glass. I wish I could have stayed to celebrate but work calls.

Selfish workaholic.

The caustic words still sting, even after all this time.

I take another drink, savoring the combination of citrus and floral flavors, pushing the burning feeling in my chest down—something I've become exceedingly good at. No one, aside from Cameron, knows about the dent in my ego.

My cell buzzes in my hand with an incoming video call from Jace. I hit accept, and Rhys's face fills the screen.

"Mom said yes!!" he screams, grinning ear to ear.

I wince at the high-pitched squeal in my earbud, but his happy face has me matching his grin.

I knew Rylann would say yes. She is head over heels for my brother.

"That's awesome, bud. She liked your surprise?"

"Uh-huh, Mom was so surprised." He bounces his head up and down like a bobblehead, making me laugh.

My eyes shift away from the phone, and my heart stalls in my chest before beating double time. An inexplicable feeling washes over me as I stare at the reflection in the mirror above the bar.

The most beautiful woman I have ever seen is standing directly behind me, unaware of my presence. Every hair on the back of my neck stands on end as I take in the striking beauty. Something about her calls to me on a base level I can't describe.

She cocks her hip—jacket folded over her arm, a rolling suitcase at her side—and shakes her head. It appears as though she's talking on the phone, and while she seems quite agitated and angry, I can't help but notice how painfully gorgeous she is.

She has these big brown eyes that shine like two topaz gemstones and warm, tawny, beige-colored skin that demands to be worshiped. Her taller-than-average height suits her, as do the curves she has in all the right places. Her long golden brown hair falls over her shoulders in waves, and the uncontrollable urge to wrap the silky strands around my fist hits me ... and my dick, causing it to twitch in my pants.

Fuck me, she's stunning.

I can't hear her, only watch as her thick red lips move seductively over the words she's speaking. I'd give anything to see if they feel as soft as they look.

"Uncle Mills? Did you hear me?"

My eyes fall back to my phone, Rhys's voice finally bringing me out of my lust-filled fog.

I'm still getting used to being called Uncle Mills. Rhys came up with it because he said my nickname, Mase, sounds too much like his mom's nickname for Jace. I don't disagree. I've heard her use the nickname in a way that makes even my cheeks blush.

"Sorry, Rhys. Can you repeat that? It's loud in the airport."

"I said we're going to have a party at Grammy's house for Christmas. But will you still come to my holiday performance? Even though I'll get to spend Christmas with you anyway?"

Damn, he melts my heart. All he wants is for me to spend time with him. Lucky for him, I'll never say no. I will always have his back.

"Of course, I will. Have your mom text me the details, okay?"

"Okay. Thank you, Uncle Mills."

I chuckle at his relieved expression. He's nervous about singing in front of all the parents—something we have in common.

Commanding the conference room? No problem.

Singing in front of large groups? Fucking torture.

Unlike my brothers, I prefer to slip into the background and observe.

Speaking of ... I look for the woman who captured my attention, my head swiveling left to right. She's gone. Evaporated into thin air.

Damn.

"Yo, Mase!"

Jace's and Rylann's beaming faces appear on the screen.

"Congratulations, you two."

"Thank you, Mills." The endearment slips off Rylann's tongue with sweetness and sass, making me chuckle. "For everything."

I'm still getting used to being called Uncle Mills, but I must admit, I kind of love it. It solidifies the special bond I feel like Rhys and I are building. I couldn't be happier that he's joined the Miller crew. "You're welcome."

"Fly safe. Oh! And don't forget to text when you get there." She's got the mom tone down to a T.

"I will." Rylann dips out of view with a nod, leaving me with Jace.

"Wish you could have stayed to celebrate," he grumbles.

"Me too. It sounds like there will be a big Miller bash this Christmas to celebrate." I lift my drink into view to toast the happy couple.

"Celebrate, we will. Thanks again, bro. I couldn't have done all this without you. I heard Rhys ask about the school performance and I'll send you the details later. It means a lot to us that here for him."

"Wouldn't miss it. He's my guy. Congrats again. I'll let you two get back to celebrating."

"Thanks, Mase."

"Don't forget, Mills," Rylann shouts in the background.

"I know, I know, Momma Ry. Text when I land." I salute my goodbyes to the phone and end the call.

I finish my drink and drop a twenty on top of the bar. Standing up from the stool, I take another look around, hoping for another glimpse of the stunning creature that made my heart stop.

"Looking for the brunette?" the bartender asks, eyebrow arched.

My hackles rise. I don't like that this guy has also noticed her.

What the fuck is that all about?

I take a deep breath and nod.

"I see her around often. Orders an Aperol Spritz every time and never utters a word. Unless she's arguing on the phone." He shrugs before walking off.

I don't know whether to be impressed that this guy remembers his customers or annoyed that he noticed her. This feeling in my gut says the latter. She's not for him to be looking at. Only me.

What?

I shake off my unease and that unexpected thought. I don't know where that came from, but what scares me the most and sends my stomach sinking is...

What if I never see her again?

TWO

Emery

DECEMBER

"Chris, please," I whine into the screen.

He vehemently shakes his head, his handsome face solemn. "Nope. No way. I'm done."

"You promised."

"*Liar,*" he hisses, pointing at me.

I am lying, but I don't want to spend the holidays without my baby brother again. I hate being away from him as it is.

My shoulders drop in defeat. I knew I would never win this fight with him.

"Fine. I'll go by myself," I whine again.

"Why are we even having this conversation? You're coming here to have a *real* Christmas before you leave me for the wasps we know as our bio parents. Same as last year—that was the deal. I told you, I'm not going back just so they belittle me or pretend I don't exist. I am not a second-class citizen, and I won't let them treat me like that anymore. Neither should you, Emmy. Our so-called parents can stop paying my tuition for all I care. I'll figure it out. My scholarship covers some stuff anyway."

I huff at his response. I never should have brought up going back east for the holiday. While he is right about his scholarship, he's wrong about who really pays for his tuition. I do, and it's a sacrifice I'd do a million times over to protect him and help him fulfill his dream of becoming a movie director. But he doesn't need to know that or how our parents are—yet again—a complete letdown.

They have been since Chris turned sixteen and brought his first boyfriend home for dinner. When he came out as pansexual, that was the end for my uptight parents. They couldn't let Chris tarnish their precious image with his—their words—outlandish and flamboyant personality.

Jerks.

Chris is a unicorn. The whole freaking package. He's incredibly smart, funny, kind, and creative, and I wouldn't change a single thing about him because he's that special.

Sinclair and Cybil Rhodes, however, disagreed and immediately shipped Chris off to a boarding school outside of Portland. "Out of sight, out of mind" should be their motto.

Since then, my relationship with them has been strained. They broke my heart the day they turned their backs on him. I'll never understand how my parents could have so easily pushed him aside, like he was an inconvenience they'd rather not deal with. He's their son, and it pisses me off when they act like Chris doesn't exist.

I'm eight years older, but it has always felt like my job to take care of him. Protect and love him. Chris and I spent one semester apart before I graduated from University of New York (UNY) and moved across the country to be near him. My parents might be heartless assholes, but I'm not. I love my brother more than anything. He's my best friend, and as his big sister, it's my duty to do anything I can to ensure he lives his best life. Case in point, his tuition.

My brother is currently attending Los Angeles California University's (LACU) film school, and I am beyond proud of him. He's super dedicated to his educational and career path. If he knew the truth about where the money came from, he'd be so angry I'd never hear the end of it. I have more than enough to deal with where our mother and father are concerned, let alone having Chris up my ass. He needs to concentrate on school. Worrying about what I'm doing to keep him there is the last thing he needs.

"You're right. I'm done bugging you about it. You don't have to come," I admit.

"That's not what I told the hot guy at the club when I was sucking his dick in the bathroom. My knees were killing me, and he was taking too long to blow. Whiskey dick is real, Em. It's a travesty, I tell you," Chris jokes.

Leave it to my brother to say something inappropriate while he's on speaker.

I jump to lower the volume on my cell, annoyed that I forgot my earbuds at home. I almost sprung for a new pair in the vending machine, but I couldn't do it. Spending money on new ones when I have a perfectly good pair at home is a waste.

Of course, my crazy-ass brother has to prove me wrong. I should have spent the money.

"Oh, gawd. Really, Chrisy?" I hide my face from view. Last I checked, I was alone, hiding in the back of the airport café waiting for my flight to Los Angeles.

I'm spending the week of Christmas with Chris before heading to our parents' estate for their annual New Year party. I only called to remind Chris to pick me up from the airport because he can be flighty and forgetful when he's working on a project, and as usual, it turned into a full-blown conversation about everything from his latest breakup, then hookup—to get over said breakup—to complaining about our parents.

"I told you not to call me that. And don't hate on me just because you're letting the cobwebs grow between your legs."

I roll my eyes at the evil grin proudly displayed on his face. He thinks he's so funny. I swear he lives to embarrass me, but the thing about big sisters is we know how to mess with little brothers right back.

"What's going on between my legs is none of your concern. Besides, Bog takes care of me just fine."

"Can you please stop calling it that?" He groans, making a retching sound.

Now, it's my turn to grin evilly. See, I can just as easily embarrass him.

"Oh, you can tell me all about giving blowjobs in bathrooms, but I can't mention that battery-operated Geralt knows exactly what spot to hit every night? Hypocrite much?"

A loud booming laugh nearby pulls me from the hot mess that is this conversation, scaring the shit out of me.

When the hell did someone sit down without me realizing?

Chris busts up while I melt into a puddle of humiliation. I try to muster up what little dignity I have left to scold the person so rudely eavesdropping on my personal conversation. When I turn to give them a piece of my mind, all coherent thought leaves my brain.

The nosy intruder is the sexiest man I have ever laid eyes on. His light brown hair falls back with his head as he throws it back in laughter at my expense. The only thing I can do is stare as his shoulders bounce jovially while his fingers lay on the keys of his open laptop sitting on the table beside me.

His gaze meets mine, and his laughter dies on his pink lips.

Fourth of July sparklers crackle and pop in my belly as he stares at me. My heart goes pitter-patter, and all I can think about is sitting on this poor man's face until he makes my body shoot off like a bottle rocket.

Just ... wow.

This man is sexy as sin. Hand to God, he puts Henry Cavill to shame with his scruffy cheeks, bulging pecs, and broad shoulders. His brilliant sea-green and hazel-brown eyes are captivating, and remind me of happier times, like summer vacations with my grandfather by the green waters of the Gulf Coast.

He speaks first. "It's you." His voice is gravelly and thick, and the seductive sound sends goosebumps prickling across my skin.

What in the world is happening?

"What?" I tilt my head in confusion.

He clears his throat. "Nothing. I'm sorry for eavesdropping. I meant no harm, but I couldn't avoid it."

He waves his large hand around in the air, and I tear my eyes away from his strong-looking forearms—that have no right to exist—and look around the café. The very public and busy café I am now occupying.

My cheeks flush as I cover my face with my hands. "Omigod. This is so embarrassing," I mumble into my palms.

Kill me now. I'm pretty sure all these people just heard about Bog and how he helps take care of my needs.

"No need to be embarrassed. I know there are plenty of women out there that enjoy the company of Henry Cavill," the sexy stranger says with a smile.

Peeking through my fingers, I stare at him. He's watching me, and the only thing I can think right now is how can this impossibly gorgeous-looking man know who Geralt is. He looks cover-model hot, and hot guys don't know about nerdy fantasy shows.

Right?

I inwardly groan in shame, and secretly in delight, at his possible Witcher fanaticism. "Please, stop. I think I'm going to die."

The stranger's husky laugh whizzes through my blood and shoots straight for my clit. My panties flood with arousal, and I squirm in my seat at the new-to-me sensation.

My body's involuntary reaction to this sexy stranger is shocking. No one has ever made me feel instantly overcome with lust before.

"You're not supposed to talk to strangers," Chris playfully chides.

The sexy intruder slowly slides his chair next to mine, bringing his face into view of the camera. His rich masculine scent of ginger and cardamom tickles my nose. He smells so damn amazing, like sex and spice. It's hypnotic, expensive, and full of possibilities.

Chris's eyes pop out of his head for a beat before he recovers. "Well, hello, handsome. I think I can make an exception for you."

Good to know I'm not the only one affected by this guy's looks.

"Thank you. I think? Let me introduce myself. I'm Mason. Stranger no longer." He rubs his chin with his fist, and the scraping sound has me clenching my thighs.

"Mason," I repeat his name, tasting the lushness of it on my tongue.

Mason's eyes find mine again, capturing me in a staring match. My eyes drop to his mouth as he swipes his tongue across his teeth before hitting me with a smoldering smile. He must practice this look in the mirror because he's got it down, and it's working.

He straight-up incinerated my panties with that look. I doubt the cobwebs between my legs survived the flood this man has brought to my body.

"I'm going to hang up. I'll see you when you land," Chris mutters.

I'm pretty sure I hear a *Fuck me, he's hot* in there somewhere before the call disconnects.

Mason and I stay staring at one another as the air around us turns heated and the sounds of the airport disappear, wrapping us in our own little cocoon. Somehow, it's not awkward.

Something briefly flickers in his eyes before slipping back beneath the sea-green depths. My gut tells me he wanted to say something but held it back at the last second.

I bet he holds back a lot. The way his eyes swirl with unsaid words makes me think he's complicated and simple, like a 'Rubik's Cube—once you figure out the pattern, it's only a matter of time before you solve the puzzle.

Knock it off. You can't afford to get involved with him.

"Did I hear your brother correctly? You're flying to Los Angeles?" he asks, breaking me from my thoughts.

"I am."

"Interesting." He runs his forefinger over his plump bottom lip, and thoughts of running my tongue over it accost me. The loudspeaker overhead blares the boarding information for the next flight.

"That's my ride." The words leave my mouth, but my body stays planted, wanting to spend more time with this handsome stranger.

Mason scoots back in his chair and begins packing up his stuff. Reluctantly, I follow suit and do the same.

Get it together, Emery. You don't know this guy.

"Well, it was nice to meet you, Mason."

He hums a non-answer, so I reach for my purse, toss my phone inside, and grab my luggage handle. I manage two steps away from the table before he's in line with me, matching my every step. He towers over me, and at 5'8", I'm taller than the average woman, but Mason has a good six inches on me.

He's got a laptop bag hanging over his broad shoulder, and I can't tear my eyes away from the way his bicep flexes, and the cords of muscles and veins strain as he carries a small duffle bag in his hand.

Mason strides confidently beside me, emitting some major badass boss vibes. He's both casual and business-like in manner and dress, with his thick chunky cardigan with leather elbow patches, a plain T-shirt, dark jeans, and expensive-looking boots.

Hot professor, maybe?

Doesn't matter, he's yummy. Chris would categorize Mason's aura as *big dick energy.*

Before I can stop myself, my gaze bounces to his crotch for proof. My face heats as I rip my gaze away.

What is wrong with me, and why am I trying to look at this man's package?

Biting my lip, I fight a groan. I hope Mason didn't see me trying to ogle his junk.

Together, we walk in silence towards my gate. My skin tingles, and my stomach dips like I'm about to get on a roller coaster. My body is going haywire at Mason's proximity.

What is it about him?

I shove that question to the back of my brain and ignore the energy building between me and this mysteriously handsome man.

"I don't mean to be presumptuous when I say this, but... Why are you following me?"

A deep chuckle rumbles from his chest at my question. He glances at me, a smug smile on his lips.

We separate to walk around a family pushing a stroller, but he keeps up easily.

"Do you want me to follow you?"

I pretend to mull over my answer. "I don't know. Are you going to kidnap me and sell me to slavery?"

"I might kidnap you, but I'd never sell you."

The butterflies in my stomach flutter in excitement at his cool answer. Why does the thought of him kidnapping me sound so hot? What is wrong with me?

So many things.

I opt to keep my mouth shut as we continue to make our way to my gate. He rubs his jaw with his hand, and the sound of his scruff sends shivers down my spine. My thighs clench at thoughts of his chin scraping the skin of my inner thighs.

My grip tightens on the handle of my suitcase, so I don't fan my very warm face. "Thanks for walking me to my gate."

Mason smirks at me like he knows something I don't. "It was my pleasure..." He pauses, waiting for me to fill in the blank.

Oh my, when will the mortification end with this man? He doesn't even know my name, and I've already thought about him in quite a few compromising positions. He has my heart racing and my hands clammy, and we've barely spoken.

"Emery. My name is Emery. My brother calls me Em."

In the past five minutes, I think I've developed a full-blown crush on this sexy, mysterious man with manners befitting of a gentleman.

"Emery," he mulls over my name, tasting it on his tongue.

I've never been more turned on than I am right now, and all it took was for him to say my name.

"Mason," I repeat. I like his name. It suits him. He looks like a Mason. Someone strong, a hard worker. Dependable. "It was nice meeting you."

He nods in agreement, fighting a smile as the last call for first-class passengers to board is announced overhead.

I clutch the ticket in my hand tighter and walk towards my plane, leaving Mason standing at the gate, with his sparkling hazel eyes boring holes in my back. The flight attendant scans my ticket before I walk down the hall and onto the plane. Without looking back, I find my window seat and take a few deep breaths.

I feel as though I've gone round for round on the punching bag, with the way my pulse is racing and the flood of adrenaline in my system has me feeling exhilarated. I take a few deep breaths, trying to calm the rush.

That man is dangerous. He might not kidnap me, but he could run off with something that doesn't belong to him.

A shadow falls over my tray table, and the spicy scent of ginger hits me. My eyes drag up the familiar body, and my heart takes off at a gallop.

Standing above me is Mason, not looking the least bit surprised to see me. He takes a seat in the empty chair across from me, his eyes locked on mine.

"Fancy seeing you here," he says smoothly.

"You knew we were on the same flight, didn't you?"

"Maybe." He shrugs.

I hum my answer, ogling the sexy way he scrapes his big hand over his jaw.

An older woman approaches, breaking our stare-off. She attempts to put her bag in the overhead bin, but Mason stands, beating her to it, and takes the bag from her hand. He lifts it easily, placing it carefully overhead for her.

"Why thank you. It's rare to come across a gentleman these days," she tells him.

"My mom taught me well." Mason inclines his head at her compliment, smiling politely at her. It's not even a full smile, but it's just as potent.

Her cheeks flush, and she clears her throat. "Well, please thank her for me, then."

Mason chuckles, amused at his effect on this poor woman, who smiles back at him and takes her seat beside me. She's as flustered as I am, and I can't stop from smiling to myself.

Another one bites the dust.

Maybe she'll be a decent seatmate, after all. I've had some real treats over the years, and by treats, I mean gross, skeevy men who don't know how to take no for an answer. I inwardly cringe in disgust, thinking about the last freak I had to sit next to.

"She'll appreciate that. I'm Mason." There he goes, introducing himself again.

Does he do this with everyone?

He extends his hand out for her to shake, which she happily accepts by placing her weathered one in his, introducing herself. "Sharon."

"Pleasure to meet you, Sharon. You know, I hate to bother you, but would it be too much trouble for us to switch seats? My girlfriend, Emery, here..."

Girlfriend? What is he doing?

Mason points to me and smiles brightly at the woman. Whatever he is doing, it's working. She's putty in his hands.

"Hi," I squeak, helping the poor woman out.

Yeah, he makes me feel stupid too.

She looks over, taking me in, and her lips lift into a sweet smile. She nods hello before returning her attention to Mason.

"...well, we've been separated, and I can't bear to be away from her for too long."

Sharon practically swoons as she places her hands over her heart. "Oh, you sweet young man. Of course. I'd hate for you two love-birds to sit apart."

"Thank you, Sharon." Mason lifts her hand and presses a kiss to the back of it.

Her cheeks flame even redder at the gesture. She stands and takes his now unoccupied seat. I watch her fan her face and mouth *wow* as Mason takes the seat next to me.

He places his warm hand on my thigh and leans into me, lips to my ear. "Play along, Emery."

His hot breath fans across my lobe, making my nipples pucker. I turn my head to his as I nod in agreement and stare at the golden streaks that break through his green eyes like lightning, our lips a hair's breadth away from each other. He's so close he could kiss me.

Invisible sparks crackle between us.

He lifts his hand, cupping my cheek as he runs his thumb under the line of my lower lip, careful not to smudge the red stain covering my mouth. From afar, it looks like he's leaning in to kiss me, even though he's not. But the act is so much more intimate than if he were to press his lips to mine.

I close my eyes as lust pools in my lower belly. For some crazy reason, I want him to do it.

Kiss me, my traitorous head whispers.

He drops his hand from my face, leaning back in his seat and taking his heat with him, leaving me wanting. My lashes flutter open to find him watching me, eyes stormy dark and lust-filled. His hand remains on my thigh, close to my knee, keeping up the charade and a respectable distance from the part of me that's dying for his touch. I'm at a loss for words.

What the hell is happening right now?

I shake away the spell he's put me under and try to lighten the mood. "So, *boyfriend,* now what?"

A coy smile takes over his face at my use of the word "boyfriend". If I didn't know any better, I'd say he liked me calling him that.

That's absurd, right?

Aside from his first name and that he knows who Geralt of Rivia is, I know nothing about this man.

He lowers his voice, accentuating the gravel in it. "Now? Now, we get to know each other."

"How do you expect to do that when your friend, Sharon, could hear everything we say?" I whisper back conspiratorially.

"Good point."

He reaches down between his legs and pulls out a sleek laptop from his bag. It looks like the newest model available. He places the obviously expensive equipment on the tray table and turns it on. I watch his fingers fly across the keyboard as he enters an incredibly long password from memory and opens a Word document.

I don't think he's a professor.

Before I can think too hard about his job or ask, Mason turns the screen to face me so I can see what he's typed.

Does this work for you?

I chuckle at his cheekiness. "It does."

I aim to please, Emery.

I roll my eyes at him and type.

Such a charmer.

Not usually. But for you ... I'm trying.

I look at him, trying to figure out if this is some kind of line. He is hot as hell, and he could easily be playing with me. He watches me watch him for a minute, letting me figure it out. My gut tells me he's not a player at all. In fact, I'd probably say the opposite.

His fingers fly across the keys again.

Do you believe me?

"I believe you."

Good. Now tell me why you're going to Los Angeles. It's not for a guy, is it?

"Oh, now you're concerned?"

His brow furrows, and my heart skips a beat. He can't possibly be jealous.

Taking my turn, I type...

Yes.

I nervously bite my thumbnail, anticipating his response.

I don't think your fake boyfriend likes that answer.

A giggle escapes me. I'm enjoying messing with him.

Putting him out of his jealous rage, I type.

I'm going to visit my brother, Chris. You met him. He's premiering a short film for film school. Then, I'll be off to visit my parents on the east coast for the holidays.

He nods and with his eyes on mine, he types his response.

What about your brother? Is he going too?

I shake my head.

No. Long story.

I've got time.

So I tell him—actually, I type—the story of why Chris doesn't visit our parents. Well, as much as I can. There are some things I can't tell anyone.

We go back and forth, chatting and laughing. It's strange. I've never opened up to someone like this before. Maybe it's because I don't have to say the words aloud. It's easier to share when my fingers do the talking. Or maybe it's just Mason that makes me feel comfortable enough to share.

Whatever it is, I shove it down and enjoy our conversation. Unfortunately, nothing can come of this. Ever.

My heart sinks, thinking about having to walk away from him when the plane lands.

But I will. I have no choice. My life isn't my own. At least, not yet.

The tiny glimmer of hope Mason gave me on the flight dies when I leave him standing on the curb of the airport, with a wave goodbye. And no way to find me.

THREE DAYS.

It's been three long and miserable days since Emery walked away from me at the airport, and I still can't get the stunning woman with the sparkling topaz eyes and the poutiest red lips I've ever seen out of my head.

My cell buzzes in my pocket for the fifth time in a row, which can only mean one of two things: my brothers are on the group chat, or it's work. Seeing as I'm sitting here on the couch with my laptop working on some code, it's most likely the former.

I pull out my phone, surprised to find Cameron reaching out. His face fills the screen as his call comes in.

With a groan, I answer because he'll keep calling if I don't.

"The answer is no. I'm busy," I all but growl.

"Mase. So glad you're in a good mood, sweet cheeks."

"What do you want, Cam?" I'm already dreading his answer. It's Friday, so there's only one thing he wants from me, and it's not to stay in.

"Why do you think I want something?"

Because you're you.

I don't even bother answering, letting my silence speak for itself. Utensils on dishes clink under the overwhelmingly loud voices of people in the background. I wait him out until he breaks.

"Okay, fine. I want something."

"What?"

"I need you to come join me at Umi." Umi? Damn. That's the most expensive sushi place in Los Angeles.

"Why?"

"Because my date brought a friend, and I need someone to distract this chick so I can get her friend alone."

"You're on a date?" I ask, shocked by that piece of information.

A date is new for my playboy brother. He is usually the "love 'em and leave 'em" type. I've never heard of him wining and dining the women he takes home—not that he has to try very hard when he's one of the best pitchers in the league and women are constantly throwing themselves at him.

"Yeah, I know. I'm trying something new, alright? Can you please come save me or not?"

"Where's Eli?" Cam usually calls him for stuff like this since he's a much better wingman, whereas I'm not.

I'm not a people person at all, and I can't even remember the last time I was on a date. Unless I count my recent encounter with a stunningly beautiful brunette.

"He's at some work thing with his number one client." That's code for "Eli is on babysitting duty". "Please. You haven't been out in forever, and this chick is ... hot. You need to let someone play with your dick before it falls off. So why not her?"

"Not helping."

"Mase, just get over here now, and I'll owe you one," Cameron growls into the phone. He really must be into this woman if he's asking me for help.

"You already owe me a thousand, but fine. Only because I know you'll keep hounding me if I don't. You're paying for my dinner, dick."

The sooner I get this over with, the sooner I can get back to work. *And back to daydreaming about Emery.*

"Done. You're a lifesaver, brother."

◈

Twenty minutes later, I arrive at the busy restaurant. I would have made it sooner, but I decided to self-park in case I want to make a quick getaway. I check in with the hostess—a young woman with slicked-back hair and a bored expression.

"Hi. I'm meeting someone."

"Name?" she asks, uninterested in our exchange.

"Miller," I grumble.

She looks at her computer and purses her lips. "No Miller here."

Fucking Cam. He's messing with me.

There's only one other name he'd use.

Jace started calling Cam "kid" back in high school and instead of complaining, he embraced it, like everything else. Cameron's every bit the quintessential last child. Wild, funny, and absolutely outrageous.

"How about Kid Fantastic? Is he here?"

The woman fights a smile, and I know I've gotten it right.

"Right this way, sir." She leads me to a table in the back, near the wall of windows that overlook the patio seating and have a perfect view of the beach. Cam is sitting next to a blonde, who is talking her head off as she rests her tits on his arm and twirls her hair around her finger.

I roll my eyes at the sight. I never should have come. I'm about to turn around when Cameron sees me.

"I see you, brother," he shouts. "Get over here!"

With an inward groan, I make my way to his table.

He gets up to give me a half hug and handshake. "Thanks, bro."

I grunt, taking the empty seat next to the girl I assume my brother wants me to distract.

Cam makes introductions. "Ladies, this is my brother, Mason. Mason, this is Stacey" — he points to the girl next to him, then across the table — "and this is Jenny."

"It's Jennifer, actually. Jenny is too girl-next-door while Jennifer sounds more Hollywood, like Jennifer Lawrence." The girl doesn't stop talking to let me answer, carrying on about wanting to sound more professional when she goes to auditions. "Jennifer sounds better, don't you think?" She finally takes a breath.

"Sure," I respond.

Her lips purse at my flat tone, but she tries to keep going with her fake friendly smile, even though the lines around her eyes and mouth give her away.

I glance at Cameron as he hides a smile with his fist.

Fucker.

A free dinner won't be enough to make up for this impromptu double date. Don't get me wrong, the girl is gorgeous with her long blonde hair and blue eyes. But her looks don't do anything for me, nor does her phony attitude.

I've dated women like this before. They are only interested in what they can get out of being with me. They don't actually want me.

The waiter takes our order as I casually sip my gin and tonic. Jennifer continues to regale us with gossip about other actresses she's met on auditions, who—quote—are "whores that spread their legs for any director or casting agent", which is why she can't seem to catch a break.

Yeah, that's the reason. More like... *You're an awful person, like the awfully cloying scent of your perfume that's suffocating me.* She smells like the inside of Victoria's Secret, nothing like the soft and sweet scent of the woman that haunts me.

"So, do you think you can represent me?" she asks without an ounce of shame.

I pause with my chopsticks midair as my tuna sashimi slips off and falls to my plate. Gotta give it to the girl—she's got balls.

"Jennifer," the blonde hisses. At least one of them has manners.

"What? You said the brother was a talent agent." She twists in her chair and grabs my wrist.

My skin itches at her touch.

"You're him, right? Can you get me an audition for the new Henry Cavill movie?"

I look over at Cameron and his face is blank, but the tick in his jaw tells me he's pissed. My brother has never witnessed this sort of thing. Me? Well, I'm not surprised at all. I'm used to this type of thing happening to me. It isn't the first, and it won't be the last. Just another reason I don't date anymore.

"Sorry, sweetheart. You're thinking of my brother, Eli." Shaking off her hold, I place the ball of rice down and drop my sticks, my appetite now long gone.

"Oh. Well, what do you do?"

"I work in technology."

Her eyebrow quirks up like maybe my stock isn't so low after all. She's barking up the wrong tree.

"Like Steve Jobs?" I can hear the hope in her voice.

I'm well off, but I'm no Steve Jobs. I own my company, a small home in a ridiculously expensive neighborhood, and a brand-new Tesla. But no way in hell am I going to break my self-appointed celibacy for a woman looking for material things.

"No." I throw my napkin on the table. "Cam. Ladies. It was nice meeting you, but I think I'm going to head out."

Cameron stands as well, his chair scraping across the ground. "I'm going to walk my brother out. Be back in a minute," he tells the blonde.

She nods and has enough grace to look agitated and ashamed of her friend.

Cameron doesn't spare her a second glance as we walk away from the table. As we reach the front desk, he stops to chat with the hostess. He pulls out a wad of cash and holds it out to her. She nods—accepting the money as Cameron slips her another, smaller stack of bills—and smiles at him, her earlier jaded mask gone in a flash of green.

I shake my head with a laugh. He's not returning to the table.

Cameron slaps me on the back. "Please tell me you self-parked."

"You know it," I say with a smirk.

Cameron chuckles as we make our way to the parking lot a block over. "Sorry about that." He's annoyed and upset about what transpired.

"Don't mention it. Seriously. Don't. Ever."

"My lips are sealed." Cameron might be a goof, but he is loyal to a fault. He might give me crap, but not when it's about something serious. I think this incident qualifies. "Wanna go grab a burger?"

"Hell yes." I point at him as I hit the key fob, unlocking the door. "You're still paying."

Cameron gasps, clutching his invisible pearls. "As if I would make you pay after that shitshow."

We slip into the car, and he turns on the radio, pulling out the extra pair of shades I keep in the glove compartment.

"Are you sure you want to ditch your date?"

"Fuck yeah. I paid for the meal before we left. I also paid the hostess to embarrass the shit out of *Jennifer*."

I look over at him, a sneer marring his face as he shrugs like it's no big deal. The casual action has us both bursting out with laughter.

I couldn't be more grateful for him to have my back.

FOUR

Emery

THE CHRISTMAS TREE GLITTERS, catching my eye, as the white stream lights reflect off the handmade gold glass ornaments adorning the beautiful evergreen.

Evergreen. The same color as Mason's eyes.

The empty ache in my chest that has taken root in the past few years has grown uncomfortably strong since I met him and walked away from him.

It's for the best. Right?

With a sigh, I sip my champagne and try to focus on the conversation at hand.

My mother is once again entertaining everyone with the story of her most recent trip to Paris. The trip was a gift from my father, no doubt reparations for another one of his marital indiscretions. It's always the same. He cheats. She finds out. He sends my mother on a shopping spree while he breaks up with whatever mistress he's been entertaining before she returns.

I don't understand how she can stand his infidelity, let alone being treated like an afterthought, instead of walking away. No amount of money is worth that level of humiliation in my book.

And yet... Here I sit like the dutiful daughter I am while my parents control my future.

I'm a fraud. I have no right to judge her when I allow my father to exert his power over me too. I'm no better than her, even if I keep telling myself it's all for Chris. I'm still taking my father's money.

A pinch to my arm has me yelping as my champagne splashes, dripping down my arms. I know better than to rub the pain away.

My mother sits next to me, patting my leg, before she whispers out of the side of her mouth at me, "Sit up. You look fat and pathetic hunched over."

Pulling my shoulders back, I tilt my chin up and plaster on the fake smile she approves of when I'm in her presence. She continues her story—about some handmade silk dress she plans to wear for this year's memorial party—like she didn't just violate me. It's nothing new, but I am growing tired of the insults and abuse. She thinks she holds all the power by hanging the agreement I made with my father over my head. With her behavior towards me, it's become increasingly clear that my time is running out.

This is why I have to let the fantasy of Mason go.

Or do you? my inner voice pipes up.

The part of me that longs to escape all this beckons me to flee. To let go of the hope that they will change their minds and leave me to live the life I want.

Everyone laughs and I force a chuckle, my smile brittle. No one sees my unhappiness, nor do they care. I'm just an ornament, a pretty thing to look at as I sit here on the settee, in an expensive pink gown my mother laid out for me to wear. A dress that's disgustingly bland and not to my taste at all.

"So, Emery, tell us what's new, dear," my mother's friend, Eleanor, says.

My mother, as usual, answers for me. "Oh, you know our girl. She's out gaining experience before she'll return home to work with Sinclair at the Rhodes Publishing."

My mask slips at the mention of working with my father. My mother intensifies her grip on my thigh, daring me to disagree. I smile and nod my assent, as required.

"How wonderful, dear." Eleanor turns to my mother, ignoring me. "Cybil, you must be excited for Emery to return home and settle down."

"Of course. Our girl knows what's expected of her."

My hackles rise, and my heart beats double time as the cage I trapped myself in closes in on me. My palms sweat, and my stomach churns. Placing my flute on the end table, I stand. "If you'll please excuse me, I need to use the powder room."

My mother waves me off as I make my leave. I doubt anyone will miss me, so I head down the hall that leads to the kitchen.

It's almost midnight, and the luxurious kitchen is empty, not a crumb of food or dish left behind. Aside from the bartender and a handful of servers who will finish running drinks for the rest of the night, the staff has gone for the night.

Grateful for the lack of prying eyes, I grab a bottle of champagne from the makeshift bar on the peninsula and step out onto the patio, overlooking the Long Island Sound. Opening the bottle, I pop the cork, the bubbles fizzing over and dripping down my hand.

The sprawling green lawns of my family estate are inky black in the pale moonlight. It looks and feels like a sad, endless abyss—just like my life.

I lift the thousand-dollar bottle of champagne to my lips and take a swig. The cool liquid pops onto my tongue as I take another huge gulp. I'll pay for it tomorrow, but it will be worth it if I can forget about the past few days for just a minute and pretend I am back at the airport.

I'd do it all differently if I could. I'd look up into the eyes of the most handsome and sweetest man I have ever met and tell him to call me. I'd give him my number and let him take me away from all of this. I'd let him own my body as he bent me to his will and gave me unimaginable pleasure.

A vision of Mason pulling my hair and bending me over as he spanks my ass has my core lighting up like the fireworks that just exploded over the water.

I take another pull from the bottle before placing it on the floor. A gust of wind blasts me, freezing me to the bone—stepping outside without a coat during winter in Connecticut was stupid.

Muffled voices on the terrace beside me catch my attention. Sinking into the shadows of the pillars that surround the kitchen veranda, I avoid getting caught listening to the seemingly private conversation.

"Does she know, Cybil?" my father's hushed voice asks.

"Of course not. She's as oblivious as ever," my mother snipes.

"Good. Let's keep it that way. Alfred still needs to get rid of ... you know who ... before we can make the announcement."

You know who? What the heck are they plotting this time? If my parents are scheming with the Westfields, no good can come from it.

"It's already in the works. Helene is planting the seeds as we speak."

My head floats, the champagne hitting me. Not wanting to lose my buzz or hear any more, I grab the bottle of champagne, slip back through the sliding glass door, and make my way upstairs to my childhood bedroom.

I open the door and memories I wish would die hit me. I hate this room. Not a single thing about it has changed since my mother redecorated it for my sixteenth birthday. I thought helping her would be fun. My excitement lasted until the interior designer showed up. Decorating this room did the opposite of bringing us closer together; it widened the gap, forcing me to realize Cybil didn't want my opinion, nor a relationship with me. In the end, I gave up. It was pointless to fight her. After that, I began counting down the days until I could leave this place.

The pale pink walls and beige furniture are a mockery. A wave of anger crashes through my body. I am so freaking tired of my parents making the decisions, forcing me to bend who I am for them and for the sake of their image.

I tear the silk gown off my body and throw it in the corner—the only act of defiance I have left in my arsenal. Well, that and my red lipstick.

A smile pulls at my lips.

Not just any red. Burgundy. The deepest shade I could find. A shade that matches my light, sand-colored skin. A "fuck you" to my overbearing and critical mother with her muted colors that wash her out, and make her look pale and white like she wishes she were.

I envision my grandfather shaking his head at his daughter in disappointment. Tears cloud my eyes as the pain of losing the only man who's ever loved me surfaces. I miss Papa so much. He loved Chris and me unconditionally, and I wish he was here now to help me get out of the mess I've found myself in.

How the heck can I pay the rest of Chris's tuition without having to sell a kidney? I have a trust, but I don't like to use it unless absolutely necessary.

You could tell Chris. There goes my dumb brain again.

I'm not telling my brother. He would kill me. Besides, paying for Chris's education is the least our parents can do, even if I have to play the game a little longer.

I put on my favorite flannel pajamas and climb into bed. Sleep doesn't come easily as I toss and turn, thinking about my predicament. And the evergreen eyes of the man who stirred something inside me that has long been dormant. What that feeling is, I don't know. It doesn't matter, though. I'll never see him again.

But if I do...

I don't think I can resist him a second time.

JANUARY

THE SOUND OF A horn blares as I glance in the rearview mirror at the asshat honking. Rolling my eyes, I turn up the volume on the radio.

"I can't go anywhere, you dick," I grumble.

Traffic is at a standstill in the arrival lanes at the airport. Of course, Cameron has to pick the busiest time of day, on the busiest day of the week, to make an appearance. Thankfully, Rhys stayed back at my brother's best friend and honorary Miller brother, Levi's house, hanging out with his twin girls.

Rhys and the girls are best friends, and they get along like family. It wasn't hard to convince him to stay back with them while I went to get his other uncle. I'm glad he did because I don't think he'd survive sitting in this clusterfuck traffic. The kid is cool, but there is no way he could sit through this nightmare without complaining. I'm barely surviving.

I've been staying with Rhys for the last few days while Jace and Rylann are on their babymoon. She's due in a few months, but since she's had a rough first trimester with morning sickness, Jace planned a surprise trip for her.

Watching Jace find true happiness here in Oregon is still taking some getting used to. He and Rylann are crazy about each other. They have a fantastic kid, with another on the way. He's finally living the life he's always wanted.

My heart stutters. The nanoscopic-sized ache I carry when I see them together has grown exponentially over the last month. Since her.

Emery.

I really thought there was something between us. We had a good time talking on the plane. We flirted and laughed. The chemistry was there. But then she walked away, without a backward glance. *Did I read her all wrong?*

I think back to the flight. The way her breath caught in her throat when I put my hand on her thigh and whispered in her ear to play along. The way her eyes stayed locked on mine, attempting to discover what lay beneath.

With anyone else, I would have been uncomfortable with such an intimate act. But with her, I wasn't. I could have stared into her topaz eyes all day, getting lost searching for all the flakes of honey mixed in. I desperately wanted to kiss her plump lips and that cute little beauty mark at the corner of her mouth.

I push thoughts of her away, blowing out a deep breath. I have got to let her go. No matter how many times I think I see her, it's just a trick of the eye. A mirage.

I check the time. Cameron should be walking out of the airport any minute. The cars continue to crawl slowly along. A break opens up, and I quickly move into the right lane along the curb.

Come on Cam.

Up ahead, a tall brunette catches my eye. Her head is down, staring at the phone in her hand.

It can't be. *Can it?*

My heart beats wildly as I drive past.

The woman lifts her head, and the world seems to stop spinning. It's her.

I slam on the brakes and throw the car in park, hazards on. Without thinking, I throw the door open and fly out of my seat, charging towards her like a bull. "Emery!"

She looks up, pinning me with her brown eyes. As much as I want to play it cool, I can't. She's finally in front of me.

"Oh my god, Mason. Hi." Her voice is breathy, and she looks shocked to see me. She pushes a lock of her hair behind her ear as I step up to her, bringing us toe to toe.

"Go out with me," I state rather than ask. I'm not usually so pushy, but thoughts of this woman have plagued me the last month.

Her cheeks flame, and the need to see how far that blush goes consumes me.

"Umm..." She's thrown off by my sudden appearance and demand.

"Don't overthink it. Just go out with me. One night. Please. I can't stop thinking about you."

A shy smile touches her lips, and I'm dangerously close to pressing mine to hers. She hesitates for a fraction of a second but nods. "Okay. Yes. I'll go on a date with you."

"Tonight?"

"Tonight." She lets out a cute giggle, warming my soul.

My face splits in a grin. I can't believe this is me right now. I never do this kind of thing. I don't date, let alone dream about and chase after a woman.

A smile spreads across my face—another thing I rarely do, and yet here I am, grinning like an idiot. I'm not only happy; I'm fucking floating. The girl I've been thinking about nonstop for the last month popped up out of nowhere and agreed to go on a date with me.

"Here. Type in your number," I command, handing her my phone.

Fuck, I sound like such as asshole. I need to take it down a notch.

I clear my throat, trying to calm my beating heart, and watch her thumbs drift across the screen as she enters her number into my contacts, a soft smile playing on her lips. Before she can hand the phone to me, it's plucked out of her hands.

"Well, well, well. Who do we have here, brother?" Cameron interjects.

I glare at my brother, but this only makes him smile more. Emery looks up at Cam, who is wearing a shit-eating grin, and back to me.

"Emery, this is Cameron, my little brother. Cameron, Emery," I introduce them and wait for it.

My baby brother is by far one of the most highly recognizable figures in sports. Women can't get enough of his pretty-boy antics. They practically fall at his feet. It doesn't hurt that Cameron is a good-looking dude. He's 6'5", built like a tank, and has the infamous Miller hazel eyes.

"Hi." She waves shyly.

"Pleased to meet you." Cameron shoots her a flirty wink.

I want to punch his smug dickface. She shakes his hand, and when she doesn't recognize him, I release my breath. Horns blare in the background, pulling my attention away from the beautiful woman in front of me.

She looks over my shoulder as some guy yells, giving me the finger. "I think he wants you to move your car."

"He can wait. You're more important."

She blushes again.

Damn. How did I not notice that last time? She's fucking sweet.

"Mase, I'm gonna hop in the car. Hurry up, man."

I wave Cam off as he heads to the car with a smirk on his face. He's going to give me shit, for sure. I couldn't give a fuck. I finally found her. Besides, he owes me after the horrible dinner I endured for him.

"I'll text you when I get back to my brother's place. Pick you up at eight?"

"Yeah. Sounds good." Her sweet, raspy voice makes my chest pinch.

What is it about her that's got me so enchanted? I'm almost desperate to find out the answer.

"Dress warm. It's going to be chilly tonight," I instruct her again, taking a deep breath.

I need to calm down. Sounding like one of those controlling assholes isn't the way to go. I don't know where I'm taking her yet, but I want her to be comfortable.

"Whatever you say, Mr. Bossy," she teases.

It usually pisses me off when my colleagues call me bossy. But her? I like the way the word sounds on her tongue. The sparkle in her eye makes me think she might get off on me bossing her around.

Hmm. Here's hoping.

"Do you need a ride?" I'd do anything to spend more time with her, even if it means letting her talk to my annoying little brother.

"No, I'm waiting for my Uber. I ordered it before you came charging out of your car."

"I didn't charge." I lean back on my heels.

"Sure you didn't." She rolls her eyes and bites her plump bottom lip.

Brat.

I rub a hand over my jaw, attempting to hide the smirk pulling at my mouth. I might have caught her off guard, but I like that she gives as good as she gets. "I'll wait with you."

The horn blares again. This time, it's Cameron fucking around in the passenger seat.

"I think your brother wants to go." She grins, nodding her chin towards the car behind me.

"He can wait. I'd rather stay here with you."

"You're cute. But don't worry, that's my car right there." She points to the black SUV that pulls up to the curb.

She reaches for her bag, but I grab it instead. Walking her to the waiting car, I carry the small suitcase and put it in the trunk. Ever the gentleman my mom taught me to be, I open the rear door for her.

She stops in front of me, placing her hand on my forearm. Her touch sends a burst of energy through my body, surprising me.

"Thank you. I look forward to seeing you later." She reaches up on her tiptoes and kisses my cheek, then gets in the car.

I watch as it pulls away from the curb. Time to face my annoying little brother.

Silently, I get back in the car and join the traffic leading out of the airport. I only make it out of the terminal before Cam's on my ass.

"That's how you're going to play this?"

"Kid," I warn.

"Nope. Don't you 'kid' me." He points his thumb out the window. "That the girl that's had you all moody and broody the last couple of weeks?"

"Moody and broody? Where the fuck do you come up with this shit?"

Cam cracks up, smacking his thigh. "Just calling it like I see it."

"No, I've been moody because you make me show up for dinners with annoying women who want Eli so he can get them auditions."

"Hey, I apologized for that, and I bought you a double-double." He places my phone in the holder mounted to the dashboard.

I might need to get one of these for my car. Jace, like the protective caveman he is, has Ry's new car outfitted with everything possible to keep her safe while driving.

"You have a date tonight. You gonna tell Rhys you're ditching him for a chick? Or am I?" He crosses his arms, waiting for it to sink in.

"Damn." I can't believe I forgot about my nephew. We have plans to play video games and eat pizza.

"Interesting." He rubs his chin like an evil villain.

The sound grates on my nerves. *He* grates on my nerves. "What's interesting?"

"Hot Airport Girl."

"Don't call her that." I don't like that he noticed how attractive Emery is.

"Oh, don't like me saying she's hot, huh?"

"Kid," I warn again as he wiggles his eyebrows at me.

"Alright. I won't tell you that your girl is hot. A smoke show. Fine as fuck."

I growl.

He barks a laugh, holding up his hands in surrender. "I'm done. Don't worry about Rhys—I'll tire him out early. He won't even know you're missing."

"Thanks," I grumble.

"So, where are you going to take her?" He changes the playlist like he didn't just throw me a curveball.

Nerves swirl in my gut. Fuck. Where *am* I going to take her? I visit often, but I rarely make it out of Pine Hills before I'm back on a flight home or to wherever work calls.

"I have no idea."

"We'll figure it out."

"We?" Out of the corner of my eye, I see him flash that mischievous grin we all know means he's fixing to run his mouth.

"Yes, we. I gotta get you laid. Maybe you'll be less of a prickly dick if you get some." He suggestively sticks his tongue in his cheek, shaking his fist.

"You're an ass."

"I'm *your* ass," he mocks, blowing me kisses. He turns up the volume of the music, ignoring me for the rest of the ride.

I don't mind it when he's quiet, leaving me to my thoughts.

My mind swirls. The possibilities for dates are endless, but I don't want just some lame dinner date. I need something better. Something to wow her.

I exhale an exasperated sigh, already frustrated with my lack of creativity. I don't know where the hell I'm going to take Emery, but it has to be perfect.

SIX

Bro-tally Awesome

TEXT CHAIN

Cam: Yo, J. Mason is ditching Rhys for a hot date tonight. Just want you to know that I'm now ranking #1 in the uncle department.

Eli: We all know I'm Rhys's fave. But what's this about a date?

Cam: Some airport chick. You should have seen his face. He actually smiled. I almost didn't recognize him.

Mase: Prick. Don't you know how to keep your mouth shut?

Jace: Nope. Should I be worried that Cam's being left alone with my son? Should I call the babysitter?

Cam: WTF? I'm perfectly capable of taking care of my nephew.

Cam: Wait! Is the sitter hot?

Eli: **GIF Will Arnet Spit-take**

Jace: Down, boy. She's in high school.

Cam: When's her birthday?

Mase: God, you're deplorable.

Cam: I'm kidding. No need to call in reinforcements. I took Rhys to the batting cages, and we played catch all afternoon. He's beat and getting ready for bed.

Cam: You're welcome, BTW. Fuckers!

Jace: Thanks, fucker.

Eli: OK, tell me about the girl. She stacked?

Mase: Don't answer that.

Cam: Not as stacked as Ry. Tall and hot AF, though.

Cam: **GIF Leonardo DiCaprio Biting Fist**

Jace: No one is. And stop looking at my woman.

Jace: Thanks, Cam. I do have nice boobs. But I should warn you … Jace is gonna smack you when he sees you.

Cam: Worth it **Eyes Emoji**

Eli: **GIF Chuck Norris Punching**

Jace: Okay, we're out. Don't bug us unless it's an emergency.

Cam: You know what that means? **Eggplant Emoji** **Water Emoji** **Cat Emoji** **Peach Emoji**

Cam: **GIF Woman Churning Butter Suggestively**

Eli: LOL. Let us know if Mason comes home with a stick up his ass or a smile on his face. Either way, at least 1 of us is getting laid tonight.

Mase: Fuck off, E.

Mase: Kid. You're dead to me, you little shit.

Cam: **Tears Laughing Emoji**

Eli: **Tears Laughing Emoji**

Jace: **Tears Laughing Emoji**

I TURN INTO THE parking lot across the street from the Science Center and find a free spot before cutting the engine. I'm nervous and excited about what I have planned tonight.

Turning to my right, I find Emery smiling, and my nerves settle. She looks excited.

An invisible string tugs at something deep in my chest, sending my pulse racing. The unfamiliar feeling is both scary and welcoming. Not wanting to dissect the emotions swirling inside me, I shove them aside and concentrate on the beautiful woman next to me.

I was done for the moment she opened the door to her house, wearing tight charcoal jeans—that look painted on—a black sleeveless turtleneck tucked into her pants like a second skin, and sexy-looking, thigh-high black boots. I almost swallowed my tongue. She looks fuck hot. The right combination of sophisticated and sexy. She has my hands itching to give her body the full attention it deserves. And those lips? They are big, red, and begging to be kissed.

My dick twitches in my pants at the thought of kissing her and letting my hands roam every inch of her body.

"Please tell me we're here for Reel Eats." Her soft, sultry voice pulls me from my dirty thoughts.

"We are. If that's okay with you."

"Are you kidding? This is amazing. I've been dying to come to one of these events. Chris and I check all the time, but the tickets are hard to come by. How on earth did you pull this off?"

"I have my ways. Connections and all that." I shrug, playing it cool like it's no big deal.

It actually is a big deal. The Science Center puts on these monthly movie nights, and they sell out quickly. Each night is catered with foods curated to represent the film playing, and people wait months for tickets.

Truth is, if it wasn't for one of Levi's twins getting sick, he and Scarlett would be using these tickets instead. I should feel bad that Lily's sick—and pray that Rhys doesn't catch anything—but she had good timing. I make a mental note to buy her a stuffed animal as a thank you. I better get three; Rhys would be upset if he and Sadie didn't get one as well.

"I don't believe you, but I'm so excited. I don't care how you got the tickets for tonight. What are we watching?"

"Jurassic Park."

Emery lets out a soft excited squeal, her shoulders shimmying.

My chest puffs. I think I nailed date night. Okay, maybe I'm going to have to get Levi tickets for another night as a thank you—the man knows what he's doing. He really saved my ass when he came over complaining about missing the event and not being able to find someone to use the tickets. It was worth having to answer Levi's questions about my date and putting up with Cameron's incessant teasing. I'm just glad Rhys wasn't hurt that I'd be leaving for the night. Cameron was true to his word and tired the poor kid out.

"Are you a fan of the movie?" I probe, trying to learn more about who she is and what she likes. I want to know everything there is to know about her.

I already know she likes country music because it reminds her of her grandfather, and pop because she loves going out dancing with her younger brother.

"Who isn't? It's a classic."

"True." I unbuckle my seat belt and reach for my door handle at the same time she does. "Stay put."

Her lips purse at my tone, making me grind my teeth.

Shit, I have to stop sounding like such a bossy dick. She brings out this primitive part of my brain that makes me want to possess and protect her at the same time.

"Please," I amend.

She nods in agreement, biting back her smile.

As swiftly as I can, I get out of the car, rush to her side, and open the passenger door. I offer her my hand, and she takes it.

Sparks crackle up my arm like firecrackers, shocking me in place when our palms touch. Her eyes widen, and her lips part with a sharp intake of breath at the charge of energy between us. I don't let go; instead, I softly squeeze her hand, letting the sparks crawl up my arm, digging into the space between my ribs. She slowly glides out of her seat to stand in front of me. Time stands still as my heart pounds in my chest.

The wind blows, whipping her hair around her face, and her sweet scent of vanilla and pears floods my senses. Without hesitation, I catch her soft locks and push them behind her ear. She shivers at my touch, confirming that she's just as affected as I am by whatever is going on here.

A smirk slips across my face. *Good.*

I take a step back, her hand still in mine, and pull her with me away from the car. I close the door and lock the car with the fob in my pocket. Hand in hand, we walk to the main entrance and get in line.

"If you could choose tonight's movie, what would you pick?" I ask as we step behind another couple in the queue.

"Oh, gee. Where do I even start? My brother is a film major, and I must tell you I've been given an education on motion pictures over the years."

I chuckle at her seriousness on the topic. "There is no wrong answer, you know. Your brother isn't here to judge you."

She smiles brightly, tucking her chin down before answering. Fuck, she's cute.

"Oh, I know. If he was, this would be a test, for sure." She bites the nail of her thumb in concentration, her pink tongue poking out.

Thoughts of what else I'd like her tongue to touch flit through my mind. I clear the thickness from my throat and softly tap her temple with my finger. "Don't think too hard."

She laughs at my teasing as I stare at her lush mouth, the red color summoning me to kiss her and never stop.

"So impatient. Why don't you tell me the movie and a dish you'd serve?" she says, flipping the question my way.

"Easy. The Matrix, and I'd serve steak. Well, maybe a steak sandwich since it's probably easier to serve and eat here."

"The Matrix, huh? Not my favorite Keanu movie, but I approve. Cop-out on the steak."

"You wound me. What was I supposed to say? Red and blue jellybeans?"

She barks out a raspy laugh, and the sound makes my cock perk up.

"Fine, I'll give you that. But there are better Keanu movies out there to choose from." She looks at me, waiting to agree with her.

"Please don't tell me your favorite Keanu movie is *The Lake House* or something equally cheesy."

"God no. I like Keanu when he's kicking ass. If I had to pick, then it's John Wick all the way."

Fuck, she got even hotter with that pick. She already had me, being a fan of *The Witcher*.

The attendant at the door scans our tickets, and hands us each two boxes of food and a bag of popcorn. Another person in a Science Center T-shirt hands us a sheet of paper with directions, explaining how each box is numbered to coincide with a scene from the film.

Emery bounces on her toes with excitement. I couldn't have gotten luckier with these tickets.

I take her food boxes while she carries the popcorn. We make our way inside, buying a couple of bottles of water before going into the theater. We chat the entire time, Emery finally revealing her movie and food picks—*The Big Lebowski* and White Russian cupcakes. She just might be my dream woman come true, or she's an apparition that will disappear at the end of the night. The jury's still out.

"These are great seats. You should thank whomever you robbed for these tickets," she boasts as we take our seats.

Now, it's my turn to laugh. My cheeks hurt. I can't remember the last time I smiled this much. "I didn't steal them."

She arches a brow at me, waiting for me to reveal my connection.

"Fine, I don't have connections. I got lucky. My oldest brother's best friend had the tickets. His daughter came down with a fever, so I offered to take the tickets off his hands. For a price, of course."

Her mouth turns into an O in understanding. "Is it wrong that I'm glad his daughter got sick and we got to use his tickets?" She cringes but can't hide her smile, nor the twinkle in her eye.

"I won't judge you if you don't judge me for having the same thought earlier."

She shakes her head adamantly. "Never. We should get her something as a thank you. But don't say that. Say it's to make her feel better."

"I was already thinking that. Maybe after the show, we can hit up the gift shop? You can help me buy a few things."

"I'd like that." She bites that sexy red lip again.

My dick perks up. It's going to be a long, painful night if he keeps responding to her every move with enthusiasm.

The lights dim, and Emery takes off her trench coat. The perfume she's wearing hits me in the face again—a man could easily get addicted to the smell of her skin. She shifts closer to me, taking her food boxes and placing them on her lap. She leans back and rests her arm against mine, sending hot prickly energy across my skin with every brush of contact.

We watch the movie, whispering and eating the entire time. It's the best date I've ever been on.

Emery is sweet and funny. If her flushed cheeks are any indication, she isn't put out by my bossy demeanor; she likes it. Nor is she put off by the fact that I travel and work a lot, which only makes me want her more. Her understanding and support—while incredibly new—are genuine, which is a first for me. She is also quite ambitious, telling me how she hopes to help expand her company, as long as her business partners are willing and supportive.

At the gift shop, she helps me pick out a couple of stuffed dinosaurs and some playing cards, talking to me the entire time about anything and everything. Our conversation flows easily from one subject to the next. Though we ask each other a lot of questions, we keep it light. She gushes over her brother, Chris, while I briefly talk about mine.

By the time I have to take her home, I'm anxious and disappointed the night is over so soon. I don't want our time to end. There is something about her that has me wanting more.

I want to explore a relationship with someone for the first time in years. I want to reach out for something that's been out of my grasp for so long. The scary part of it all is that I only want that with her.

I LOOK UP THE street as my little bungalow with its white siding and green shutters comes into view. I'm almost sad to see it because it means that my night with Mason is over.

Never have I ever pulled up to my home and felt sad. I love my little house. It's a small two-bedroom-two-bathroom home I got for a steal nearly four years ago. It's nothing special, but it's all mine. I have never felt more at home than I do here, in this quiet neighborhood in Pine Hills.

I had hoped Chris would move in with me and go to college at U Portland, but when he got a scholarship to LACU film school, he moved south and never looked back. I'm so proud of him, even though I miss him like crazy. He deserves to chase after his dreams, and I plan on helping him get there any way I can. At least until he turns twenty-five. Then, the trust fund our grandfather left him will be released.

It's not a lot of money but enough for us to be comfortable. I used mine to put a down payment on my house. I love that when I come home every day, I'm reminded of my Papa's loving heart and generosity. Losing him was really hard. He was a wonderful man and more of a parent to me and Chris than our own father. We spent summers on the Gulf Coast with him until he passed away from a heart attack over ten years ago. I know things would be different if he were still alive. He never would have allowed my parents to manipulate me and send Chris to boarding school.

While I wish my parents truly cared about us, I know they don't. I doubt they even wanted us to begin with. We were just another box to check off. Another familial expectation to fulfill. The same expectations they are forcing on me now.

Movement to my right pulls me from my thoughts. Turning my head towards the man who showed up out of nowhere, I find him watching me as we sit parked in my driveway. Mason's sea-green gaze is intense and the burnt honey streaks in his irises glimmer in the dimly lit car as they bore into mine. The butterflies in my stomach soar.

He's so freaking sexy.

I never expected to see him again, even though he's all I've been thinking about since we shared that flight all those weeks ago. I don't think I can keep resisting him, nor do I want to. Without even realizing it, he's urging me to choose myself for once. With his scruff-covered angular jaw, tentative smile, and smoldering gaze, he already had me smitten. But now?

After this incredible date and getting to know him better, I don't want to stay away from him. I want to know every little detail that makes him the sweet, thoughtful man he is. I'm even drawn to his slightly bossy attitude. It's hot, and I'm here for it.

I'm completely compelled by everything about him. He intrigues me on so many levels, and the chemistry between us is off the charts. I just know, down to my soul, that one night with Mason wouldn't be enough. He's already taken an ax to my control, and all it took was one date with him.

He's shown me just how lonely and unhappy I am. It hurts knowing that we have to end this before it even starts because it would be selfish of me to start something with him when my life is more complicated than it appears.

Why does Mason have to be so damn irresistible?

"Thank you so much for tonight. I had a wonderful time," I whisper.

"It was my pleasure. I had a great time too." His voice comes out thick and gruff as he leans closer and pushes a stray hair behind my ear. "Thank you for going out with me."

I freeze as he slowly follows the shape of my jaw with his lips, his mouth hovering over mine. All I want is for him to kiss me. My breath stalls in my chest, waiting for him to finally close the fraction of the space between us.

Oh god, what is he doing to me? I shouldn't want this so badly.

Seconds pass before Mason opens the door, climbs out of the car, and sucks the thick air out with him, allowing me to finally breathe. He walks around the front of the car, headlights illuminating his gloriously tight butt as he makes his way to my door.

Ten out of ten, I recommend checking him out. My thighs clench at the naked images of him I conjure up in my head.

Mason's eyes catch mine, and he smirks. He totally caught me staring. He slows his pace, taking his time walking the rest of the way to my door, making a meal of my leering. My face heats as I chuckle and shake my head at the roguish smile pulling at his mouth.

Gah. I'm in so much trouble.

Biting my lip, I wait for him. Watching. My stomach flips with anticipation as he gets closer, his smile growing. Something in me tells me that Mason doesn't smile without reason or often. It has this secretive quality to it like you only get a smile if you earn it. Being on the receiving end of it makes me feel like I've won the lottery.

Mason opens the door and extends his palm to me. I take the invitation, letting him help me out of the car. I exhale a tight breath as pinpricks brush across my skin at his touch. His fingers thread through mine as he leads me to the front door. With my free hand, I reach into the pocket of my coat, clasping my hand around my keys.

Mason steps close, crowding my space, enveloping me in his warm spicy ... cologne? Body wash? Whatever it is, it's intoxicating. I don't think a man's scent has ever turned me on before. But with Mason? Everything about him makes me hungry for more.

My clit tingles, and my heart beats wildly in my chest as the anticipation of his next move wraps around me, making the air crackle with energy. I'm dizzy. My body's reaction to him is new; I have never reacted to a man this way before.

Stepping away, I try to create space between us and take a deep breath. Mason steps forward with me, meeting me step for step until my back hits the cold wood door, refusing to let me flee. Tilting my chin up with his knuckle, he leans forward, stopping when his lips are a hair's breadth away from mine, his eyes locked on me.

"Emery." His breath fans across my lips. My knees wobble at the lustful way my name rolls across his tongue.

"Yes?" I whisper, barely getting the word out. My throat feels dry, and yet my mouth is watering at the possibility of kissing this sexy man.

"If you don't want me to kiss you, now's the time to push me away, baby doll." The endearment rolls off his tongue seductively, and I can't stop the approving hum that rumbles low in my throat.

Baby doll? Why does it sound so sweet and hot at the same time?

"So, what's it going to be?"

Instead of pushing him away like my brain knows I should, my traitorous body refuses and arches into his, bringing us closer together. My breasts brush against his chest. He weaves the tips of his fingers through my hair at the base of my neck as both his strong hands cup my jaw. My skin pebbles at the electrifying touch of his thumbs as he caresses the sensitive skin between my neck and jaw, and my nipples harden to peaks as my lower belly tightens with unfurled lust.

Mason slowly turns my chin to the side before covering my mouth with his.

Fireworks explode in my stomach. Mason swallows my moans, deepening our kiss. He tastes sweet and tangy, like the lime Jello in our food box, and something more ... masculine. He tastes delicious. Like home.

Alarms blare as his tongue expertly slides against mine, making my knees weak. If this man fucks like he kisses, there is no doubt he will ruin me for all other men.

Mason devours me possessively, gently taking what he wants while giving me exactly what I need. I'm putty in his hands. Powerless against him and this inexplicable pull he has on me.

He slowly glides a hand down my side, resting it on my hip, burning my skin through my clothing. With his knee, he nudges my legs apart, forcing me to straddle his thigh.

The heat and friction between us are my undoing. I drop my keys to the ground and wrap my arms around his neck, pulling him closer. Tangling my fingers in his soft locks, I finally stop thinking and start feeling.

Wild desire snakes through my body as his arms tightly wind around my waist. My hips jut forward of their own accord, grinding against his thick thigh, seeking relief. Mason releases my hair, slamming a hand against the door with a grunt, his mouth never leaving mine.

Small yapping barks startle me as I rip my mouth away from his. Clinging to him, I drop my head back against the door, trying to catch my breath. What the hell was that witchcraft?

Did he feel it too?

"What in the world is that?" he grunts.

Opening my eyes, I find Mason's chest heaving. His lips are swollen and wet from our kiss, and he's staring through my side window where a tiny dark shadow is jumping up and down.

"Oh, that's just Henry."

Mason looks at me in question.

"My toy Yorkie. I adopted him. Well ... more like inherited him since he belonged to Chris's ex-boyfriend. 'Boyfriend' is extreme;

he was more like a one-weekend stand," I yammer on, slightly embarrassed by my dog and the intense heat my pussy is emanating onto his thick thigh.

I shift, but Mason holds me in place.

"Henry?" He arches a knowing brow at me.

My face warms. He's going to realize how crazy deep my and Chris's Henry Cavill obsession runs.

He already knows about Bog, so I guess it can't get any worse.

Biting my lip, I nod.

A slow smile stretches across his face, and I almost fall to my knees.

"Well, then. I guess I have my work cut out for me if I want you to be obsessed with me instead," he says smoothly.

I bark out a laugh. He can't be serious. Superman doesn't hold a candle to him. Mason is the real deal. Sexy, smart, and boy can he kiss. My thighs clench around his thigh still parked between my legs.

He smirks before running his nose from my collarbone to my ear as my eyes flutter closed.

"You smell good enough to eat." He kisses my jaw before stepping back, taking his heat with him.

I glance down and watch as he adjusts the extremely large bulge in his jeans.

Damn. I open my mouth to invite him in when he shakes his head.

"Not tonight." He bends down, picks up my keys, and hands them to me.

Our fingers graze, setting my body on fire and my stomach tumbling. When I look into his green eyes, I can see the same fire within me is burning him too.

He does feel it.

"Open the door, Em."

I do as he says, unlocking the door and opening it wide as Henry dashes across the threshold, jumping and pawing Mason's shins.

He leans down and picks up my little dog, cradling him sweetly. Scratching Henry's little ears, he looks the pup in the eyes and says, "Don't get used to keeping her all to yourself, you hear me?"

Henry yips like he's telling Mason to get lost while my heart leaps in my chest at his words.

"Mason?"

He looks at me and shakes his head again, refusing to let me talk. "I'll pick you up tomorrow at nine for breakfast. Be ready, and wear something you can walk in."

Grabbing my dog from his clutches, I pop a hip and glare at him. My body might be turned on by his bossy attitude, but my brain rebuffs that nonsense real quick. He won't come inside, and now he's demanding I go out again with him.

Something snaps in me. I have enough people telling me what to do; I will not add another to that list.

"You're not my boss, and who says I'm going anywhere with you?" No matter how sexy he is. I stand firm, waiting to see how he reacts.

His shoulders drop as he closes his lids and takes a deep breath before opening his eyes, which have softened in intensity. "You're right, baby doll. Care to join me for breakfast and a hike tomorrow morning?"

My body relaxes at the change in his tone. His apology and body language assure me he's being genuine. I know Mason is a leader and used to giving direction, but he's going to need to keep that behavior for the boardroom. I have no problem letting him know I won't be pushed around.

Might want to work on that with your parents, my head screams.

I sigh. "Better."

Mason chuckles, amused by my attitude, and I can't stop the smile pulling at my lips.

"So, breakfast?"

"Breakfast sounds nice," comes barreling out of my mouth before I can think better of it. Henry wiggles in my arms, so I place him on the floor.

Mason wraps his arms around my lower back and stares at me with earnest eyes and says, "I want you to know I will always treat you like my equal. I'm sorry for being bossy."

I nod as he steals a kiss. It's not as intense as our first, but it still packs a punch, knocking me breathless. He breaks away, peppering kisses along my jaw.

Pressing his lips to my ear, he whispers, "But make no mistake. In the bedroom, I am the boss, and I look forward to showing you how much I appreciate my employees."

A moan rattles in my chest at his innuendo. I know his words sound like all kinds of sexual harassment, but my body doesn't seem to care. It wants him to boss me around. Bend me over the couch and ravage me. My panties flood with arousal and all I want to do is pull him into my house, and ride his face and his dick all night long.

Oh shit. I'm horny, and Mason is not helping.

"Good night, Emery." He pulls away with a smug smirk.

He has every right to be cocky. I almost came in my pants from his dirty insinuations alone. And that kiss? I don't stand a chance against him.

"Good night, Mason."

He waits on the porch until I step into my house and lock the door. I watch as he walks towards his car, climbs in, and drives away.

Squealing, I do a little dance. He yips at me, not into being trampled on.

"Sorry, buddy."

He jumps on the couch as I plop down against the fluffy pillows next to him. My tiny pooch jumps back in my lap, licking my chin. I push him away as my phone buzzes in my pocket.

In my Mason fog, I forgot to remove my coat. Shrugging it off, I pull out my phone and see a text from Chris. Swiping it open, I chuckle to myself as I read his message.

Chris: **Megan the Stallion Twerking**
Chris: I'm off to the club with Dirk to get my dance on.
Emery: Dirk?
Chris: Don't judge. I met him at the gym.
Emery: Cliché meeting, no?
Chris: **Middle Finger Emoji**
Chris: He's hot.
Emery: Be safe. Talk tomorrow?

My stomach flips as I bite my thumb at the thought of our weekly catch-up call. As much as I want to tell Chris all about my date tonight, I shouldn't. My life is too complicated to get involved with someone like Mason. He's the perfect blend of intense and broody, with a swirl of sweet and thoughtful. My catnip. And this pussy wants a taste.

Oh gee, I really am hot for it. Maybe Chris was right and there are cobwebs growing between my legs.

With a sigh, I rest my head on the back of the couch. My thoughts are all over the place. I can't get how amazing the date was or how amazing Mason is out of my head. He was attentive, checking to see if I needed more food or something to drink. The way he looked at me in awe as I watched the movie, reciting a few lines...

Not gonna lie, I loved the way he watched me with hooded eyes. Like he was holding back the need to kiss me. I've never had a man look at me like I was the only person in the room. If he doesn't stop with all the sexy swoon he's throwing my way, I can see myself falling for him.

Or, at least, riding him into next week.

I press my cool hands into my flush cheeks at the dirty thoughts I keep conjuring up. My phone beeps again.

Chris: Always. I'm hoping Dirk has a big dick. He certainly has big feet.
Chris: **Photo of ankles and very large feet**
Emery: **Eye Roll Emoji**
Emery: His dress shoes are pointy. His dick size could be deceiving.
Chris: Why are you putting bad juju out into the world? He needs to have a big dick, Em. I need a good dicking-down tonight.

I shake my head at my brother. I might have been thinking of getting a dicking-down by Mason, but I would never tell Chris that.

Although, lately, he's been more outrageous than usual. He's taking his breakup with Sierra harder than he's let on. I don't know why—she was the worst. She was needy, clingy, and way too jealous.

Anger churns in my stomach. That girl said something to him. It's the only explanation for his wilder-than-usual behavior.

Shaking my head, I text my baby brother back. I know this will pass. I'll just have to wait out his storm and let him do his thing.

Emery: Hope you're right. Good night, Chrisy. **Kiss Emoji**
Chris: Good night, Emmy. **Heart Emoji**

NINE

Emery

My heart pounds like a drum in my chest at the ringing of my doorbell. Henry races to the door, barking at the person on the other side.

"Relax, little guy," I say in a soothing tone as I pick him up and -pat him on the head.

My stomach dips like I'm riding a rollercoaster as I open the door and take in the sight before me.

On my doorstep is Mason, looking hot as sin. Ready for the cold Pacific Northwest day, he's wearing a black puffer jacket with the zipper undone, a tight gray shirt that molds to his bulging pecs and firm abs, charcoal joggers that leave little to the imagination—and have me desperately trying to keep my eyes off of the crotch area—paired with some black sneakers. The matching black beanie on his head leaves his shaggy hair curling at the ends around his ears, and my hands itch to touch the soft strands.

"Hi." My greeting comes out choppy, like my breath.

What is he doing to me? I feel like a crushing teenage girl when I'm around him.

"Good morning."

Mason leans in and kisses me on the cheek while I stand frozen and tongue-tied. Thank goodness for Henry, who leaps out of my arms, searching for attention and breaking me out of my stupor.

Mason takes him from me, scratching him behind the ears, as he steps into my home and closes the door behind him. "Good morning to you too, Henry."

My Yorkie barks in response, making me chuckle. Henry has a knack for talking back as if he understands every word spoken to him. On some level, I think he does.

Mason brings his green eyes to mine, looking right into me. My knees wobble, and my cheeks flame at his intense gaze. He smiles, and holy shit-balls... If I was a popsicle, I'd be melted.

Yeah, I am definitely crushing on this sexy man.

He breaks the silence first, crouching down to put Henry on the floor before bringing us chest to chest. "Are you ready to go, or do you need more time?"

"I'm ready. I just need to grab my jacket." I point at the closet behind him.

He steps to the side, leaving me enough space to pass him. My arm brushes against his, and sparks crackle to life between us, exploding across my arm and up my neck. Taking a deep breath, I try to calm my nerves and grab my jacket.

Mason takes it from my hands, helping me to slip into the sleeves. He pulls the coat over my shoulders and spins me around, clutching the zipper and pulling me closer, our bodies flush.

His minty breath fans across my lips. "You look beautiful."

His compliment has my cheeks warming.

"Thank you," I whisper, my voice hoarse as his heavy-laden eyes linger on my body, sending shivers down my spine.

I'm wearing black fleece leggings and a long-sleeve thermal in my favorite burgundy shade. It's nothing special, but it's tighter than skin and accentuates every curve on my body. The weather might call for warm clothes, but I made sure to give Mason a nice view of my long legs and ass.

Thank you *5 Rounds Cardio Kick-boxing*. With the way his eyes eat me up like he'd rather eat me for breakfast, I think those classes have paid for themselves.

Before I can think it through, I raise onto my toes and kiss him.

He doesn't hesitate to grasp my ribcage beneath my coat, pulling me closer to deepen the kiss. His hands slide up over my breasts before gripping my jaw and tilting my head to his will, taking charge.

My thighs clench, and my center slickens as he continues to ravage my mouth, slowly and purposefully, like there is nothing else he'd rather do. I like bossy and in-control Mason.

Damn. He's a good kisser.

My clit pulses with need at the taste of him on my tongue. He explores my mouth, setting the pace, and I let him, allowing myself to get lost in the spell he has on me.

Mason wrenches his mouth away with a pained groan like it's physically painful to stop. His chest heaves as he cups my jaw, running his thumb over my wet puffy lips, and mumbles, "This mouth."

"What about it?" I murmur, leaning into his touch.

He sucks in a deep breath and shakes his head before spearing me with his sea-green eyes. "Let's get some food in that pretty little mouth of yours," he growls.

I swear it sounds like he wants to stick something else in my mouth. Visions of my lips wrapped around his cock flood my brain, and my nipples pucker. Thankfully, my stomach grumbles, lightening the mood.

We laugh, and just like that, the intense sexual tension between us boils down to a simmer.

"That's probably a good idea," I mumble because I'm pretty damn sure I might let Mason take me to the bedroom right now and have him do whatever he wants to me.

He releases my face and steps back, taking his heat with him. I miss his touch immediately.

Deep breath.

I turn and pick up Henry, putting him in his bed by the couch. I head for the door and lock up the house before letting Mason lead me from the porch to his car. The palm of his hand lands on the small of my back, burning my skin through the thick layers of my clothing. My face is flushed, and my body is in a heightened state of awareness at Mason's proximity. It takes me a minute to stop thinking about that kiss as the sexy man who broke my brain drives us to our destination.

"You said you work in marketing. What's that like?" he breaks the silence.

"It depends. The place I work does a little of everything: graphic design, updating websites, helping businesses get on social media, stuff like that. The ladies I work with are awesome. They hired me right out of college, and I had no experience. But they took a chance on me and have recently extended a partnership to me."

"That's amazing. It sounds like you love your job."

"I do ..."

"But?" he asks with a pause, waiting for me to answer.

How does he know there's a 'but'?

I have never told anyone this, but Mason makes me feel safe and I know he would never judge me. "Well, I'd really like to expand our business into events, but I've been too chicken to suggest it."

"If it's something you really want, you should. It probably seems scary but if you don't take a chance, it's a missed opportunity.

He's not wrong. My stomach churns at the prospect of my partners saying no. "I'll think about it. Tell me about your work. You said technology, right? Does that mean computer stuff?"

He chuckles, glancing my way, and my stomach churns for another reason this time.

"I work in tech security, so yes, in this instance, it's all about computers. My best friends and I are software developers and coders, specializing in bank security."

Mason continues talking and I listen, lost in the deep timber of his voice as he tries to explain what he does. It's too technical for me, but it's hot as heck listening to how passionate he is about his work. He's extremely dedicated to his business.

It also seems like he travels a ton for his job. I know that would be a red flag for most women, but I don't mind. Mason is out there making a difference, and he's proud of what he does, which makes me proud too. To know someone cares about others so much that he dedicated his life to this calling, it's commendable.

Our conversation flows throughout the rest of the drive and our breakfast.

❧

As I look around from the top of the trailhead Mason and I just hiked, I'm a little somber. The heavy dark clouds getting ready to roll in from the distance are darkening my mood.

Or maybe it's the fact that you've been missing out on so much.

Closing my eyes, I take a deep breath. Peeking through the trap of lush green oak and maple trees is the stunning vision of St. John's Bridge and its gothic steel. Like the bridge, I'm trapped too.

I have been missing out on ... my life. I live in this charming small town, and I've yet to explore all it has to offer. It took the man standing next to me, who doesn't even live here, to get me to eat brunch at the little spot my colleagues rave about. My life is ... sad. Lonely. Boring.

"Penny for your thoughts?" Mason's deep tenor cuts my introspection.

"You couldn't afford them," I respond, focusing on the view instead of the way the gorgeously sweet man beside me brushes his arm against mine, making the hair on my arm prickle with recognition.

"Name your price, Emery."

I turn to Mason. The look on his face hits me in the gut. His eyes take in every inch of my face with a furrowed brow, trying to read me. To figure me out.

My pulse jumps. I have to be careful around him. He sees too much, and it's dangerous. He can easily rip away my carefully constructed walls, created to spare Chris the pain of knowing the truth. Mostly, Mason's dangerous to my heart. He has the ability to ruin me.

And worst of all, I want him to.

"Mason..." I reach for his hand and my shoulders sag in defeat, knowing what I have to do.

"No." He shakes his head, his eyes unwavering in whatever decision he's already made. He wraps his arms around my waist and pulls me close.

I want to put up a fight, but with his arms around me, I feel safe and let him hold me up—something no one has ever done for me.

"I know what you're thinking, and no. Believe me, I know this isn't the right time. We both work too much. You have your brother to take care of. My business is taking off, taking up almost every minute of my life. But those other minutes, when my mind wanders, it's you I think about. Ever since that flight, I've thought of you. When you walked away..." He shakes his head.

My heart pinches, thinking about that goodbye in the airport all those weeks ago. I didn't want to say the word, but I had to. I had to push through the unfamiliar feeling of loss that formed like a lead ball in my stomach. A ball that grew heavier with every step I took away from him. It took every bit of willpower I had to keep from looking back.

Did he feel the same loss?

"Then I saw you at the airport, standing on the curb looking like a vision, staring at your phone, and I knew I had to take a chance. This is our chance. What are the odds of me finding you again?"

"Pretty good, seeing as I'm at the airport every other weekend," I tease.

His lips turn up slightly, fighting his smile. "Smart-ass."

"Charmer."

Mason flashes me a wide grin, and my heart flutters.

"Only for you." He taps my cold nose with his warm finger. "Our timing might be shit. I'm leaving for work tonight. I travel all the time. I don't live here. All things for the cons column. But I don't want to let you go. I want to get to know you. I want to spend whatever time I can with you. Please tell me you do too."

"I do, but—"

"Nope. None of that," Mason cuts me off.

I hold back my smile and bite my tongue.

"Let's just see what happens. Let's take a chance. Take things slow. What do you say?"

"So, you want to be casual?" I think I can do casual.

A growl rumbles in his throat at the word, and my stomach dips. Is he ... jealous? We've been on one freaking date. Okay, two if you count this morning. Three if we count the plane.

That's more dates than you went on last year, my brain snarks.

Visions of Mason going on dates with another woman make my stomach twist. *Oh crap.* Now I'm the jealous one.

"If by 'casual' you mean we talk and see each other when we can, then yes." He drags the last word through gritted teeth, sounding like he's in pain agreeing to my terms.

His eyes bore into mine before dancing to my mouth. He watches intently as I slowly swipe my tongue across my bottom lip—a plea for him to kiss me.

He returns his gaze to mine. "Just so we're clear, my definition of casual also means you are casually *not* bringing other men to your bed."

"Is that so?" I arch a brow his way in defiance.

If he thinks he can tell me who I can and can't go out with while he's off banging chicks in whatever cities he's visiting for work, he has another thing coming. There is no way this will be a one-sided agreement. It's not like I go out on dates and sleep with men regularly. Yes, Bog keeps me fulfilled most of the time. I'm a woman, and I have needs. So yes, I've had the occasional one-night stand over the years to alleviate the loneliness, just not lately.

"Does that mean you will casually *not* be bringing other women to your bed?"

"Baby doll, the last time I brought a woman to my bed was over two years ago. So, no, I will not be bringing other women to my bed. Only you ... if you let me."

My jaw drops at his admission. He hasn't had sex in over two years? How is that possible? Mason is freaking gorgeous. Like, "bite your lip, pick your jaw up off the floor, fan your face, and replace your wet undies" sexy.

"Okay," I choke out.

"Okay? Like, okay, we can be casually monogamous? Or like, okay, I can take you to my bed and ravage you?"

Words escape me as I think about him ravaging my body. He chuckles at my hesitation and presses a kiss on my cheek.

"Good to know where your head's at," he says with a smirk.

I'm stuck frozen in place, confused by what I just agreed to and a whole lot turned on by it.

"Come on. It's time to head down." He grabs my hand, never letting it go as we walk down the trail back to his car.

He tells me all about his nephew, who suggested this hike and breakfast spot. How he plans to spend the rest of the day with him before he has to fly out to some client meeting. I listen intently, nodding along as he leads our conversation. I find it so sweet that he spends what little free time he has with his family.

When we reach my place, he walks me to the door and tells me he'll text later, before covering my mouth with his. We make out on my front porch for a long while before he pulls away and leaves me standing there dazed, waving at his taillights.

I'm not sure how I thought today was going to go, but I sure as hell didn't foresee myself getting dropped off at home and being kissed to within an inch of my life by my now "casual boyfriend".

I'm so fucked.

And for once, I think I'm okay with it.

TEN

Mason & Emery

TEXT CHAIN

JANUARY 10
    Mason: I made it to Chicago.
    Emery: How was the flight?
    Mason: Long and boring. It was lacking a gorgeous brunette.
    Emery: Charmer.
    Mason: Only for you.
    Mason: I'm meeting the gang for dinner, and I have client meetings all day tomorrow. Can I call you tomorrow night?
    Emery: I look forward to it. Night, Mason.
    Mason: Night, baby doll.

January 11
    Mason: I'm in my room. Can I still call you?
    Emery: I might be waiting for you.
    Emery: **Selfie with a bowl of popcorn**
    Mason: You're beautiful.
    Emery: Charmer.
    Mason: Only for you.

January 15
Mason: What's your favorite color?
Emery: Hello to you too, mister.
Mason: Hi, brat.
Emery: Hi, bossy. It's burgundy, by the way.
Mason: Like that skin-tight shirt you wore on our hike?
Emery: Like that, did you?
Mason: Fuck yeah. Showed off your rack quite nicely.
Emery: **Shakes head** I didn't know you were so crude.
Mason: Only for you.
Emery: Charmer.

◍

January 18
Mason: How was your day?
Emery: Great, actually. I finally got up the nerve to talk to my business partners about expanding into events. They are completely supportive. It will be a huge task, but if all goes well, I think we could be successful.
Mason: That's awesome. I'm proud of you.
Emery: Thank you for encouraging me to speak up.
Mason: That was all you.
Emery: So, how was your day?
Mason: Lacking...
Emery: Lacking what?
Mason: You.
Emery: Charmer.
Mason: Only for you, baby doll.

◍

January 20

Emery: What's your favorite meal?

Mason: Can you keep a secret?

Emery: **Crosses heart**

Mason: It used to be my mom's pot roast, but my sister-in-law's mom makes the best tamales I've ever had. They're so good I dream about them.

Emery: **Rubs hands together**

Emery: Thanks for the blackmail info.

Mason: That's cold.

Emery: **Laughing Emoji**

Emery: I promise, mum's the word.

Mason: What about you?

Emery: Hands down cinnamon rolls for breakfast.

Mason: I bet you'd taste delicious and sweet for breakfast.

Emery: **Shifts in seat uncomfortably**

Emery: Charmer.

Mason: Only for you.

💋

January 23

Mason: Loved seeing your face last night.

Emery: Really? I was a sweaty mess after my boxing session.

Mason: I like you sweaty and wet.

Emery: You're incorrigible.

Mason: Only for you.

Emery: Charmer.

💋

January 25

Emery: I need a vacation.

Mason: Why's that?

Emery: It's cold and rainy, and I'm tired of wearing my jacket every day.

Mason: Where should we go?

Emery: Who invited you?

Mason: Me. Problem?

Emery: You paying?

Mason: Sure.

Emery: In that case, Hawaii.

Mason: Really?

Emery: Yeah, my colleague was talking about it and I've never been.

Mason: Me neither. It's a vacation date.

Emery: Deal. **Sun Emoji**

January 28

Mason: FaceTime tonight? I need to see your smile.

Emery: Charmer.

Mason: Only for you.

Emery: I'll be home in 30.

Mason: See you later, baby doll.

ELEVEN

Mason

I RACE THROUGH THE back door of my home, slamming it shut behind me as I check my watch for the tenth time in less than five minutes.

Fuck.

I'm running late for my call with Emery. It's already after nine, and I hate the idea of having less time to talk with her. All I want is more time.

I hang my garment bag in the closet, leaving my suit inside for me to deal with later. Stripping out of my clothes, I chuck them in the hamper and head to the bathroom for a quick shower. Turning the faucet to hot, I wait a minute before stepping under the spray. The warm water heats quickly, relaxing my tightened muscles. I quickly wash my hair and body, before rinsing and hopping out. Grabbing the towel off the rack, I dry my hair before wrapping it around my waist. I rub on some deodorant and head for my closet, pulling out some boxer briefs and a pair of athletic shorts.

Phone in hand, I flop onto my bed, letting the cool fabric of my comforter envelop me. If I wasn't amped up to talk to Emery, I might pass out. Between the exhaustion of traveling and the headache the new client is giving me, I'm beat.

Since I last saw her, it's been two endless weeks of nonstop travel, and I can't wait to see her tonight. We've been texting almost every day since our first date, and I've been lucky enough to pull a few calls and FaceTimes too. But it's not enough. I crave her messages and voice, and it only grows stronger with every passing day.

She's put a spell on me. A spell I welcome with open arms. I need to see her in person, soon.

The team and I are going over the February schedule after the weekend, so I'll know more then. Pushing all thoughts of work out of my head, I slide open my phone—ignoring the texts from my brothers—pull up FaceTime, and press Emery's name.

It only rings twice before her gorgeous face fills my screen, taking my breath away.

"Hey, baby doll."

A smile pulls at her deliciously plump lips that are slightly stained pink from her red lipstick.

Fuck, I wish I could wrap her in my arms and kiss her right now. She's so damn beautiful. She doesn't have a stitch of makeup on, and she still takes my breath away.

"Why hello, Mr. Bossy."

Her raspy voice makes my dick twitch when she uses the moniker. It twitches when I see it written in text. Hell, my cock twitches at the mere thought of this intoxicating woman.

"How was your day?" I clear my throat.

She licks her lips, and I have to bite back a groan.

"Better now." She sighs, resting her head on the side of the couch, giving me an appetizing view of her slender neck.

"Same, babe. Same." I lick my dry lips, wishing they were on her soft skin.

Her eyes follow the movement as she does the same. My lips quirk up in a smile because I know the feeling. I couldn't keep my eyes off of her mouth if I tried.

She clears her throat, her cheeks pinkening. "Are you in bed?"

Fluffing my pillow, I sit up and lean against the headboard. "Yeah, I just got home and was too tired to walk back to the living room."

"Hold that thought."

The screen goes black, and I can hear the muted rustling of her movements. Her face appears again, and this time, she's sitting back against a gray tufted headboard.

"Okay, now that's better." She swipes the little hairs falling from her ponytail away from her face and smiles at me.

My heart does a little pitter-patter at the sight, and I subconsciously rub at my collarbone.

"Taking me to bed so soon, Emery?" I joke but secretly yearn for it to be true.

She bites her lip and rolls her eyes at my innuendo. "You wish."

"I sure as fuck do." I'm not lying. I am dying to know what this woman tastes like. What she sounds like as she comes all over my cock.

"Promises, promises," she teases.

My dick twitches at her sass. Fuck, it's hot. "Brat."

She beams at me with fire in her eyes as the collar of her shirt falls over her shoulder, exposing her succulent skin. Is she getting off on this? Because I sure as fuck am.

"I'm teasing." She bites the tip of her finger.

Visions of me putting something else in her mouth send my blood flowing south. "I'm not. I'm going to rectify this distance between us real soon."

She lifts her perfectly manicured brow at me, begging me to continue. She wants me just as badly.

"We'll figure that out later. Tell me something good?"

She laughs at my quick change in conversation, and the sweet tinkling sound is music to my ears as it warms my chest.

Oh yeah, I'll be closing the distance between us as quickly as possible. I'll make it happen if I have to.

"Chris called, and his short film got picked for some festival in April." She sounds so proud of her little brother, and it only makes me like her more.

My brothers are my best friends, so I understand the sentiment. But that's not why I called. I want to know about her.

"That's great. But I asked about you."

"What about me?" Her brow crunches in confusion.

"Tell me something good about you. What's going on with you?"

Her eyes widen in shock for a fraction of a second before she shrugs.

Does no one ask this amazing woman about her day? About what's going on with her? How she feels? I'm going to have to change that.

"Umm. I don't know," she whispers.

"Can I tell you about my day?"

She nods tentatively for me to continue.

"First, my alarm rudely woke me up this morning, ripping me from my dream about this gorgeous woman with sparkling brown eyes and lips that could kill a man."

Emery bites the corner of her lip fighting a smile, doing what I hoped my story would do.

"Then I had to deal with some frustrating clients today, but every time I tried to work, I kept getting distracted by that dream of mine."

"What was your dream about?"

Here's the thing. I did dream about her. It just wasn't PG-rated. Emery and I flirt and tease when we talk, but it hasn't gone beyond that. This is uncharted territory for us. If I tell her about my dream, this takes our relationship to a whole new level. I'm ready to go there with her, but I'm not so sure she is.

"Are you sure you want to know?" My voice is thick and has gone down an octave.

She squirms, and her breaths get shorter, quicker.

Does she dream about me too?

"I mean ..." Her eyes flit away from the screen.

Oh, she's ready. I'd pound on my chest like a gorilla if I didn't think it would stop her from going down this road with me.

I keep my voice low, but firm. "Look at me, Emery."

She returns her heavy-lidded gaze to mine, and I don't miss the way my command racks her body with shivers.

Oh yeah, she dreams about me.

Fuck it. Here goes nothing.

"In my dream, you were in my bed and I had your legs spread wide as I ate your delicious pussy, feasting on you until you came screaming my name and your cum ran down my chin."

Instead of freaking out, Emery's eyes close and a soft moan vibrates in her throat as she no doubt imagines my dream in that pretty head of hers.

My length grows, thickening with need. I run my hand over the tip of my cock, giving it a squeeze over my clothes, fighting the urge to lower my shorts and stroke myself as she watches.

I watch her chest heave as she lays back, her eyes closed and lips parted. She's so fucking sexy.

"What happened next?"

This woman. How did I get so lucky? She surprises me with her responses at every turn, digging her claws deeper into me.

"If I had kept dreaming, I would have kissed my way up your body, stopping to lick and suck your nipples until you begged for me to slide my cock inside your tight wet cunt."

She moans louder at the picture I paint of us for her, spurring me on.

"I would have fucked you slowly, bringing you to the edge over and over until you were a needy, panting mess, before fucking you with long hard strokes, watching your tits bounce with every deep thrust until you came on my cock."

Emery pulls on the collar of her shirt before sliding her hand down her body and out of view. She bites her lip as her eyelids slowly slide open. The heated look in her eyes has me on the verge of coming in my pants.

"Emery," I warn.

Her body stiffens, and I might fucking die a happy man right now. This gorgeous woman is touching herself while I'm on the line telling her about my dirty dreams.

"Mason," she groans my name.

I can't stop from slipping my hand into my boxers, gripping my shaft. I want her to say my name like that every day.

"Yes, baby doll?"

"Are you touching yourself too?" Her voice is breathy and laced with desire.

That sound will now be my fuel every time I jerk off to thoughts of my girl.

My girl?

"Fuck, yes," I grunt, not sure if it's an answer to her or to my own wayward thoughts.

"Good, because I'm about to come."

"Keep that phone on your face and those eyes open. Show me how fucking stunning you look coming to thoughts of my thick cock buried deep inside you, fucking you hard."

She groans, panting and squirming, as she shakes her head from side to side, nearing her orgasm.

"That's it. Imagine it's my fingers, my tongue, my cock making you come."

"Yes," she keens, forcing herself to look at me.

My balls tighten, tingling with my impending orgasm as I pump my hand up my shaft faster, harder.

Forcing my eyes open, I watch Emery get herself off to my voice. To thoughts of us together.

As much as I want to see her fingers coated in her arousal and pushing into her pretty pussy, seeing her like this—vulnerable and open to me—is hot as fuck.

I see when her climax hits. Her eyes pinch tight, her muscles contract, the breath in her throat catches, and her body shudders. The sight of her coming is better than I imagined.

"Fuck," I growl.

Two more pumps and I come, hard, shooting my load over my stomach. That was possibly the best orgasm I have ever experienced.

Her eyes open, and a light sheen of sweat coats her forehead. "Well, that was new."

Her comment catches me off guard, and I bark a laugh. She chuckles, her smile bright and shy. She's never looked prettier than she does right now, all sex flushed. I can't wait to see her like this again.

"That was new for me too."

"Really?"

"Really. I don't make it a habit of jerking off while on the phone to a gorgeous woman on the other line."

"So this ... umm ... was your first time?"

The idea of having a first something with Emery sends a thrill through me, making me wonder what other kinds of firsts we can share.

"Yes, and hopefully not the last."

She grins, shooting me in the chest. Or maybe it's cupid. I don't know. But I like it. It's new and exciting, and I want more of it. I want more of her.

"Ready to tell me something good that happened to you today?"

She tugs on her ponytail, releasing her long hair in waves over her shoulder.

"Well, there was this hot guy..."

I growl playfully at her, and she giggles. That sound. Fuck, it does all the things to me.

"He called me and told me a sexy story, which led to the best orgasm I've ever had."

"Yet."

"Yet?"

I nod. "Yup, best yet. I plan on giving you more orgasms than you can count while making you come so hard you see stars. I'm going to own your body, Emery, and bend it to my will."

"So bossy."

"You haven't seen anything *yet*, baby doll."

TWELVE

Mason & Emery

TEXT CHAIN

FEBRUARY 2

Mason: Football or baseball?

Emery: Neither. **Boxing Gloves Emoji**

Emery: You?

Mason: Soccer.

Emery: Interesting. Bourbon or beer?

Mason: Neither. Gin.

Mason: ...

Emery: Aren't you going to ask me about mine?

Mason: Aperol Spritz.

Emery: What? **Shocked Emoji**

Mason: That's your favorite drink.

Emery: How'd you know?

Mason: I have my ways.

Emery: Evasive much?

Mason: I'll tell you about it when I see you. Speaking of, when can I see your beautiful face in person and not on my phone screen?

Emery: Depends. Will you be in L.A. next week?

Mason: SF. What about the weekend after? I can be in Portland.

Emery: You'd come here for me? The only weekend you have free?

Mason: Yes.

Emery: You know that's Valentine's Day weekend, right?

Mason: So, then be my Valentine, baby doll.

Emery: Charmer.

Mason: Only for you.

Mason: Is that a yes?

Emery: Yes, Mason. I'll be your Valentine.

February 3

Mason: My plane is delayed.

Emery: My feet hurt.

Mason: Ha. Hit me with it. Why?

Emery: Wore heels too long. But I signed a client for a marketing event next month. It's just a conference, but it will be my first big event.

Mason: That's awesome. Pick up.

Emery: Okay, Mr. Bossy. Give me a second. I just got home, and I'm changing into comfy clothes.

Mason: Maybe we should turn this into a video call. Keep your top off.

Emery: Perv.

Mason: Only for you.

Emery: Charmer.

February 8

Mason: Deal breaker...

Emery: ???

Mason: NY or Chicago-style pizza?

Emery: It's not pizza if it's not made in NY.

Mason: Good answer.

Mason: *Picture of large pepperoni pizza**

Emery: **Drooling Emoji** That looks good. Where are you?

Mason: In NY for a quick client meeting. Just stopped by my favorite place before Kenzo and I hop on a flight back to L.A..

Emery: I'm jealous.

Mason: Don't be jealous, baby doll. Kenz means nothing to me.

Emery: Funny. I meant the pizza.

Mason: I know. But don't worry. You're my only girl.

Emery: Charmer.

Mason: Only for you.

February 12

Emery: Thank you for the flowers. They're beautiful.

Emery: **Selfie with burgundy bouquet**

Mason: You're beautiful.

Emery: Charmer.

Mason: Only for you.

Mason: I'm glad you like them.

Emery: Love them. Is it still casual if I say … I can't wait to see you?

Mason: We are anything but casual, Em.

Emery: Mason…

Mason: I'll see you tomorrow, baby doll.

FEBRUARY

My phone rings, and I groan at the name flashing across the banner. What the fuck does he want right now? I hit ignore, but less than a minute later, it's ringing again.

"What do you want?" I bark.

"What's up your fucking ass?" Cameron snaps.

Shit, I shouldn't be so short with him, but my flight's delayed and I'm irritated as fuck. I hate being stuck in Seattle. I was hoping to land early so I could see Rhys before I spend the rest of the weekend with Emery.

"Sorry. Shit's just messed up, and my flight's delayed."

"Yeah, that sucks balls. So you won't be home this weekend?"

"Nah."

"Where are you headed next?"

I don't want to let on where I am, but if I do manage to see Jace and his family, Cam will find out anyway. "Portland."

"No shit. Why didn't you say? I would have met you there."

That's exactly why I didn't tell him. He has too much time on his hands during the week of his off-season and with nothing to distract him, all he wants to do is hang out.

"Last-minute decision," I mumble, hoping he doesn't read too much into it. There is no way in hell I'm telling Cam about my real reason for dropping into Oregon—Emery.

"Why don't I believe you? You never do anything without planning it first." He's clearly suspicious.

Am I that fucking predictable? *Yes.*

I run my hand over my jaw in frustration. Cam's right. I have been planning this trip for the last two weeks, and it was never to see my nephew. When we spoke the other night, something didn't sit right with me knowing I would be close by and wasn't going to spend time with him. Before I could stop myself, I was promising I would have an early dinner with him.

The last thing I wanted to do was delay getting to Emery, but I knew if I didn't see my family before spending the weekend with her, I wouldn't be able to fully enjoy our time together.

"Yeah, well, believe it."

The voice crackling through the overhead speakers finally calls my flight number, saving me from my kid brother's probing.

"Cam, my flight is boarding. I'll call you when I get back to town."

"Yeah, yeah. Alright. Fly safe, brother."

"Will do, kid."

With another delay on the runway before take-off and the hour flight, I land in Portland to a message from Jace, letting me know that Rhys isn't feeling well and that they were all going to stay in and rest.

Mason: That sucks. Hope he feels better. I'll be back around. Take it easy.

Jace: Thanks, man. See you soon.

If it were any other weekend, I'd be more upset about missing time with my family, but a bigger part of me is grateful for the extra time I get with Emery. I shoot her a text.

Mason: Just landed. Lots of delays. Would you mind meeting me at the restaurant for our 9pm reservation?
Emery: Okay. See you soon.
Mason: Can't wait.

I shove my phone in my pocket and rush off the plane to the taxi stand. When I arrive at the hotel, I check in and confirm the dinner reservation with the concierge before heading to my room for a hot shower.

I'm nervous about tonight. It's been years since I've had a date on Valentine's Day. When our schedules didn't line up until this weekend, I didn't even hesitate to ask her to be my Valentine.

Since the moment I saw Emery's reflection, I've been captivated by her. Our texts and calls have only made the pull stronger. She's fucking amazing. I look forward to getting her messages with random questions. I count down the hours until I can hear her voice over the line or see her beautiful face on video chat. I fall asleep every night and wake up every morning thinking about her.

Without even trying, she's consumed me.

Fifteen minutes before I'm supposed to meet Emery, I'm dressed and ready to go. I opted for my charcoal suit, a black button-up dress shirt, and a maroon tie. I want tonight to be special for us, which is why I chose the restaurant offering a special Valentine's menu for dinner.

I grab the single long-stem rose I set aside on the table for Emery and look around the room. Everything is set up perfectly. I hope she joins me after dinner to see it.

I make my way to the elevators and head down to the restaurant bar. I originally planned on renting a car and picking her up, but the plane delays ruined my plan.

Emery has no idea I'm staying here, and I don't want her to know. The last thing I want her thinking is that I'm trying to get her into bed.

Do I want her there? Hell fucking yes.

I want to run my hands over every square inch of her body and memorize every freckle, every moan, every cry of pleasure that escapes her as I bury myself inside her.

All. Night. Long.

My cock grows thick in my slacks at thoughts of Emery beneath me. Discreetly adjusting myself, I step out of the elevator and walk through the lobby. I remind my dick to cool it. I want more than just sex with her.

For the first time in years, I can see a future with someone. With Emery, I know this is more than just a good time, a stop on the road. She already means more to me than I can explain. I want her to feel the same way. My goal this weekend is to not only tell her how I feel but to show her too. I want her to take a chance on me. On us. Hence the room decor waiting for her.

Taking a seat at the bar, I order both of us a drink. Gin and soda for me, and an Aperol Spritz for her. I chuckle to myself, remembering how I shocked the hell out of her with that little bit of knowledge.

That fucking bartender. I can't believe he was right. I shake my head and take a sip of my drink.

The hair on the back of my neck stands on end, bringing my eyes up to the mirror behind the bar.

Like the first time I saw her, Emery stands at the entrance of the restaurant, face down towards the cell phone in her hands. She's wearing a burgundy cocktail dress that cups her breasts perfectly and flares at her hips. Her light caramel hair lays in soft curls that hang right above her waist. She looks absolutely stunning.

My pocket buzzes, and I know it's her. I don't bother reaching for it as I turn around on the stool and watch her. She must feel my gaze because her head snaps up, and her eyes connect with mine.

Everything clicks into place, and my chest feels lighter as I watch a radiant smile pull at the plump burgundy lips I dream about, and spread across her face. While I've seen that smile on my phone screen, it's nothing compared to seeing it in person.

I stand—my heart pounding in my chest—and like a moth to the flame, I make my way to her. I close the distance between us in quick long strides, sweeping her into my arms and crushing my mouth to hers in a searing kiss.

Her hands find my hair, and I'm about to pick her up and carry her upstairs when I hear a throat clearing. I break the kiss and stare down at the girl that's captured me by surprise. Swiping my thumb across her bee-stung lips, her lipstick mostly intact, I admire how wet and swollen they are from our kiss. Her cheeks are tinged pink as her chest heaves.

She's never looked more beautiful.

"Hi," I mumble into her mouth, stealing another quick peck.

"Hi," she whispers, her breath fanning across my lips. Her eyes dart over my shoulder to where the hostess is surely watching, and she giggles. "That was some greeting."

I can't help but chuckle at how sweet it sounds and how good it feels to hold her. "What can I say? I missed you."

And that's the fucking truth. These past few weeks getting to know Emery have been some of the best I've ever had, but I want more. All the texts and calls aren't enough anymore. The sexy phone call we shared only multiplied my need to see her. To touch her.

I thought the way she made me feel was all a dream. Something I conjured up to help me get by, but that's not the case at all. She is very real. As are the feelings I've developed for her.

For the first time in a long time, I've let myself begin to fall for someone that I can see a future with. That should scare me since we've only been on two dates weeks ago, but with her here in my arms, it feels so right. She feels right.

"I missed you too, Mason."

At her confession, I pull her closer, hugging her to my body, relieved that she's finally in my arms. I kiss the top of her head and breathe in her intoxicating vanilla pear scent.

"I ordered us a few cocktails while we wait for our table." With my hand on her lower back, I lead her to the bar, where our drinks sit waiting for us.

"For you." I hand her the rose sitting on the bar.

She gives it a sniff. "Thank you."

I pull out the bar stool for her to take a seat, before sitting beside her and pulling my stool as close as I can to hers. Turning her body to the side, I capture her knees between mine. She bites her thumb—in that cute way I like, where her red lips wrap around her slender digit and her pink tongue pokes out—and watches me.

I can see the question lingering in her eyes. She's been dying for me to tell her this story.

"Go ahead. Ask."

"How do you know this is my favorite drink?" She holds up the wine glass filled with orange liquid to me before taking a drink.

Her pretty, pouty lips wrap around the straw, and I can picture them wrapped around me instead. I cover my impending groan by taking a sip of my drink.

She watches me, waiting for me to give her the answer. She wiggles in her seat impatiently, and I can't help but make a meal of it.

"Well? I'm waiting, Mr. Bossy." She puts her drink down and slowly crosses her legs, her dress riding higher and granting me a better view of her toned thighs. She smiles at me coyly. She knows what she's doing.

I give her a smirk of my own before I give in. "You know, I'm about to lose all my cool points with this story."

"I doubt that." She leans forward and puts her palm on my chest, running it down my tie. "I must say, you clean up nice in this suit."

I place my hands on her thighs, her skin burning mine. "Baby doll, it's nothing compared to how fucking sexy you look in this dress."

Goosebumps break across her skin as she squeezes her thighs together. She places her hands on mine and lifts my mitts off her thighs. "Thank you. But stop distracting me with all your sexiness and tell me how you know about the Aperol Spritz," she smarts.

"You think I'm sexy?"

"That's what you took from that sentence?"

"Hell yeah. What man wouldn't when a gorgeous, intelligent woman tells him he's sexy? I'd be an idiot."

She purses her lips and lifts a brow at me not taking the bait.

"Fine." I rub my scruffy jaw, deciding whether or not to tell her the whole story. But honestly wins out, as it will every time with me, so I tell her, "The first time I saw you was back in October. I was sitting at a bar like this." I point to the mirrored wall behind the bar.

Her eyes follow mine and return to me, completely captivated by my story.

"I only caught a glimpse of you while I was talking to my nephew on the phone. You were staring at your phone and talking into your earbuds. You looked angry and frustrated. I thought to my-self, 'Damn that woman is the most beautiful creature I have ever seen.'"

"Mason." She sighs, biting her lip.

My heart does that skip again. I can hear the appreciation and wonder in her voice, and I want to hear her say my name like that again. Only breathier while I'm deep inside her, claiming her as mine like she did on the phone.

"I looked down at my cell to finish my call, and when I looked up again, trying to find you, you were gone."

"That's so sweet. But what does that have to do with knowing my favorite drink?" She tilts her head to the side.

"As I searched the crowd for you, the pervy fucking bartender came over. He told me he'd seen you around and that you always order Aperol Spritz while you talk on the phone."

"Does this bartender have salt-and-pepper hair and look like a beefed-up Zaddy?"

"What the fuck is a Zaddy?" I growl.

She bursts out laughing. "It's the new version of DILF. It means a hot old guy who may or may not have children. Chris is determined to get with that guy. But he's out of luck. Bartender Zaddy is strictly into women."

"And how would you know that?" I grit out. Jealousy tinges my vision green. I swear if she says he's laid a finger on her, I might break his fucking face.

"Oh, I've seen him staring at the big boobs of a fake blonde while she rested them on his bar top. Pretty sure she'd have let him take her home with pleasure. If you know what I mean." She pumps her eyebrows at me.

I laugh, relieved to know he's never touched my girl. Not that I could blame him—she's fucking perfect.

"Get jealous there for a second?"

"Uh, yeah. I was envisioning pulling him over the bar and punching his teeth out."

"Don't worry, Mr. Bossy, you're the only guy I've picked up at the airport." She pats my hand.

I squeeze her thigh. "I thought I picked you up."

"Okay, we can go with that story if you want," she says with a shrug.

We both know I'm the one who initiated our conversation. I'm about to fight her on it when the hostess comes over, letting us know our table is ready. Grabbing Emery's hand, I help her off the stool and watch her calves flex as she places her feet on the floor.

I take her in, from her sexy stiletto-covered feet to her pretty topaz eyes. She's utterly stunning and without a doubt one of a kind.

"You're fucking beautiful, baby doll."

"Thank you," she whispers, blushing.

We follow the hostess to our table, Emery's hand still clasped in mine.

If the rest of the night continues this way, I'm pretty sure I'm going to fall for her completely. I might already be there.

FOURTEEN

Emery

"How's Henry this evening?"

Nervous butterflies flutter in my stomach at Mason's probing question.

"Probably living his best life and being spoiled by a couple of six-year-olds," I say with a shrug.

His fork stops midair as he arches his brow in question. I chuckle at his surprise.

When he asked me to meet him at the hotel restaurant, I assumed he booked a room here ... and I would stay with him.

Over the past few weeks, we've gotten to know each other very well. Mason is funny, in a dry humor kind of way, and genuinely sweet. Even though he is busy with work, he checks in with updates on his day and makes time for us to talk. I look forward to getting his texts and hearing the way his gruff voice says my name or calls me baby doll. Our texts and calls have become flirtier, and our last FaceTime was definitely not suitable for work.

When he suggested we meet this weekend and asked me to be his Valentine, I figured this was it. We'd spend the weekend together. Alone. Doing all the things I've been imagining us doing every night before I go to bed.

So, I planned. I sent my dog to stay with some work friends, packed my overnight bag—which is sitting in my car—and wore the sexiest bra and panty set I own.

"You don't need to go home tonight?"

"Nope." With a smirk, I take the last bite of my chicken, exaggerating the way my lips wrap around the tines and the way my tongue swipes across my lips.

Mason stares at my mouth hungrily.

The waitress approaches our table, breaking our trance, and tops off my glass of wine. "Can I interest either of you in the dessert menu?"

"Please."

"No, just the check."

The waitress freezes at Mason's curt tone, unsure of what to do while we engage in a stare-off. My mouth pops open as he shakes his head at me, like the bossy man he is. The urge to fight him is strong, but the dark look in his eyes stops me.

My body shivers at the heat of his glare. He has something else in mind. My stomach dips in anticipation.

"Just the check, please," he repeats with a grunt at the server.

I nod in agreement, and she leaves without a word.

"I really wanted dessert," I pout. I mean, I do want dessert, but I want this sexy man more.

"So do I, but they don't have what I want here."

My center clutches air at the insinuation spoken in the same rough voice he used during our naughty phone call.

"What do you want for dessert?" I whisper.

"You."

I bite back a groan. Something tells me Mason is about to ruin me and I'm going to enjoy every single second of it.

"Where will you be having this dessert?" My question leaves me in fragments as I pant, my heart racing.

Mason places his hand on my wrist and leans forward. "Upstairs in my room, where only I will have the pleasure of hearing you cry out my name as you come."

He runs his tongue over his teeth, and the horny part of me wants to jump on the table and lay out on it, for him to eat me right here and now.

"Hmm."

My body flares to life as he smirks at me, all too aware of how turned on I am. Not that I care. I want him so badly I physically ache. Hell, I'd probably do anything he asked me to. He makes me feel special and seen, and unbelievably wanted and desired.

While most of our time together has been through calls and texts, we get one another. I feel like we've known each other longer than weeks. The connection we are building is special, and it grows stronger every day.

We might have only shared a few kisses, but holy freaking shit were they amazing. Our physical chemistry is there. If tonight's date is any indication, the tension built up between us is at an uncontainable boiling point, waiting to combust. My body feels heavy with desire, and it's driving me wild.

Mason drives me wild. He's unlike anyone I have ever dated, and I'm not about to let him slip away. I'm close to having everything I've ever wanted, and Mason has become a big part of that.

He was right. Our timing might not be ideal, but when I'm with him, it feels right. We feel right.

The waitress drops the check. He releases my wrist and quickly takes care of the bill.

Mason stands, reaching his hand out to me. I grab my clutch and take his hand. Sparks lick up my arm as I place my palm in his. Every time he touches me, my body responds knowingly, like he's the live wire my body craves to come to life.

He leads me out of the restaurant, through the hotel lobby, to the bank of elevators. The elevator dings its arrival, and Mason pulls me to his chest, wrapping his arms around me.

"Are you sure you want to join me? It's perfectly fine if you want me to walk you to your car and kiss you goodnight."

I run my free hand under his jacket and over his muscular chest before grasping his tie and pulling, bringing us nose to nose.

"You can walk me to my car," I murmur.

He nods, pulling away.

I yank his tie harder, keeping him in place. "To get my overnight bag. Then, you can carry it upstairs to your room."

Mason closes his eyes as his hands grip my waist. His fingertips dig into the flesh of my backside. When he finally opens his lids, his sea-green depths have turned dark and stormy. The small strips of golden brown in his irises glow like lightning streaking across the night sky over the ocean, taking my breath away. The hungry expression in his gaze makes my knees weak, and my heart cracks open wide for him to take.

"I need you to be sure, baby doll. Because if we go upstairs, I'm going to devour you and your sweet pussy. I'm going to fuck you so hard that you'll be feeling me for weeks. I'm going to be the boss of your body and reward you with orgasm after orgasm. All. Night. Long. Is that what you want?"

My knees wobble at his declaration. I have never wanted anyone more than I do him. I want to be his in every way possible. For the first time in my life, I'm okay with him not only setting fire to my body but to my entire world. I welcome it. A part of me would love to watch it burn to the ground around me, as long as he is by my side.

This is it. There's no turning back now.

"Yes. Please, Mason. I want that and more. I want you," I confess.

My chest heaves, and I have a feeling that if I kiss him now, we won't make it to his room before my clothes hit the ground.

I release his tie and smooth it down as my other hand grips my small clutch. His eyes never leave mine as I catch my breath.

"Fuck it. I'll get your bag later. Right now, all I want to do is get you upstairs, naked and spread out on my bed." Mason wraps his arm around my waist and pulls me onto the elevator, my feet barely touching the ground as he sweeps me off them.

I let him in every sense of the word. Our gaze never breaks as we ride the elevator. I couldn't tell you if there are other people sharing this small space with us because all I see is him.

Before the doors fully open, he's lifting me through them and down the hall. He pulls out his phone and unlocks the door with it. He really is tech-savvy. Before I can utter a single word, Mason has me in the room and pushed up against the door, crushing his mouth on mine in a fierce kiss.

His fingers grip my hair tightly as he tilts my head to the side and slips his tongue into my mouth, deepening our kiss. I drop my clutch. My hands roam his hard body, pulling him closer.

I fall. Into him. Into my feelings for him. Into his heat as his body presses into mine. All of it.

He feels so good. But I need more. I need him naked. Now.

I slip my hands over his shoulders, shoving his jacket off. Working his tie next, I rip it off and start unbuttoning his shirt. When I finally get it open, I can't help but push him away to get a better look.

I gulp, taking in his body. Fuck, he's hot. I knew my broody computer nerd was fit, but damn. FaceTime didn't do him justice. He puts Henry Cavill to shame. Mason is all hard lines and thick corded muscle. A small scattering of sandy brown hair runs across his chest and below his belly button. He's the sexiest man I have ever seen.

As I score my nails over his chest, he hisses. As my eyes devour him, I lick my lips, thinking about running my mouth over every inch of his tan skin.

"Like what you see?"

I nod, lost in the gloriousness that is this Adonis of a man.

"Your turn."

His lips find my neck, and my eyes close at the contact with a moan on my lips. He sucks and licks his way down to my collarbone as his hand finds the zipper of my dress. I arch into his hold, my body begging for him to lower it.

He slowly unzips my dress, letting the straps fall over my shoulders. Gripping the soft fabric, he glides it down my body and over my hips. My dress falls into a pool at my feet, leaving me almost bare, except for a black lace bra, matching panties, and black heels.

Mason steps back, taking in the sight of me with an approving growl that singes my nerve endings and makes my core tingle. My chest lifts with pride. I'm curvy, but I work hard for my body, training at least four times a week at a boxing gym. His reaction makes all my hard work feel damn good as he palms his straining erection over his pants. I love knowing it's me turning him on. That he wants me, just as I am.

"You're so fucking beautiful, Emery."

I shiver as he runs his feverish hands up my side, cupping my breasts. He licks, and runs wet kisses over my chest and collarbone, before burying his face between my boobs. I'd laugh if it wasn't so fucking hot.

"Mmm... Thanks," I mumble as his lips wrap around my nipple through my thin lace bra. I can hardly think when he touches me. Each brush of his skin against mine sends me reeling with need.

"Get on the bed. Now," he growls, stepping away. "And keep the heels on, baby doll."

"So bossy," I rasp, running my finger down his chest to the top of his slacks.

"This is nothing. Just you wait."

Holy hell.

I've never been dominated in the bedroom, but with Mason, I look forward to handing over my control to him. I have a feeling it's going to be a high unlike any I've ever experienced.

Heels on, I walk over to the high bed and sit on the edge. Sliding back, I let my feet rest on the box spring, before leaning back on my elbows and spreading my thighs open for him to get a better look.

He licks his lips as he stares hungrily at my center, my arousal obvious. He's barely touched me, and I'm already dripping wet for him. He steps between my legs, his pants grazing my sensitive skin.

"Well?" His gaze drops to his belt and looks back at me, waiting.

"So bossy," I sass again, biting my lip.

I sit forward and reach for his belt. Taking my time, I undo the buckle, letting it fall open to the sides. My fingers deftly flick the button on his slacks before slowly dragging the zipper down. As I slide my hands into the waistband of his boxer briefs, I look up to find him watching me. He looks brutally handsome, looming over me with his jaw clenched and eyes burning with desire. Dragging his boxers and pants over his hips, his cock springs free.

The sight sucks the air from my lungs. Mason is perfection personified. His cock is long and thick, and the broad tip makes my mouth water.

The head of his cock bobs, brushing the tops of my breasts, eliciting a groan from the both of us. The contact of his hot, silky skin against mine has me licking my lips. Mason's large hands cup my breasts over my soft lace bra, lifting them and smearing his precum across my skin.

"One day, Em. One day," he grunts.

Mental images of him fucking my chest flash before me. "Yes." I nod, wanting everything from him.

"Lay back."

My body immediately responds to his demand. My back hits the cool fabric of the sheets without hesitation. Mason toes off his shoes and kicks off his pants before kneeling between my legs. My eyes close as he runs his nose up my center, inhaling my scent over my soaking wet panties.

"You smell so good. I bet you taste even better." He pulls my panties to the side and flicks his tongue across my swollen, needy clit. "So wet and so sweet," he mumbles, burying his face between my legs like a man starved, grunting in satisfaction at my taste.

I force my eyes open, watching as Mason kneels before me and licks, nips, swirls, and laps at every inch of my pussy. My muscles quicken as my orgasm builds to a crescendo.

The urge to taste him while he tastes me hits me hard, leading me to yank Mason's hair and pull his face away from my throbbing center. He looks up at me in confusion.

"Your mouth is magical, but it hardly seems fair that I can't taste you while you're tasting me."

His tongue flicks my clit again. "What do you propose we do to remedy that?"

Without a word, I throw my leg over his head and turn around, letting my head hang off the bed. Wrapping my hands around the back of his neck, I bring his mouth to mine in an upside-down kiss, tasting myself on his lips. He groans into my mouth as I nip his bottom lip before soothing it with my tongue.

"Stand up and put that big, beautiful cock in my mouth." The words that leave my mouth surprise me.

But that's what Mason does to me. He makes me feel. There are no other thoughts running through my brain except for him. All that matters is him and me. Right here, right now.

He drops his forehead to mine and closes his eyes. "You're fucking perfect, you know that?"

"Whatever you say, Mr. Bossy."

Mason's head snaps up, and that dark look in his eyes is back. My thighs clench and my pussy weeps for his attention.

With panther-like mobility, Mason stands tall above me. He pulls my panties off and throws them across the room. "Better. Now, my little brat, spread your legs and wrap those pretty lips around my cock."

My legs and mouth fly open as I latch my hands onto the firm muscles of his ass and pull him forward. Doing exactly what he told me to do, I wrap my lips around his broad tip and flick the tip of his cock with my tongue before taking him deep into my mouth.

"Oh fuck," he grunts.

Mason's hands skim over my legs, resting on my inner thighs before spreading me open. His mouth finds the juncture of my thigh and pussy, and he sucks hard. My body bows off the bed, and the head of his cock hits the back of my throat, choking me. The simultaneous mix of pain and pleasure has my core growing wetter and my clit pulsing, begging for his touch.

As if he knows what I need, Mason returns his attention to my aching clit. Of course, this man right here knows how to work me into a frenzy. His tongue swirls and laps at me like I'm the most delicious thing he's ever eaten.

The pressure of my orgasm builds slowly and deep inside me, and I'll be damned if I come alone. His hips move in unison with mine, snapping forward at a punishing pace, and I love it. I love getting him to lose control for me. I relax my throat and take him deeper, loving the taste of him on my tongue. I lock my arms around his thighs, holding him in place and hollowing my cheeks, sucking him. I swallow around his thick shaft when he reaches the back, and hum. I can feel his glutes flex, and his balls tighten.

"Do that again, and this will be over before it starts," Mason growls.

I smirk around his cock, and he pulls out of my mouth with a pop.

"Maybe that's what I want. Make you lose control."

"I already told you, baby doll. I'm the boss when you're in my bed," he states. His breath fans over my sensitive core, making my flesh pimple. "Now, tell me who's the boss."

He swiftly swings me around again and drops to his knees before throwing my legs over his shoulders, my heels digging into his back. His stormy eyes find mine, and the sexy smirk on his lips has my stomach tensing. He looks like a predator between my legs, begging me to fight him.

I ignore his request. I'm nowhere ready to admit he's the boss and he knows it, at least not yet.

He drives two fingers deep inside me, making me cry out. My hips lift off the bed, begging for more.

"Answer me, Emery. Who's the boss?"

The sound of his fingers gliding in and out of me is lude and wet, and hot as fuck. My orgasm coasts to the edge again.

Overwhelmed by the way he's working my body over, all I can do is shake my head, still not ready to give in.

"Use your words or I stop." His hand stills.

"No... Don't stop. Please," I beg. "You. You're the boss, Mason." I finally concede, needing him to finish what he started.

"Damn right," he grunts before diving back in and devouring me, his hand pumping into me harder than before. "You taste better than dessert." Lick, taste, swirl, suck.

"Oh god."

Inhuman moans escape me as my muscles coil tight, and he works his mouth over me. Lick, taste, swirl, suck, spear. Repeat. My body soars at his ministrations. Lick, taste, swirl, suck, spear. And...

I shatter spectacularly into a million sparks, like fireworks on the Fourth of July. My pussy flutters as he wrings out every drop of my orgasm, owning my body like a sex god.

"Holy shit..." I pant, my breaths choppy. "That was" — I take a deep breath — "By far the best orgasm I've ever had."

Mason chuckles, kissing his way up my stomach, my breasts, and my neck. His lips find mine in a passionate kiss. Grabbing his hair, I pull him closer, kissing him harder and wrapping my legs around his waist. His erection glides through my wet slit.

"You're so wet and hot. I can't wait to feel you wrapped around my cock."

I feel his words vibrate in his chest. "Please," I whine.

I need him so badly I think I might combust if he doesn't get inside me now.

Lifting me higher onto the bed, he reaches over to the side table and pulls out a strip of condoms. He rips one off, before tearing open the foil package with his teeth, and rolls it down his impressive package. He strokes himself over the thin rubber, and my pussy pulses in anticipation.

Mason is huge. I've never been with anyone as big as him. *How on earth will that fit?*

Biting my lip, my nerves shaken, I look up into his warm hazel-green eyes. My heart skips a beat, and butterflies take flight in my stomach at the look he's giving me. So much goes unsaid between us, but I can feel it—this is it.

We are more than a long-distance fling. There is no more space between us. My soul has found its home with his.

My heartbeat slows as he covers my body with the weight of his.

"You feel it, don't you?" He settles himself between my legs, his lips brushing mine.

"Yes," I whisper.

"Good." He crashes his mouth to mine in a hungry kiss as he notches the tip of his cock at my entrance.

His hips slowly move forward, one glorious inch at a time, and my body spreads around him like he was made to be inside me. Pulling back, he starts the delicious intrusion over and over, sinking into me at a leisurely pace.

"That's it. Open up for me. Let me into this sweet tight cunt."

My body complies, melting at his crude words. My knees fall open, and my fingers grip his shoulders. He feels so good. We feel so good together. I'm eager to watch as he takes me to a place I've never been.

Breaking our kiss, I push his chest away, lift onto my elbows, and stare as his cock moves in and out of my pussy. Both of us stare at our connection before our gazes collide in a deluge of unbridled lust and something more. I don't know how or why, but my pussy gets wetter with every thrust, my arousal dripping down my ass. Mason reaches between us, cupping my pussy around his cock as he enters me.

"You feel so good, so wet. Your pussy looks so pretty spread open and taking my cock like she was made for me."

"Hmm," I groan. Fuck, his dirty talk is on point and I am here for it.

I close my eyes as he continues his unhurried pace, getting lost in the sensation and pleasure he's giving me with his touch. Mason moves his hand to my thigh, lifting it over his hip. His thrusts increase in speed as his other hand finds mine, threading our fingers together and lifting it over my head. He lavishes my neck with his mouth, kissing and nipping at my skin.

"More," I beg, lifting my hips to meet his. "Harder."

"Did you forget who's the boss?" He slows, driving into me with deep, hard strokes. "I know what you need." Thrust. "Now be a good girl and take what I give you." Thrust.

"Oh fuuu..." I moan as he sinks into me, giving me exactly what I need.

"That's it. I can feel your muscles tightening. You're so close. Give it to me, baby doll. Come all over my cock."

Pushing up onto his knees, Mason moves both his hands to my hips and lifts me, pulling me onto his dick. He increases his pace, and the primal sound of our bodies connecting fills the air.

Unlike last time, this orgasm feels tighter and builds higher. His thumb finds my clit, and the pressure is exactly what I need to go flying over the edge. White sparks fire behind my eyelids as I come with his name on my lips, and my muscles contract in delicious waves around him.

"Fuck, yes. Just like that." Mason pistons in and out of me, faster and harder.

My eyes snap open in time to watch him throw his head back in ecstasy. His hands dig hard into my ass, no doubt leaving bruises behind, as he comes with a shout. I've never seen him look sexier than right now as he comes inside me.

He pumps his hips a few more times, riding out his orgasm, before falling onto his elbows beside my head and slamming his mouth to mine, kissing me hard. His tongue delves into my mouth, twining around mine in a sultry dance.

With him inside me, we make out, holding onto each other, completely wrecked by what has got to be the best sex ever. Pulling back, he slides out of me and rolls on his side, pulling me with him.

Despite just having him fill me, an emptiness settles in my stomach. I miss him inside me already. I push that thought away and kick off my heels, snuggling into his side. Breathing in his spicy scent, I rest my arm on his chest and my thigh across his hip. My knee nudges his cock, and I'm rewarded with it twitching.

"Keep that up, and I'll be fucking you again real soon," he grunts as I draw circles on his chest with my fingers.

I can't help the smile that pulls at my lips. I kiss his chest and mumble, "Fine by me."

Mason removes the condom and ties off the end before throwing it on the floor. "Is that right?" he drawls.

I look up, and our eyes lock. I swing my leg over and straddle him, gliding my pussy over his already hardening cock.

"Yep." I bend down, hand on his chest, and kiss his jaw. My hair falls around us like a curtain, hiding us away from the rest of the world.

He crosses his arms under his head and flashes me a cocky grin. "Then, by all means, take what you want. I'm all yours."

His words are taunting, but they also hold the truth. He is mine.

Without a word, I grab a condom, bring the foil pack to my mouth, and rip it open. I pull out the rubber and shift back on his thighs. He grows harder as I stroke his cock with my hand.

Licking my top lip, I moan at the sight of him, my greedy mouth watering and my pussy slickening. I admire his perfect dick as my grip tightens. Fighting the desire to put him in my mouth again and suck him off, I keep stroking him from root to tip.

"Well..." He's watching me hungrily stare at his cock.

His jaw ticks, and I know he's fighting the urge to take over. His restraint is commendable as I continue to stroke him.

"Who's the boss now?" I ask.

He reaches up, trapping my bottom lip between his thumb and forefinger, pulling it down with a smug smirk that I don't know whether to smack or kiss off his face. His fingers drift down my throat and through the valley of my breasts until his thumb settles on my clit.

"It's still me, baby."

"Is that so, Mr. Bossy?"

I gasp as he rotates his finger in circles over my sensitive bud, lighting my core on fire.

"Always, but you can ride my cock like you're the boss right now."

That's exactly what I do until we both combust together in a burst of white-hot heat. And my body isn't the only thing that falls over the edge with him.

So does my heart.

FIFTEEN

Mason

I READ SOMEWHERE THAT there are instances in life when the world slows and time freezes. Those frozen moments are remembered forever, burned into your soul. Every color, every smell, every emotion, every detail. All of it. A picture-perfect image your brain holds onto with absolute clarity.

For me? This is that moment.

The sun filters into the room through the half-open curtains covering the wall of windows, illuminating the gorgeous creature next to me in an ethereal glow.

I know, without a doubt, that as soon as I walk out that door today, the memory of waking up with Emery in my arms will never fade. Not the way the sweet scent of her skin lingers on mine, not the way her long silky hair splays across the pillows as her soft breaths fan across my chest, nor the way her full pink lips purse in slumber and beg me to kiss them. How her naked body wraps perfectly around mine, or the way her heart beats in time to my own as we lay in the soft white sheets of this hotel bed. And definitely not the way my chest floods with warmth at the mere sight of her lying beside me.

Breathing her in, I sink into the warmth of Emery's body and glance around the forest-green walls of our hotel room—the room that will forever contain the memories of our beginning. We've only left it once to retrieve her overnight bag from her car, and even then, we couldn't keep our hands off of each other.

The memory of us climbing into the backseat, where we made out and fooled around like horny teenagers in nothing but the hotel's complimentary terry cloth robes, has me smiling.

We've spent the entire weekend in our own little bubble, ignoring calls and texts from the outside world, and I wouldn't change a thing. Being wrapped up in Emery was a gift, and I didn't waste a minute on anything other than her.

Between work and my family, I'm pretty sure I will walk into trouble when I leave this room, but I couldn't give one fuck about it.

My eyes bounce around the room again, landing on last night's room service cart that held our meal. We enjoyed our dinner out on the terrace while laughing, sharing stories, and kissing. Okay, mostly kissing. And touching. I can't stop touching her.

Emery stirs in my arms, and I look down and see her eyes flutter behind her eyelids.

What are you dreaming about, baby doll? Us?

Yeah, I don't give a damn about the problems I might face after this weekend. Emery is worth it.

I close my eyes and soak in the peaceful feeling settling inside me.

Fuck, now that I've had a taste of her, I'll never get enough. The beautiful woman in my arms has enchanted me from the start. It might have been her beauty that first caught my attention, but it's her big heart that keeps me in a chokehold. Emery is kind, funny, sassy, independent ... perfect. She's everything I never knew I wanted.

She moves again, her thigh grazing my cock and making my morning wood an even bigger problem. I hiss at the contact and attempt to move my girl's leg off my aching dick. Emery groans as I slowly lift her leg trying not to wake her, but she removes it from my grip before burrowing her head in my chest and rubbing her knee over my hard-on again.

"I know you're awake, baby doll," I whisper, kissing the top of her head.

She tilts her head back and cracks open an eye, looking up at me with a smirk playing on her lips. "Hmm ... Good morning." Her sleep-riddled voice is sexy as fuck and not helping my situation.

"Good morning." I brush the stray hairs on her face behind her ear and lean in to kiss her.

She pulls away, covering her face with the sheet draped over her chest. "No way, mister," she mumbles, pushing my face away with her hand. "I need a tooth brushing before you kiss me."

"Babe, I had my head between your legs for hours, and you kissed me after. Now pucker up." I twist us, rolling her onto her back beneath me.

She giggles, shaking her head behind the sheet, refusing to kiss me.

Yeah, that won't do.

"Unacceptable." I grab the sheet and rip it away from her face before crashing my mouth to hers.

Her body melts into mine and I take full advantage, deepening our kiss. She tastes like herself, sweet and sultry. Mine.

My hands roam over every inch of her soft skin, reveling in the way her hips find mine. Her fingers dig into my shoulders and her legs wrap around my waist, evaporating any irrelevant thought but the present.

I let myself get lost in her. The feel of her soft body under mine. The scent of her sugary skin infiltrating my nose. The heat of her pussy encased around my cock. The sound of her moans as I make her come. The way she feels like home.

I hate leaving today, not knowing when I'll see her again.

"This isn't goodbye, it's an ... 'I'll see you soon'."

"Mason—"

"No." I shake my head at her. "Not this again."

I don't know when it happened, but somewhere along the way, I've decided that I want to be with Emery. I want to make us work. I want to put in the energy to make *us* happen.

"But—"

Cutting her off, I press my mouth to hers. She melts into me, letting me kiss away the negative thoughts.

"Did you have a good weekend?"

She nods, biting that delicious plump lip of hers.

"Did I give you enough orgasms to hold you over until I can see you again?"

"Yes." She rolls her eyes.

Brat. I wish I had more time to take her back upstairs so I could bend her over the couch and fuck the sass out of her.

Instead, I pull her to my chest and tilt her chin up. "Are you sure you don't need one more to hold you over?"

She slaps my chest. "You're so bad."

"Only for you."

"Charmer." She drops her forehead on my chest.

"Look at me, please."

Her eyes snap up to mine, giving away all her thoughts.

Gripping the back of her neck, I stare into those topaz orbs that make the organ in my chest pinch. "I know this isn't ideal, but this weekend... I know you felt it. Focus on that feeling. On us. That's all that matters. The rest is just details. Trust me, we'll get there, okay?"

"Okay."

She slides her arms around my shoulders, and I can't help but lift her up in my arms. She wraps her legs around my waist as I push her back against the car door.

"Now, how about we seal the deal with another kiss?"

A beaming smile spreads across her face, right before I swoop in and kiss her senseless. When we break apart, my dick is harder than stone and she looks dazed, all traces of doubt gone.

Good.

She drops her legs to the cement with a contented sigh and turns her sparkling brown eyes on me. "Will you text me when you get home?"

As if I could go more than a couple of hours without talking to her.

"I'll text when I get to the airport." I kiss her forehead. "When I take off." I kiss her cheeks. "When I land." I kiss her nose. "When I get home." I capture her lips and kiss her sweetly. "Now, I need you to get in your car and get home safely. Okay?"

"Yes, Mr. Bossy."

I growl, and she laughs. The sweet sound burrows into the spot behind my ribcage. She gives me one last peck before getting into her car and rolling down the window.

I lean down, bringing us face to face. "Can you do a video call tomorrow night?"

"Yes."

"Good. Wear nothing." Just picturing a naked Emery has me ready to blow.

"Perv." She rolls her eyes at me again, but the flush on her cheeks is proof she approves of my perversion.

"Only for you."

"Charmer." She puts the car in reverse. "I'll wear nothing if you won't either."

"Deal. I can't wait to see your beautiful face."

"I doubt that's what you're looking forward to seeing." She licks her bottom lip as her eyes dip to my cock like she's thinking about seeing him too.

"I won't complain if I get to see your naked tits and sweet pussy too."

Her eyes widen in shock as she looks around. The parking lot is empty, but it doesn't stop her from reprimanding me.

"Omigod, Mason, you can't say stuff like that. Someone could hear you."

I shrug.

Good. I want people to hear. Then they'll know she's mine, and I take care of what's mine.

"Why not?"

She smirks. "Because it makes me horny, and then I'll have to use Bog."

Jealousy has me snarling. "I'll punish you if you use Bog without me."

"Promises, promises," she snarks, letting the car roll back.

I grab the window and lower my face to hers. "I keep my promises. Don't test me, baby doll." I give her one last kiss and step away.

She finishes backing out, and with an ache in my chest, I watch my girl drive away.

SIXTEEN

Mason & Emery

TEXT CHAIN

FEBRUARY 18

Mason: I can't stop thinking about last night.

Emery: Me neither.

Mason: I'm pretty sure everyone thinks I'm crazy because I haven't been able to stop smiling.

Emery: Oh no. We can't have that. Think grumpy thoughts.

Mason: Brat.

Mason: Can we have a repeat? I need to see you come again while you pet that pretty pussy and chant my name.

Emery: OMG. Mason, you can't text me things like that when I'm at work. I'm pretty sure my colleagues know what kind of texts you're sending me.

Mason: Sext, babe. I sent you a sext. Did it make your panties wet?

Emery: Who are you, and what have you done with the stoically sweet tech nerd I met?

Mason: He died when he tasted the sweetness between your legs.

Emery: **Blushing Emoji**

Mason: If it makes you feel any better, I made myself uncomfortably hard at my desk.

Emery: It does.

Mason: You didn't answer my question.

Emery: Yes.

Mason: Fuck, that's hot.

Emery: Go back to work.

Mason: Fine. Talk to you tonight, beautiful.

Emery: There's my charmer.

Mason: Only for you.

February 23

Emery: Thank you for the cookies. They were so good.

Emery: **Picture of Henry eating a dog cookie**

Mason: You're welcome.

Emery: What's your favorite dessert?

Mason: You.

Emery: **Kissy face Selfie**

Mason: Cute. Wish I could lick the chocolate off your lips.

Emery: I don't have chocolate on my face.

Mason: I can dream.

Emery: Charmer.

Mason: Only for you.

February 27

Emery: Good night, Mason.

Mason: Night, Em.

March 1

Mason: Miss you, baby doll.

Emery: I miss you too. Good luck at your conference.
Mason: Thanks.

❦

March 5
    Mason: Call me.
    Emery: I can't. I'm at that event I told you about.
    Mason: Text me when you get home.
    Emery: Okay.

❦

March 12
    Mason: Good morning.
    Emery: Good morning.
    Mason: What are you doing tonight?
    Emery: Talking to you?
    Mason: Damn right. Have a good day.

❦

March 15
    Emery: I'm home.
    Mason Video Calling.

❦

March 20
    Mason: When will you be in my town?
    Emery: April. Chris has an event.

Mason: I have no travel for April scheduled. Can I see you?
Mason: I miss you.
Emery: I miss you too. And yes.
Mason: Fuck yes. I can't wait to get my hands on you.
Emery: Charmer.
Mason: Only for you.

○

March 23

Emery: **Selfie in low-cut shirt, with a spoon between lips**
Mason: Please tell me you're home, eating that ice cream.
Mason: Em??
Emery: I'm home, Mr. Bossy.
Mason: I'm going to punish you for being a brat.
Emery: Promises, promises.
Mason: I promise to lick that ice cream off of your tits next time I see you.

○

March 24
Mason Video Calling.

○

March 26

Mason: **Selfie in gray sweatpants**
Emery: Is this my punishment? Because I think I need to be bad more often.
Mason: Now who's the charmer?

Emery: Charmer? No. Just a horny girl drooling over the hot guy that keeps calling her.
Mason: I'm more than that, babe.
Emery: Oh yeah? What are you, then?
Mason: Yours.

❦

March 27
Emery Video Calling.

❦

March 29
Mason: You up?
Emery: Who dis?
Emery: Is this my Friday booty call?
Mason: If I wasn't so far away, this would be funny.
Emery: Relax, Mr. Bossy. I'm watching TV. ALONE.
Mason: What are you watching?
Emery: The Witcher.
Mason: Fuck, you're hot.
Emery: Charmer.
Mason: Only for you.

APRIL

My phone buzzes on my desk, and a smile pulls at my mouth.

Mason: How is your day going, baby doll?

I shake my head at the screen, fighting the giddy sensation in my stomach as I reread the term of endearment Mason has called me since our first date. I've never dated a man who called me anything other than my name, and I must admit... I like it.

Emery: Good.

It's been too long since I've seen Mason in person, and I'm not talking about "on the phone". We haven't been with each other since the amazing, sex-filled weekend we shared in February. I figured after we spent Valentine's Day together, Mason would have moved on. He's constantly traveling for work and working crazy hours, but he's proved me wrong. He calls and texts me almost daily. Some nights, we even video call.

While I wish I could see him in person, I look forward to seeing his handsome face. Okay, I also like seeing his naked chest and his hand wrapped around his enormous cock as he jerks off, all the while telling me the dirtiest things to help me get off.

Mason: Just good? I thought it would have at least been great after last night.

I can still hear his silky deep voice demanding that I pull my vibrator—the infamous battery-operated Geralt—out of my drawer and use it while he watched me pleasure myself.

I traced the vibrator through the valley of my breasts, down my stomach, until I reached my clit. My eyes fluttered closed as the vibrations rippled from my center to the tips of my toes.

"That's it. Spread those legs wider. Let me see how wet you are for me." Mason's words were like kindling on a fire.

I spread my legs, dipping the toy inside my soaked core.

"Imagine it's my cock pushing into your tight pussy."

It didn't take me long after that to come to the sound of his gruff voice. It was by far one of the hottest moments of my life. I've never felt more vulnerable and confident in myself than I did with Mason's hungry eyes on me as I experienced one of the most intense orgasms I've had.

Every single one with him is the best orgasm of my life. Mason has unlocked this kinky side of me that totally gets off on being watched ... by him.

Emery: Last night? What happened last night?
Mason: I watched you come all over that horrible substitution for my cock. It was the best part of my day.
Emery: Really?

I bite my lip, waiting for his response. I look at the time, and I try to recall where Mason said he would be today. I hope he's working from home. I hate it when he sends me dirty texts while he's with his colleagues.

Sure, you do.

Fine, I admit it. I get off on receiving his texts any time of day.

Mason: Any time I get to watch you come is the best part of my day. I love watching you touch that sweet pussy and chant my name as you break apart.

My heart races, and my breaths pick up as I read his sweet, dirty words.

"I know that smile."

I jump at the sound of my business partner behind me. Clutching my phone to my chest, I take a deep breath, praying she didn't just see my messages. She's been extra nosy lately.

"What smile?" I ask, playing innocent.

"Oh please. I know that face. Is your secret luv-ah sexting you again?" Scarlett throws her head back and laughs at her own joke, her pregnant belly jiggling.

She is by far one of the most beautiful women I've ever met, except for my other business partner, Rylann. Where Scarlett is tall and blonde with a yoga mom body, Rylann is short and brunette with the body of a bombshell. You wouldn't think women as gorgeous as them would be the sweetest, most genuine people you'd ever meet, but you'd be wrong because they are. I lucked out in the boss department. They took me under their wing, and gave me the space to grow and flourish at their—our—company. As much as I fight it, they are my work family and I adore them.

"Scar, leave her alone. She'll talk to us when she's ready. Right, Em?" Rylann comes to my defense before turning her big warm brown eyes on me and shooting me a wink. "Hopefully, soon. Because I've never seen you smile as much as you have these past couple of months."

It's always been a struggle for me to open up and make friends. Coming from a wealthy family, I've found that most people either want or expect something from me in return. It's not *what* you know, but *who* you know.

Not with Scarlett and Rylann. They expected nothing from me besides hard work and dedication. All they've wanted is my friendship, beyond our work camaraderie.

"I will, promise. It's still early days," I defend.

"Early days, my ass. The only reason for you to blush like that from a text is because it's a dirty text."

"Scarlett," Rylann scolds.

I swear my face blushes tomato red at being busted reading and sending sexts at work.

"Fine." She throws her hands up in the air. "I'll leave her alone. For now." Scarlett narrows her eyes at me.

I almost squirm at their glare, but I hold still.

Scarlett walks away, but Rylann sticks around. She sighs and rubs her swollen belly as she watches Scarlett slip into the bathroom. "Ignore her. She means well. We want you to be more than just our business partner. We care about you. I know you don't like to talk about your family and what brought you out here. While I wish you would share, I understand being guarded. I wasted a lot of time grieving, and it left me empty. If I didn't have Scarlett by my side, supporting me and forcing herself on me, I don't know where I'd be. Without her and her husband's help, I wouldn't have been able to reconnect with the love of my life."

I only know bits and pieces of her story. She had this glumness about her, even before her first husband passed away from cancer a couple of years ago. Then, she was a walking zombie. Her once sad eyes are now warmer and brighter than ever. She's practically a ray of sunshine these days.

"We're here for you. You know that, right?"

I nod, not sure how to respond to her kindness.

"When you're ready to open up, we are waiting for you."

My throat closes, and my eyes well with tears as Rylann waddles off down the hall to the bathroom to join her equally pregnant friend, leaving me with a lot to think about.

I've only ever had one friend, and even then, it wasn't like what my colleagues were offering. Chris is my best friend, but he's my brother and it's not quite the same as sharing things with girl-friends.

The problem is, I don't know how to have real friends or how that works.

EIGHTEEN

Mason

EMERY: I JUST BOARDED the plane. I'll see you tonight, Mr. Bossy.

I hold back my grin as I reread the text Emery sent me. "Excited" is putting it mildly for how I feel about seeing her tonight. It's been two months too long since we've been in the same town. Since I've been able to hold her.

Kiss her.

Despite our great weekend, Emery was hesitant when we said our goodbyes in the hotel parking lot. She had me worried for a minute. I was prepared for her texts to become infrequent and eventually taper off. I mean, what would a woman like her want with a guy like me? I travel too much and work too hard.

But I was serious when I told her I would see her again soon. I've kept in constant contact, never letting her forget that she's on my mind. For every text I send, she sends one in return. My efforts have been working, and even though we agreed to be only casual, we're more than that.

For once in my life, I will not give up on what I know we can build together. Especially when I've only had a small taste of her. I want more.

No. I *need* more. She's all I've craved since I saw her from afar, in the mirror at the airport.

Her messages are the best part of my day. When I miss them, there's this ache in my chest, like a mix of heartburn and emptiness. It's the same ache that grows the longer I go without seeing her.

I push the uncomfortable feeling down and look around the restaurant, making sure my idiot brothers aren't around, before I return her message.

I'm meeting them for lunch today. It's been a while since us brothers—Eli, Cameron, and I; not counting Jace since he now lives in Oregon—have gotten together.

Mason: I can't wait to see you.
Emery: Me too. When do you want to meet? Chris's event should end around 9pm.

I look at my watch. Eight and a half more hours until I lay eyes on her in person.

I'm not the sappy guy who falls for a girl and moons over her, but with Emery, I am. There's just something about her that feels different. When I'm with her, it feels right.

My ex, Brittany, would be pissed to know I am making the effort to make a relationship work. My crazy work hours were one of the biggest gripes she had when we dated years ago. That, and the fact that I never "paid her any attention".

I was just starting my company, and things were off to a rocky start. The code Kenzo and I had been creating wasn't working, so yeah, I pulled crazy hours. She wanted to move in together and a proposal. She dropped hints constantly, but I wasn't there yet. I was hurt when she broke things off. Well, I was more hurt by the way she ended our relationship.

She came to my apartment—with her new boyfriend—to collect her stuff and to rip me a new one, letting me know it was because of my selfish, workaholic ways that she was leaving me for someone else. Someone who put her first.

I cared about the girl. She was beautiful and smart, but there was always something lacking between us. Maybe I wasn't ready. I don't know. Since then, I've dated on and off, but no one has stuck with me like Emery.

Then, there are the dates like the one Cameron made me go on, where the women I meet are only there to get closer to one of my brothers.

Not Emery. She's into me because she genuinely likes me, no other reason or agenda.

I still have a demanding career, but with her, I want to make her a priority. Emery understands my passion for the work I do and has been supportive without judgment. She's a game-changer.

My phone is snatched out of my hand, and before I can beat the culprit's ass, he's sitting across from me with a smug smile.

"Well, well, well. What do we have here?" Eli looks down at my phone curiously.

I flash him a cocky smirk. He might have taken my phone, but I always lock it. He can't read the messages.

Cameron takes the seat next to me and smacks me on the back. "What'd I miss?"

"Oh, nothing. Just grouchy Mason here, smiling at his phone." I wasn't smiling. *Was I?*

Whatever. Eli is just trying to rile up Cam, who takes the bait. "Please tell me it's because of a girl."

The waitress arrives, interrupting Cameron. She takes our orders and leaves, promising to return with our beers.

"So, Cam, when do you leave for your next away game?" I take a sip of my water, evading his interrogation.

"You know I leave next week." He points at me. "Don't change the subject. You've been in a rather good mood lately, which means you're getting laid. So, tell me... Who is she? Hot airport girl? Please tell me it's Hot Airport Girl."

The server places our beers on the table and runs a hand up Cam's arm as she walks away. He doesn't seem affected by it anymore, but that can't be easy—strange women always touching him without permission. I cringe at the thought.

"Who's Hot Airport Girl?"

"No one," I grunt at Eli. I reach out to grab my beer, taking a big gulp. The cool liquid does nothing to soothe my irritation.

Fucking Cam and his big mouth. I don't want my brothers in my business. The less they know about Emery, the better. I'm not ready to share her with the group yet. We don't even live in the same city.

Cameron snaps his fingers, a huge grin on his face. "What's her name again? Emily? Everly?"

"Emery." I blurt.

Fuck. He's got me.

"Ha! Gotcha fucker. I remembered her name. How could I forget? That chick was fucking hot. I do not forget hot chicks' names."

My hackles rise and before I can stop myself, I cuff him behind the head. "Shut the fuck up, kid."

"Oh, this is serious, Cam. Mason's getting angry," Eli taunts. He turns to me and shakes his head. "Can't believe you fell for that. You know how he is."

"Fuckers," I grumble, sagging in defeat.

I totally fell for it, but the thought of my brother—or anyone for that matter—thinking about how hot Emery is pisses me off. Because she is hot.

Fucking hot.

And there is nothing I can do about it. Emery turns heads wherever she goes, with her big topaz eyes, thick caramel-colored hair, long muscular legs, and plump red lips.

She's gorgeous. And mine.

Eli picks up his beer and takes a sip, watching my face as my thoughts play out. I try to school my features, but Eli is a master at reading people.

"Tell me about her."

"Yeah. Tell us about her." Cameron props his head on his big hands and bats his lashes. "Then we can have a slumber party, braid each other's hair, and paint each other's toes."

Eli barks a laugh. "You're such an asshole, Cam." He throws a napkin at Cameron, who beats it away with a laugh. Turning back to me, Eli says, "But seriously. Tell us about her."

I glance at Eli, and he seems genuinely interested.

"I met her at the airport, back in December. We were on the same flight. I thought we hit it off, but when we got off the plane, she walked away. I didn't see her again until the weekend I went up to watch Rhys while Jay and Ry went on their babymoon."

"Remember? I texted everyone about his hot date," Cam tells Eli, who nods in understanding. "Don't leave out how you were mysteriously in Portland back in February." There goes that big mouth of his again.

I throw Cameron an evil glare, but instead of taking it as a threat, he smiles. He's been piecing all this together for weeks, trying to get me to spill. Now, I don't have a choice.

"She lives in Portland?" Eli asks.

I nod, not wanting to divulge the fact that Emery lives in the same town as Jace, which was quite a shock.

"Interesting. Continue." Eli waves his hand at me and takes another sip of his beer, all while Cameron sits there with a smug look on his face.

Bastard.

"We've been talking, and she's in town this weekend. I'm supposed to meet her after her brother's event. He has some art premiere at LACU film school."

"You mean, the Experimental Short Film Screening that's happening all weekend?" It figures Eli would know about this.

He's a talent manager at Blaze Talent Agency. When Eli's best friend broke away from his father's agency, he convinced Eli to leave with him. Since then, the two have made quite a name for themselves. Especially Eli, who manages a few household names—including one TV sweetheart turned pop princess.

"You would know." I shrug, even though my chest tightens.

Why didn't I ask her about the event?

Because I'm an idiot. Here I am, thinking about what a great job I'm doing keeping her a priority, and I didn't bother to ask her about her brother.

"Dude." Cameron looks at me and shakes his head in disappointment. "You aren't going?"

"She didn't invite me." Fuck, I sound like a dickhead.

Honestly, I didn't even think anything of it. Her brother is all she has, and I didn't want to intrude. When we talk, she doesn't mention her parents. From what I remember of our conversation on the plane, she and her parents have a tumultuous relationship because of their lack of acceptance of Chris's sexuality.

"You like this girl, right?" Cameron asks.

"Yeah." I more than like Emery. I can see her being the one. I just don't want to jinx it. I haven't had much luck in the relationship department in the past.

"Then you show up, idiot. And take her some flowers, for fuck's sake," Cameron grumbles.

Mr. Doesn't Do Repeats is over here giving me dating advice. I think hell froze over.

"I don't even have a ticket," I grumble.

Cameron looks at me like the dumbass I am. "Hello, have you met our brother? I'm sure he can get you a ticket. Right, E?"

Eli leans back with an air of superiority and rests his arm on the chair beside him. He might be an inch shorter than me, but he looks ten feet tall right now. His creepy half-brown eye twinkles, and I know this is going to cost me.

"For a price." He runs his tongue over his teeth, sucking them, knowing my inevitable answer.

"And that is?" I already know the damage. Eli loves collecting things. And when I say "things", I mean "favors".

"A favor—to be determined—when the time comes, with no questions asked."

Of course.

Seems straightforward enough, but with Eli, it's never that simple. But...

"Deal."

I'll worry about the consequences later. Right now, all I want to do is surprise my girl. Maybe this gesture will show her how serious I am about us.

●

My simmering irritation makes me itchy as my chance to find Emery ends with the dimming lights. It took me longer than expected to get the ticket from Eli and drive through L.A. traffic, and now I'm stuck with taking a seat in the back row of the theater.

I place the small bouquet of burgundy dahlias under my seat, hoping they don't get crushed, as the program director introduces the various films being shown. I tune him out as a hundred questions and doubts flit through my mind.

Was this the right move? Why did I listen to Cam?

My palms sweat, and I can't stop fidgeting. I told her we were more than casual, but showing up at her brother's event without an invitation is different. This makes our relationship serious, right? Am I ready for us to be serious?

Yes, my brain whispers.

We text daily. When we aren't texting, we're talking on the phone or video calls, all of which have progressively gotten hotter. I love watching Emery touch herself and get off on the sound of my voice. I want more of those moments with her. I want them all.

I don't know where she's at, and it's confusing. Sometimes, she will pull back and put up her guard with me, and then other times, she lets her walls down and we really connect.

I bounce my knee while I continue to analyze my relationship, causing the hipster sitting next to me to give me some major side-eye. He can fuck right off. The only person I am here for is Emery, and I want nothing more than to make us official.

Fuck.

Realization slams into me, and my nerves slip away. I let the peace of my decision wash over me. I am ready. I've been ready since the moment I saw her reflection in the mirror at the airport. I want her to be mine and no one else's. I know being long-distance isn't easy, but maybe I can travel to see her more. I can make more of an effort for her.

The credits roll, and the lights turn on. Voices in the theater rise as everyone starts to stand and make their way through the aisles, filing out of the room.

I follow their lead, picking up the bouquet I brought, and scan the room, searching for her honey-brown locks. The hair on the back of my neck stands on end, and my heart beats wildly in my chest. Damn, seeing her on video calls pales in comparison to seeing her in real life.

My girl is fucking stunning. She's wearing skin-tight black jeans and a burgundy top that hangs off her shoulders, showing off her elegant neck and the tops of her breasts. Her clothes hug every curve of her body with perfection, and my cock takes notice, jumping at the vision of her mere feet away from me. Her mouth is painted to match the deep red fabric of her blouse, and all I can imagine is kissing those big, pouty lips.

I watch as she strides up the aisle of the theater, her arm linked with her brother. She looks young and carefree as she animatedly talks, waving her hand wildly in the air. Her brother says something that has her throwing her head back with a laugh.

As if she knows someone is watching, her head snaps my way and her eyes land on mine. All doubt disappears as we stare at each other from across the room. Emery's lips turn up into a smile so bright it takes my breath away.

She releases the arm she's holding and serpentines through the crowd towards me. My feet move just as quickly as we make our way to each other. I'm about to scoop her up when she leaps into my arms and wraps her legs around my waist. Without a care in the world, I wrap my free hand around the back of her neck and bring her lips to mine in a searing kiss that ignites every nerve in my body on fire.

As I hold Emery in my arms, the lonely ache in my chest—that's taken residence in the cavity when she drove away from me—fades away. My tongue delves past her lips as I deepen our kiss and explore her mouth. She tastes even better than I remember, and I can't help but grunt as my dick grows hard at the heat of her core resting on my lower abs.

A throat clears, and a voice pops our bubble. "Holy fuck, it's a live sex show."

Emery breaks our kiss and the spell she had me under, and shouts, "Chris, seriously!"

I bark a laugh. Hugging her tight, I kiss her neck as she drops her head to my shoulder and her legs from around my hips. Placing her on her feet, I bury my face in her hair and inhale her sweet scent, like the addict I am.

I turn around and come face to face with the most mischievous grin I have ever seen.

Chris bounces his eyebrows at me and crosses his arms. He is basically the male version of Emery, with the same honey-brown hair and topaz eyes. Where his sister's eyes are more serious, his are more playful. It's obvious he is the more carefree sibling while Emery looks like she carries the weight of the world on her shoulders.

"Well, well, well. Looks like my sister has been holding out on me." His gaze flashes to Emery's, and her cheeks pinken.

Trying to divert the conversation, I stick out my hand and introduce myself, "Mason."

"Oh, I know who you are."

I smile at his snark. She either told him about me, or he remembers me from the airport.

"What I don't know is how long this has been going on." He moves his finger between me and Emery. "Or how you got into the theater without an invite."

"My brother called in a favor and got me a ticket," I interject, bringing the focus back to me as an embarrassed Emery shifts foot to foot under her brother's watchful eye. I wrap my arm around her waist and pull her to my side.

"And who, pray tell, is your brother?" he asks.

I'm not about to answer that question. Maybe another time.

"Chrisy, stop being a brat," Emery chides.

He turns a snarling face her way, and her shoulders drop. My hackles rise until Chris laughs and I know it's all in good fun. I'm familiar with annoying younger siblings.

I stifle my laugh. I like this guy. He reminds me of Cameron always giving me shit. While my brother is a pain in the ass, I love him. It's clear that Emery feels the same about her brother.

"Who are those for?" Chris points a finger at the bouquet in my hand.

Shit. I forgot all about it.

Emery looks up at me and bites her now lipstick-free bottom lip. She uses her thumb and wipes around my mouth, trying to clean the red stains off my face. I wrap my fingers around her small wrist and lay a kiss on the soft skin.

"Hi."

She smiles at my late greeting. "Hi."

Emery wraps her arms around my neck. I lean down to kiss her.

"Hello!" Chris interrupts, throwing his hands in the air.

I push the flowers out at him. "You. These are for you."

He rolls his eyes and grabs them. "You're a smooth fucker, you know that?"

I shrug at him while the beauty beside me snorts a giggle.

"These are Emmy's favorite color, but since she gets you tonight, I'm taking these as a consolation prize."

"How about dinner too?" I offer.

Chris gives me a wide smile. "Now we're talking, Mr. Smooth. Follow me." Chris turns on his heel and heads out of the now-empty theater.

With him gone, I pull Emery close and put my hands in her back pockets, squeezing her firm ass. "Surprised?"

She nods.

"Good surprise?"

She nods again. "The best." She lifts onto her toes, kissing me softly and slowly as her tongue seductively swipes mine in a sensual dance.

My cock grows thick against my zipper as her hands run over my chest and neck. I grope her ass tighter and she moans into my mouth, reminding me of the night she moaned my name as she came riding my face.

"Yo! Knock that shit off. I'm hungry!"

Emery and I break apart. I press my forehead to hers and close my eyes, attempting to calm down my racing heart and my raging hard-on.

"Is he always this much of a pain in the ass?"

She shakes her head. "No, he's worse."

We both laugh at that.

Yep, he's definitely like my little brother. I don't know if those two should ever meet.

With a heavy sigh, I release her and take her small hand in mine, and lead us out the door to what I can only imagine to be an interesting dinner.

MASON PULLS DOWN A small street in Venice Beach, and I'm a little confused by our location. I visit the Los Angeles area often, but I haven't explored the city or its sites like I should have.

He clicks the garage door opener as he pulls the car into a short, narrow driveway. The white door lifts, and Mason drives into the small carport.

"Wait here." Mason kisses my hand.

I watch him climb out and walk around the car, appreciating the way he moves with such grace. I could watch him all day. There's something erotic in the way his muscles flex that has my thighs clenching in anticipation.

He opens the door and holds out his hand to me. I place my palm in his, gasping at the heat of his touch. Flames lick up my arm, my stomach flips, and I shiver. Pushing the burning desire in my belly down, I step out of the car. The sexual tension between us is palpable as the air around us turns thick and heady. Our reunion has been months in the making. The particles in my body vibrate with excited lust.

It's clear Mason feels the same.

Neither of us utters a word as we exit the garage and make our way across his small backyard. I attempt to look around, but Mason's feet move too quickly across the stone-covered space before he leads me into the backdoor of his home. From what I can see, it's a cute little cottage with an outdoor dining table, six matching chairs, and a surfboard leaning against the siding of his one-story home.

With his phone, he unlocks the door and turns the lights on low before pulling me inside. I glance around, taking in the modern space of his open-concept kitchen/living room.

It's exactly how I thought it would be. Minimal and warm. It feels like home, with its beautiful cream-colored walls that are adorned with large landscape photography pieces, a rich brown–colored sectional, and a walnut dining table. I love the juxtaposition of the modern interior design to the older, craftsman exterior of his home. The way he's turned the classic cottage into something modern while keeping its original charm is gorgeous.

"Em." Mason's gruff voice cuts through my thoughts, bringing back the heat of the moment.

One of his warm hands lands on my hip while the other wraps around the back of my neck. He tilts my head back, staring into my eyes. My knees shake at the fire in his gaze. The streaks of gold glow and break through the green of his irises. My hands glide up his arms and squeeze his shoulders.

He leans forward his lips inches from mine. "Can I offer you something to drink?"

Drink? Umm, no.

What I really want is for him to carry me to the bedroom and have his way with me. I've missed him so much. These past few months have been hard, being without him. I know it seems silly since we only spent one weekend together, but it was the best weekend of my life. I enjoyed our time together, talking and getting to know each other. When I'm with him, he makes me feel special. Seen. He listens attentively when I talk, and while he's a bit gruff and matter-of-fact, he's also very sweet and considerate. Even when he's dominating me in the bedroom, he makes sure my needs come first.

I swear Mason made it his goal to give me three orgasms to his one every time. I've never been with anyone like him before. Sex with him is an experience. Together, we are explosive, like a match to a powder keg.

He owns my body—a fact my body is very much aware of. His proximity to me right now has my skin pebbling and my heart racing. Since that kiss in the theater, I've been craving his touch. It was hard to sit still at dinner while Chris spoke, and Mason ran his hand up and down my thigh under the table.

"Okay." Maybe a drink would do me some good and help cool off the heat building between my legs.

Every part of me wants Mason. Now. I want to give him everything I have to offer, and not just physically. It's a dangerous thought, but I'm more afraid of not giving into him, into us, and regretting it for the rest of my life.

Mason hinges over, throws me over his shoulder, and carries me to the kitchen, quieting my thoughts.

"Mason! What are you doing?" I cry out with a laugh.

"Getting you something to drink." He shrugs and playfully slaps my ass.

I bite back a moan as my panties flood with arousal.

Mason places me on the kitchen island and spreads my legs wide, standing between my knees. My clit pulses against the tight fabric of my jeans as he pushes me back, and my palms land behind me on the cool marble.

We might not be using words, but our bodies are speaking loud and clear.

I hook a leg around his hip and pull him closer. His hand drifts from my knee up my leg, and he digs his thumb into the tender flesh of my inner thigh as he stops at the juncture of my hip and my pussy.

"Behave, baby doll."

I drop my leg as Mason steps away and opens the refrigerator. He grabs two bottles of water and places them on the counter beside me before turning his back to me. He pops open a cabinet and pulls out a small glass, and then fills the cup with ice from the dispenser. My skin pebbles at the prospect of him using that ice on my overheated body. He places the glass on the counter and opens my bottle of water, letting it hover over the glass.

"Ice water?" He arches a brow at me.

"No." I bite my lip.

He smirks, placing the mouth of the bottle at my lips instead. "Drink?"

My heart beats erratically as I do what he asks without a second thought. I'd do anything he wants right now. I am putty in his hands, and he knows it as he slowly pours the water into my mouth with a coy smile on his delicious lips. I take a small sip, my eyes on him the entire time. Water dribbles down my lip as he pulls the bottle away, and my tongue pokes out to catch the drop.

Mason watches the movement. As if he has all the time in the world, he caps the water and pushes it aside.

"Aren't you thirsty?" I ask, hoping this little display leads to what every nerve in my body desires—him.

"Absolutely parched." He leans over me and places his hands next to mine. "Are you ready to quench my thirst?"

So fucking ready.

I wrap both my legs around his waist and pull us flush together, his hard cock to my wet pussy. I nibble his square jaw as I place my index finger on his chin, then run it down his throat and chest before hooking it over the top of his jeans. "How can I quench your thirst?"

His breath fans across my lips. "Oh, Em. I'm going to enjoy taking my time drinking you tonight."

Mason molds his lips to mine in a fiery kiss. I groan into his mouth as his tongue tangles around mine. His hands roam my body, setting my skin on fire. My back hits the hard marble top as Mason's lips move to my neck, sucking on the tender flesh that sends my body arching into his. Aching for more.

He cups my breasts over the fabric of my shirt and I whimper, "More."

He grips the bottom of my blouse and pulls it over my head, throwing it behind him. His hungry eyes glide over my exposed skin. "You're fucking gorgeous."

Another man's watchful eye would have me reaching to cover up, but not Mason's. The way he stares down at me, like I'm a gift from the heavens, has me dropping my arms to the counter, baring more of myself to him. He makes me feel confident and stronger than ever, like I'm more than just a pretty face meant to grace someone's arm like a trophy.

His big hands caress the sensitive skin up my stomach, over my breasts, and behind my back, where he deftly unhooks my bra. I pull the straps down, revealing myself to him, my nipples taught and needy for his mouth.

"Fucking perfect," Mason mumbles before his mouth covers my hardened peak. He swirls his tongue around the stiff bud, sucking, before nipping the tip between his teeth.

I hiss a breath as he moves to the other, lavishing it with the same attention. My clit pulses, and my core drips with lust.

If I learned anything, it's that there is no rushing Mason. If he wants to take his time, that's exactly what he'll do. Even if it drives me crazy.

"Mason," I beg, my voice hoarse.

"I know."

He runs his hands down my sides, gripping my hips tight. He releases the button of my jeans and undoes my zipper. My hips lift as he slides the offending material down my legs, leaving me in just my thong.

Mason pauses his movements, groaning at the sight of me. My body flushes as he fists his hard shaft over his pants. I love that I do that to him.

Mason falls to his knees and throws my legs over his shoulders—my pants stuck around my ankles at the top of my boots—capturing himself between my thighs. His eyes find mine as he leans forward, his nose hovering over the thin scrap of silk separating my pussy from his face.

He breathes me in. "You smell so good. Like vanilla and tart pears. You make my mouth water; you're so fucking delicious." He runs his nose up my slit before grabbing the side of my underwear that rests at my hip. "I hope these weren't special."

Before I can answer, he tears through the fabric with his fingers before ripping them from my body. He stares at my glistening core, admiring the display before him, and licks his lips.

"You're so wet for me. Such a good girl, saving me all this sweet cream to drink." He buries his head between my thighs and grunts into my sensitive flesh as he eats me out like a man starved.

My eyes roll to the back of my head as he fucks my pussy with his mouth. His tongue finds my throbbing clit, and within seconds, I'm brought to the edge.

"Oh god," I moan.

"That's it, baby. I can feel you getting close."

I grip his soft hair between my fingers, tugging his face closer. He chuckles, returning his mouth to my aching bundle of nerves.

My muscles quiver as I mumble, "So close. More."

"You come when I say."

Mason spreads my knees wide as he slides a finger deep inside my pussy, curling it towards my front walls, rubbing that magic spot only he's been able to find. The hot tension inside me grows as I clench around his fingers.

"Now, Emery. Now you can come for me."

My body obeys, bowing off the counter as the coil constricting my clit snaps and sends a rush of fire through my veins. Warm liquid gushes from my pussy, streaming down my crack. Mason growls in approval, lapping at my tender center as my body trembles from the freefall of the most intense orgasm it has received.

What the fuck was that? Did I just...?

I look down to find Mason watching me, his chin glistening with wetness and a satisfied smile on his face. He slowly stands between my legs, still trapped by my jeans, and licks his fingers clean. "I knew you would be able to quench my thirst."

Yep. I did.

My cheeks flame in embarrassment and his salacious display. I can't believe he made me squirt. I've never done that before. I didn't even know I could. I throw my head back on the counter, covering my face with my hands.

Mason laughs, grabbing my wrists and bringing my hands over my head. "Open your eyes, Em."

I shake my head, squeezing my eyes tight.

"Yes. Now."

My eyes snap open at his command, my traitorous body complying with his every demand. It knows who owns it, even if my brain fights it.

"That was by far the hottest, sexiest fucking thing I have ever experienced. Now that I know I can make you come like that, make you squirt, it will be my mission to do it every time I put my mouth on your sweet-as-fuck pussy."

Fuck me dead.

"I—"

He shakes his head at me. "I'm not done. Are you going to be a good girl and pay attention?"

I nod, waiting for him to continue.

"Good. Now listen, and listen carefully. After that, there is no way in hell I am ever letting you go. You're mine now. You hear me?"

My poor invested heart lurches all while screaming, *Yes, yes, yes.* My stupid brain tries to sound the alarm and raise a red flag. For once, I shut those thoughts down, flip my brain the finger, and listen to my heart.

I want to be Mason's. I want him to be there for me. I want to be there for him. Even when work pulls us in different directions.

I just hope I can fix everything before it all crumbles and he finds out the truth.

Even if my world falls apart, I will always be his. I don't know when it happened, but somewhere along the way, he claimed my heart. Now, I have no choice but to do everything in my power to make him mine too. And keep him.

"I'm yours," I answer.

"Damn right, you are."

Mason pulls off my shoes and drops them to the floor. He peels my jeans off the rest of the way, letting them land next to my boots, then toes off his shoes and rips his shirt over his head.

He stares at my aching wet slit and licks his lips. "I think it's time for dessert now."

He snaps open the button of his jeans and pulls down the zipper. He removes his pants and the tight boxer briefs I know he wears in one fell swoop. His big cock springs free, bobbing in the air, hard and pointing straight at me.

I reach for his thick length, but he steps back.

"Nuh-uh. You know the rules."

I roll my eyes. Always so bossy and in control.

He gruffs a laugh and lifts my legs up to rest my ankles on his shoulders. "Who's the boss, Emery?"

He opens the drawer below and pulls out a condom, tearing it open and rolling it down his shaft. I watch as he notches his cockhead at my entrance.

"Answer me. Who's the boss, Emery?"

A stronger woman would fight him on it. But staring into his smoldering hazel-green eyes, I've been brought to my knees by him and his magical cock.

"You're the boss, Mason. Now, fuck me already."

Mason slams deep inside me in one thrust. I'm so wet from the orgasm he gave me that my pussy opens for him, wrapping around him like a glove.

His fingers grip my neck as he tilts my head back. "Say it again."

I grip his forearm for leverage as he pounds into me. I lift my hips meeting him thrust for thrust, allowing him deeper access to me. To everything.

"You. You're the boss," I pant. "My boss."

Mason drops my legs to his side as he threads his fingers through the hair at the base of my neck and pulls me up to a sitting position. He slams his mouth over mine in a searing kiss. Bringing his other hand between us, he rubs circles over my clit. My arms and legs wrap around him as he picks up his pace. My body shutters as my orgasm builds.

"That's it, Em. Come on my cock. Show the boss who owns this pussy."

His words set me off, and my orgasm hits me like a freight train of serotonin to my system. Pure euphoria slides through me as I cry out his name.

His cock swells as his pumps become erratic and he follows me over the edge, coming deep inside the condom with an animalistic grunt.

Dopamine spreads over me like a warm blanket as I come down from the high of my orgasm. A high I have become addicted to. A high only Mason can deliver. I fall limp in his arms, resting my head on his shoulder, our bodies heaving in time as we catch our breaths.

"I think I'm thirsty now," I whisper, kissing his shoulder.

He throws his head back and laughs. "Here."

Mason hands me the water from before as he slips out from between my legs. I watch as he ties off the condom and throws it away, reminding me of something.

"Why are there condoms in the kitchen drawer?"

He looks at me, a serious expression on his face. "There are condoms everywhere. My brother thinks it's funny. It's a long story, but Eli has taken it upon himself to make sure we are all stocked up. It used to irritate me, but after today, I might have to thank him."

"That's pretty funny." I chuckle.

But he doesn't laugh. The face he makes sobers me up.

"I'm guessing it's more than just a long story?"

"You can say that. It's complicated. But a lot of heartache could have been prevented if people were more honest with each other."

I swallow down the lump forming in my throat as he wraps my legs around his waist.

"Promise me. If there's a problem or something's going on ... you will talk to me. Can you do that for me?"

I nod, tears clouding my eyes as I lie to the man I've fallen in love with.

Fuck. I love him.

A pit forms in my stomach, and I know I should tell him now. I'm so close to everything being over that I don't want him to get involved. It will make things harder for me to walk away. I just need to protect him a little longer. Mason's not the only person that will be hurt by what I've been doing.

I have Chris to think about. He's the one I'm more worried about. Everything I've done was for him. To help him. I can't break my promise to protect him, not yet. I need a little more time and for everything to fall into place.

I push my thoughts and worries down like I always do, and focus on now. These wonderfully sweet and stolen moments I've been able to carve out with the man I've come to love.

I kiss the sweet caring man between my legs and savor the attention he's offering me. "Take me to bed, Mason"

"No place I'd rather take you."

Mason carries me to his bed, where he shows me who's the boss while he worships my body all night long, and I fall even more in love with the man holding me.

I QUIETLY CLOSE THE door behind me so I don't wake up the beautiful woman, who—I hope—is still sleeping in my bed.

The floor creaks as I sneak across the room to the kitchen, carrying a bag of breakfast burritos from my favorite place. Grabbing some plates from the cabinet, I set them on the counter and pull out the food, placing the foil-wrapped goodness on them. I ordered four different burritos, unsure what Emery likes to eat in the morning. The last time we ate breakfast together, we had French toast and fruit—not much of a choice when it comes to hotel food. I reach into the fridge and grab two more water bottles and the orange juice.

When I turn around, I almost drop the bottles to the floor. Standing in my kitchen, wearing nothing but my college t-shirt, is Emery. The words Cal IT never looked hotter.

"Good Morning." She tugs at the bottom hem of the shirt that hits her upper thigh. "I couldn't find my clothes. I hope this is okay?"

"My t-shirt has never looked better." I give her body another slow perusal.

She looks beautiful and perfectly fucked. Her hair is tied up in a wild knot on top of her head, her lips are swollen, and her long legs are begging for me to wrap them around my waist as I impale her with my cock.

My dick jerks in my sweats, loving the thoughts running through my mind.

"Charmer." Her cheeks turn pink as she smiles at me and takes a step towards me. She checks out the food I brought and hums in approval. "So, what do we have here?"

I clear my throat, trying to focus on her question. "Breakfast burritos." I point at each one as I describe them. "This one is eggs with veggies. This is chorizo, bacon and cheese, and machaca. My favorite."

"Chorizo, please."

I place our food on the plates and guide her to the barstools on the other side of the island.

"Thank you."

"You're welcome. I don't know about you, but after last night, I'm starving."

She chokes on her bite, and I hand her a bottle of water. She takes a sip as I pat her back.

"You okay?"

She nods, wiping her lips with the back of her hand. "Yeah. All good."

I hide a smirk as I take another bite of my burrito. I love that I can make her flustered with just a few words or the mention of the naked activities we performed together. We were up until three in the morning, exploring each other's bodies and making up for lost time.

Emery moans around a bite of her food. "Wow, this is good." She wipes her mouth on a napkin before opening her mouth to take another bite.

My cock comes to life at the sight, and I have to force back a groan as she moans again. She has no idea of the effect she has on me. How unassumingly sexy she is when she does anything.

I close my eyes and breathe, trying to bring the conversation back to food, and not throwing her on the counter and eating her for breakfast.

"The food's great. I found the little place when I moved in a while back. I hadn't gone to sleep the night before because I was up, working on a code, and I was starving. I went for a walk at six in the morning, and it was the only place open and they had a line out the door. I took a chance and got in line. Best decision I ever made. They do all kinds of breakfast, but burritos and sandwiches are their specialty. I even have my brothers addicted."

"That's awesome. This reminds me of the food I would eat visiting my grandpa. He was from Texas. Every summer, he would take me and Chris to Galveston." She goes quiet, getting lost in her memories.

"I thought you were from Connecticut."

She exhales. "I am. My grandfather met my grandmother in college. She got pregnant, and they got married right after graduation. She was from old money. Her family wasn't happy that she ran off and married someone beneath her." Her shoulders sag, and she takes a sip of her orange juice before continuing, "My grandfather came from a rich ranching family, and they even dabbled in oil, but to my grandmother's family, they were still considered low class."

I push a strand of hair behind her ear as I listen to her tell the story of her family.

She turns to face me, her eyes clouded with tears. "When my grandmother left my grandfather, she took my mother with her, cutting him off. For years, he was estranged from them. He tried to fight it, but eventually, he gave up. My mother didn't want a relationship with him. She became what my grandmother should have been—a dutiful wife with a degree, who stays home and sits on charity boards planning galas. Her only job is to stand beside my father, on his arm, and be quiet."

That sounds fucking awful. I can't imagine my mom ever keeping quiet or not having a career of her own. It clearly bothers Emery too, though I'm sure there is more to unpack there. Aside from her brother, this is the most I have heard her speak of her family.

"It wasn't until Chris was five or six that my grandfather started to come around again. Don't get me wrong, Papa—that's what we called him—always sent cards and presents, but I wasn't allowed to see him."

"Why not?"

"My family wanted everyone to forget that he was a Mexican rancher from nowhere, with no name."

"That's awful." It's no wonder Emery doesn't talk about her family; they sound like uptight assholes.

"It is. But when Chris was old enough, my parents allowed us to visit Papa. At first, it was a week at a time. But eventually, it turned into the whole summer. They loved having summers to themselves. No kids. Charity events and parties. All the glitz and glam without the responsibility. Not that it mattered—Chris and I felt the same. We counted down the days until school ended and we would be in Texas, where we could run free and be kids. Where there were no expectations to act a certain way. Where a grown-up actually cared about our well-being and loved us. Papa loved us so much that it made up for the lack of care we received the rest of the year. He's the best, and I miss him."

She hangs her head in grief, and it breaks my heart. I stand and swoop her up into my arms. She wraps her arms around my neck and rests her head on my shoulders as I carry her to the couch.

Taking a seat, I keep her in my lap. "Why didn't you tell me this before?"

She looks at me with sad eyes, and it hits me. She doesn't share this information with anyone.

I kiss her forehead and hold her tight. "I'm honored that you shared that piece of you with me."

"Mason?"

"Yeah, baby doll?"

"I'm not like them, you know." Her voice cracks, as does my heart at her pain.

How could she even for a second think I would lump her into the same box? She's kind and beautiful, inside and out.

"I know." I kiss her nose.

Her lips turn up into a soft watery smile. "Tell me something about your family."

She rests her cheek back on my chest as I run my hand up her legs, reveling in her soft skin and the way her shoulders have relaxed after telling me something so personal.

Her family isn't the only one with hardships, but in comparison, ours seem so small and trivial. Jace might be the exception, but that's not my story to tell.

I flip the conversation and go with something easy. "Do you remember my brother, Cam? The one from the airport?"

She nods, trailing her fingers around the color of my shirt. "I do."

"Well..." I clear my throat. I don't know why I hate bringing this up. It's not Cameron's fault he's a famous baseball player. He deserves it. I never met a person more dedicated to the game than him. "He plays for the Los Angeles Evaders."

"What's that?"

I almost laugh at her response. Never in my life have I met someone who didn't know who the Evaders were.

"It's a professional baseball team."

"Oh, cool." She shrugs.

I bark a laugh at her nonchalance. Well, fuck, that was easier than I thought it was going to be.

Threading my fingers in her hair, I pull her head back. "Not a baseball person?"

She shakes her head and smiles. "Not a sports person. I like kickboxing to work out, but that's mostly because I get to punch a bag. Cheaper than therapy."

"You're cute." I boop her nose, making her giggle, then down and kiss her pouty lips.

"That's all you have? Your brother plays baseball. What about your other brothers?"

"My oldest brother is a lawyer, and my second oldest brother owns a talent agency with his friend."

"Ah. Normal people. I like it."

Normal, she says. She wouldn't think that if she knew more about them, but I let it go. I want her to keep thinking that we are a regular family. In a lot of ways, we are. We have Sunday dinners, we go on family vacations together, and we text almost daily. But when one of your brothers is a pitcher for one of the biggest baseball franchises and your other brother knows half of Hollywood, "normal" isn't the word I'd choose.

"Chris is normal," I tell her.

She snorts a laugh and rolls her eyes at me.

"Okay, maybe not normal, but he's a cool dude."

"He's definitely something. Thank you for taking him to dinner with us."

Dinner with Chris was an experience. He is loud, unapologetic, and has a wicked, sharp sense of humor. It felt like hanging out with my own brother. I wouldn't mind keeping him around. In fact, I want to keep the woman in my arms around more than anything.

"My pleasure."

She gives me a wide smile, her earlier gloomy demeanor gone. Shifting in my lap, she rubs her ass against my cock. I couldn't stop the fucker from getting hard if I tried. She bites her lips, holding back a laugh.

"Stop moving. Or I'm going to bend you over the coffee table and fuck you senseless."

Emery closes her eyes and hums at my threat.

My hand crawls up her inner thigh, my fingertips inches from her slit. She responds to my touch instantly. Her knees fall open, offering me an invitation to go further. I slide my hand under the hem of her shirt and cup her naked mound.

"Do you want me to bend you over and fuck you, baby doll?" My fingers trace her wet seam. I pause my ministrations. "Answer me."

Her eyes open and land on mine, topaz irises sparkling, and there is no mistaking the intensity behind them. The air around us becomes stifling as the heat between us ramps up.

"Yes."

"Yes, what?" I swipe my thumb across her plush bottom lip.

She visibly swallows—anticipation at its finest because we both know where this is going.

"Yes, Boss."

I don't know how this little bossy game started, but it gets me hard as fuck. When she says I'm the boss, the animal in me comes to life and all I want to do is rip into her and devour every inch of her body. I want to fuck her hard enough that when she gets up, she'll feel me between her legs for days.

With my foot, I push the table away from the couch and lift Emery off my lap, placing her on her knees in front of me. "Turn around."

She obeys immediately and faces the coffee table, placing her hands on the flat surface.

She's so fucking perfect.

I reach into the end table drawer beside me and pull out a condom, then stand behind her. She squirms, and the bottom of my shirt lifts, teasing me with a view of her pert ass cheeks. Shoving down my pants, I rip open the foil packet and roll the latex down my painfully hard cock, before getting on my knees behind her.

"Such a good girl, waiting patiently for me to fuck you."

Emery moans, her chin falling to her chest. I place my palm between her shoulder blades, pushing her chest down to the table.

"So fucking beautiful." I run my hand up the back of her thighs, over her ass, her back, and her arms. Twining my fingers with hers, I guide them to the edge of the table. I hinge over her taught body and whisper into her ear, "Hold onto the edge, and don't let go."

She wiggles her ass, and I bite back a groan as my cock slips between her crack. Fighting the urge to shove my dick inside her tight wet hole, I take a deep breath and lift my shirt over her butt.

"Mason, please," she whimpers.

"Shh. I'll give you what you need when I'm ready." I stroke my cock while running the tip through her slit, bumping her clit—teasing us both—before notching my cock at her dripping entrance, pushing in just the tip before pulling back.

"More. I need more. Please." Emery begs, her knuckles turning white as she grips the table's edge.

I slip in an inch, stilling. Pulling the tie from her hair, I release the silky strands before wrapping them around my fist and turning her head to the side so she can watch me as I fuck her. Without warning, I snap my hips forward, impaling her tight pussy with my cock.

She cries out, shoving her ass back against my hips. "Oh fuck. So good," she whines.

"Fuck yes. Your pussy was made for me." I look down to watch my cock move in and out of her body as she takes every one of my thick inches. "That's it, baby doll, take my cock. Take it all."

The sound of our flesh slapping together fills the room, and I can't help but keep riding her harder, pushing in deeper.

I'm never going to want another after her. She's all I want. Every moment, every kiss, every touch—I want them to all be with her.

With my free hand, I reach around and slip my fingers around my cock, gathering her arousal before bringing them to her clit, working the sensitive bundle of nerves as I fuck her. My balls tingle, and I know I'm about to come, but I can't until she does. I won't.

"I need you to come. Let go for me, and come on my cock like a good girl, Emery."

As if she needed permission, tremors wrack her body and her pussy squeezes my dick, choking it. Emery comes with a guttural groan, her pussy spasming around me, taking me over the edge with her. Spots color my vision, and I come in a burst of white-hot heat.

Releasing her hair, I collapse forward and wrap my arms around her waist. I bury my face in her neck, inhaling her fruity vanilla scent, catching a whiff of my own on her skin. My cock jerks, and the scratch of fabric between us draws my attention.

"You know, my brother would call this the 'Winnie the Pooh'."

What the fuck is wrong with me? Why on earth would I say that right now?

Because you have shirts and no bottoms on.

Emery chuckles as I slip out of her tight wet heat. "Okay, two things to unpack here. One... What's a 'Winnie the Pooh'?"

I sit back on my heels, pulling her with me and wrapping my arms around her. "It's when you have sex with no pants on but keep your shirts on."

Seriously. Shut the fuck up.

Emery laughs, making me feel like less of an idiot.

"Okay, that's funny. But why on earth are you thinking about your brother right now?"

"I have no fucking clue. I think you broke my brain," I grumble.

"That's kind of hot. What other types are there? Maybe we can add a few to our list."

She giggles, and I laugh along with her. Emery tilts her head back and looks up at me with a smile. My heart flips at the soft, freshly fucked, smiling face staring up at me. I lean down and press my lips to hers in a sweet kiss.

She breaks away and switches position, straddling me on the floor of my living room. Lifting my shirt, she pulls it over her head, chucks it to the side, and presses her palms to my chest. "What's it called when you have a shirt on and I don't?"

"It's called perfect, just like you."

Emery leans down and captures my lips with hers as she glides her soft wet slit over my cock, bringing it to life. When I enter her next, it's slow and sweet.

Yep, I am definitely wrecked. I am in deep with this woman, and there is no one else I would rather be in the deep end with.

TWENTY-ONE

Emery

MASON'S PHONE RINGS FROM the counter. He glances back at it but ignores the chime and buries his face in my neck instead.

My skin pebbles, and I naturally tilt my head to the side, giving him more access. He doesn't disappoint as he kisses and sucks the delicate skin. We are snuggled up on his couch, watching *The Witcher*, but a screening of our favorite show has turned into more of a Netflix and Chill situation.

We can't keep our hands off of each other, not since I jumped into his arms in the theater. I wanted to invite him, but I wasn't sure where we were with the whole "meeting each other's family" thing. A small part of me wanted him to just show up, and he didn't disappoint. I couldn't contain the joy it brought seeing him standing there with a bouquet.

It's so unlike me to show affection in public, but everything is different with Mason. I want to be near him, I want him to touch me, and I want him to kiss me. I want to experience the desperate need to be in the arms of a man who adores me, and wants to be near me all the time. To love me, hold me, kiss me. I want it all.

I've put myself last for so long that I didn't know how badly I've been missing someone special in my life. Someone who just wants me.

I hope I'm not mistaken, but it seems like that's the direction Mason and I are heading. Every moment with him is brighter and livelier. I get tunnel vision when I'm with him. He's all I see and want.

I snuggle in closer to Mason's side. Today has been amazing. After two rounds of seriously hot living room sex, we took a shower and went for a drive up the coast. It all felt so normal, just the two of us talking and driving, coasting along, without a care in the world. We ate at a cute little seafood spot, where we shared our meals, testing each other's food choices. We took a walk on the beach, holding hands, and shared a kiss under the warm California sun. We shared apple pie with a scoop of vanilla ice cream for dessert at his favorite diner.

Like our weekend back in February, we easily fell into each other. It's like we've been in a relationship for years. The comfort I find when I am with him is new to me. Being with Mason is as easy as breathing. The simple moments we have shared together mean everything to me. They remind me of the summer days I spent in Texas as a child when I felt loved and cared for. I know it's too soon, but the way Mason looks at me stirs up those same feelings.

The weight buried in my chest pinches as my mind drifts. Aside from Chris and Papa, there hasn't been a person in my life who has cared about me ... until now.

Mason's hand caresses my thigh, and I push away the dull ache in my heart and focus on this moment right here, with him. I burrow deeper into his side and inhale his spicy ginger scent, letting it warm my insides, soaking up the time we've shared in our happy little bubble.

"Em?" Mason places his palm on my cheek and turns my face to his.

"Mase?" My eyes meet his hazel-greens that are filled with so much heat my lungs forget how to breathe. Mason is devastatingly handsome and a complete hazard to my health.

"Breathe, babe." He flashes me a sly, knowing smirk. He leans forward, and his breath fans over my mouth as he runs his over mine.

I inhale, lips parted, waiting for him to kiss me.

His phone rings again, breaking the spell.

"I'm sorry. I think I need to get that."

"It's okay."

He gives me a soft peck before lifting my legs off his lap and getting up. He picks up his phone, and I watch as his caramel-brown hair falls over his eyes. The soft strands are all messy from where my hands have been lazily pulling on the ends as we watch TV.

I try focusing on Geralt and Yennifer's banter, but I can't help but hear pieces of Mason's conversation. It's clearly work calling. I sit patiently and wait for him to finish. When he sits back on the couch, his entire demeanor has changed. It's clear his mind is elsewhere now.

"Is everything alright?"

Mason's shoulders sag at my question. Like a record scratching, I know our weekend is over.

"That was work. The deadline for a project I've been working on just got moved up."

"You need to go to work?" I say more to myself than him. Memories of my father cutting weekends and vacations short for work sting my heart.

He looks at me, and it's almost like he doesn't want to say it but does anyway. "Yes, I have to head into the office."

"Okay."

I get up, but he grabs my wrist, pulling me into his chest.

"Em—"

I cup his scruffy cheeks and stare into his eyes. "It's fine, Mason. I understand. Your work means a lot to you. You're the boss, and your team needs you."

I need you, that little voice in my head screams, but I shut her up. I can't let my inner insecurities dictate how I feel about him. I have to remind myself that he's not my father. He's not working for the money or the notoriety. He's not keeping late hours because he's having an affair with another one of his assistants.

"I don't want our weekend to end."

His words calm the storm of emotions brewing in my chest.

"Me neither, but they need you."

He places his hands over mine and closes his lids. "Thank you," he says, opening them, his previously stormy eyes now calm, the streaks of gold glinting. "You have no idea how much I needed to hear that."

"You're welcome."

I don't want our weekend to end, but I know how invested he is in his work and company. What he's doing actually helps people, and I never want to prevent him from doing that, from pursuing his passions.

Mason wraps his palm around the back of my neck, tilting my head to the side before pressing his mouth to mine. He kisses me with an intensity that burns from the inside out. Heat spreads across my body, and my knees shake. I grab onto his shirt and cling to him as his tongue wraps sensuously around mine in a kiss so hot my lips will be tingling for days. A kiss that means so much more than I think either of us is prepared for. But I willingly take it and return it with the same intensity. The same unspoken words of affection.

When we break apart, he places his forehead on mine, and I can almost feel the words he has yet to say. The ones I'm simultaneously scared and greedy to hear. While he doesn't say anything—and he doesn't have to—the gesture alone fills some of the holes that live in my heart.

"I'm going to miss you," he whispers, bringing a smile to my face.

"I'm going to miss you too."

"Just because I have to work doesn't mean I want to. I'd rather spend my time with you, but I made a commitment and I need to follow through."

"I know." And I do. I can see it in his eyes, hear it in his words. I matter to him. He's trying to keep me in his life, to make us work, but he has commitments that he can't break. I wouldn't want him to.

"You do?" he asks. For once, my bossy man sounds vulnerable.

I think back to last night when he made it clear that I was his and he wasn't going to let me go. It had hope blooming in my belly. That, or I was drunk on orgasms. Maybe both.

"Well, you did make me promise to be yours while your dick was inside me, so you kind of made it clear that you want me," I try to joke, but I think I miss the mark when Mason growls.

"Don't talk about my cock being inside your tight wet pussy when I can't do anything about it. I would rather be buried balls deep inside you than leave for work."

I suck in a breath at his declaration. I almost want to beg him to stay and do just that. But I can't.

He gives me a quick kiss and smacks my ass. "I'm going to change. Grab your stuff, and then I'll drop you off at Chris's before I go."

All I can do is nod as I watch him head into his room. He just blew my mind with his sweet, dirty words and an almost confession that I might mean more than his work. I'm not going to get my hopes up, but I want that to be true. If not now, at least someday.

For both of us.

Because there are some things I still need to figure out and I'm running out of time.

◈

Chris collapses next to me on the couch, a bottle of white wine in one hand and two glasses in the other. "So why did lover-boy have to drop you off? I thought you were staying with him all weekend."

Ignoring his question, I take the glasses from him and place them on the coffee table. He twists off the top and fills our glasses.

Sliding a glass my way, he knocks his knee to mine, waiting for me to spill.

"There was an emergency at work."

"Mm," Chris grunts, his concern clear.

My hackles rise. I understand where Chris is coming from. Growing up, we saw how our father always put work ahead of his family.

"I know what you're thinking, but Mason isn't like that. What he's doing helps people," I scold my brother, defending Mason.

Chris side-eyes me, taking a sip of his wine. "What does he do for work?"

"He and his team are building software for banks that helps people from getting their identities stolen."

"Okay, that's pretty cool."

"It is cool. He's not Father. I swear. Mason is passionate about this topic. It's..." I pause, thinking of how his face lit up talking about the project he's working on. The way he speaks so intensely about why he got into tech security is actually kind of... "It's hot, in that nerdy kind of way."

"You mean, *he's* hot?" He fans his face and pretends to swoon.

I shove him away, and he bursts out laughing.

"You're such a perv."

He pushes me back, and my wine sloshes over the edge. "Well, I'm happy for you. He seems like a good guy. Dinner was fun. He didn't bat an eyelash at me—or my crazy—so if you say he's not like that asshole *you* call a father, I believe you."

I roll my eyes at Chris, disregarding the jab at our absentee parent. He's not wrong—our father is an asshole, but I can't let that kind of thinking get in my way. I have a plan that I need to stick to.

"What's that look for?"

"What look?" I take a sip of wine and curl my feet onto the couch.

"The look that said you have something going on that I don't know about. What are you hiding from me?"

At times, I hate that he can be so perceptive—the minuscule downfall of your brother being your best friend. "It's nothing, Chris. Just drop it."

He eyes me warily. I can see the questions he wants to ask.

My phone dings, and I am almost grateful for the distraction, hoping like heck it's Mason. My hopes are dashed when I see who sent me the message.

I slip on the mask I've honed over the last few years, wiping away my emotions. Sliding open my phone, I open the message and read it while Chris stares daggers at me, carefully studying my every move.

Mother: Your presence is required next month for the annual Beginning of Summer Soirée.

Ugh. Why does she have to be so damn cold?

I am not looking forward to this event. She throws a horribly chic party that's catered to the nines. It would be fun if everything wasn't beige and everyone in attendance wasn't fake. My parents and their friends all act like they love each other but, in reality, can't stand each other. They all talk about each other behind their backs. My head hurts already, having to plaster on a smile and nod at all the inane small talk I'll have to put up with.

I respond to her with my usual clinical tone. Not that it matters—my mother doesn't expect to have a real conversation with me. All she expects is for me to do my father's bidding.

Emery: I'll be there.

I turn off my phone and throw it on the table. I'll probably regret missing a call from Mason, but I need to put my mother out of my mind. Grabbing my wine, I finish it off before pouring another glass. I'm glad I don't have to fly out until tomorrow morning.

"Why are you going to their Summer Soirée, Emmy?" My brother leans back and crosses his arms, agitated at my participation in our parents' lives.

"Chris, I taught you better than to read other people's texts," I chide, trying to lighten the mood.

"You're not other people, and now I for sure know something fishy is going on."

I know I should tell him, but I have spent so long protecting him that I can't stop. At least not now, when I'm so close to the end. I only have a few more months of pretending.

You mean lying.

I run my hands over my face, trying to ignore the annoyingly accurate voice in my head. This is getting harder to do, especially since Mason has come into my life.

I exhale. "Chrisy, I promise it's nothing. I'm taking care of it, okay?"

"What does" — he uses finger quotes — "you're taking care of it mean?"

"It means that, right now, I can't tell you all the details, but I will. I'm figuring it out. The end is near. I just need you to finish college so we can be done with everything, and then I can tell you what's been going on."

He shakes his head. He's getting angry at my evasion. "Why can't I know now?"

I want so badly to tell him the truth, but...

"Because I know you," is all I say.

There is no way Chris would let me do what I need to do in order to help us get away from our parents. *We* need me to do this. Then, when we cut them off. Then, there will never be a need for them to come back into our lives.

"Chris, I need to do this for you and for me. It's the only way."

For everyone. I think about my childhood friends back home, who need me too.

"I don't like it," he grumbles.

"I don't like it either, but this is how it has to be. It's only for a little bit longer, I promise."

"How much longer?"

The original plan was until Chris's final tuition payment was paid, but I don't know if I can wait that long. "At least until the end of summer, and then I'll tell you everything."

His gaze flicks over my face, but I give nothing away.

His shoulders sag. "Okay. When you're ready to talk, I'm here. I won't judge you. I never would. You're everything to me, Emmy. You, my dear sister, are all I need in this world. I don't care about anything else. You know that, right?"

Tears well in my eyes, and I clear my throat. "I know, Chrisy. You mean everything to me too. It's me and you against the world; I haven't forgotten. That's why I need a little bit more time. It's going to be okay."

I don't know if my words reassure him, but he accepts my answer.

I take a deep breath, pushing away my negative thoughts. Everything has to work out. I have to believe that in order for me to keep doing what I'm doing.

Chris pulls me into a tight hug, and I can't help the tears that fall down my cheeks as I think about the cage I inadvertently trapped myself in. Instead of walking away all those years ago, as I should have, I let my parents manipulate me. I let them scare me into submission. Only now, I have more to lose and I won't let that happen.

I can't lose Mason. I don't think my heart could handle the loss.

TWENTY-TWO

Mason & Emery

TEXT CHAIN

APRIL 6

Mason: I'm sorry for cutting our weekend short. Can I make it up to you?

Emery: I'm listening.

Mason: I have a thing in Seattle next week. I have to be back in L.A. on Monday, but I'd like to spend my Saturday with you. Can I see you?

Emery: You can see me.

Mason: I can't wait to boss you around.

Emery: **Eye Roll Emoji**

Emery: Me too.

April 20

Mason: I can't get the image of you sprawled out on the bed and crying out my name while I was eating your delicious pussy out of my head.

Emery: Mason...

Mason: Emery...

Emery: I'm at work.

Mason: So?

Emery: You're so bad. I told you not to send me filthy texts during work hours.

Mason: I never agreed to that.

Mason: Did I make your panties wet?

Emery: Stop.

Mason: I'm waiting...

Emery: Yes. I'll call you tonight.

Mason: Until then, baby doll.

Emery: Charmer.

Mason: Only for you.

April 20

Mason: I have to be in Seattle again. Please come meet me?

Emery: For the weekend?

Mason: Friday and Saturday.

Emery: I don't know. I have work.

Mason: When was the last time you took a day off?

Emery: When was the last time you took a day off?

Mason: Touché.

Emery: I'll see what I can do.

Mason: I'll make it worth your while.

Emery: Oh, I bet you will.

TWENTY-THREE

Bro-tally Awesome

TEXT CHAIN

A<small>PRIL</small> 30

Cam: It's that time again. Who needs tickets?
Eli: Me. I'll email you the dates.
Jace: Same.
Cam: Yo, Mase. Tickets?
Cam: Where are you, dude?
Jace: Not here.
Eli: Interesting.
Cam: Very interesting.
Eli: Is he really ignoring us?
Jace: Looks like it.
Cam: Fucker.

TWENTY-FOUR

Mason

MAY

"UNCLE MILLS, WHEN ARE you coming to visit me?" Rhys asks.

His golden-brown eyes are narrowed my way through the phone—my only means of seeing his face these days. Between work and spending every free weekend with Emery, I haven't seen my nephew in far too long, and in my absence, Cameron has rubbed off on him.

Rhys's current kick is becoming both a professional soccer and baseball player, like his uncle. I don't think anyone besides Bo Jackson has managed to play two separate professional sports in well over a decade, but I cheer on the seven-year-old and his big dreams nonetheless. He'll figure it out when he's older.

"I don't know, little man, but I will definitely be in town when your sister is born."

"But that's not for a long time." He sticks his sad little lip out, and my heart sinks.

I hate that I haven't prioritized him, but for once, I've found someone other than family that I want to dedicate my time to. I can't go without seeing Emery for very long. She's become my obsession. Being away from her is agony, and the small pockets of time we've managed to carve out are the only thing keeping me sane.

"I know, buddy. I have had a few projects for work that keep me out of town." I'm bummed and miss the kiddo too.

I wasn't lying when I said I've been traveling. This week I'm in Chicago, and instead of spending Memorial weekend with my family, I'm stuck in a conference room from morning until night, trying to get this code working just right with the bank's software. We keep running into a glitch. Kenzo and I have been trying to code a patch within the network, and being onsite is critical for running diagnostics.

After next week, work should calm down a bit, at least until fall.

A thought pops into my head and has my wheels turning. Next month is June. Not only is Rylann giving birth to my niece in a couple of weeks, but it's also Emery's birthday. I might be able to stick around Pine Hills for longer.

"Hey, Rhys?"

"Yeah?" His dejected little voice pulls at my heartstrings again.

"How about when your Mom has the baby, I come and stay with you guys for a little while?"

"Say, what now?" Jace's voice cuts in as he pulls the iPad away from Rhys to talk to me. "Repeat that for me?"

I roll my eyes at him but can't help my smile. I think I just broke my brother's brain. I am not known for taking time off—at all—so this is a shock for him. Me too, if I'm being honest.

"Need a Q-Tip? I said, when Rylann—you know, your soon-to-be wife—gives birth, maybe I can come stay with you. Help you out with Rhys and stuff."

"Are you serious?" He still sounds skeptical.

"Yes. Gee, you act like I don't take time off or something. Did I not stay with Rhys so you could take my beautiful future sister-in-law on a babymoon?"

Jace growls at my compliment directed at his fiancée. He hates knowing we all think she's gorgeous. It's funny because Cam, Eli, and I met her first on our guys' trip to Mexico. He's just the lucky bastard that won her heart later.

"You did," he grits out. "But that was planned months in advance."

I shrug. "Well, I have free time next month. Do you want my help or not?"

"Yes!" Rhys screams in the background, jumping on Jace's back.

He picks up Rhys, both their faces now in my sightline. The image of them together has my brain jumping to scenarios.

What would a future with Emery look like? Does she want kids? Would she move to L.A.? Could I move here?

I shove those crazy thoughts away as Jace says, "I will have to speak to my wife."

"I'm not your wife." Rylann's sweet, raspy voice pipes up from somewhere.

Jace practically snarls, "You wear my ring, you have my babies—you're my wife."

"Not yet," Rylann sings and steps into view.

Jace grabs her by the back of her neck and pulls her close. I feel like a voyeur watching them share a silent conversation.

"Later, Sunshine."

Her cheeks turn pink, and I cringe. I think I witnessed their foreplay.

"Can you two not right now?" I groan.

They kiss, and Rhys wretches.

"Why do they always do that?" he whispers to me.

His cheeky remark has me laughing.

"Because they love each other," I tell him.

He looks back at them and smiles, then turns to me. "So, are you coming or not?"

Jace and Rylann speak at the same time.

"Not."

"Yes."

"Awesome!" Rhys yells.

Jace turns and points at me. "The wife has spoken. But you can't stay here."

"Fine by me." I'm pretty sure I have somewhere else I can stay anyway.

As long as she'll have me.

MY NERVES SHOOT THROUGH the roof as I glance at the time again. Twenty minutes until I have to make my way towards the airport.

I review my notes again for Mandy, the temp worker we hired to cover the front desk tomorrow. We've already gone through everything she will be handling—mostly fielding calls and updating clients—while I am away.

Guilt gnaws at my stomach. I hate leaving a pregnant Rylann here alone to handle everything. With Scarlett being on maternity leave with her twin boys, I should have found a way to get out of my parents' party this weekend.

Fat chance.

I shake my head to myself as I reorder my notes and put them in a manilla folder. There's no way I could miss it; I'm already on thin ice where my parents are concerned. Who knows what they would do if I didn't make an appearance?

It's only one day, I remind myself.

Anxiety courses through my system at the mere thought of having to put on a show. Every part of my soul despises my hometown, the fake people that live there, and the reasons keeping me from cutting ties.

Standing from my desk, I grab the file and place it at reception, where Mandy will be sitting. I watch as she trails a waddling

Rylann around, taking notes. As Rylann chuckles, cradling her stomach, a flash of me swollen and pregnant pops into my head. I never really entertained the idea of having kids before. My parents aren't exactly the best role models, and with the way things are, my sole focus has been one attempt after another to escape my parents' grasp—a slow process that has become increasingly difficult to follow through with, even if it's for Chris's sake.

But with Mason? A future with him flashes before me.

As if she can feel me staring, Rylann turns around and gives me a soft, knowing smile. She's perceptive and all-knowing yet never judgmental. She never pushes me for answers or details, unlike Scarlett, who would prefer to tie me down and water-board me for answers. No, Rylann is a gentle soul, and I couldn't be more grateful for her to be my boss. *Partner.*

Who am I kidding? Those two women will always be my bosses. That's how it started for us. They hired me, just like Mandy here, to help cover while they went on maternity. Only then, it was Rylann first. Those two seem to do everything together, even have their children at the same time.

Rylann walks over to me and pats my hand. "I'm going to be fine, Em. Remember, we did this before, you and me."

"I know. I just... Well, that's just it. It was you and me."

She chuckles, squeezing my hand. "It was." Shrugging, she jerks her head at the newbie headed towards the bathroom. "But I like this one. Maybe we'll get lucky, and she'll become another you."

My cheeks heat at her compliment. She always knows what to say to calm me down and ease my fears. I love working here. It's been a dream come true.

"Thanks, Ry."

"Of course, girl. You know we love you. You're one of us."

My chest tightens, and my eyes cloud. Rylann always tells me this, but I've always ignored it. Lately, though, I've really wanted to be one of them. I have been carrying a load of heartbreak, guilt, and secrets for so long that it's hard for me to let people in, for me to trust.

I don't know what comes over me, but I lean in and give Rylann a hug. Her belly bumps me as she hugs me back. Her sweet citrusy perfume soothes my heart ache as she holds me tight.

"You're the best boss ever," I whisper, pulling out of her grasp but feeling ten times better.

She rolls her eyes at me. "I'm not your boss."

"You'll always be my older, wiser boss-lady. Scarlett too."

"Don't let her hear you call her old, or she'll kick you in the ass."

We share a laugh, thinking about how Scarlett would, indeed, kick my ass for calling her old.

"True, and I kind of like my ass."

"Me too. It's my inspiration after I have this kiddo. Maybe I'll be joining you at one of those crazy kickboxing classes you take."

"You're perfect just as you are, but I'd love for you to come with me to one." I really mean it.

Rylann's eyes widen in shock, but she quickly shakes it off. "I'm holding you to that. Now, why don't you get out of here and have a good weekend already."

I make a face, and her smile falters for half a second.

"I'm always here if you need me."

Nodding, I give her another hug before heading to my desk and grabbing my suitcase.

I feel lighter as I head out. It's nice knowing I have someone in my corner when I'm ready to let her in.

Tonight's affair is the same as always, lavish and artificial. The air buzzes with idle chatter as everyone drinks and nibbles on fancy hors d'oeuvres, sipping thousand-dollar bottles of champagne while a jazz band plays in the background.

My mother outdid herself, as usual, going above and beyond with her theme—beige. The tablecloths, the flowers, the food, and even the twinkling lights overhead are beige. It makes everything look so ... lifeless and boring, like her.

My stomach flips as I observe her and my father with their friends from the other side of the dance floor. Leave it to Sinclair and Cybil Rhodes to put on a spectacle. They are all fake smiles and forced hearty laughs as they drink and schmooze with each other. The sound of their synthetic joy grates on my nerves and makes me sick.

Bubbles pop and sparkle on my tongue as I take another sip of my champagne, hoping the cool liquid soothes the anger licking at my skin. Don't get me wrong, the estate—which has been passed down for generations on my father's side—is gorgeous, with a beautiful view of the Long Island Sound. The community is located on a privately owned peninsula, and many of the estates here in Heaven's Point have this view. A view that is highly sought after and revered.

Except for me and Chris. Growing up, this place was—and still is—a soulless prison. A place where you're expected to act and dress a certain way.

A hand lands on the small of my back, bringing me out of my thoughts. I look up into the clear blue eyes of my friend, Alexander Westfield—Lex to me. He is classically handsome with his strong jawline, sandy blond hair, and perfectly straight white teeth. He's got that all-American-boy quality to him, and I adore him. He's been helping me with my parental problems my entire life.

"Emery, you look beautiful tonight," he appraises my pale pink–colored gown and smirks.

He knows I didn't pick out this dress. Another "gift" from my mother. It was hanging in my room, with a note telling me to wear this for tonight's festivities. She does it on purpose. She knows how much I hate the color pink.

"Hey, Lex." I give him a hug and catch a whiff of his leathery-scented cologne. He smells expensive, rich, and all wrong.

I gently push him away, hoping the smell doesn't linger on me all night. There is only one man's scent I want to breathe in like oxygen.

Mason's.

My heart flutters just thinking about him and how he plans on having an extended stay in Pine Hills next month. He was so sweet, asking if he could stay with me. I didn't even bother asking why before saying yes.

"Where's Lizzie? I haven't seen her," I ask about his longtime girlfriend, and I look around the lawn, trying to catch a glimpse of her red hair.

"She couldn't make it." Lex uncomfortably tugs on his blue silk tie.

"Is everything okay?" I ask my friend.

He seems out of sorts. Now that I look closer, he has dark circles under his eyes, and his hair is slightly disheveled and longer than usual.

He clears his throat and takes a sip from his flute. "Yep. Everything's good."

"Is she working?"

He nods, sipping his champagne again. He averts his gaze, and I shake it off.

It's not unlike Lizzie to miss an event. She recently started a pediatric fellowship at the hospital in Greenwich—the town over.

My parents catch sight of us and head our way.

"Incoming." I nudge Lex.

He turns in time for them and his parents to sidle up to us as well.

"Alexander, it's wonderful to see you. I see you found Emery," my mother coos.

"Yes, ma'am."

"Are you ready for the announcement?" my father asks Lex.

My friend's back stiffens, and the hairs on the back of my neck stand on end.

"What announcement?" I ask.

"Alexander is taking over the company at the end of summer," his father, Alfred announces. "Isn't that right, my boy?" He smacks Lex on the back.

"But I thought—"

Lex shakes his head at me, and I bite back my question. We made a promise never to question each other in front of our parents for fear they might figure out what we have been doing.

Unlike me, Lex wants to run his family's empire. He has been working tirelessly to prove that he can run the family business. And when I say their business is huge, I mean it. The Westfields own the largest media company in the world. Their media portfolio is beyond diversified, owning everything from newspapers to news channels, and everything in between.

Both my father and Alfred pull Lex away to mingle, leaving me with a million questions. Lex takes another look back at me over his shoulder, his blue eyes flashing with regret before he walks away.

"He's doing the right thing, listening to his parents," my mother says, her voice grating on my nerves.

I say nothing, sipping my drink instead. This is just another dig at me my mother can't help herself from taking.

"You'll see," she snips. "This is the only way. The right way. You will fulfill your duty any way you can since you decided not to run Rhodes Publishing." Cybil fluffs her hair before disappearing into the crowd. Her pungent flowery perfume lingers behind her like a cloud of toxic fumes, choking me.

Her comment plays on repeat, not quite sitting right with me. Why does it feel like everyone else knows what's going on? My head won't wrap around everything that's been said and done tonight, but I suspect I'm not going to like what's been happening here without me. I need to talk to Lex about it.

For the rest of the night, I search for my friend in the crowd of the famously wealthy people who live here, but I come up empty. A sense of dread lingers within me as I give up my search and return to the main house.

When I'm in my room, I strip off the silk and sequined dress—that probably costs more than my monthly mortgage payment—and leave it on the floor before heading to the bathroom for a quick shower.

Once I'm clean and rid of every particle of cloying perfume and cologne that clung to me, I lie down and pick up my phone.

My earlier unease is forgotten as I see Mason's name on the home screen, notifying me of two missed text messages. I slide open my phone to read them.

Mason: I can't stop thinking about you and how you taste. I get hard just smelling vanilla. And pears. You've ruined me.

Mason: When I see you, I'm going to ruin you like you've ruined me, baby doll.

My breath hitches, and my eyes fall closed as I think about Mason's hands roaming every inch of my body before he buries his face between my legs. My body heats, and my core gets wet.

He doesn't need to try to ruin me; I'm already ruined. I have been since I met him.

TWENTY-SIX

Mason

JUNE

MY PULSE RACES AND my palms sweat as Jace walks toward me, holding a tiny bundle wrapped in a pink muslin blanket. I'm scared I'm going to drop her. I've never held a baby this small.

My brother places his daughter in my waiting arms. "Meet your niece, Sariah."

Exhaling a breath, I hold the sweetest girl in the world, staring at her chubby face. She has cute bow-shaped lips, dark brown eyes, and comically long lashes that coat her lids.

"I didn't know newborn babies had so much hair."

Rylann chuckles, drawing my attention. "Not all babies, but mine come out with full heads of hair."

Jace leans down and kisses her temple, whispering, "Our babies," in her ear.

Ignoring the painfully sweet moment between my brother and his wife, I return my attention to Sariah as she coos and roots.

I picture holding a different little girl—one with honey-brown hair and wide doe eyes the color of warm topaz. The same color as the woman I dream about at night.

Would our kids look like her? Fuck, I hope so.

"Mase, I have to head down to grab Rhys from Rylann's parents. Are you coming or staying?" Jace interrupts my daydreaming.

"I'm good right here with this precious girl in my arms." I glance at Rylann as she sits back in the hospital bed with a sigh, no doubt tired from giving birth in the middle of the night. "Is that okay with you?"

"Of course, Mills." She uses my Rhys-given nickname, making me chuckle.

I won't admit it to anyone, but I like the nickname; it's grown on me.

"I'll be right back with our boy." Jace gives Ryann another kiss before leaving.

"How are you feeling, Ry?"

She smiles widely, her eyes shining bright, and sighs. I can't imagine how exhausted she must be, but here she is, looking like a million bucks. She is one of the strongest women I know.

"Tired. Sore. But nothing I haven't gone through before."

I can feel her eyes watching me as I stare at Sariah, who is now snoozing soundly in my arms, but I keep my attention on my niece.

I owe this little princess for arriving earlier than expected. Emery doesn't know I'm in town yet, and I want to surprise her for her birthday tomorrow.

What the hell do I buy her? It needs to be special.

"Can I get some advice?"

Fuck, this is awkward. I'd scratch my jaw if my hands weren't holding a baby, but there is no fucking way I would ask my brothers for advice. I would never hear the end of it.

"Sure. What can I help you with?" Rylann twines her fingers together and places them over her stomach.

"Well, what are some good birthday present ideas?"

Rylann grins. "Who's the girl?"

"What girl?"

"Oh, please. Like you'd ask for advice on what to buy a guy."

"Fine, you got me." I shift forward on my seat and push to a stand. "There's this woman I've been seeing, and it's her birthday tomorrow. I'd like to get her something nice." I hesitate, looking down at Sariah.

I've only just met her, and I love holding her in my arms. She's going to have the rest of her uncles wrapped around her finger too. I place her tiny body in Rylann's arms and take the seat next to her bed.

"Is she special?" Rylann tilts her head, trying to read me in the silent way she does.

My throat tightens. Why do I get nervous talking about Emery to my family?

Because everything seems too good to be true.

I push that thought back, not wanting to pull on that thread. Lately, Emery has been ... off, maybe? A little skittish since visiting her parents. I want her to forget all about them and focus on the good. I want her birthday to be special.

There's that word again.

"Yes, she's special." As soon as I speak the words, my shoulders feel lighter.

Emery *is* special. Hell, I was just picturing what our daughter might look like.

"I'm so excited for you."

"You're not going to ask" — I hold up my hand, ticking off the questions I'm sure my family will throw at me with my fingers — "who is she? Where did I meet her? What does she look like? When are you going to meet her? When's the wedding?"

Rylann lets out a hearty laugh that has her head hitting the pillows behind her. "I can just see your mom asking every one of those questions." She wipes the tears from her eyes. "But no. I'm not going to ask you. When you're ready, you'll tell us." She shrugs, adjusting her hold on Sariah.

"How do you do that?"

"Do what?" She lovingly runs a finger over Sariah's baby-soft cheek.

"Act so calm and patient?"

"Mm, you know, I've been through a lot." She pauses, looking down at her daughter again.

My stomach dips, knowing I'm making her think about how she lost her previous husband to cancer.

Before I can stop her, she continues, "When I walked away from your brother all those years ago, I never thought we'd find our way back to each other. We both married other people and had separate lives to live. Yes, we endured unimaginable heartbreak between then and now, and yet I wouldn't change a thing. We had to go through all that to get here. Now, we have a beautiful growing family and our relationship is stronger than ever. I honestly believe everything works out the way it's supposed to. So if this woman is your person, take your time and follow your gut. Be open and honest, and for the love of God, listen to her. She might be telling you things without you knowing. I have faith your heart will guide you."

"Thank you." I do trust my gut, and it's working with my heart, pointing at Emery being the one.

"You're welcome. And to answer your question: sometimes it's about the thought that makes a birthday special, not the gift."

The door bursts open, and Rhys comes rushing through.

"Uncle Mills!" He launches himself at me, sending my chair back on two legs at the force of his body as he throws himself in my arms.

"Hey, buddy." I ruffle his hair and breathe in his sweet orange and syrupy scent, hugging him tight. "You had waffles, didn't you?"

Rhys gasps. "How'd you know?"

I tap my nose. "I can smell it, and you're making me hungry." My stomach rumbles in agreement, so I tickle Rhys's.

He squeals and the sound hits me soul deep. I love this kid.

"Congratulations, you're a big brother now," I tell him, pointing at Sariah.

"Thanks. I love my sassy so much already." He jumps out of my arms, climbs onto the bed, and cuddles Rylann and his sister.

"Sassy, huh?" I chuckle. Rhys and his nicknames.

"Yup. She's going to be just like Mom."

Rylann gasps in mock offense while both Jace and I laugh our asses off. Rylann *is* sassy as hell.

This kid, man. He really makes our family complete.

"I agree, son. Sassy and beautiful, just like your mom," Jace states, staring at his fiancée.

Rylann's cheeks pinken, and her eyes water as she stares up at Jace. The look they share is so full of love that it's impossible to miss.

Instead of jealousy burning my intestines like acid, love warms my stomach and radiates up my torso. Hope blooms in my chest as I get a glimpse of the future I could have.

Emery is the only woman who has urged me to try and reach for something more than work in life. She's the one I want to share my life with.

⚬

I pull the rental car along the curb outside Emery's house and park. Peering through the passenger window, I look at the quiet little two-bedroom home with white and green shutters.

Double-checking, I spot her car sitting in the driveway. I was a little afraid she wouldn't be home from work yet. When we texted last, she was busy taking care of the office while her partners were out, and had planned to stay a little late. I gave her an extra couple of hours before heading over here to surprise her.

My heart rate speeds up, and my palms begin to sweat. Fuck, what if she hates surprises?

It's too late now.

With a calming breath, I open the door and get out of the car. Opening the rear passenger door, I reach into the back seat and with one hand grasp the handles of the bags I packed for Emery's birthday celebration. With my other hand, I grab the balloons and the bouquet, and using my butt, I slam the door shut and make my way up the stone path to her door.

I can hear Henry yapping his little head off through the door as I approach. Shaking my head with a smile, I picture the tiny furball bouncing in the air like he has springs on his feet.

"Quiet, Henry," Emery's muted voice calls out from somewhere in the house.

I knock on the door and step back as Henry goes absolutely wild at the sound.

"Damn dog."

I chuckle as Emery curses him out.

Without even checking the peephole—something I'm going to have to talk to her about later—the birthday girl opens the door. Her jaw drops, practically hitting the floor in front of her.

I spread my arms wide. "Happy Birthday, baby doll."

Emery's breathing turns ragged, and her eyes start to shine with unshed tears.

Fuck, I got this all wrong.

I drop my arms as a giant tear rolls down her cheek, tearing my heart in two.

"I'm sorry. I should have called. I—"

Emery grabs my shirt, twisting the fabric in her fists, and presses her chest to mine in a tight hug. "No." Her voice cracks. "You caught me off guard. I love my surprise. Aside from Chris, no one has ever done anything like this for me for my birthday."

"You mean, surprise you. Right?"

She shakes her head, and my heart breaks for a completely different reason. If my arms weren't full, I'd wrap her in my arms and hug her tight. Take away the pain in her eyes.

"My parents aren't the touchy-feely types, and they certainly do not celebrate birthdays. I had one party when I turned sixteen, and that was more for them than for me."

What the fuck is wrong with these people? How could they not celebrate their child's birthday? My chest aches for the little honey-haired version of the beautiful woman before me.

"Well then, I better make this a birthday you won't forget."

"I'd like that."

Before I can hand Emery the bouquet of burgundy peonies I bought for her, she tugs my shirt and pulls me through the door. I kick the door shut, determined to give her a night to remember.

If I have my way, this goddess of a woman will never go another birthday without someone—that someone being me—celebrating her and the amazing woman she is.

A woman who works hard and takes care of her brother without a second thought. A woman who is sweet and kind, and deserves the world. The woman who knocked me on my ass and flipped my lonely world upside down.

The woman I have completely fallen for.

WHEN HENRY WENT CRAZY at the knock on the door, I wasn't expecting the six-foot-two sexy man who has taken over my every thought to be standing on the other side. To say I was surprised to find him on my porch is an understatement.

I shake my head at him, smiling. "I still can't believe you're here."

I drop my hands from his shirt as he kicks the door shut, carrying a couple of canvas bags in one hand, and a beautiful bouquet of burgundy flowers and balloons in the other.

"Believe it, Em. I'm here." He kisses my cheek and walks past me toward the kitchen, calling over his shoulder, "Get in here, birthday girl. It's time to unwrap your presents."

My feet freeze, and my throat tightens. "You got me presents?" I choke out, tears clouding my eyes.

"Of course." He shrugs.

I appreciate his casual tone—he's doing me a favor by not making a big deal out of this. But inside? Inside, I'm melting and on the verge of breaking down.

Aside from that horrible Sweet Sixteen, I was serious when I told Mason that only Chris has ever celebrated me on my actual birthday. I've only known Mason for a little over six months, and here he is, with an armful of presents just for me. On my birthday.

As if I couldn't be more head over heels for the thoughtful man in front of me. He has done what no one else has been able to do in years—break down my walls and capture my heart. I'm glad his back is turned to me because I doubt I could hide the hearts in my eyes right now.

The clang of bottles catches my attention as Mason places the bags and flowers on the kitchen island. I take a deep breath and watch as he releases the balloons, letting them float to the ceiling above, and turns around to face me.

His heated gaze lands on mine as he leans his lower back against the marble's edge and crosses his thick arms over his chest, taking me in from head to toe. I'm barefoot, wearing tattered purple and white flannel shorts with my college emblem and an oversized gray t-shirt with the same design, and have no makeup and no bra on.

My face burns at his attention as I stand before the sexiest man alive, wearing the least sexy outfit I own, and yet ... he's looking at me like I'm his next meal. Fighting the urge to cover myself with my arms, I let Mason finish his perusal, my nipples hardening under his watch as he licks his bottom lip so slowly that my panties almost combust. Memories of that tongue on my sex have my clit pulsing and my center slick with arousal.

His eyes find mine, and my cheeks are on fire for a different reason. My chest rises and falls in the same rapid beat as my heart.

"It's not a birthday without ... presents." The husky tone Mason uses to enunciate "presents" has my pussy throbbing. "Do you like presents, Emery?" His voice, like his body, oozes sex.

It's erotic, and I am completely hypnotized, my body begging for him to touch me. My mouth feels thick, and the words stick on my tongue like a fly trapped in honey.

I nod my assent and the gold streaks in his eyes glint as he smirks at me.

"Would you like to see what I brought you?"

"Yes, please," I croak out, finding my voice around the beating of my heart in my throat.

"Come here first." He reaches out a hand for me to take.

I place my palm in his warm one, and those tell-tale sparks skate across my skin, making my body tingle.

"Before we celebrate, I think I owe you a birthday kiss, don't you?"

"Yes," I exhale, stepping into his body, bringing us chest to chest.

There's that smug smirk on his lips again. He's enjoying his effect on me, and while I'd love to push back just a little, I don't. I've missed him, and it's my birthday, dammit. I want him. His presence is the best birthday present I have ever received.

With his knuckles, Mason tilts my chin up and presses his lips to mine in a soft, tender kiss. He licks the seam, and I open without hesitation, inviting him in as he invades my mouth with his wicked tongue. My body bursts into flames as he dives in, gripping my neck and threading his fingers through my hair, tugging enough to make my scalp sting. My soft moans fill the air as I grip the fabric of his dress shirt in my fists, and my knees tremble under the weight of his control on me. The control I so willingly hand over to him every time we are together.

I never thought I would be the surrendering type, but when I'm with Mason, I don't think twice about it. He can do whatever he wants with me. My body craves his bossiness, his possession. Mason likes having all the control. He gets off on it, and I get off on giving it to him.

Mason's warm hands land on my hips, surprising me as he lifts me into the air and spins me around. Instinctively, I wrap my arms and legs around his body, holding on tight as he continues to kiss me like I'm his reason for living.

Needing more of him, I dig my heels into his firm ass and roll my hips, aligning our centers. Searching for relief, I rub my clit over the ridges of his cock. He's hard, and all I want is to release him from the confines of his jeans and let him take me right here on the counter.

I'm so lost in my thoughts of riding this sexy man that I barely register Mason's strong legs shifting under us. My butt lands on the suede cushion of my stool before he breaks our kiss and rests his forehead against mine.

"Fuck, I've missed you, baby doll." His quick breaths fan across my wet lips, sending shivers down my spine. "As much as I would love to bend you over this counter and bury my hard cock in your sweet pussy, let's start with some presents."

My pussy contracts, begging for him to do just that, but he pulls away instead. My body screams in opposition, begging for me to rip off his clothes and mount him in the middle of the kitchen.

Oh goodness, Mason turns me into a horny mess.

I take a deep breath. I need to cool it.

Unable to hide my discomfort, I pout. "Fine."

With a chuckle, he pecks my lips once more before moving back around the other side of the island. He has my body humming and he knows it, the smug jerk.

Yeah, but you like it.

Ugh. I do. In fact, I love it. I love *him*.

The words stick on the tip of my tongue, and my fear stops me from saying them aloud.

Mason pulls out two pink bakery boxes—one large and one small—and opens them. Inside the large box sits a white cake sprinkled with what looks like cinnamon, with the words *Happy Birthday* written in frosting across the top.

"What kind of cake is that?"

"Cinnamon roll, with cream cheese frosting."

"What?" My eyes pop out of my head.

Holy shit. He remembered my favorite meal and found it in cake form for me.

"Do you like it?" He rubs his chin nervously, a far cry from my confident, bossy Mason.

My nose tingles as I push back my tears. "Are you kidding? It's—" My voice cracks. My emotions are at the surface, waiting to break free. "It's perfect. Thank you."

"You're welcome."

Henry barks, reminding us of his presence.

Mason grins and opens the smaller box. He pulls out a cookie cut in the shape of dog paws and kneels down. "I didn't forget about you, you little furball." He hands my yorkie a dog treat the same size as his hairy head.

Henry snags it with his teeth before running out of the kitchen.

Mason goes back to unloading the bags, like he didn't just make me swoon with that little display, and pulls out four plastic food containers and utensils. Garlic, chili, and cumin fill the air, making my stomach grumble and my heart skip a beat. He continues to move around my kitchen like he belongs here, washing his hands and setting up our dinner.

I stare at his corded forearms as they ripple and flex with his movements. You would never know Mason was a computer nerd if you saw his body. He hides a work of anatomical art under the crisply pressed slacks, dress shirts, and cashmere sweaters with suede elbow patches he wears. He looks like a hot professor. You know, the one that all the girls fight over so they could be his TA.

Sorry, ladies. He's mine.

The last bag clangs, and once again, my interest is piqued.

Pointing to the bag I ask, "What's in that one?"

He shoots me with a smoldering smile, and it's like a shot of liquid lust straight to my pussy. He's sex on a stick and a detriment to my libido.

"That is part of my surprise." He pulls out four bottles of champagne and places them—labels facing away from me—on the counter. "Where can I find glasses?"

I move to stand, but he clicks his teeth at me.

"No, no, birthday girl, you stay seated. I'm taking care of you tonight."

With a smile on my face, I sit and direct him to the cabinet that has the champagne flutes. He takes four glasses down and places one in front of each bottle.

"Champagne? Fancy."

Mason chuckles. "A quality beverage for a quality woman."

I push past the compliment that burns my cheeks.

"So, how does this work?" I wave my finger around the bottles.

"First, we're going to taste each one of these champagnes. Then, you're going to tell me which one is your favorite, and that one will become our champagne of choice when we have something to celebrate."

My heart beats wildly in my chest. His tone and choice of words suggest that this isn't a one-time thing.

I'm done for.

Not only did he bring me food and dessert, but he remembered all of my favorites. He's standing here, for me, not because he's obligated to be here or because he needs something. He's here for *me*.

"I love that."

I love you.

I let the words dance in my head. I want to tell him how I feel, but I don't want to confess my feelings while my parents continue to throttle my freedom.

Soon.

I jump at the sound of the cork popping, and Mason shoots me a coy smile. He pours the buttery bubbling liquid into the flute and licks the droplets off the rim of the bottle. He repeats the process three more times, seductively licking the bottle each time. He's gone from turning me on to making me swoon, and back again.

"Mason." His name slips past my lips like a plea.

Or maybe it's a warning. I don't know. What I do know is that I couldn't care less about the drinks in front of us. All I want is for him to lick me like the bottle in his hand. He's got me dripping, and he hasn't even touched me yet. The little erotic show he's put on with the bubbly has me all hot and bothered.

He shakes his head. "Not yet."

Anticipation settles in my stomach like butterflies. My skin prickles. *What does he have up his sleeve?*

He hands me the first glass. "Sip."

As usual, I heed his command without a second thought.

"Too sweet," I say, licking the drop off the bottom of my lips.

Mason follows my tongue as he takes the glass from my hand and sips it. "Agree."

He places it on the counter and hands me the next. This time the flavor is tart, almost sour, and I shake my head in disapproval, returning the glass.

He gives it a try and grins. "Agree. Bottle two is also out."

We repeat the process twice more.

"So, birthday girl, tell me... Which one is your favorite?"

I roll my head from side to side, pretending to mull it over. "I'm going to have to go with the third one. It has a nice balance between sweet and dry."

"It was pretty good." He lifts the bottle, revealing the label to me, but my eyes are on the sexy man in front of me. "But ... I think we need to test it again. Make sure it's the right fit. Come here."

He crooks his finger at me, and like the moth to his flame, I slip off the stool and walk around the counter, obeying him without hesitation.

"Stop."

Again, I comply, stopping mere inches from his hard body.

He grips my hips, squeezing, and bends his knees, running his nose up the length of my neck, inhaling my skin. "So fucking sweet," he mumbles, kissing my neck. "I think it's time we get rid of these clothes, yes?" He arches a brow at me in question, waiting for my answer.

"Yes."

His fingers find the hem of my shirt, and in one quick go he removes it, throwing it to the floor. His eyes burn with hunger as he explores my naked torso. "You're fucking beautiful, Emery."

My eyes close as he slides his fingertips down my chest to the tips of my breasts, my nipples turning into diamonds under his touch. Hooking his fingers over the waistband of my shorts, he pushes them over my hips, letting them fall to the floor in a pool at my feet. He hisses at the sight of me completely bare for him.

"Fuck, I take it back. You're a goddess among men. I'm not worthy of such perfection."

I preen. His praise is a balm, soothing my jagged edges. I've lived a life of constant criticism—from my parents, from society, from myself—about my looks, my career, and my choices. Everything. I have to live with unrealistic expectations held over my head. It's an exhausting, lonely way to live.

But all those criticisms and expectations melt away when I'm with Mason. He doesn't want me to be someone I'm not. He doesn't want or need anything from me. He only wants me. Just as I am.

He wraps his large hands around my ribcage and lifts me onto the counter. I hiss at the cold sting of the marble hitting my ass. My eyes fly open to find him staring at my body in awe, his lip trapped between his teeth.

I tug at the bottom of his shirt. "Since it's my birthday, I think it's only fair that you should be naked too."

"That can be arranged." He steps back, making a show with his striptease, and slowly takes off his button-up, dropping it to the floor. "Better?" he asks.

"Nuh-uh." I put my hand out, palm up, with a silent demand for his shirt next.

He grins and removes his shirt. Of course, he does it in the only way a hot guy can. With one hand behind his back, he tugs the collar, pulls the fabric off of his body, and drops it next to his dress shirt.

What is it about the way men take off their clothes that makes it so sexy?

My hands itch to touch the man standing before me. Instead, I lean back onto my hands and take in every hard ridge of his torso, from his firm pecs, down the lines of his abs, to the delicious V of his adonis belt. I lick my lips, hungry to lick every peak and valley of his body.

I point to his slacks. "Those too."

Mason slips off his socks and shoes, kicking them to the side. He unhooks his belt and one-handedly pulls it out of the loops, dropping it to the floor with a clang. Flicking open the button of his slacks, he unzips them, sliding the material over his hips and letting them fall at his ankles. He stands before me in nothing but a pair of tight charcoal boxer briefs. The head of his cock peeks out the waistband as a bead of precum glistens from the tip, tempting me.

Needy groans bloom in my chest as I reach for him.

Mason steps back, shaking his head as I drop my hands.

"It might be your birthday, but I'm still the boss and these are staying on." He snaps the elastic of his briefs, baiting me.

I want to put him in my mouth and suck. But since I want to see where this is going, I won't be a brat and I'll let it go.

Mumbling under my breath, "For now," he smirks, stepping between my legs.

"Now, where were we?" He lifts the bottle of champagne to my lips. "Drink."

I part my lips as he pours the cool liquid into my mouth, and the mix of dry and fruity flavors hits my palate like a sensual blast. I swallow, but the champagne overflows my mouth, effervescing on my tongue, and dribbles down my chin.

Mason dips down and laps up the line of alcohol before kissing me. "Delicious."

He's delicious.

I hum in agreement.

His green and gold eyes lock on mine as he brings the bottle to his mouth and takes a drink. The bubbles spill down his chin, and I lean forward returning the favor, tonguing the drops off his stubbled chin before pressing my lips to his. Champagne floods my mouth as he opens his and kisses me. I swallow the pink champagne as our tongues tangle and sparkle from the bubbles.

My head dances, and I'm not sure if it's from the instant effects of the alcohol hitting my system or the sultry way Mason wraps his tongue around mine, fucking my mouth like I wish he'd fuck me.

We break apart, gasping for air.

"I'm not quite sold yet. Lay down." Mason presses a palm to my chest, pushing my back to the counter. He bends my knees and places my feet on the edge. Tipping the bottle, he pours the champagne in my belly button.

I jolt at the cold sensation, causing a stream to spill over the side of my waist.

"Stay still."

As motionless as I can be, I watch him tongue a wet trail up my curves back to my belly button. He lifts his glowing hazel eyes to mine and dips his tongue in the small pool with a grunt before he sucks down the alcohol in the most erotic way possible.

Arching my head back, I attempt to control my breathing and focus. My body is on fire, and my pussy is quivering with need as cold liquid hits my heated skin again with a fizzle.

I force my eyes open. I don't want to miss a single moment.

I watch as Mason dribbles champagne in the valley between my breasts and runs his finger through the puddle.

"So fucking tasty." His pupils are blown, and his voice is thick, low.

I watch with rapt attention as he cleans the drop off his finger with his mouth. Bending down, he slurps the pool, sucking my skin.

"Mason," I exhale his name, my body bowing, begging for his touch.

"I'm starting to agree—this might be the best-tasting champagne I've ever had."

He pours another stream—over my breasts this time—before lavishing them with his lips and tongue. With every pull of my nipple, my clit tingles and pulses. I'm on the verge of coming when he pops off and switches sides.

Pour, lick, moan, suck.

Down the path of my body he goes. Frustration begins to boil in my belly as his mouth roams every inch of my body, avoiding my slick center—the place I am desperate for him to suck. His process is methodical as he pours the champagne down the crease of my thigh and hip.

"So sweet." He pulls my pussy lip into his mouth, teasing me.

"More," I pant.

My core gushes, needy for his touch as he pours more champagne down the other crease of my thigh. Inhuman moans vibrate in his chest, and my knees fall open for him. He repeats the same sensual tease.

"You smell like pears and a hint of vanilla."

Pour, lick, moan, suck.

I'm a writhing, panting mess, completely under his spell.

Mason places the bottle next to my head and kisses me. He tastes sweet and tart, like the champagne he's been drinking off my body. My nipples pucker and my hips lift. Mason rips his mouth from mine and drops to his knees. Gripping my thighs, he spreads my legs wide and shoves his face in my pussy.

"Yes, yes, yes." I thread my fingers through his hair and tug, grinding into his mouth.

Mason eats me out like a starving man finding his last meal.

"Mmm. Yes, right there, don't stop. Please don't stop."

"Never."

My thighs contract as he spears me with his tongue, fucking my hole.

"This pussy is mine. So good, so wet. It's time to give me what I really want, Em. I want to drink you in. Every. Last Drop."

He drives two fingers inside me, so deep it almost hurts, but with a twist of his wrist, the pain turns to pleasure as he hits that spot deep inside me—the one only he controls. My hips buck as my insides lock up, coiling tight before snapping in the most intense orgasm.

"Mason!" I cry out, screaming his name all while chanting *I love you* in my head.

The words take a backseat as every fiber in my body vibrates with hot energy. My pussy spasms, and the intense fire I felt last time hits me as my cum pours down my crack, and all over Mason's hand and face.

As promised, he drinks up every drop, growling in satisfaction.

Holy fuck. How does he do that? And why do I want him to do it again?

"Fuck yes. That's my good girl, squirting all over my tongue. You taste so fucking delicious I could drink every drop of you, every day, for the rest of my life, and still be thirsty for more."

My sex clenches at his vulgar words. Everything's a blur until I feel him notch the tip of his cock at my entrance.

"Baby doll, I don't have a condom, so if you want to stop, tell me now."

I shake my head. "No, I want this. I want you. Nothing between us. I'm on the pill and clean."

"I'm clean too. Are you sure?"

"Yes. Fuck me, Mason."

With a growl, Mason pushes his thick shaft into my core in one thrust, filling me completely. My eyes roll to the back of my head as I get used to his size. When I open them, I find him watching me with a look I can't describe.

I wrap my legs around his waist, pulling him into me. "Move, please," I beg.

He moves, taking long languid strokes, fucking me with purpose. His fingers dig into my thighs as his thumbs spread my pussy's lips apart and his gaze falls on our connection.

"Look at us, baby doll. You look so fucking good wrapped around my cock. This pretty cunt was made for me. So hot, so tight, so wet."

Lifting onto my elbows, I watch as my pussy swallows his huge cock. His dick glistens with my arousal, beckoning me to touch it. Wrapping my fingers around the base, I grip him tight and stroke him while he fucks me.

"Oh fuck, babe. Don't do that, or I'm going to come."

"Yes." I love knowing that I can get him to lose control. To take what he wants from me.

I tighten my grip, but he swats my hand away, making my skin sting. With two hands, I grab his hair and pull his face to mine, kissing him with everything I have to give. I fuck his mouth while he fucks me on my kitchen counter, and it's everything.

He is everything.

Waves of pleasure build inside my lower belly.

"That's it, baby. I can feel you clenching. Come for me." His thumb lands on my clit and presses down, circling the sensitive bud as he pounds into me.

"Yes," I hiss as he sends me over the edge again.

"Bed," Mason grunts, wrapping his arms around me and lifting me off the wet, sticky counter. He only makes it a few steps before he stops and pumps up into me.

Gripping his shoulders, I dig my heels into his ass. I lift myself, only to drop down, impaling myself on his cock.

"So good, Mase. More," I chant.

My back hits the wall as he slams me against it and possessively wraps his hand on my throat, gripping me firmly and tenderly.

"Mine." With a single word, he claims me forever.

"Yours," I confirm.

He slams his mouth to mine in a scorching kiss as he ruts into me as animalistic, almost feral growls rumble in his chest. He grinds his pubic bone into my clit, and the combined friction and pounding have me soaring over the edge again.

"Yes, squeeze my dick. Just like that."

"Oh fuck," I keen as my arousal drips down my ass crack and his balls continue to slap against my sensitive flesh.

Mason's pace doesn't falter, and my body feels like Jello.

"I don't think I can take any more," I groan, my pussy still fluttering with the aftershocks of my orgasm.

"You can, and you will. You will take every thick inch I have to offer you. You will come on my cock, my face, and my hand, over and over, and when I'm done, you'll beg for more, birthday girl. By the end of the night, your pussy will be addicted to my dick like he's addicted to your sweet tight cunt."

I drop my head to his shoulder and nod. I'd agree to anything right now. I'm already addicted to him.

Mason swings us around and finishes carrying me to my bedroom, where he spends the rest of the night inside me, worshiping me, telling me how beautiful I am, and calling me his.

My birthday cake and dinner might be long forgotten, but this moment—this man—will be seared into my memory and my heart for all time.

TWENTY-EIGHT

Mason

JULY

MEMORIES OF EMERY INVADE my mind as I sit in this hot plastic chair, roasting my nuts off and watching my brother play a doubleheader.

It's getting harder and harder to leave her after every trip. I feel like a part of me is missing when she's not around. I was so close to telling her how I feel, but it never seemed to be the right moment. It doesn't come off as the most romantic way to tell a woman you love her while you're balls deep inside her. And I was inside her every moment I was with her.

For a week, I split my time, helping my brother out with Rhys while Emery was at work. But I made sure to spend my mornings waking her up with my head between her legs, and my nights putting her to sleep with my cock buried nine inches deep inside her perfect pussy.

Fuck, I have to stop thinking about her while I'm in public.

I shift in my seat and take another sip of my beer. I'm wedged between Eli and Rhys, who is eating a miniature helmet full of frozen yogurt, most of which is dripping all over his chin, and the new baseball jersey Cameron bought him for today.

My entire family has flown to Chicago to watch Cam pitch at one of the oldest baseball fields in America. Well, not the entire family—Rylann stayed back home with the baby.

I wanted to spend the holiday with my girl, but she had plans to visit her parents again. Something about a party her parents host every Fourth. The way she explained it, the event sounds stuffy, with a bunch of old, snooty rich people and their equally entitled offspring.

When we spoke this morning, something didn't feel right. Emery sounded wooden and sad. I wanted to rush to her side, pull her into my arms, and promise to fix everything for her. Not that she would let me. She's still keeping some distance between me and her family.

You're one to talk. Why haven't you invited her to meet your family?

I smother my groan and annoying thoughts with another drink of my rapidly warming beer.

"What's that face for?" Eli bumps my shoulder, sending my beer sloshing in my cup.

"E, you're lucky you didn't spill this all over my shorts. What the f—"

My head is clipped from behind mid-sentence. I rub the spot and turn to find Jace glowering at me. He glances down at Rhys, who is slurping away on his dessert, eyes locked on the mound where his uncle is pitching.

"Watch your mouth, brother, or I'm going to have to beat you senseless."

"Sorry," I growl.

He's right. I should watch my mouth, but no way could he beat my ass. Jace is a big softy, and I'm grown now. I could easily kick his ass.

Eli chuckles beside me. "It's funny, you know."

"What's funny?"

"You, getting in trouble with Jay. You're always the good brother, kissing his a-s-s all the time."

Rhys leans across my lap and whispers "I can spell, you know." He smiles proudly, a chocolate mustache painted across his face.

Eli pushes his little head back. "Get out of here, you nosy little turd, or I'm not going to sneak you cotton candy."

Rhys jumps back in his seat and stares ahead. He must really want that cotton candy. Rylann is going to flip when she learns about all the junk we let this kid eat. His uncles aren't even the worst ones—it's Jace. He's a full-fledged sucker, and Rhys has him wrapped around his little finger. All he has to do is pout, and Jace is buying him whatever he wants.

"I need a refill." Eli hits my shoulder and stands. "Anyone want anything?"

Rhys gives Eli the look, and Jace shakes his head, a grin plastered across his face. He knows about the candy.

"I got you, little buddy."

Rhys smiles and bounces in his seat.

My chest warms watching his face light up. I love him so much. Our life is better with him in it.

I stand with Eli and shuffle out of the aisle, up the stairs, and through the crowd to the concessions stand. We get in line and wait.

"Where's your girl this weekend?"

I roll my eyes at Eli's question. Nosy fucker.

"With her family. They have an annual party."

"Why didn't you go with her?"

"I'm here with my family. This is Rhys's first time in Chicago for a game on the Fourth."

Eli nods as we inch closer to the front. "How are things going with her?"

"Good."

"Getting serious?"

"I guess."

"You guess?" His eyebrows meet his hairline. "What do you mean, you *guess*? You've been seeing this woman since January."

"It's long-distance," is all I say.

He's right, though. I have been seeing Emery for the past seven months, and my heart says it's serious. Very serious. Seven months is a long time, but when you only get to see the person you're dating a couple of days a month, does it even count as real dating?

This long-distance thing we have going on is getting old. My need to be with her every day grows deeper.

"So?" He shrugs. "You talk every day?"

"Yes."

"Do you have phone sex?"

"I'm not answering that."

Eli grins at my non-answer. "That's a yes. Do you love her?" My brother stands beside me, arms crossed, waiting for my answer.

I look at him, and his usually playful persona is gone. Right now, he's Eli, the concerned big brother. The big brother that would do anything to make me happy. He only reserves this side of himself for his family.

I drop my shield and nod. He can't help me, but it feels good to admit it. "Yes, I love her."

He grins. "Thought so."

"You going to give me shit for it?"

"Nah, I'm happy for you."

"What about you? Are you seeing anyone?"

"This isn't about me, Mase. It's about you. If you want her, make it happen. If she's who you want, you're going to have to do the work. No half-assing it. Tell her how you feel."

The line moves and we step up to the cashier, putting in our order.

A million questions run through my mind as my phone buzzes in my pocket. I pull it out to find a text.

Emery: I miss you. I wish you were here.

Like a message from the heavens, I know what I need to do.

After we returned to our seats, I gave my nephew a kiss on the cheek, a new hat, and a promise to see him soon, then booked it out of there. No one questioned my need to leave, probably assuming I had work to do. I do have my work cut out for me, but not in the way they think.

I'm going to find my girl and tell her I love her.

The overhead announcement crackles our descent into the greater New York area. It only took me two hours to book a flight, pack up my hotel room, and hop a plane east. My mind's sole focus has been getting to Emery as quickly as possible. Something deep inside me tugs at my chest, pulling me to her like a gravitational force.

Our call this morning plays in my head.

Her voice cracks. "I hate being here."

My heart breaks for her, knowing how cold and detached her parents are. I don't understand why she visits them if all they do is criticize her. "Just leave. Come here, baby doll."

I hear her take a deep breath over the line. "I can't. I have something I need to do."

"What is it? Can I help?"

"No. I have to do this alone."

I turn on my dominant voice, the one she can't resist. "Emery."

"Oh god, don't say my name like that right now," she moans.

"Then tell me what's wrong. I want to help you."

"I need to do this. For me, for you, for everyone. After, I promise it will only be us. I swear it. I just need you to trust me," she babbles, confusing the fuck out of me.

"I trust you."

She sniffles, and my stomach dips. I hate being so far away from her when she's upset like this. She's crying on the other end of the line, and there isn't a fucking thing I can do about it.

After a minute, she takes a deep breath and clears her throat. "I have to go."

"Okay."

"Mason." I can hear the words laced behind the sound of my name on her tongue. The words I've been dying to say too.

In the same tone, I reply, "Emery," praying she understands the depth of my feelings for her.

TWENTY-NINE

Emery

MY HANDS SWEAT, AND my heart pounds in my chest as I scan the grounds searching for my parents. I lost track of them while I was playing Dutiful Daughter and making idle chit-chat with people I have nothing in common with.

I don't know why I'm still bothering to do so. I know once I tell my parents the charade is over, I'll be cut out of their lives forever. I press a hand to my stomach. I dread what my parents are going to say to me. I'm expecting the worst, but no matter what, it's still going to hurt—they are my parents, and I love them.

But, I need to rip off the proverbial Band-Aid. I can't live like this anymore. Now that I've tasted what real love feels like, holding onto some small thread of hope that my parents will love me is naïve. They are never going to change.

I think back to Papa. He tried to show me what love was all those years ago. I see that now, but then? I just wanted my parents to love me, and in some ways, I still do. I sought their love and affection any way I could, even if it meant crushing my individuality, crushing my soul in the process.

When Chris came out and they shipped him off to boarding school, I stopped trying so hard to earn their approval. For the last eight years, pretending to be a good daughter has been about survival. I had to survive for me, for my brother.

Not anymore. I don't need them. I'm pretty sure I can cover the last semester of Chris's tuition on my own. It's time for me to move on. For the first time in my life, I have someone besides my brother who means more to me. This is my life, and I will not let my parents get in the way of my happiness. Cybil and Sinclair will not get in the way of me building a life with the man I love.

It kills me that I haven't been able to tell Mason yet. When I do tell him, I don't want the situation I've landed myself in to be hanging over our heads. I want to be free from the chains.

A round of laughter to my right pulls my attention. I scan the glistening, synthetically youthful faces of the "who's who" here in Heaven's Point.

Nope, not them.

Their disappearance is pretty suspect, seeing as they make themselves the center of attention at every party they throw.

Striding across the lawn, I head back to the main house. There's only one other place they could be—my father's office. I enter through the back door that leads to the kitchen.

The chef, in his pristine white coat, shouts as plates clatter and servers load their trays with tiny bites of pretentious food. The smell nauseates me as I hustle my way through the chaos, and I head towards the other wing of the house. Muffled voices become clear as I approach the door.

Is that Lex talking?

What the hell is he doing here? I didn't see him at the party.

Lifting my hand to knock, the door swings open. Lex stands on the other side, his eyes widening at my appearance and his smile faltering.

Glancing over his shoulder, I see my father sitting at his desk, with my mother at his side. He files some papers into a manilla legal folder.

My eyes bounce back to Lex, who shifts side to side. My friend stands before me, wearing a suit like he just came from work instead of the classic chinos and white button-up he usually wears to the Rhodes "red, white, and blue" party. As always, he looks good, but his blue eyes have lost their sparkle, and the dark circles that surround them are dark and deep like he hasn't had a good night's sleep in ages.

"Emery, I-I wasn't expecting to see you." He runs a shaky hand through his hair and adjusts his tie.

The hair on the back of my neck stands. Something was off the last time I saw him, and the guilty look on his face makes my stomach churn as acid burns my throat. "Lex?"

"Emery, darling, come in. You're just in time. We were discussing the announcement with Alexander. Everything is all set."

My blood freezes at my mother's elegant voice calling me from inside the room.

"Lex, what are they talking about?" I want my friend to explain what he's doing here and why it feels like I'm walking into the lion's den.

He doesn't get a chance as my father approaches, laying his sweaty hand on Lex's shoulder and squeezing, his knuckles turning white. Lex winces at the contact.

"Alexander was just leaving. We'll speak soon, son," my father says, dismissing my childhood friend in the same haughty tone he uses when speaking to people he deems beneath him.

Lex's mouth opens like he's going to say something, but he thinks better of it and slams it shut. He nods and rushes past me, closing the door behind him.

"Take a seat, Emery." My father's tone is hard as he points to an empty seat at his desk.

Without thinking, I take a seat.

Lex's presence has me shaken. I'm curious, and at the same time, my chest feels heavy with dread. I'm not going to like what I'm about to hear.

"What's all this about? Why was Lex here?" My head swivels to my mother, expecting her to answer me. Stupid, I know.

As usual, her expression gives nothing away—not that it could with her overly botoxed face.

"It's time, Emery," Sinclair states flatly.

Pieces of the last conversation I had with my mother hit me like a hammer to the chest, knocking the wind out of me.

You will fulfill your duty.

"No." I shake my head.

"You will do as I say. That was the deal we made. I gave you money and time, but you've run out. Of both. Lex has agreed to the terms. You will go to Oregon to pack your belongings and return within the next week." He shuffles the stack of papers on his desk.

Blood pounds in my ears as my father continues, but I hear none of it. This is not happening. I came here to tell them that, and they've beaten me to the punch.

No more.

"We will make an announcement next month. Then—"

"The hell you will!" I shout, jumping from the chair, sending it flying back to the floor.

My mother rolls her eyes at me like I'm a petulant child. I ball my fists, fighting the urge to lay into her. It would be a waste of my breath.

"I will not be going through with our deal."

My father's mouth opens to argue, but I cut him off.

"I said no. I didn't sign any legal documents, so you cannot hold me to it. What you are doing is against the law."

"We had a verbal agreement."

"Sue me. I'll be sure to make a spectacle for all your friends to see. I came here to tell you it's over. All of it. I don't know what you have worked out with Lex, but it doesn't matter. I'm not following through with this farce any longer. I'm out. I only put up with you for Christopher. You remember him, right? Your son."

"You will not speak of that ... that thing to us," Cybil yells, her eyes bugging out of her head.

Red tinges my vision as my mother calls my brother "a thing". Her son, her flesh and blood. I turn my glare on her, wishing it would burn her alive. How dare she speak of him that way. He has more class in his pinky toenail than her and all the soulless upper-crust assholes attending this party have in their entire being.

"Chris is not a *thing*. He is a wonderful man with a kind heart. Who he loves is none of your business. Why can't you just be supportive of him? Of me? We are your children, and yet you have never treated us with an ounce of love or care. Chris was right—you two are toxic, and I can't wait to walk away from you. Because make no mistake, when I leave today, I will never come back. I have spent my life bending over backward, looking for your approval. But nothing will ever be good enough for either of you."

My father scoffs. "You will have nothing if you walk away from this. There will be no more money for you or your brother."

I force an angry laugh. The gall of this man. He knows nothing about me.

"Every penny I've taken from you has been to pay for both my and Chris's education. So you can take your money and shove it. I am a partner at a successful marketing firm. The money I have, I made myself through hard work and with absolutely no thanks to you. You can threaten me all you want. I don't need you. Besides, I still have money Papa left me, and so will Chris when he turns twenty-five. So unless you plan to take legal recourse, I will be walking away because I refuse to end up like the two of you, trapped in a loveless marriage with your affairs and fake friends."

"Must you be so uncouth?" Cybil flips her hair, and my father leans back in his chair. He's checked out of this conversation. If I'm not going to do his bidding, he's done.

Well, guess what, old man? I'm done too.

I stand tall and pull my shoulders back. "Cybil, Sinclair. I'd say it was nice knowing you, but we know that would be a lie. Goodbye."

The heavy chains of pain and neglect they've forced me to carry fall away. I never wanted it to end this way, but I can't say I'm not relieved. Head held high, I make my escape and race into my new life.

"If you walk out that door, don't bother coming back," my father shouts, his final parting words hitting their mark on my heart.

I knew it was coming, but it hurts all the same.

Throwing open the door, I walk into my future and into a solid wall of muscle. The familiar scent of ginger and spice surrounds me as thick arms wrap around my waist.

"Mason." His name leaves my lips like a benediction. Looking up into his green and gold-streaked eyes, my body relaxes.

I'm home.

THIRTY

Mason

THE CAR PULLS THROUGH the gates of the biggest fucking mansion I have ever seen, and a pit forms in my stomach. I don't know what I was expecting, but it wasn't this.

Emery's childhood home isn't a mere mansion; it's a fucking manor, like one I had envisioned while reading *The Great Gatsby* as a teen.

Exhaling a breath, I pay the driver, promising him a five-star rating, and step out onto the stone driveway. Music and voices from the back of the estate draw my attention. I glance down at my clothes—khaki slacks and a linen button-up.

I hope these people aren't dressed to the nines tonight.

I lift my gaze up at the formidable stone and vine-covered home, with its white columns and art deco detailing. Yeah, these people are going to be wearing clothes that cost more than any average person's paycheck. I make good money, but I have more sense than to spend thousands of dollars on a piece of fabric I'll only wear once.

My shoulders sag, thinking about my sweet girl growing up in a home like this. She shuts down at any mention of her family unless she's talking about her brother or her grandfather. Aside from the time she said she was nothing like her parents, Emery has never mentioned how well off her parents are and where they live, let alone how they live. She's never acted like she was raised with a silver spoon in her mouth. Emery is kind, compassionate, and hard-working; nothing like how I'd imagine people who grew up with the uber-rich would be—entitled.

Something niggles in the back of my brain, telling me there is more to her story than I could ever understand. Memories of our first plane date come to mind.

She mentioned that her parents don't approve of Chris because it didn't fit into their *values*. She said she felt like they expected too much from her and that she still feels obligated to continue a relationship with them, even though they have pretty much cut Chris out of their lives.

The story of her grandfather is starting to make a lot more sense. I suspect I'm about to meet some of the most snobbish, old-world–thinking people in the state.

I take a breath and adjust my collar. I can take anything as long I have Emery.

She sounded broken and sad on the phone, and it gutted me. I could hear her anxiety and the tears she was fighting over the line. After my talk with Eli, I knew I had to come and be here for her. She needed me. I wanted to surprise her, let her know that I will always have her back.

She's mine, and it's my job to support her, protect her.

The front door opens, and a guy with blond hair, a square jaw, wearing—as Cam would say—a "fuck me, I'm rich", expensive-looking suit and loafers, steps out onto the colonnade. His blue eyes widen in shock at my presence. "Can I help you?"

"Yeah, I'm looking for Emery."

He nods and looks back at the door before returning his gaze to me, taking in my appearance. He frowns, looking sad and tired as fuck, like life's been beating him down. Something about the way he looks makes me feel bad for the guy.

"She's in her parents' office. Just follow the hallway down to the back of the house. You can't miss the double wood doors." He adjusts his suit, walks around the porch, and disappears into the night.

I suck in another deep breath, attempting to calm my frayed nerves, and step through the door.

The grand entrance I'm greeted with matches the exterior of the home—white walls with expensive paintings and lighting hanging on them. A wide staircase with an intricate iron banister to the right leads to the second floor, and a matching chandelier hangs above the marble floors. On the left sits a never-been-used sitting room with a fireplace, antique chairs, and coffee tables.

Fuck, this place is insane.

Accepting the guy's directions, I follow the hallway to the back of Emery's home. About a minute passes, and as he said, a dark wood door with more ironwork comes into view. Behind the entrance, I can hear raised voices but the words are muffled, making it hard to discern what's being said.

Lifting my hand to knock, the door swings open, and a body collides with mine. A body I know as intimately as my own.

Emery gasps, shocked at walking into me and my surprise presence. Instinctively, my arms wrap around her waist, holding her tightly to my chest. Over her head, I see a man and a woman—who I assume are her parents—standing behind a large antique oak desk.

Emery grips my forearms, and my eyes find her wide topaz gaze on mine. My heart rate slows now that I have her in my arms.

She looks over her shoulder and shakes her head before focusing back on me. "Let's get out of here."

She steps out of my hold and laces her fingers with mine, pulling me away from the office and the people in it. Emery leads me down the halls, through the kitchen, and onto the back deck overlooking the great lawns covered in white tents and people.

I step toward the railing and watch servers carrying food and drinks hustle about, while people—dressed in what I can only describe as expensive yacht-wear—mill about, chatting.

I shake my head. I can't believe this is where Emery grew up. It seems so contrary to the woman I've gotten to know and fallen in love with.

"Wow, this is ... something." My stomach tightens as unsettling thoughts start to form in my head.

Why did she keep all this from me?

"Yeah." She steps beside me as the breeze catches her hair, whipping it around. The scent of vanilla and pears I've come to crave does little to soothe my racing heart.

"Emery—"

She cuts me off, her eyes glassing over. "Not here, please."

I nod as she laces her fingers through mine and leads me down a hidden staircase, to the boat deck sitting above a boat garage and private dock. She takes a seat on the bench by the balustrade overlooking the Long Island Sound. I take the seat next to her and pull her close. She rests her head on my shoulder as we watch various-sized boats and mini yachts float along the water, waiting out the time until the fireworks.

"Mason, what are you doing here?" she asks, breaking the silence.

Tilting her chin up, I stare into her eyes. "I came for you. It sounded like you were crying when we spoke this morning. I was worried about you." I brush my thumb across her temptingly sweet, pouty bottom lip. "The thought of you being sad and alone killed me, so I hopped on a plane. I want to be the person supporting you when you need it most."

"I don't know what to say. No one has ever shown up for me before. I—" Tears leak out the corner of her eyes, the streams glistening down her cheek in the moonlight.

"Shh. I'm here." It breaks my heart that she's been alone in her struggles.

Not anymore.

With my thumbs, I wipe away her tears and press my mouth to hers. She tastes sweet, like champagne and all her. She melts in my arms, letting out a soft moan as I deepen the kiss, exploring her mouth with mine. My cock stirs to life as her hands slide up my arms and her fingers snake through the ends of my hair.

Emery kisses me back, but the eagerness at which she returns the kiss scares me. It feels frantic, like she's afraid I might evaporate into thin air.

Pushing past my apprehension, I let Emery take over. Based on the loud voices I heard before she came barreling out the door, something must have happened with her parents.

A throat clears, breaking us apart. When I glance over at the intruder, it's the same guy who told me where I could find Emery. Dropping my hands from her waist, I stand.

"Lex, what are you doing down here?" She stands up, gripping my hand in hers.

Lex? What kind of a name is that?

My hackles rise as her eyes nervously bounce between me and Mr. Fancy Suit.

Who the fuck is this guy? And who the fuck wears a suit to a Fourth of July party?

A pretentious asshole, that's who.

My earlier sympathies slip away as his demeanor changes before me.

He tugs at his tie, pulling his shoulders back, attempting to exude confidence. "I didn't realize you had company. I know you like to sit down here when things get ... hectic." He turns to me and smirks. "If you'll excuse us, I need a word with my fiancée."

His words are like a shot to the chest. *Fiancée?*

I shake my head. I can't have heard that right. "What did you say?"

"I'm sorry, did you not know?" He looks at Emery, a look of confusion on his face.

"Lex, what are you doing?" Emery shakes her head as she sobs into her hand, tears pouring down her face.

Every insecurity, every hint of doubt I've pushed away since laying eyes on her comes rushing back, and a pain like I've never felt slices through my heart as I watch them talk. The words don't register as the beat of my bleeding heart pounds in my ears.

This guy isn't lying—he's her fiancé.

All the hints she's dropped over the last six months hit me. How the fuck did I not see the signs? They were all there.

The way she walked away that first day and tried to tell me we couldn't be serious when I saw her again. Her resistance and mood swings when things got a little intense. The way she never spoke about this place. It's no wonder—she was harboring a whole separate life. Another man.

Her small palm squeezes my hand, and I rip it out of her grip, away from her touch, my skin searing as if burned from the contact.

"Mason, listen to me, please," Emery pleads.

Bile rises in my throat. "Is he telling the truth? Is he your fiancé?"

Please say no, baby.

My heart pounds in my chest as I turn to the guy, looking for answers. He has enough sense to keep his mouth shut as the woman I thought I knew shatters my soul.

Rather than denying it, she shakes her head while her words betray her, and she croaks out, "It's complicated."

Her answer cuts through me like butter, flaying me open. I'm at a loss. I don't know what to say. All I know is that I need to get the fuck out of here. Fast.

I spin away from her and make my way to the stairs. Lex steps to the side, avoiding eye contact.

That's right, motherfucker.

Anger courses through my veins, looking for an escape. She fucking played me. How could I be so stupid?

I'm halfway down the dock when fireworks scream their ascent and explode above, the sounds of their release reverberating in the night sky. Colors flash and sparkle as I quickly stride away from everything I thought I had in the grasp of my hand.

"Mason!" Emery screams.

I stop on instinct at the sound of her distress.

She rushes in front of me and presses her hands to my aching, hollow chest. The one she just took a melon baller to.

"Please don't go. I need you to listen to me. It's not what you think."

I shake my head. "No. We have been together for seven months. Seven. You had plenty of time to come clean. To talk to me. You promised me no secrets."

"I know—"

"You lied!" I bellow, heaving, my anger taking over. "You fucking lied to me, Emery. Everything I thought I knew about you was a lie. Everything we've built was a fucking lie."

"No, it wasn't. You know me. You're the only one that does."

I scoff, waving my arms around. "Sorry to break the news to you, baby doll," I mock, using the endearment now to hurt her. "But I don't know anything about you."

"This is nothing. This..." She swivels her head around the acres of land and the giant elegant home. "It means nothing to me, Mason. You mean everything to me. Everything."

My heart wants to believe her, but my head is screaming at me to run, reminding me that she lied for months about being engaged to another man.

Has she been with him the whole time?

Oh god, I think I'm going to be sick.

I lash out. "Yeah, well, you mean nothing to me."

The blood drains from her face as she clutches her middle. The lie I spewed burns like acid on my tongue. Walls erect themselves around my heart, staunching the wound I'm about to inflict on us both.

"We're over. Go back to your fiancé, Emery. Turns out, you do have someone to support after all, and it isn't me."

A sob breaks from her body as I watch the woman I love crumble before me. My hands itch to hold her up, but I remind myself that she did this to us. She's the one who lied. She's the one who cut me first.

Rubbing at the pain in my chest, my eyes water. The need to hold her grips at the edges of my breaking heart as my conscience begs me to hear her out. I rush past her before I say or do something else that will hurt us. Hurt her.

I can't console her when she's the one that broke us. I need to protect myself, and her, by getting as far away as possible.

I race across the lawn, around the extravagant house, down the stone driveway, and out the wrought-iron gate. Every painful step away from her rips a piece of me apart. It's like running away from home when you're a kid—you know it's wrong, but you do it anyway.

Ignoring the invisible string pulling me to her, begging me to go back, I keep walking. Leaving my home. Leaving pieces of me behind.

THIRTY-ONE

Emery

STRONG ARMS WRAP AROUND my waist as my knees give way and the man I love rushes away from me, leaving me broken.

"I got you, Emmy," Lex soothes, his cologne invading my nose as a wave of nausea hits me.

The smell is wrong. His arms are wrong. Everything about this is all so wrong.

"No," I cry, pushing him away.

It should be Mason, the man I love with every cell in my body, holding me up.

Sucking in a breath, I straighten my spine and wipe my face, turning on my oldest friend—the friend who promised to help me, not hurt me. "Why, Lex? Why did you do this?"

"I didn't do anything we didn't already agree on. This is how it has to be. You know that." He sighs as his shoulders hunch.

I step back, shocked at his answer. When did he turn into this? He's given up.

"No. This isn't real." I point between the both of us as tears cloud my vision and his betrayal weighs like a lead ball in my stomach.

"It can be."

What fresh hell have I walked into? I know he doesn't mean this.

"That's not the deal we made, and you know it. I never interfered when you were with Lizzie." I yell, my pain morphing into anger.

Lex looks around, but we're alone; everyone has gathered on the blankets laid out at the edge of the lawn overlooking the Sound.

I bark a bitter laugh. "Really, Lex? Now you're concerned with who hears us?"

Fireworks crack and pop overhead, no doubt keeping everyone's attention.

Alexander has been my best friend since we were kids. We concocted this stupid plan when our parents sat us down to let us know we would be married after Lex graduated from business school. We were twenty-two and naïve, thinking we could change their minds. When they dangled Chris's college fund over my head, threatening to cut him off if I didn't agree to their terms, I didn't know what else to do. I only agreed after Lex promised to get us out of this. Now, without a word, Lex has flipped the tables on me. I thought he was better than to fall for these games. To act on this insane plan.

Has he always wanted to run his family company? Yes. But enough to marry me? No.

I thought Elizabeth was his whole world. Hell, they've been together since high school. I know this entire debacle with our parents can't be easy for him, but trying to make an arranged marriage with me isn't going to help either of us. Especially when both our hearts belong to someone else.

Right?

"Lex, where's Lizzie?"

"I'm sorry." He looks away in shame, his body caving in on himself. "Forget I said that."

"You're keeping something from me. Where is Lizzie?"

"She-She's gone. She left me, and I've gone too far. There's no way to back out of this. My parents won't allow it."

My chest caves in at his admission. I'm a horrible friend; I should have seen the signs. They were all there—Elizabeth's mysterious absences, the dark circles under his eyes, the stupid suits. None of this is Lex. His meeting with my father makes everything clear. He put the company first and signed the papers.

Idiot.

No wonder Elizabeth left him. I love my friend, but when it comes to his parents, he's a spineless coward. I feel for him, I do. But when you come from families like ours, getting what you want always comes with strings.

"You promised me that we would get out of this arrangement and it would never come down to us actually getting married. How could you hurt me like this? How could you hurt Mason? He didn't deserve that, and neither does Lizzie. The woman you love. Remember her?"

"Of course, dammit! I know, okay? I said I'm sorry. I assumed he knew, like she did."

My shredded heart flaps lifelessly in my chest, reminding me that I was the one who lied. I kept Mason in the dark—something Lex never did with Elizabeth.

"Well, he didn't, Lex. I didn't want to bring him into this mess. I kept him out, like Chris. I never thought you'd change the script and try to marry me." My voice cracks, a sob breaking free, and my knees buckle.

"Shit." He catches me and wraps me up in a hug—my head on his chest—rubbing circles on my back, soothing me. "It's going to be okay."

"You've ruined everything, you know," I mumble into his six-thousand-dollar Tom Ford suit. I rub snot over his lapel and hope it and my makeup ruin this ridiculous get-up.

He chuckles. "I know."

"He's never going to forgive me."

"If he loves you, he will."

"Doubt it." Stepping back, I take a breath. My eyes fall on the path Mason took. He couldn't run away fast enough. I glance back at my friend, and he has enough sense to look ashamed. "Lex, I need to know. What changed? Why do this now?"

He runs his hands through his hair and tugs. "Fuck. I-I'm tired, Emmy. So fucking tired. I've wanted to take over the company since I was a kid and went with my grandfather to work." He turns away, dropping his chin to his chest.

"I know." Reaching out, I place my hand on his shoulder in comfort.

"Everything started to unravel at work. My father wants to retire, but you know he refuses to hand it over while I'm still unmarried. I brought up Lizzie to him and told him I was ready to marry her. But he shut it down. He said he would rather die than hand over the company to me if I was" — he uses his fingers to quote his father — "with that gold-digger. I was shocked. I figured, with time, he'd let our arrangement go. Lizzie begged me to stand up to him. We got into a huge fight. She said if I didn't put my foot down with my father and put us before the company, she was done. I didn't. I couldn't. I'm so close to having everything I have ever dreamed of."

"How's that working out for you?"

He laughs at the irony. He's not happy; I can see it in his eyes. "I fucked it all up, didn't I?"

I nod. "Yeah. But if she loves you, she'll forgive you," I use his earlier words against him.

The difference is, Lizzie might forgive him. She might not come from as prominent a family as ours, but she's a part of this world. She understands our way of life, his struggles, and the pressure he's been under.

"I love her so much." His voice breaks, and his shoulders shake.

While he might have just blown up my love life, I can't help but comfort my friend. My heart aches for him. Pulling him in for a hug, he drops his head on my shoulders and cries.

"I know you do."

Lex's parents are as bad as mine, if not worse. The way they have treated Lex's longtime girlfriend is appalling. She's one of the smartest, sweetest women I know. She's kind and compassionate. Who wouldn't want a doctor with the biggest heart as their daughter-in-law?

Yeah, but she doesn't come with a dowry in the name of Rhodes Publishing.

I'm done with our parents putting business before their children. It's not uncommon in our world, but I won't live like this. It's why I finally said no.

I know what real love feels like. *Knew.*

I doubt Mason is going to give me the time of day to explain. He told me secrets were his hard limit.

I love that man fiercely, but he is stubborn as hell. My bossy man.

Tears spill down my face as I picture the devastation on Mason's handsome face. The betrayal of my lies cut him deep.

"What the hell am I going to do now?" Lex sniffs, and I can't help but hug him tighter because I feel the same way.

But for once, I know what we need to do and who we need to call for help. I don't know if it will be enough to fix the damage and hurt we've caused to the people we love, but it's worth a shot. I might have made my choice, although too late, but Lex still has time to fix his. It's going to hurt like hell for him. I've prepared myself for this day for years. I might not have given up hope my father would change, but deep down, I knew it would end like this for me—outcasted in his eyes.

"I made my choice, Lex. I've accepted the consequences. I am not going to pretend anymore. I can't. It hurts too much. That's why I came tonight. After you left the office, I told them it was off."

"What did Sinclair say?"

I shrug. "The usual. If I leave, not to come back. Blah blah blah."

"Wow. You really did it, didn't you?"

"Yes. It feels like the noose around my neck has been cut. I can breathe, but..." My heart sinks, remembering Mason's stinging parting words. "It doesn't matter now. I was too late."

"That's nothing. I signed the agreement. I'm so fucked."

"How? I didn't sign anything." See, this is exactly why my friend is an idiot. He's so focused on the company. he doesn't think things through.

Lex's head snaps up. "What?"

"I didn't sign the paperwork. So even if you did, and accepted the terms of our marriage and the merger of the companies' terms, it's not valid if I don't sign. No matter what deal our parents have or try to pull behind our backs, they can't do a damn thing if we both don't sign the marriage license or the contract."

"They said you signed them both."

"Figures." I scoff. Of course, Sinclair and Alfred were playing head games with Lex, trying to use me for their own gain. "Why didn't you talk to me?"

"I—" He scratches his chin, thinking. He flings his arms in the air. "Fuck if I don't know. It felt like the company was slipping through my fingers."

"You're an idiot."

"I am."

"The company can't be worth all this suffering. The head games, the control, the money, the parties, the fake people, the expectations that come with it all. What you had with Lizzie was real. I had it too, and it was beautiful. I'd trade it all for another chance with Mason."

"I don't know how to let it go."

His confession truly breaks my heart because I understand. This is all he's ever known. I left to be closer to Chris, and Lex stayed behind. He has yet to break free from his chains while I've been slowly severing mine without anyone becoming the wiser.

"You have to let it go, or you'll never be happy. Is this really what you want? A pretend marriage with me because our parents say so, just to keep our businesses within the families? Or do you want a life full of happiness and love? Don't you want to spend your life with the one person who owns your heart? Who gets you inside and out? Who makes you happy? Who you can't spend a day without? Can you honestly tell me you can live without Lizzie?"

"No," he confirms what I already knew. She's his person; he just lost sight of what's more important.

"Let's start there. Let's go find her."

"I don't know where she is. She's not at her place. She won't answer my calls. No one will tell me where she is. Not even Flip. I don't know what to do, and I'm losing it."

I'm not surprised Flip has been tight-lipped. He's protective of his sister, Lizzie. They protect each other like Chris and I do.

"We'll find her."

"You're really going to help me? Even after I fucked you over and scared off your man?" He raises a brow at me.

"You know I will, you idiot."

As for my man, I don't think he is anymore. I'll figure that out later. Right now, I need to help the people I know need me.

"All you had to do was ask. I will help you find Lizzie. I might know someone who can get Flip to talk." Flip's best friend.

"Chris," we both say. The one person who was forced out as a teen and never looked back is Lex's only hope.

The irony is not lost on us as we share a laugh, and for a fraction of a second, the pain in my heart lessens. If I can't get my happy ending, I'll at least make sure my friends do.

"We'll figure it out. Together."

"Promise?"

"I promise. You owe me big time, though."

He hands me his pocket square, and I wipe the smeared mascara under my eyes.

"If you help me, I'll be indebted to you for life. You can have anything you want."

If looks could kill, he'd be dead. He has nothing to offer. All I want is the man who walked away with my heart and soul.

Lex hisses and throws his hands up in surrender. "Sorry."

"It's my fault. I should have told him."

That's the truth. I was afraid that if I told him, it would taint our relationship. I've watched Lizzie's face firsthand when our parents would make comments about Lex and me getting married. It killed her. I thought that by keeping this farce away from Mason, I would be protecting him from that kind of pain. Instead, I probably made things worse.

"Ready to make things right with the people we love?" I ask him.

"Yes, but..." His shoulders lift with his inhale and as he exhales, a smile falls over his face. "First, I have to tell Alfred to fuck off."

I wince. "That's not going to go over well."

"No, it's not. But it's time."

I nod, agreeing. But it has to happen for him to move on and live the life he truly wants.

"Can I stay with you when my father inevitably kicks me out of the company, I'm penniless and homeless, and Lizzie tells me to fuck off?"

I lace my hand through the crook of Lex's elbow with a laugh—a real laugh because his prediction might come true—and lead him down to his car parked in the circular driveway. "You can always stay with me. Or Chris. He'd love that."

"Oh, god no. Not Chris. He'd rake me over the coals, and I don't think I'm strong enough to take that kind of torture."

"True. Chris is mean. He cuts you deep with the truth."

Lex hums as we reach his car. He pulls out the fob and unlocks his ugly-as-hell sports car. "Speaking of ... are you going to tell him about all this?"

I bite my lip, unsure. I know I'm going to have to tell Chris, but not yet. Right now, I just want to get away from this horrible place and break down. My brother will only point out the obvious—I had it coming, playing games with the Rhodes and Westfields.

"I will. But tonight, I just want to be alone and lick my wounds."

I regret not immediately chasing after Mason and falling to my knees, begging him to listen and forgive me. When he said I meant nothing to him, it was like taking a knife to my heart and cutting it from my chest. I hurt him so deeply. I doubt he would have even listened to me. He was so angry, it's probably for the best if he has some time to cool off. I hope he'll give me a chance to explain. I did try to tell him, but I knew he wouldn't understand.

I was barely an adult, with no real money, trying to take care of my brother, who at the time had just been ostracized for being queer. It was my job to protect him when no one else would. This was only supposed to be until Chris was done with college and Lex took over the company. I should have known better, but hindsight is 20/20 and all that.

I don't know if I would have been strong enough to say no if not for Mason. He came along and made me fall in love with him. He might have forced himself through my walls and destroyed my carefully constructed plans, but I let him. I'd do it again.

He means more to me than anything else in the world. I've only ever cared about taking care of my brother and helping my friend. I never thought I would fall so completely for someone that I'd throw my plans out the window.

The moment I met him, I knew he was dangerous to my plans, my future, my heart. These past seven months with him have been life-changing. He's opened me up and showed me what true love is. Love that is given freely, not earned.

I just hope I haven't lost him. I'm not sure how I'll go on without him.

THIRTY-TWO

Mason & Emery

TEXT CHAIN

JULY 4
    Emery: I'm sorry. Please let me explain.
    Emery: Pick up, please.
    Emery: We need to talk.

July 5
    Emery: Talk to me … please. I'm sorry.
    Emery: Call me back.

July 6
    Emery: I'm sorry.
    Emery: It's not what you think. I swear. Call me.

July 8

Emery: I know I hurt you, but please talk to me. Let me explain everything.

○

July 9

Emery: I'm not going to give up. I'll keep texting.
Emery: I miss you.

○

July 10

Emery: Why won't you talk to me?
Emery: I'm sorry. Please let me explain.

○

July 11

Emery: I was never with him. Only you. I promise.
Emery: It will only ever be you, Mason.
Emery: I miss you.

○

July 15

Emery: Please pick up your phone. Talk to me. Don't cut me out. Let me explain.

○

July 22

Emery: I'm begging you, please talk to me. Give me a chance to explain.

July 26

Emery: ANSWER YOUR PHONE, DAMMIT!

July 31

Emery: I miss you.

August 5

Emery: Just talk to me, please. I need you.

August 13

Emery: Happy birthday xo

August 14

Emery: Goodbye.

THIRTY-THREE

AUGUST

I RUB THE BURNING sensation from my eyes as the words on the screen blur together. For the last hour, the same open spreadsheet on my computer has been staring back at me.

My phone buzzes and I reach for it, swiping it open. *Nothing.* I slam my phone down. Of course, it's nothing. I'm going crazy, imagining the notification sounds and buzzing. It's never him.

Mason hasn't answered my calls or text messages in six weeks. I've spent every night since he walked away from me crying myself to sleep. I miss him so much that my body physically aches for him. I can't eat, can't sleep, hell, I can't even watch my favorite show without thinking of him and crying.

Despair courses through me like ice, freezing me to my core. I've never experienced this level of loss after breaking up with someone.

Not a breakup. This is a savage ghosting.

Ugh, my inner Chris is annoying. Thinking about my brother reminds me of what a horrible sister I've become in the last few weeks. I've been ignoring his calls, preferring to text him with fabricated stories of being busy. For the first time in years, I skipped his last event in favor of wearing sweatpants and Mason's shirt while curling up into a ball on the couch, watching Keanu Reeves kick ass while crying my heart out.

Tears fill my eyes as I drop my chin to my chest. I try to stave off the tears attempting to bubble up to the surface. I'm a mess.

The pain has only worsened since I called Mason and left a drunk message on his voicemail. After downing a bottle of wine by myself, I found the courage to call. Of course, it went straight to voicemail. My memory is a little foggy, but I remember the words "sorry", "fake fiancé", "I love you", and "miss you". It's not exactly how I wanted to tell the man how I felt, but the alcohol in my system had me disclosing like a sinner on Sunday in the confessional.

I cringe at the memory. Not only at the call but the hangover too. I had a headache for days. *Stupid wine.* I'm never touching the stuff again.

Freaking voicemail. I bet he never even listened to it. He probably deleted it, along with all my texts. I wouldn't be surprised if he blocked me. It would explain why all my messages go unread.

A week after the voicemail incident, with still no word, I officially threw in the towel. I can't take the silent treatment anymore. It cuts deeper than if he had yelled and fought with me face to face.

I know I hurt him by lying, but I had hoped he would hear me out. Give me a chance to explain. Instead, he's cut me out of his life without a second thought.

I might have stopped reaching out to him, but it's done nothing to change how I jump at the sound of my phone or how I see his face everywhere I go. Reaching for my phone has become second nature since the beginning of our relationship. Good morning texts would greet me when I woke and good night messages would send me off to dream about him.

Now, there are no more texts, no more calls, no more Mason at all.

"Okay, enough is enough." Scarlett slams a stack of files on my desk, snapping me out of my somber spiral into the darkness that lurks in my lonely heart.

"What?" I ask.

She points at me, glaring.

I flinch at the intensity of her attention. I don't want her to see how broken I am. I'm supposed to be the rock. The unflappable co-worker who can handle it all with no distractions. No emotions or personal life. Just work.

"Nope, nice try. Rylann isn't here to save you, missy. It's time to spill, or so help me God, I'm going to kick your ass and fire you."

"You can't fire me," I snap back. I bite my lips, shocked at my own snark. I've never spoken to Scarlett like this before.

A wicked grin spreads across her face. "Oh, getting sassy now, are we?"

"I'm sorry, I—"

"Oh save it. Sass all you want; it doesn't bother me. I'm just glad you're alive in there. Now, are we going to talk about why you have been a" — she waves her hand in my general area with a look of repulsion — "hot mess, with your sad eyes and horribly drab outfits? You look like you're dressed for a funeral."

I look down at my clothes to see that I'm wearing a silk blouse with a matching pencil skirt and pumps. I didn't look at my clothes when I was putting them on this morning, but they definitely look like how my heart feels. Black.

This isn't me. My outfits are always planned out and impeccably chic. I pride myself on looking and acting like a professional at all times. Over the years, I have used my look as a shield of armor.

Before Mason found me and tore down all my walls, making me fall in love with him. Before I lost him. Nothing matters anymore, but I can't tell Scarlett that, so I stay quiet. Being vulnerable isn't my strong suit.

In the upper echelons where I grew up, being vulnerable was tantamount to spilling blood in the water while swimming with sharks, who attacked and used your weaknesses against you. It's how my father was able to trap me in an arranged marriage with a man who was in love with another woman. He used my love and need to protect Chris against me, and in the end, it all backfired. Spectacularly.

I lost the love of my life because I was too slow to walk away. I'm all alone.

I can't stop the flood of emotions that hit me with that thought, and the tears I have been keeping at bay spill over, the pit in my stomach growing and choking me.

"Oh shit. Emery, don't cry. I'm sorry. I didn't mean to upset you. I just thought this was about a guy." She wraps her long arms around me, and her strawberry scent invades my nose.

Her affection feels both foreign and strangely comforting.

"It is. But..." I sob, tears streaming down my cheeks.

She pulls back, her arms on my shoulders, squeezing. "But what? You can talk to me, you know. No judgment."

While it scares me to open up, I don't think I can do this on my own. I'm exhausted. My self-imposed seclusion from forming relationships has made me lonely as hell. Having Mason in my life showed me that.

He was my safe space when the world felt heavy on my shoulders. If I had let him shoulder the weight with me, things might have ended differently between us. We might still be together.

I hate that it's taken me so long to see that I have people here, people who care about me, who have been patient and kind. Rylann and Scarlett have always been on the sidelines, waiting for me to open up and let them in.

"It's about more than just a guy—"

"Wait! Hold that thought. This calls for an emergency meeting." She whips out her cell, taps the screen, and brings it to her ear. "Ry, it's happening." A scream on the other end has Scarlett pulling the phone away from her with a laugh. "Get your fine, just-had-a-baby ass to Blue Cantina. Stat." Scarlett disconnects her call. "Rylann is going to meet us for lunch at our favorite restaurant."

I look at the time on my phone. "Lunch? It's three o'clock."

"Fine, call it an early dinner." She throws her hands in the air dramatically like I'm a moron for questioning her.

"We have work," I say dumbly.

"Nope, we are done for the day." She turns and shouts towards the reception, "Mandy, can you please watch the phones for another thirty minutes and then lock up? Tell everyone there was an emergency and either Em or I will get back to them tomorrow."

"You got it, Boss." Mandy salutes Scarlett with a grin.

I really like her. Rylann was right—she's a good addition to the office. Not only is she a hard worker and quick at picking things up, but she is sweet as pie.

"What have I told you about calling me that?" Scarlett places a hand on her popped hip.

"You said not to." Mandy smirks.

"That's right. Because it's Boss *Bitch*." She snaps her finger, and for the first time in weeks, I throw my head back and laugh.

Mandy chuckles, and Scarlett looks beyond pleased with herself.

"Let's go, Em. It's time to drink a pitcher of margaritas and spill your guts.

"Whatever you say, *Boss Bitch.*"

I take another sip of my mango pomegranate margarita in a vain attempt to push away my tears. I've been sitting here for the past hour, eating chips and guac, while I tell my business partners all about my family drama. I still haven't explained the true root of my despair.

"Holy shit, you've been like … engaged this whole time." Scarlett's jaw is hanging open.

I mean, I don't blame her. My life is like a soap opera.

I shake my head and hold up my left hand. "No ring, no engagement. All fake."

"Semantics, girl. You were *betrothed* to another." She takes a sip of her virgin margarita.

Both she and Rylann opted for alcohol-free drinks, seeing as they have infants back home waiting for them.

Guilt swirls in my belly for pulling them away from their families. These women have just given birth, and yet here they are listening to my sob story, giving me a comforting shoulder to cry on.

Rylann glares at Scarlett. "She did it for her brother and to help her friend," she defends, placing her small hand on mine. Turning her attention to me, she looks me in the eye and says, "I'm sorry you had to go through all that alone. It was very selfless of you. I can't imagine how hard carrying this burden alone must have been for you. It was very brave."

"Thank you." My voice cracks. I take another sip of my drink, stirring the straw.

Rylann doesn't know how much I needed to hear those words. Her kindness warms my cold soul, and her deep brown eyes shine as she smiles, giving me a nod.

"More like stupid," Scarlett snarks.

I choke on my margarita. I want to laugh and cry at the same time.

"Scarlett," Rylann snaps.

"What? It's true."

So true.

"Sometimes, I miss the shy quiet girl you used to be," she laments, trying to hide her smile.

Scarlett sticks her tongue out at her best friend. "No, you don't."

Rylann laughs. "You're right, I don't. But ... be cool, or you're going to scare Emery away again."

Scarlett turns to me. "You're stuck with us now, girly. You should have come to us before now. We would have helped you."

Thinking back, I was so young when I moved here and started working for them. Trusting doesn't come easy for me, and I didn't think the plan Lex and I had would come to this. I figured he would have grown a pair and married Elizabeth when she graduated medical school.

"How could you have helped?"

My question is met with rolled eyes.

"We would have given you the money for Chris's tuition, dummy."

My eyes bug out of their sockets at Scarlett's statement. I glance at Rylann who nods, agreeing.

"You would have done that for me?" I ask, still not comprehending. It's hard to understand when you've grown up in a home where love was conditional and always out of reach.

"Duh," Scarlett deadpans.

"Of course. You're a part of our family," Rylann says, smacking Scarlett on the shoulder. "We would have helped any way we could. I just hate that it's taken you so long to let us in."

"Truth," Scarlett interrupts. "Do you think you're the only one with problems? Look at my friend here. She lost her husband to cancer and spent years separated from the love of her life until they saw each other again last summer. I lost my parents and my grandmother, and I'm not sure I would have met the love of my life if those things hadn't happened to me. But through all that, you know what we did have?"

I shake my head. There is so much I don't know about the ladies sitting with me, baring their souls to me. Not getting to know them sooner will be something I regret for the rest of my life. These women are smart, resilient, and incredibly strong.

"We had each other's backs. We held the other up when we were too weak to do it ourselves," Scarlett says seriously, all traces of humor gone.

"She's right," Rylann confirms. "We have your back now too, Em. Whatever you need, we are here for you. We've just been waiting for you to see us."

My eyes mist over as I take a deep breath. "Thank you." I mean it.

Thin ropes that held me back snap as I fully accept that I'm not alone anymore. I've always had Chris, but in some ways, I've felt like his parent, not his sister. I've never had true friends that listen to you like a therapist would, or help and support you when things get too hard.

Scarlett's right. I'm so stupid. I could have put the whole arranged marriage thing behind me a long time ago. With their help, I could have been strong enough to end the agreement I made with Lex and my parents years ago. I was stubborn to think I had to go at it, alone and now it may have cost me the love of my life.

Mason and I had so much potential. Our chemistry was off the charts, and the ease with which we fell into our relationship wasn't an everyday occurrence. People search for that kind of connection all their lives. Until him, I had never experienced that level of intimacy with someone.

"It was stupid." I can't stop the sob that tumbles from me. Now that I've started, I willingly let the rest of my truths flow. "So stupid that I didn't tell the man I am in love with about it, and when he found out, he couldn't run away fast enough."

With him gone, a piece of me is just missing. My heart, my body, my soul—every cell in my body aches for him. I miss him so deeply I'm falling apart at the seams without him.

"See, stupid." Scarlett points at me while Rylann rushes to my side of the table and wraps her arms around me.

I breathe in her coconutty scent, letting it cocoon me in a warm blanket, and sink into her comforting embrace, returning her hug. She gives really good hugs. I'd have given up anything to have a mom like her. So understanding and compassionate, loving and affectionate.

"It will be okay," she soothes, rubbing my back. Her tone is hopeful and almost has me believe things might work out. Rylann hisses at her best friend, "Scarlett."

I know they are having one of those weird silent conversations over my head. I wish I had a friendship like theirs.

My chest twinges. Something tells me I could have had it with them sooner if I had let them in and talked to them about something other than work.

"Sorry, Emery. I didn't mean to blurt that out," Scarlett says.

I pull away from Rylann with a chuckle as I wipe my eyes. I know Rylann just forced her to apologize.

"No need. You're right, I am an idiot. I should have told him. I just... I don't know." I shrug. I have been staying up at night, wondering why I didn't just tell him. All I can come up with is, "I guess I wanted to keep him out of it. What we had was special, and I didn't want to taint our relationship with my old life. I figured with us being long-distance, I could keep us in our bubble and handle everything on my own. Then, when I walked away from my parents, it would be a clean break and I could be with Mason without my past hanging over my head." I leave out the five weeks of ghosting. They don't need to know how pathetic I am for still pining after someone who clearly doesn't want me anymore.

It takes me a minute to hear the silence hanging over the table.

I look up to find Scarlett gaping at me and Rylann's mouth hanging open. She snaps it shut and shakes her head at Scarlett. I wish I knew how they communicated like that. Bestie telepathy?

Rylann clears her throat. "How did you meet Mason?"

Her question has my lips turning up at the memory of our meeting at the airport. I tell them about how Mason was listening to my call with Chris, how he walked me to my gate and then surprised me by boarding the same plane right after, our computer conversation, and every moment we've shared since then. Well, shy of a few details because some moments are just for me to cherish.

"Wow," Scarlett whispers.

"Yeah." I exhale and take another sip of my drink.

Everything with Mason really was wow. He had me falling for him faster than my panties could hit the floor.

"You know what?"

My eyes bounce to Scarlett's.

"You should come to Rylann and Jace's joint bachelor and bachelorette shower."

"What sho— Ow. Shiitake mushrooms," Rylann grouses as she leans down and rubs her leg.

I glance at Scarlett curiously.

"The shower I've been planning for Labor Day weekend. Remember?" Scarlett stares are Rylann.

"Oh, right. That shower. I forgot. Mom brain." She points to her head and laughs with a shrug.

"That sounds like fun. Can I help with anything?" I will do anything to take my mind off of everything going on. Or lack thereof now that Mason is no longer in the picture.

"Actually ... there is something you can help us with," Scarlett says, a wicked grin on her face.

Uh-oh. I don't know that look. I've worked with her for years, and the look she's giving me scares the shit out of me.

"You can plan it for us."

Okay, I was not expecting that.

"I can do that," I agree, easily.

These women have taken me in when I was looking for a new start. This is the least I can do for them. Besides, keeping busy will be good for me.

At least, I hope it will be because I can't stop thinking about the man with electrifyingly green-gold eyes who owns my heart. The man I might never see again.

SEPTEMBER

TONIGHT IS JACE'S BACHELOR party, and while I am super happy for my brother, this is the last place I want to be.

I peel the saturated label off my beer bottle, barely listening to everyone laugh and crack jokes. I'm not in the mood. I haven't been since I walked away from Emery after finding out she had a fiancé the entire time we were together.

A fucking fiancé.

I scoff and finish rest off the warm beer in my hand.

Eli pushes the blow-up woman sitting in the chair beside me to the floor and plops down on her place. Eli went all out with the decorations for the day: condom necklaces for us all to wear, with matching t-shirts that say *Dad in the streets, Daddy in the sheets*, cheap blow-up sex dolls, and light-up cock rings. Normally I would have a good laugh at Jace's expense—because, let's face it, Eli is ridiculous—but my heart isn't in it.

He takes a swig of his beer. "What's with you, brother?"

I grunt a noncommittal answer. Besides the fact that I want to leave, he knows what's wrong—I've just been refusing to answer him.

I was close to not coming today, but Eli and Cameron got on my ass and guilted me into being here for Jace. They reminded me that we didn't get to do this for his first marriage, and it was different this time. They aren't wrong. This time around, Jace has it right.

I couldn't be happier for my big brother, but I'm not in the right headspace for celebrating.

I'm pissed off and, quite frankly, sad. My heart feels like it got run over by a Mack Truck, and then the said truck backed up and ran it over again. But for my brother, I came. I'm wearing this stupid-ass shirt, and have been all day, starting with beers and burgers at the local brewery that Jace loves, and now here, at a small lounge in their small town.

My eyes dance around the room. This place seems like an interesting choice for my sister-in-law, who is pure sunshine, but Rylann said that when she and Scarlett were younger, it was their favorite place to go dancing and to celebrate their biggest wins.

The lounge, aptly named The Red Room, is one open room with a dance floor in the middle, surrounded by tables and chairs. In tribute to its moniker, everything is covered in red—the walls, the chairs, the floor, the bar top, the lighting. Everything. It's giving me heartburn, reminding me of a certain someone's matching red lips.

Cameron ambles over and takes the seat on my other side as a waitress drops a tray of shots on the table in front of us.

"Are you still all up in your man-feels?"

Glaring at him, I grab a new beer from the ice bucket and crack it open, taking a sip. Fucking smug asshole, giving me shit. Cam and I are close, being the two youngest of the group. We've always shared a special bond, which means he can read me like a book.

"Leave him alone, Cam," Eli warns.

"Nah, I'm done leaving him alone. He's made himself non-existent since the Fourth. Did something happen with Airport Girl?"

My plans to avoid my family so I don't have to talk about what happened have been too obvious. I have thrown myself into work and even convinced my partners to take on a new project, only after I promised to be the team leader and would do all the travel. No matter how far I fly or how busy I keep myself, I can't outrun her tear-streaked face or the way it feels like half of me is missing without her.

The night I walked away, I was fuming, anger coursing through my veins like lava. Livid, I tried to find clues in every conversation we had, every meeting. The only thing I could come up with was her mentioning the expectations her parents had for her. Other than that, nothing. Believe me, I tried. I played it over and over, from every angle.

When the car service finally picked me up, I was so mad I rashly blocked her number. I wanted to make her and the pain disappear, and I've been too stubborn to undo it. Did my ego take a hit? Yes. Am I afraid to see what kind of messages she's left me? Yes. Do I miss her like crazy? Also a yes.

I just don't know if anything she has to say will take away the sting of the betrayal her lies have made on me. I don't know if anything will be enough to take away the empty ache in my chest.

She lied to me, and getting over that seems ... impossible.

Secrets were the one thing I told her I had no room for—I needed complete honesty in our relationship. After everything I've seen happen with Jace and the shit with Brittany screwing me over, I needed full transparency. I might be a grouchy, grunting bastard, but I'm not like my oldest brother. I'm not equipped to handle heartache and move on like him.

Fuck it.

I grab a shot of tequila off the tray and put down the same beer I've been nursing since we got here. "Yes. We're over."

I lift the warm shot before bringing it to my lips and throwing it back. The liquid burns like fire down my throat as Eli and Cameron follow my lead, each grabbing a shot and taking them down.

Slamming the glass on the tray, Cam sits back and starts bobbing his head to the music blaring from the old jukebox, looking too casual. "What happened?"

She has a fucking fiancé, that's what happened.

"It didn't work out. Long distance." I shrug, trying to play it off. I don't want my brothers to know I was played for a fool. Nor do I want their pity—they get half the truth.

Eli's watchful eyes burn the side of my face. He knows I'm lying through my teeth. Weeks ago, I was confessing to him that I loved her before racing off to get on a plane to be with her. He hasn't pressed for answers, but he knows something is up.

Jace and Levi—Jace's childhood friend, who is married to Rylann's best friend, Scarlett—join us at the table.

Levi pulls out his phone, reading something on his screen. "The ladies are here. They are looking for a parking spot."

"Finally," Jace grumbles, his eyes on the door waiting for Rylann to walk through.

The women spent the day at a spa for the bachelorette portion of the day, taking advantage of both sets of grandparents being in town, who no doubt are spoiling my nephew and niece rotten. A part of me wishes I stayed back with Rhys and Sariah to spend more time with them before I head to Chicago for client meetings tomorrow morning.

The lounge door swings open and Jace stands, his chair sliding back behind him. I watch him race to Rylann, her face lighting up at the sight of him. My brother wraps his arms around his woman and pulls her in for an over-the-top kiss.

I look away. Their love is like lemon juice on a paper cut. Listen, I'm happy for my brother, but right now, jealousy digs into my chest and squeezes. Behind my eyelids, I recall getting the same reception from the woman I had fallen madly in love with. How Emery's brilliant topaz eyes sparkled with the same loving shine as she ran into my arms in that crowded theater and kissed me.

"Holy shit, is that..."

My eyes snap open at the shock in Cameron's voice and find his head turned toward the crowd of women who just entered the bar. Standing beside Jace and Rylann is Scarlett, with Levi's arms wrapped around her waist as he greets his twin sisters, Laci and

Lexi. The twins step away in slow motion, and every molecule of air in my lungs is expelled from my chest like a jab to the diaphragm.

"Airport Girl," Cameron mumbles in disbelief.

As if my mind conjured her up, Emery stands behind the twins, with a nervous smile, wearing a burgundy cocktail dress that molds to her body like second skin and what looks like the same sexy black stilettos I fucked her in on Valentine's Day. Standing there, achingly beautiful, she shakes hands with Levi and Jace.

My eyes laser in on her, and I watch as her shoulders stiffen. She must feel my stare because her eyes snap to mine. Her little mouth forms a perfect O, and I can't help the memory of her thick lips wrapped around my cock as she took me to the back of her throat from popping up.

My dick thickens at the sight of her. *Down, boy.* Fucker knows who he belongs to, no matter how hard I try to tell him no.

My body is drawn to her. Without thinking, I stand and my feet move in her direction, her mere presence a beacon calling me, bringing us toe to toe. What the hell is she doing here?

"Mason," she exhales my name, and I fight the urge to touch her, to kiss her soft, luscious lips. "What are you doing here?"

I can feel everyone's eyes on us. "I could ask the same of you."

"My bosses invited me."

"Business partners," Rylann coughs.

The corner of Emery's mouth twitches. "Right. I forgot. Business partners."

What the fuck?

How did I not put this together? Not only does Emery work with my sister-in-law, but she's their business partner as well. When we met, I recall Emery telling me it was fairly recent and that she had been working with them for years, but they weren't close.

So much has changed since I've seen her. Emery is opening herself up and making friends. She couldn't have picked two better women to have her back. While that's good for her, for me, it's fucked.

My stomach dips. A piece of me is proud of her for breaking out of her shell, and the other part of me hates it. It's like she's ... moving on.

What did you expect? You blocked her number and haven't spoken to her in almost two months.

Like a shock, I remember why we aren't together and take a step back. If I didn't know her, I would have missed the way her face falls at the distance I put between us.

She's quick to recover and plasters a fake smile on her face.

"Emery! It's shot time, girl!" Laci yells, oblivious to the tension between us.

"If you'll please excuse me." She turns, making her way to the bar, glancing over her shoulder at me.

Our gazes lock, bringing that explosion of fireworks with it. She shakes her head as if she's trying to make sense of my presence, before meeting up with the twins.

Me too, baby doll. Me too.

My heart races double time, my mind and body at war with each other. Stay here or go to her? Kiss her or yell at her?

A hand lands on my arm. "Are you okay?"

I look at Rylann in confusion. "Did you know?"

She weighs her answer. "I figured it out a couple of weeks ago. I never realized Jace hadn't come to the office in a while, or that I hadn't mentioned his last name. You know how closed off she can be."

I nod. I do know. It took me months to rip away at her walls before she opened up about her grandfather, and that was the tip of the iceberg.

"Are you going to be okay?" Rylann asks, her eyes worried.

"Did you do this on purpose?"

She laughs. "No, that was all Scarlett."

Speaking of the devil, Scarlett throws her arm over Rylann's shoulders with a wide smile. "Surprised?"

"Scarlett, behave," Rylann scolds her.

Jace was right. Scarlett is a nosy shit-stirrer. He just doesn't mind because it worked out for him.

I return my attention to Emery standing at the bar, her long hair waving behind her as she chats with Lexi. "I'm fine."

"'Fine'. We'll see about that," Scarlett huffs, mumbling under her breath as she walks away.

"Mason."

I rip my eyes away from Emery to my soon-to-be sister-in-law, who is watching me. "Sometimes, everyone needs a little push. Look at me and Jace." With those parting words, she heads toward the bar, towards my girl.

Not your girl, asshole.

Growling at myself, I return to my seat and take another shot off the tray, shooting it down.

Fuck. What the hell am I going to do now? I can barely keep her off my mind when I picture her a thousand miles away from me. Now, she's only feet away, and my body is screaming for me to grab her and kiss the living hell out of her, to dive in and lose myself in her all over again.

Rylann's words ring in my ears. *Sometimes, everyone needs a little push.*

I think about how fate played a part in bringing her and my brother together the first time, and how it wouldn't have happened again without the help of their best friends. Too bad it doesn't work that way for everyone.

Emery lied to me. How can I ever trust her again?

"So, that's her, huh?" Eli asks.

I nod, shaking myself out of my thoughts.

"Small world." Cameron whistles, shaking his head, no doubt as shocked as I am.

"You can say that again," I grumble. I still can't believe she works with Rylann and Scarlett.

"You should talk to her."

I shake my head as Cameron sips his water. He doesn't drink much during the season, and since his team is looking to get into the playoffs, I'm not surprised he's already made the switch.

"Why not? It doesn't seem like you two had a clean break."

Because we didn't. Our break was anything but clean. A messy fucking disaster is what it was.

Following Cam's lead, I grab a water bottle and chug. That last shot was a mistake. I need to keep my wits about me, or I might do something stupid, like scoop her up in my arms and take her to my hotel room.

For the next hour, I watch her. I couldn't rip my eyes away from Emery if I tried. She's heart-stopping beautiful as she dances and laughs while nursing her favorite drink.

My eyes follow her as she slips away to the bathroom.

This is it. I need to talk to her. I need to know if she didn't know Jace was my brother. My gut says she didn't, but my brain says she can't be trusted. That she's a liar.

I stand, but a hand grips my wrist.

Eli pulls me back. "Be cool, Mase. Don't cause a scene."

"What makes you think I'm going to cause a scene?" I scoff, ripping my hand away.

"Only the angry glares you've been shooting at her all night. Take it down a notch, man."

I ignore his warning and march my way to the bathroom, following her down the dark hallway. Leaning against the wall, I cross my arms and wait for Emery to step out of the restroom.

The door flies open and I move, blocking her way.

"Are you avoiding me, baby doll?"

Emery flinches at the endearment that slipped off my tongue with ease. "I'm not avoiding you. I was invited to hang out with the girls. Which is what I'm doing. It's a bachelorette party, after all."

"Did you know?"

"Know what?" she asks.

"That you work with my sister-in-law."

"No."

"Don't lie to me."

The double meaning of my jab lands hard and her face pales as her eyes glass over.

"What do I have to gain from lying about knowing your family?"

I sneer, "Who knows with you. You have a habit of lying and keeping secrets."

Just stop talking, asshole. What is wrong with you?

"Wow. That's what you think of me? That's low, even for you." I shrug.

She pulls her shoulders back and lifts her chin. *There's my bratty girl.* "Mason, I'm here with my friends and colleagues. I can't talk to you about this here. Maybe if you had answered one of my many calls or texts, or even listened to my voicemail, we could have hashed this all out before running into each other like this. I will not fight with you here. I will not ruin Rylann's night."

"Who said I want to fight with you?"

She closes her eyes and takes a deep breath. "That's right. You don't like to fight. You like to run away from your problems."

Shots fired.

I did run away. I know it was a mistake, but I was angry. Before I knew it, a day turned into a week, then into a month. I couldn't go back at that point. She hurt me.

"What was I supposed to do, watch you walk off with your *fiancé*?"

"I tried to explain, but you didn't let me. Instead, you ghosted me, Mason. You cut me out of your life like I didn't matter—"

Instead of letting her finish, I grab the back of her neck and slam my mouth to hers in an aggressive kiss. I don't want to hear her explanations and lame excuses. I might be angry and unable to forgive her, but she's wrong. She does matter.

I fucking love her. Still.

Her fists land on my chest as I push her back into the bathroom. Twirling us around, I slam her back up against the door and flip the lock. My lips never leave hers as I devour her mouth like a glutton, hungry for more, and she opens for me willingly. My cock turns to steel as her taste explodes on my tongue.

Fuck, I missed her so much.

My free hand roams over her curves, groping and squeezing her tight body as the other controls her head, allowing me to take what I want. She moans into my mouth, and my hips find hers on instinct, grinding against the heat of her pussy.

Emery's height is an advantage, but Emery in heels is fucking hot. The apex of her thighs aligns with my cock just right as she lifts her leg, her knee on my hip. I slide my hand up the back of her thigh and grope her ass before gliding my fingers over her lace-covered pussy. She's wet and hot, and all I want to do is bury myself inside her tight heat.

I miss you. I miss this. The words are on the tip of my tongue, but I push them back, kissing her harder, blocking them from slipping out.

"Mason," she whimpers against my lips.

I don't want to hear her utter a word, or I might snap out of my haze and stop what's about to happen. Stopping is the smart thing to do, but I'm not going to. I'm too far gone. Every cell in my body settles with her in my arms, so I kiss her harder, fucking her mouth with my tongue. Refusing to face the truth.

Emery's hips thrust forward as my fingers move her panties to the side. I slide two fingers inside her and place my thumb on her clit. She moans at the contact, arching her pert tits into my chest. My cock grows harder, begging to feel her wrapped around the thick shaft. Her body shivers as I run circles over her swollen bundle of nerves. I know her body better than my own—she's close. Her pussy quivers, and her cum soaks my hand.

Her fingers land on the waistband of my jeans and I buck my hips forward, encouraging her to take my cock out, moving my hand faster and deeper inside her, just the way she likes.

She does what I want and unbuckles my belt. I thrust my hand harder, edging her closer. She undoes the button and zipper, diving into my boxer briefs. She wraps her hand around my girth and squeezes, pumping my hard shaft from root to tip.

Fuck. Her hand on me feels so good I might blow.

"Show me where you want my cock, baby doll." I quickly cover her mouth with mine, cutting off her words.

She guides my cockhead to her entrance, letting me know where she wants me. Her arousal coats my tip, dripping down my shaft, and I snap. Without warning, I propel my hips up and into her, sheathing every thick inch of my cock deep inside her pussy. She's hot, wet, and ready. Her body wraps around me like a glove, like she was made for me.

I shove that thought away, letting the anger and hurt that lance my heart take over. I gather every emotion weighing me down and take it out on her body. Gripping her ass, I lift her up and piston into her with abandon, impaling her with my cock.

She groans, wrapping her legs around my waist as she takes every thrust, every pump, every single thing I have to offer. Her muscles contract around me, coaxing my orgasm from my body like the witch she is, wrapping me up in her spell. My balls tingle, and fire shoots down my spine.

She comes, squeezing my dick like a vise and screaming into my mouth, sending me over the edge with her as I come hard, emptying thick ropes of cum inside her, draining my balls dry.

I rip my mouth away from hers, gasping for breath, and my cock slips out of her slit. I watch my cum spill out, and it's like a bucket of cold water.

Shit. What the fuck did I just do?

Dropping her feet to the ground, Emery steadies herself on shaky legs.

I step away, tucking my cock back inside my boxer briefs and zipping up my jeans. "Fuck," I mumble.

I can't believe I let it get this far when I know it changes nothing for me. For us.

Emery shimmies, pulling the hem of her dress down. She's a panting, beautiful mess. A mess I have no business getting involved with right now.

Not after she lied to me, breaking my trust. And my heart along with it.

THIRTY-FIVE

"MASON," I PANT, MY breathing still labored after our explosive encounter.

I don't know what I was thinking, letting it get this far. There is still so much left unsaid, but per usual, when it comes to us, we can't fight the physical connection that binds us together.

Mason's back is to me, but from the muttered fucks he keeps repeating, I know he's freaking out over what just happened.

"Mason," I repeat his name.

He shakes his head, refusing to turn around.

"Please look at me."

"No." He runs his hands through his hair, tugging on the ends. "This was a mistake. Fuck!" he yells, spinning around, his eyes wild. He looks like a caged animal—scared, angry, and in pain.

It breaks my heart seeing him like this, knowing I did that to him.

"Let's just talk. Please," I plead.

He schools his features; the way I'd imagine he does when he's in charge at work. "No. Just because we *fucked*, doesn't mean things are magically fixed between us. Like I said, this was a mistake. It never should have happened. It was nothing," he declares harshly, leaving no room for argument.

He's already decided to throw in the towel. Any hope I held onto that we could fix us evaporates, and in its place, anger takes over.

After everything, he still won't let me explain the dumpster fire that is my family and the situation I got myself into after college.

"Nothing? Wow. You really know how to drive home that we're done. I get it. It's fine. I hope you enjoyed your cheap fuck."

"Em—" He reaches for me, but I step back.

If he were to touch me now, I might break down and cry.

"No. You're right. It was just sex, right? It meant nothing. We mean nothing." I run my hands over my dress and pull my shoulders back.

I will not shed another tear for a man who thinks I'm nothing but a meaningless fuck in the bathroom of a shitty bar. I am *so* done with people treating me like I'm worthless. I refuse to let people use me anymore. I have had enough of people using me and making their love conditional. I know I fucked up, but I don't deserve this. I deserve more.

"Listen—"

I scoff, cutting him off. He did not just seriously say that to me. After weeks of ignoring me. The fucking balls on this guy.

"No." I shake my head, allowing the anger coursing in my veins to take over, and push back the pain he has inflicted on my heart. "Just... You know what? Fuck you, Mason. I'm done. I won't let you treat me this way. I thought you were different. Joke's on me. You're just like everyone else in my life—an undependable, self-serving, selfish asshole."

"Yeah, well, I thought you were a good person. Honest. Instead, I come to find out that you're a liar. You're all smoke and mirrors, baby."

"Thank you."

"For what?"

"Showing me exactly why I don't rely on people. Why I don't let them in. You can fill in whatever narrative you want about me to justify your actions. There is so much more to what happened than you know. But you won't let me explain. *You* don't want to listen. So, I hope you feel good about yourself. Don't worry about me. I'm going to be fine without you."

Where did that come from? I'm a little shocked, but damn, it felt good to say all that.

How dare he? He ghosts me for weeks, fucks me in the bathroom, and then refuses to discuss what went down.

Yeah, I'm good.

Mason stands there in stunned silence at my outburst as I turn, unlock the door, and shove it open. Without a backward glance, I head towards the bar. I need to get the hell out of here and as far from that infuriating, sexy asshole as possible.

Rylann spots me first, and her smile falls.

I probably look like a slutty, angry mess. No doubt in my mind that everyone knows what just went down in the bathroom.

"Are you okay?" Rylann asks.

"No, but I will be. I think I'm done for the night. I'm going to head home if that's okay?"

"Of course. Thank you for planning such a lovely day. I'm sorry things didn't work out like I had hoped they would."

Jace steps behind Rylann and wraps his arms around her waist.

How did I not see it? Mason looks almost exactly like him—tall, brown hair, the same jawline, and those eyes... They are the same shade of green, but instead of a ring of gold, Mason has streaks.

I'm so fucking stupid.

"Do you need a ride home, Emery?" Jace asks.

"No, I'm good. You two enjoy your last hurrah. I drove here and only had one drink." I thank them again for the invite.

Luckily, everyone is out on the dancefloor, distracted, as I grab my purse from the stool and race out of the bar.

Henry yips from his crate as I walk through the front door and throw my keys on the entry table. I lock the door and make my way over to the little furball. At least he loves me no matter what.

Okay, that's not true. Henry would love anyone who gives him a treat, but at least he listens to me. He's loyal and can't leave me. My dependable little pooch. I lift him into my arms and give him a scratch behind his ear.

"I missed you too, Henry," I coo as he licks my cheek. "Love you too, buddy."

I carry Henry to my room and deposit him on my bed. Grabbing the hem of my dress, I lift it over my head and catch a whiff of Mason's scent. The ginger and spice that once brought me pleasure make me nauseous as I remember the awful conversation we had in that horrible bathroom.

I throw the dress in the laundry and head to the bathroom. I need a shower. As much as I don't want to wash away Mason's smell, his touch, his cum, I absolutely need to.

I turn on the shower and step in, not bothered by the chilly water as it warms, washing away the pain of losing Mason all over again.

With the water burning my skin, I sink to the floor and let myself fall apart.

♥

A shrill ring wakes me from a fitful sleep.

My swollen eyes feel like I have sand in them as I blink them open. A look around my dark room tells me it's still dark outside. My cell stops ringing, only to immediately start again.

Ugh, Chris.

My finger slides across the screen, and I lift the phone to my ear. "Hello?"

"Emmy, wake up. You will not guess who I just met," Chris shouts over the sound of music and people in the background. He must be out, having the time of his life.

"Chrisy, it's too late for this," I groan.

I'm not in the mood for his happiness. I just want to curl back up in my blankets and forget last night ever happened, maybe even the last eight months.

Is it possible to start the year over again?

"It's never too late for Henry Cavill, Emmy. Never."

That catches my attention and I spring up to a sitting position, knocking over my poor Henry, who growls and stalks out of my room, pissed at being woken up.

"Did you hear me? I met Henry Cavill, Em. Henry freaking Cavill."

"Holy shit, Chris, really?"

"Yes! And he's just as hot in real life as he is on screen. He's also cool as fuck. He loved that we named our Yorkie after him, and he totally chuckled when I told him about Bog."

"Wait, what?" I can feel my face burning from absolute embarrassment. "You didn't really tell him about my vibrator, right?"

"Oh, I *sooo* did," Chris chuckles. My brother has no fucking shame.

"You asshole."

"He thought it was funny."

"I hate you."

"No, you don't."

"Ass."

"Biotch," he quips back.

I sigh. We could do this all night if I don't stop first.

I've missed this. Save for the one conversation I had with Chris for Lex, I've missed my brother and our talks these past few weeks. With his internship, the tumultuous end of my relationship, and being cut off by my parents, I haven't felt like burdening him with all my problems.

"Ems, what's wrong?" he asks.

Throwing myself back on my pillows, I cover my eyes with my arms and take a few deep breaths. He's out, partying and living his life the way I've always wanted for him. He doesn't need to be on the phone listening to me cry over my parents or a man who clearly doesn't deserve my tears.

"It's nothing. We can talk about it later."

"Liar. Don't think I don't know something's wrong with you. We haven't spoken since you called and asked me to call Flip so he could help track Lizzie down for you. Tell me what's going on."

"It's a long story."

"Fine. Go back to sleep. We'll talk in the morning."

Tears tickle their way up my nose, a little sad at his easy acquiescence. "Okay. Love you, baby bro."

"Love you more, big sis."

THE BED SHIFTS UNDER me, and I roll over searching for Henry.

Wait. Henry doesn't move the bed when he jumps up to snuggle. In fact, he has to lick my face to make his presence known.

That means...

I fly out of bed with a scream like my ass is on fire. Grabbing my black stiletto off the floor, I hold it overhead like a knife ready to plunge into the creep-ass motherfucker in my bed. "What the f—"

"Emmy." Chris cackles. "It's just me, relax."

"You almost gave me a heart attack, you needle dick."

My brother only laughs harder. "Put down the shoe, you crazy woman. What can that shoe do if I really was some perv trying to sneak into your bed?"

I look at the shoe still raised over my head. "I was thinking I would use this pointy part right here to stab said perv and run away." I throw the shoe at him, and he falls over laughing, tears wetting his lashes. "You suck."

"I do." He wiggles his eyebrows at me and pats the bed.

I roll my eyes at him and climb back in beside him. Now that my heart rate has returned to normal, I'm shocked to see Chris.

"Why are you here? Don't you have work?"

"Nope. If you had picked up the phone, you would know last night's *wrap* party was to celebrate the end of my internship.

School starts next week, so I thought I would come visit my favorite sister."

"I'm your only sister." I drop my head on his shoulder.

I have no idea what I'm going to do. I have enough money set aside for his tuition, but I don't have enough for his books or incidentals, at least not until next month when I get my trust stipend.

Buying this house depleted my savings. I figured, in the long run, it would pay off to have a lower mortgage, and the bank offered me a great interest rate for a larger cash sum as the down payment. Then Chris ruined it by moving to California for college.

"Tell me what's going on." Chris leans his head on mine and throws his arm over my shoulder, hugging me tight as he waits for me to speak.

When did Chris's arms get so ... big and muscular? I can still remember him having scrawny teen arms just a few months ago. *Right?* But now, sitting next to my little brother, he's not so little. He's a man. He's all grown up.

Chris is an adult. He's about to graduate from college, and he received an amazing internship this past summer, putting him closer to his dreams of directing films. He's perfectly capable of taking care of himself.

Why do I still look at him like he's a helpless kid? Chris has been there, urging me to cut ties with our parents for so long, and I kept making excuses because I wanted him to have the best.

"Chrisy, how did you get here?" I ask.

"I took a plane. You know, those big metal tubes that defy all logic."

"Jerk. No, really. Why are you here?"

"I could hear it in your voice, sis. I know you're not okay. You need me. So I figured the only way I was going to get your stubborn ass to talk was to get up here as soon as possible."

My little brother flew to me because he knew I needed him. He's here to take care of me.

Tears flood my eyes. Rylann's right. I've been blind to the people who have been here, silently supporting me. Waiting for me to ask for help. I'm not alone and never have been. I have people to help me get through this.

"Mason broke up with me," I confess.

"Oh, babe. I'm so sorry. That sucks."

"You're telling me." I rub my sternum, the ache of his loss still sharp as a knife.

I'm not alone.

"It's my fault. But the good news is I finally divorced Cybil and Sinclair," I croak out, my voice thick with emotion as tears tingle my nose.

"You did what now? And can you *please* start from the beginning? It seems you've kept a lot of information from me these last couple of weeks," he says, his breath fanning across my hair.

I have been keeping things from him, but no more. I'm done holding it all in.

"Fine." Sitting up, I twist around and cross my legs, wiping the tears from my cheeks.

I face my brother. It's time. I owe it to him to share everything that's been going on these last couple of years.

"But first, you have to promise me you won't get mad."

Chris twists around, mimicking my position, as Henry jumps onto the bed and sits in his lap like he, too, is waiting for me to finally spill. Chris is going to be pissed.

"Well, if you ever want someone *not* to get mad, don't start a conversation like that. Now I know it's bad."

My mouth waters, and I choke back the sour acid burning in my stomach. It is bad. I let everything get too far and, as a result, I lost Mason. I didn't realize it then, but agreeing to this stupid plan ruined my future. I still remember that day like it was yesterday.

"Seven years ago, I struck a deal with Cybill and Sinclair."

Chris opens his mouth to interject, but I cut him off, covering his mouth with my hand.

"Nope. No talking. You want me to start from the beginning?" I remove my hand, waiting for him to agree.

He huffs, "Yes."

"Okay, so I had just graduated with my Master's degree. Cybil and Sinclair were livid with me for not accepting a role at Rhodes Publishing. Instead, I informed them I was moving to Oregon to be closer to you."

"Wait, what?"

"Let me finish." He nods, so I continue. "They immediately threatened to cut me off. But I didn't care about the money. I knew I could find a job."

I was determined and ready to accept the consequences of my decision. I felt so sure and confident at that moment. All that mattered was being near Chris. He had just been thrown out of our home and shipped off to live on the other side of the country. He was alone, and I couldn't bear the thought of something happening to him and being unable to get to him in time. Chris was all I had. Still is.

Being his sister has been the only thing I've ever known how to do right. He's the only person who understands what it's like growing up as a Rhodes. Living with parents who don't give a damn about their children isn't for the faint of heart. We had to train ourselves to be strong, to hide our weaknesses. But my weakness has always been Chris, and it was easy for my parents to use that against me.

"When I didn't take their threats seriously, they threatened to hurt you instead. They vowed to stop paying your tuition and cut you off completely. You were sixteen, Chris. I couldn't let them do that." Hot tears stream down my cheeks at the memory.

He wipes them away. "It's okay, Emmy. I know how they are. So what did they want from you?"

See? He gets it. Since the day he was born, my brother has brought solace and meaning to my life. The loneliness I had always felt melted away as I held him in my arms for the first time. In my little eight-year-old brain, I knew he would need me, and I promised I would always be there for him. I became not only his sister but also kind of his mother in a way. I protected him from anything and everything, and that extended to our parents.

"The deal was that they would continue to pay for the prep school, all of your college tuition, and housing until you turned twenty-five and had access to the trust Papa left you. In exchange, I would..." It's hard to admit this next part because this is where everything started to fall apart, even though it was a no-brainer for me to agree to their terms. "In exchange, I would marry a man of their choosing, to keep RP in the family and help the business grow. I agreed. They let me move, and I almost forgot about it. I was happy here. I saw you all the time. You were safe and taken care of. It wasn't until they required my presence at their stupid Memorial Day party, a year after the agreement, that things started to change. I didn't think they would go through with it, you know?"

"That's insane, Em. Why would you do that?" Chris moves Henry to the side and jumps off the bed. He paces across the room, running his hands through his hair. "I can't believe you agreed to marry some stranger and be in a loveless marriage just for me. Why?"

"Chrisy, it was the easiest thing I ever did. I had to protect you."

He shakes his head. He's freaking out, but he doesn't need to worry.

"It's over, Chris. It's not happening."

His eyes snap to mine. "You got out of it?"

I nod.

"How? Wait! Who did they want to marry you off to?"

I pat the bed. "Come sit down, and let me finish the story."

He rips off his sweatshirt, revealing his very tattooed arms, and sits back down.

When the hell did he get the ink? *Another time, Emery. Concentrate.*

"Alexander Westfield," I state cooly.

"What?! Nooo." He gasps.

"Yup."

"But..."

"I know."

"Lizzie," we both say.

"It shocked the hell out of me too. Lex and I sat in the office while our parents laid out the timeline. After Lex graduated from business school and worked for the company, we would announce our engagement, and then Lex would be appointed as CEO. Turns out, Alfred was holding the company over Lex's head, and the only way he would receive his birthright was if he broke up with Lizzie and married me so that we could unite the companies."

"Holy fucking shit." Chris shakes his head in shock.

"I know. It would have been huge. Westfield Media and Rhodes Publishing uniting."

"Uniting" is an understatement. Their union would be beyond lucrative. They would become a powerhouse in the industry and could expand globally.

"Anyway, after the meeting in the office, Lex and I met up separately. We figured we could fake this whole thing. I would live here, and he would work on his parents. He thought he could get them to accept Elizabeth with more time. So while they thought they had the upper hand, they didn't. It was only a matter of time until it all blew up in their faces. Instead, it blew up in my face."

"What do you mean? I thought you were getting out of it."

"I was. I did," I clarify with a huff. This is harder to explain than I thought it would be. "I knew Lex would never go through with this. He has been in love with Elizabeth since we were children. But then—"

"Lizzie left him," Chris interrupts me. "That's why you needed my help, right? Why you wanted me to call Flip?"

"Yup. She was tired of Lex being a coward and not standing up for her and their relationship. But instead of chasing after her, the dummy pivoted. He decided to go all-in on the fake engagement and arranged marriage with me."

"What a dumbass. So, where does Mason breaking up with you fit into all this?"

"Fourth of July, he showed up at the party, surprising me. I had just finished telling Sinclair and Cybil to shove it up their asses, which of course ended in us getting cut off, and I ran into him. He was standing at the office door when I opened it. We went out onto the overlook to talk. Lex, of course, picks that time to show up and call me his fiancée. Mason blew a fucking gasket. We argued. He walked away, and I haven't heard from him since."

I leave out the part of me finding out he's related to my business partner's husband, and the goodbye-fucking in the bathroom. Some things, a little brother just doesn't need to know.

"Damn. I'm sorry, Emmy. I thought he was different." Chris wraps his arm around me and pulls us back against the headboard.

Taking comfort in his hold for once is a nice change to our dynamic. I always felt like I had to be the one there for him, not the other way around.

"So did I. The worst part is that Mason never let me explain. He just automatically assumed I was a cheating liar."

"His loss," Chris states flatly.

Then why does it feel more like mine?

My insides are hollowed out, and all I want to do is sit around and cry into a box of cookies and a bottle of wine.

"I swear, if Lex doesn't find Lizzie and grovel, I'm going to kick him in his balls for his role in all this."

"Ha! Can you imagine Lizzie kicking him? She's so tiny. I doubt her dainty foot could do damage." Chris cackles, making me laugh at the picture he's painted.

It feels good to finally laugh with my brother, even if everything else in my life feels dull without Mason.

"Thanks."

"For what?"

"For being here. For hopping on a plane to see me. For not judging me."

"Never, Ems. You're my girl. I'll always be here for you."

Just like all those years ago, my loneliness melts away. Only this time, it's my baby brother holding me.

I drift off to sleep, tired from confessing, from being sad and lonely. I'm free after letting go of all the secrets and burdens I've been carrying over the years.

But the freedom from the past doesn't stop me from dreaming about a different pair of arms holding me through the night. I doubt it ever will.

THIRTY-SEVEN

Bro-tally Awesome

TEXT CHAIN

OCTOBER 6

Cam: Yo, Mase. What's up, sad sack?

Eli: He's still wallowing. Leave him alone.

Cam: Lame. Either get her back or get over her by getting under someone else.

Jace: Cam, you're absolutely the fucking worst. Mase, please do not take his advice.

Mase: Wouldn't dream of it.

Cam: Are you coming to the game or not?

Mase: Not.

Cam: Figures.

Eli: You're still going with me to that event next week, right?

Mase: Do I have to?

Eli: Yes, dick wad.

Jace: What event?

Cam: And why wasn't I invited?

Eli: A studio party. Cam, you weren't invited because you have zero chill.

Cam: I have chill. I'm the fucking chilliest of the chill.

Jace: If you have to say you're chill, you're not chill. Besides, don't you have a pennant series to worry about?

Mase: I'm working, you dicks. Stop texting me.

Cam: So touchy.

Cam: **GIF of Rizzo from Grease**
Eli: **Laughing Emoji**
Jace: **Laughing Emoji**

October 15

Eli: Dude, Cam. Sorry for the loss, bro. That hurt.

Cam: Yeah, but whatcha gonna do? I can't believe that asshole Rivera charged Thompson and broke his leg. Who does that? Now we are out a catcher. WTF are we going to do next season?

Cam: Tell me something good. How was the party? Did you get laid? Better yet, did Mase get laid?

Mase: Shut the fuck up, kid.

Cam: Kid? Oh damn. Don't poke the grizzly, boys. He's grumpy.

Eli: Yeah, because he saw Emery's brother at the party and ran out of there like his ass was on fire.

Eli: Fucker. You ditched me. Now you owe me another favor.

Jace: Another favor? Shit, Mase, how many do you owe E?

Mase: Apparently 2.

Jace: Yeesh.

Cam: Ha! You deserve to be indebted to the devil, running away like a bitch baby. What did you do, Mase?

Mase: Nothing.

Eli: Exactly.

Jace: I did nothing once. Worst mistake of my life.

Mase: **Mase has notifications silenced**

Eli: I think we hit a nerve.

Jace: Do you think he realizes he'll see her at the wedding?

Cam: He does now. **Laughing Emoji**

THIRTY-EIGHT

Emery

NOVEMBER

WHY ON EARTH DID I let Scarlett talk me into attending this stupid event? There is no way in hell this is a business mix-and-mingle like the event ad said. The way the women are dressed tonight, it looks like they are here looking for a date, not to make business connections. Even the men are dressed like they are ready to go out clubbing.

Tightening my blazer around my waist, I make my way to the bar and order a white wine. I'm going to have one drink and then head out of here. My pajamas, reruns of *The Witcher,* and a bowl of popcorn are calling my name.

Someone bumps their arm against mine as I sip my wine, sending the cool liquid sloshing over the side and down my chin.

"Oh, shit. I'm so sorry." A large hand holds out a few cocktail napkins.

I take them, sopping up the wine. "Can I get that dry-cleaned for you?"

I glance up at the owner of the large hand—prepared to tell him not to worry about it—and lose my train of thought when a pair of brown, almost inky black eyes stare at me with concern, trapping me like a fly in a web. His gaze is intense but not unkind, and the deep rich color reminds me of the night sky, dark and endless. He smiles, and I can't help the way my eyes take him in.

He's tall with long curly black hair, a jaw full of scruff, and dressed in a three-piece black suit that probably cost more than my mortgage payment. He smiles at my obvious checking him out, and damn, if I wasn't still in love with a man with green eyes that pierce my soul, I might let this one take me home for a night.

But I am, and my lady bits only come to life for one man. I can't even come fantasizing about Henry Cavill anymore. Mason has ruined me for all men. The sexy jerk.

At that thought, my brain synapses start working again. "No dry cleaning necessary. I wore black for a reason tonight. I figured at some point, I'd slip out, grab a slice at the pizza parlor on the corner, and eat it on my way to my car."

"That sounds like my kind of plan." He smiles and holds out his hand. "I'm Graham, by the way," he says, introducing himself, and I swear I detect a slight accent.

"Emery."

"Nice to meet you, Emery."

"Nice to meet you, Graham."

"This is going to sound like a line, but I swear it's not. Do you come to events like this often?"

I can't help but chuckle as he tugs on his collar, looking about as comfortable as I am in this place.

"God no. This is the first and last time for me." I look around and lower my voice. "These people look desperate for dates, not connecting about work."

"Thank fuck. I thought it was only me who thought that. When I arrived, some woman with a perfume that made me sneeze ran her fingernail down my chest and asked if I wanted to *do* business with her."

He mock-shivers, and I throw my head back with a laugh.

"Damn, that's bold."

"Too bold for me." He chuckles. It's nice, deep and throaty.

Too bad it still does nothing for me. Not a spark or a butterfly in sight. Absolutely nada.

The bartender approaches, and Graham orders us another round, refusing to let me pay since he spilled my first glass. I accept, and we fall into an easy conversation.

He proceeds to tell me he's only in town for a few months to help take care of his aging grandmother, who recently fell and broke her hip. She's the only relative he has here in the States since his father passed away. His mother lives in Spain, and he's currently working remotely out of Seattle.

I tell him about my job in marketing and events, and how I moved here from the East Coast after my brother came here for boarding school. I keep it light and have a great time with him.

"So, where are you with this pizza thing?" he asks, his thick brow arched and a playful smile on his lips.

I look at my watch. It's only nine-thirty, but I did manage to stay forty-five minutes longer than planned.

"I haven't been able to stop thinking about it since you mentioned grabbing a slice. Mind if I join you?"

Do I want him to join me?

He's been nothing but kind the entire time we've been talking. His eyes have stayed on mine, never dipping to my chest, and he's been genuinely into just talking to me. Nothing more.

Going with my gut, I say, "I can eat a slice."

We grab our coats from the hostess, and I lead him to the pizza place a few blocks away. We end up ordering a whole Margherita and sitting down at a high-top table.

"So, why were you at tonight's event if you're only going to be here for a short time?"

He shrugs. "I was hoping I could snag a client or two while I'm here. My plate is a little empty with it being close to the holidays, and I like to stay busy. What about you?"

"I was forced to attend tonight by my business partner. I think it was a ruse. She's just trying to get me out of the house."

"Ah." He nods his head in understanding. "Recent breakup?"

"Yeah." I sigh. "Am I that obvious?"

"Nah. I just recognize a kindred spirit," Graham says, and it's clear there's a story there.

I don't want to pry, so I take another bite of my pizza.

"So, any chance you want to hang out again?"

"Graham—"

He cuts me off. "As a friend, Emery. I'm new in town, and the only people I've spoken to lately are women over the age of seventy-five. Please, I'm begging you, throw me a bone and be my friend. It would be nice to hang out with someone my age for a change. The last thing I need is to have another meal with a bunch of gossiping old blue-hairs that either try to set me up with their granddaughters or hit on me. Have mercy on me, and have lunch with me this week, please." He bats his thick black lashes at me and pouts his lip, making me snigger.

"Fine, you win. We can have lunch."

"You won't regret it. I'll even pay."

We exchange numbers, and Graham promises to get in touch soon. We end up chatting for another hour before calling it a night.

I might not have gotten business out of the event, but I might have just gained a friend.

❦

"Where are you off to?" Rylann asks as I grab my coat and layer up.

"Um..." I look away, shifting nervously.

What should I say? She's marrying Jace. Mason's brother. I don't want to put her in an awkward position. Not that it matters. Mason and I aren't together. I can do and see whomever I want. But guilt forms like a lead ball in my stomach.

Her face softens as she reaches out and places her hand on my arms. "Emery, it's fine. You're allowed to move on."

"It's not like that. I'm just going to lunch with a friend. He's—"

"He," Scarlett whoops. She's way too excited over nothing, but I don't tell her that. "Go on with your bad self, Em. Where did you meet him?"

"We met at that mixer-event you made me go to last week," I confess.

"What mixer?" Rylann asks, confused.

"It was that networking event at the cool bar in Portland," Scarlett says, looking away.

Rylann gasps, shaking her head. "Scar, you know people only go to those events to hook up."

I knew it was a setup! Freaking Scarlett, butting her nose in my business.

"So?" Scarlett shrugs. "Emery needed a night out, and it looks like it paid off."

"Like I said, it's not like that. Graham is my friend. He's only here temporarily, taking care of his grandmother."

"Graham, huh? Sounds like a hot guy's name. Tell me, is he hot?"

I shrug. "He's ... handsome."

Liar.

Is Graham hot? Yeah. He's everything a girl could want physically, and he just so happens to be a genuinely nice guy too. Our friendship feels like the one I have with Lex, totally platonic and sexless. There are zero sparks flying between us.

"You should bring him to the wedding," Scarlett says.

Rylann gasps again, clutching her throat. "Scarlett," she hisses.

"What? He's new in town. He should at least come to the reception," Scarlett persists like it's no big deal.

Rylann looks over at me with worried eyes, no doubt thinking about Mason, then turns back to Scarlett. They have one of those silent stand-offs, and this time, it's really uncomfortable standing here watching them.

My stomach churns. I knew things were eventually going to get awkward. Not only am I helping her plan her wedding, but she's also forced me to be an honorary bridesmaid.

As it is, every time I see her, I find it hard not to ask about him. What's he doing? How he's been? Any breadcrumb she'd be willing to drop, I'd take. But she's revealed nothing.

As we get closer to her wedding day, anxiety blooms in my stomach, keeping me up at night. I don't want a repeat of what happened last time. The way we hurt each other still haunts me.

I miss Mason like crazy, but I don't think I can handle going through all that again.

Scarlett must win whatever argument they are having because Rylann's shoulders fall. "Jace and I would love for your friend to join us at the reception."

"Thank you, but that's not necessary," I assure her.

While having Graham there as a buffer might help me get through the night, I would never do that to Mason. It would kill me to see him with someone else.

I rush out of the office, not wanting to make things more awkward.

Climbing into bed, I grab my phone and lean against my headboard, and same as I do every night, I scroll through old texts between me and Mason. I know I should have deleted them a long time ago, and rereading them only makes me more sad and lonely, but I can't bring myself to do it. I'm not ready. I don't know if I ever will be. I miss him so damn much, my heart aches.

Our texts disappear as the screen flashes with Chris's name. I accept the video, and his face fills the screen.

"Hey, Chris."

"Hey, Ems."

"How are your classes going?"

A smile spreads across his face, and I already know the answer.

"Going great. My final projects are due the first week of December, then I'm done. I can't freaking wait. Don't worry, I'm still coming to you for Thanksgiving."

After I spilled my guts about Mason and cutting ties with our parents, Chris and I fell asleep. The next day, we laid everything out on the table and managed to find a way to pay for his last semester of school and books. Turns out, my baby bro is resourceful, and had a chunk of money saved from his internships and other side jobs he's picked up. I am so freaking proud of him and the man he is turning into.

"That's great. Want to eat out or stay in?"

"In?" he hedges, no doubt still unsure of my state of mind these days.

I'm slowly getting there, but I definitely don't want to go out. Thanksgiving is for staying home and eating a whole pumpkin pie while watching *The Wizard of Oz* on TV.

"That works for me." I sigh, wishing the holidays would be different, or rather, spent with someone else.

Rylann mentioned going to Los Angeles for the holiday, and I'd bet my paycheck that's where Mason will be too.

"Oh no," Chris interrupts my thoughts.

"What?"

He groans. "I know you're thinking about him. Please tell me you aren't reading your texts again."

"I wasn't." The lie slips easily off my tongue.

"Liar," he hisses.

I am a liar. A huge one. I wish I could stop, but I can't. It's a sickness I'm not ready to get over. Yet. Or any time soon.

"Just drop it," I plead.

"Fine. How was that event last week?"

"Horrible. It *so* wasn't a business thing. Scarlett tricked me. Everyone was there to hook up."

Chris cackles, almost falling off his chair. "Scarlett's awesome. So, did you meet anyone?"

I don't want to tell him about Graham, but I vowed never to keep secrets again. "Yes and no."

He rubs his hands together like a nefarious villain. "Ooh. Spill it, woman."

"I made a friend." I hesitate too long, and Chris catches on.

"Friend or *friend*?" he sings, kissing the camera.

I roll my eyes at him. "Just a friend. He's going through some stuff too. He's only in town temporarily to take care of his grandmother."

Why do I feel the need to keep telling everyone this? Even if I was interested in him, it's no one's business. I'm single as a Pringle and can date whom I want. I shake my head at myself, skipping over the thoughts of dating anyone but Mason.

"Well, I'm proud of you for making friends. That's a huge step for you."

"It is." I smile in appreciation that Chris recognizes my accomplishment because this is a big deal for me.

I don't let people in easily, but with Graham, it was effortless. He's kind of in the same boat as me since he also just got out of a relationship. Though, I think it might be easier for him to move on since his ex moved away for a job in another country. Mason left me because I was an idiot for lying and keeping secrets from him.

"Rylann said I could bring him to the wedding. Is that weird?"

"No. You're allowed to make new friends, man or woman. You're also single as fuck, so if you wanted to date this guy..." He pauses, waiting for me to fill in his name.

"Graham. His name is Graham."

"Oh, let me guess," he snaps, weighing his thoughts. "Older guy, super hot, and rich as fuck."

"How do you do that?"

He grins and pumps his brows. "It's a gift."

"You're ridiculous."

"And yet you wouldn't change a thing about me."

"True. I love you just as you are." I grin back at my baby brother. He really is perfect.

"Okay, Bridget. Back to this whole date thing. I think you should do it."

"Why is that?" I groan.

"Well, if Mason is truly over you, it's a non-issue. But if he isn't over you, he's going to be hella fucking jealous if you show up with another guy."

I roll my eyes at him again. I hope that the old wives' tale isn't true because I am about to get these eyeballs stuck in the back of my head with this conversation.

"It's been months. I'm pretty sure he's moved on."

"Doubt it," he grumbles, covering his mouth with his fist, piquing my interest.

"Why do you say that?"

"Okay, I wasn't going to say anything. *But...*" he sings, exaggerating the word like he usually does when he has gossip or wants to make a show of things. "A couple of weeks ago, I saw him at an event. He was with Eli Miller, who I assume is his brother because they look exactly alike, and as soon as Mason saw me, he peaced out faster than you can come on a ten-inch cock with a vibrator up your ass."

I cringe. "Gross."

Chris cackles, loving that he can still make me uncomfortable. "Gah, I love messing with you."

"I know. But, why didn't you tell me about seeing him before?" I ask, curious about this new development.

"You had finally stopped crying yourself to sleep. I didn't want you backsliding." He gives me a sad smile.

He knows how hard this break up has been on me. I get why he kept it from me, I really do. But I can't just erase my feelings. I truly loved Mason, and a part of me always will.

"If Mason was over you, he wouldn't have run out of the hotel like a fucking coward when he saw me. Also, why didn't you tell me his brother is a hotshot talent agent?"

"Didn't know he was," I answer honestly.

"Jeez, Em. Did you even talk to Mason, or did you just climb up on his dick every chance you got?"

"We talked." Over text and, of course, when I wasn't riding his dick.

"Then why are your cheeks turning red?" he questions my reddening face as I turn away.

No way in hell will I talk about my sex life with my brother. He can share all he wants, but I think of him as my kid, so it's hard for me to get past that.

Thinking back, Mason and I kept our relationship in a bubble. Every text, conversation, and meet-up was about us. The outside world didn't exist when I was with him. Aside from Chris and the one story I told him about my grandfather, I didn't bring up my past and especially not my parents. That would have only led to questions I couldn't answer.

I have a feeling Mason felt the same way. At times, he was just as evasive as I was. He never used names, and the one brother I did meet was in passing, back in January.

"Em, I gotta go. I got a hot date tonight," Chris says, interrupting my runaway brain.

"Alright, Chrisy. Be safe."

"Always. Love you."

"Love you too."

We hang up, and I throw my phone on the pillow beside me, replaying what Chris said about Mason being jealous.

There is no way he'd be jealous of me bringing someone. We haven't been together since July, and I refuse to count our bathroom encounter. That little rendezvous was born out of longing, anger, and desperation, and according to Mason, it meant nothing.

The little devil on my shoulder wonders if he would be green with envy if I showed up with Graham.

Never gonna happen. No way would I bring a date to Rylann's wedding. Picturing him with another woman on his arm makes my gut roil, and tears prickle my eyes. I'd probably die from heartbreak right there, in the middle of the room, if I had to witness that in person. Just thinking about him moving on hurts like a dagger to the heart.

Mason might have walked away from me, but I still love him, and hurting him is the last thing I want to do.

Mason

THANKS-FUCKING-GIVING.

Okay, so maybe I'm grouchier than usual. But this year has been shit. I'm just waiting for another kick to the balls at this point. I'm tired, moody, and I miss my girl.

Scratch that. I have no girl.

In order to avoid thinking about Emery and the fact that we aren't together anymore, I've been overworking myself and my team to the bone. So much so, that they officially banded together to form a mutiny and have refused to take on any more work until next year, and when this project ends next week, I won't have anything to do until February.

I have no idea what I am going to do to keep busy at this point. As soon as I stop whatever I am doing, my mind drifts to her.

The last time I saw her still haunts my dreams.

It's always the same. She's standing there, with tears pouring down her cheeks, reaching for me as I walk away. When I turn back around, I find her in the arms of that blond douche, who kisses her. Without fail, I wake in a cold sweat and an ache in my chest.

When I'm not dreaming about her with him, I'm dreaming about her sweet naked body plastered to mine while I'm balls deep inside her as she comes, screaming my name.

Every. Fucking. Night. It's always her. It's always torture.

I know it's a combination of the anger from being lied to and missing the woman I love. It all started after the way things went down in the bathroom. I haven't felt right since then. Guilt gnaws at my insides for treating her the way I did.

"If you had answered one of my many calls or texts, or even listened to my voicemail..."

I've agonized over our conversation, but I've been too chicken-shit to unblock her and call her. I'm not even sure she'd talk to me at this point. I can't even tell you the number of times I've picked up my phone and pulled up her contact, on the verge of unblocking her to listen to her voicemail, or the number of times I've wanted to pull up her credit card records to see what she's been up to.

I only did that once, right after the Fourth. It didn't give me any information, only that she was back in Pine Hills. Kenzo busted me while I was being a stalker. I was in a bad place, and I missed the fuck out of her. The devil on my shoulder got the better of me when I was alone in the conference room one night. I thought everyone had left, but he came back just as I was pulling her information up in our security program. He didn't say anything to me, but the look of shock on his face shamed me from ever looking up her personal information again.

I had never abused my hacking skills or our program before. I've worked hard at protecting people's identities, not looking up their information.

The doorbell rings before the door opens. Jace's voice travels through the house announcing his arrival.

Fuck.

I don't know how to look at Rylann in the face. She knew instantly what happened in the bathroom when Emery raced out of the bar. I've been avoiding my sister-in-law ever since. I could see the disappointment in her eyes.

I take a deep breath and force myself to remember that Emery lied to me. She had a fiancé the entire time we were together. Probably still does.

Right?

I groan in defeat. My excuses are getting weaker with each passing day. The anger I felt then has dwindled. If she had a fiancé, why did she let me fuck her in the bathroom?

That fucking bathroom. The memory of her quiet moans as I stuffed her full of my cock has the greedy bastard jumping in my slacks. The smell of her sweet pear scent still clings to my nose. I should have a carpal tunnel with the number of times I've jacked off to visions of her in the shower over the last couple of months. Because, of course, my dick only works with visions of her. Her pouty lips, the rasp in her voice as she says my name while she comes on my cock.

Fucking shit.

I throw my head back against the couch and breathe, willing my half-chub to die down.

"Uncle Mills!" Rhys screams right before landing on my chest. He jumps, and his little knee lands right on my balls.

"Oof." That will do it. Mister Hard Dick is completely gone, and just like I predicted, there's that kick in the balls I've been waiting for. "H-hey, buddy."

"I missed you so much." His little arms wrap around my neck as he squeezes.

"Me too. But I promise, next month I don't have work, so I will come visit, okay?"

"Promise?"

"Promise."

"Good, because I have that lame Christmas show again. Will you be there to see me sing again?"

"Wouldn't miss it."

"Yay!" Rhys jumps off my lap and tears out of my parents' living room as Jace and Rylann enter.

My parents are hosting Thanksgiving this year, seeing as Jace and Rylann will be getting married on New Year's Eve and will be hosting Christmas.

I haven't even let my mind drift to their wedding. My brothers were right—I didn't think about Emery being there, which is dumb on my part. She was at the bachelorette party, and she works with Rylann and Scarlett. Of course, she will be at the wedding.

I stand from the couch, thankful Rhys didn't do any permanent damage, and give my brother a hug and slap on the back.

"Jace, good to see you." I check my watch and see that it's almost time for dinner, and I've been sitting in the living room alone for over an hour.

Cameron's and Eli's voices carry from the kitchen as they joke around with Rhys and my dad in the dining room.

"Back at you, brother. It's been too long." He steps back, and my eyes fall to Rylann.

She has so much personality I forget how short she is. My five-month-old niece, Riah, sits on Rylann's hip, looking like a spitting image of her mother.

"Ry, how are you?"

Her lips form a line for a fraction of a second before she puts on a smile. See? Disappointed.

"I'm great, thank you for asking, Mason. You?"

Mason. Ouch.

Fair. I'm not her favorite brother-in-law at the moment.

"I've been better." I decide to go with the truth, hoping it softens Rylann to me. I don't want things to be weird between us.

"Hmm." She hugs me and then holds out Riah for me to take. "Here is your niece. I need to use the restroom."

She rushes out of the room while I hold a drooling Sariah in my arms.

"Sorry, Mase." Jace takes a seat on the couch. "She's a little annoyed with you."

"Yeah, I kind of figured that out."

My niece coos, pulling a smile at my mouth. She's fucking adorable.

"It will pass. She just cares about Emery. That girl has been through a lot." He mumbles the last part under his breath, but it catches my attention.

She's been through a lot.

What the fuck does that mean? Is she hurt? Did something happen with her fiancé? Did she marry him? The questions swirl in my head, but I play it cool.

I can't stop myself from asking, "Is Emery okay?"

"Oh, yeah. She's fine. Nothing for you to worry about." Jace looks away before standing and heads toward the rest of our family in the kitchen, leaving me alone.

Nothing for me to worry about.

Why do those words feel like a bloody knife to my heart? She's the one that broke my heart. Not the other way around.

Because you love her?

My mother calls out that dinner is ready as Riah slaps my cheek with her wet drooly hand, stopping my head and my heart from spiraling.

"Thanks, baby girl. I needed that." I wipe the slobber from my face and blow a raspberry on her cheek.

She giggles, wiggling in my arms like a worm as I make my way to the table.

I place Riah in her highchair, strapping her in, before taking my seat between Cam and Eli, and across from Rhys. The little testicle-kicking turd grins at me, flashing me a gap-toothed smile.

Dad holds up his wine glass. "Before we eat, I just want to say a few things. First, boys, thank you for being here. Times are changing, but it means a lot to your mother and me that you spend the holiday with us. Second, let us welcome the new addition to the Miller clan, Sariah. My sweet girl, you complete us."

"For now," Jace not-so-subtly whispers into Rylann's ear, making her blush and the rest of us groan.

"Heard that," Dad says with a chuckle. "Rylann, I know I said this last year, but sweetheart, thank you for making Jace happy and bringing Rhys into our life. Rhys, my number one grandson, I love you, kiddo."

"Love you too, Granddad!" Rhys shouts.

"Happy Thanksgiving!"

We all raise our glasses and get to eating.

"Gee, Pop, what about the rest of us?" Cameron asks, sipping his wine.

"Find a woman and give me some grandbabies, and you'll get a special shoutout."

"Pass." Cameron piles food on his plate like the glutton he is, hoarding all the potatoes.

"What about you, Eli, any prospects?" Mom asks. The poor woman is obviously tired of her sons being single.

She and my father met and fell in love in college. They've been together ever since. My dad always said he knew instantly that my mom was the one, and as she looks across the table at him, I understand. There is so much love between them. True, unconditional love.

I thought I had that with Emery. I thought she was different. Joke's on me.

"Too busy with work, Ma. Maybe one day." If I hadn't seen Eli in action, I would call bullshit, but he truly is one of the hardest-working guys out there. He's built something great with his business partner. He takes his work seriously, and it's nice to see a different side of him while he's working.

With us, Eli's the jokester, always keeping it light while he watches everything, always knowing more than he lets on. At work, he uses those skills to his advantage. Eli's hard-working and determined to make a name for himself and his clients. It doesn't hurt that everyone and their mother owes him a favor. He uses his connections in Hollywood to his advantage. He's good at connecting people and getting what he wants. It feeds his need to help people, and whether he likes to admit it or not, he's a giver. He's always been that way.

I probably owe him more than two favors, but he has never actually asked for anything in return. I doubt he ever will.

"You aren't getting any younger. You don't want to be an old man when your kids are born," Dad pipes in, and Rylann chuckles.

"Hush, Sunshine," Jace huffs. If we go by his earlier remark, that must be a hot topic for them.

Lucky fucker.

"We get it, Dad. We will try to bring home women for you to meet next year." Eli sips his beer. "Maybe one of them will want to date you."

"Boy, I'm going to kick your—" He looks over at Rhys, who has a mouth full of mashed potatoes. "Butt. You know your mother is the only woman I need."

He shoots Mom a wink. He and Eli go back and forth as I drown them out and push the food on my plate around.

"Mason? You're awfully quiet over there," Mom says, sipping her wine.

I look up, and all eyes are on me.

"Yeah, Mason. Why are you so quiet?" Rylann pipes up.

I look over at her, a little shocked that she's calling me out. I think she might be a little more than annoyed about what happened with Emery.

"Oh damn." Eli coughs.

"Ry's pulling out the big guns." Cameron claps his hands and rubs them like he's ready for a show. Not gonna happen. "Go, sis."

Rylann looks at me, eyebrows raised. "I'm not pulling out anything."

"Like, Jace, am I right?" Cameron says, laughing at his own joke.

Jace chokes on his food. "Hey, leave me out of this."

"I'm not quiet. Just nothing to report." I shrug and shovel food into my mouth.

I don't want to talk about my relationship status or lack thereof. I thought things would work out with Emery, but they didn't.

Rylann harrumphs and goes back to eating, but of course, Cameron can't let shit go. He has to keep poking.

"Really? Nothing to report? No girlfriend at all?"

"I have a girlfriend," Rhys chimes in, saving me from shoving my kid brother's face into the gravy bowl and drowning him.

"Oh yeah? What's her name?"

"Sadie, duh. She's my bestest friend, and she's a girl."

The table erupts into laughter. I doubt if Levi were here, he'd think this was funny. He's a protective dad when it comes to his girls.

"You're right, kiddo." Jace ruffles his head. "Make sure I'm there when you tell Uncle Levi about your girlfriend."

"Okay." He shoves a huge piece of turkey in his mouth, ending the conversation.

We all slip into talk about Cameron's teammate who broke a leg. He's worried about who management will bring in to take Thompson's place. He's been the team's catcher since Cameron started in the league, and building a rapport like theirs takes time.

After a while, I zone out, and my mind drifts back to Emery.

Is she in L.A. with Chris or back in Oregon? Is she with her fiancé? What the hell did Jace mean when he said she's been through a lot? And the question that bothers me the most …

Why does it feel like I'm missing a huge piece of the story?

FORTY

Emery

DECEMBER

I FINISH PUTTING THE final touches to the center pieces for tonight's dinner, ignoring my friend's question. He knows about my and Mason's story, and how Mason turned out to be Rylann's soon-to-be brother-in-law, which is still a little shocking.

"Are you ready for tonight?" Graham asks again.

When the florist called to say their delivery van broke down and the other wasn't nearby to deliver the order, I panicked. Luckily, I remembered Graham had rented a truck while he was here. He was quick to answer my call, easily offering to help me out. As a thank you, Jace and Rylann invited him to stay and join us tonight, as well as tomorrow for the wedding reception, effectively turning him into my date, after all.

Graham fit in quickly with Jace, Levi, and Rylann's dad, as well as with Rhys as they all helped set up the room, while Rylann nursed Riah and Scarlett dealt with the twins.

I don't know what I would have done without my friend. I'm just relieved this won't be a problem tomorrow. We used a different florist—one closer to the venue—for the wedding center pieces.

"Well?" Graham asks for the third time, following me as I double-check the table setting's centerpieces for the hundredth time.

"I think so," I say, evenly, desperately trying to hide how nervous I am about tonight.

Twisting the vase this way and that, I dare not look Graham in the eye. He'll know I'm lying through my teeth. He's good at reading people—it's one of the many things I find endearing about him, and I'm glad to have formed a friendship with him.

"It's no big deal, right? He's here for the wedding, just like I am."

I adjust the candles again. I haven't been able to get the seed Chris planted in my brain out. Would Mason really act jealous? Is he really not over me yet? At the thought of him not being over me, butterflies flutter in my stomach and my pulse speeds up.

"You're a terrible liar, Emery. It's okay to be nervous to see him. Things were complicated when you two ended," he says.

Last week we met up for dinner, and over a bottle of wine, we ended up spilling about our exes. He's been supportive, helping me to understand where Mason is coming from while also understanding my decision to keep the fake engagement a secret. Graham has become a wonderful friend. He's one of the good ones, that's for sure.

Too bad he doesn't make your nether regions tingle.

Ugh. Stupid brain. And traitorous hussy of a vagina who only weeps for one man. The same man I am currently freaking out about seeing tonight.

I don't want a repeat of what happened on Labor Day weekend. My clit pulses at the memory of Mason taking me in the bathroom and pushing me up against the wall. Sex with Mason was never the problem. Our problem was opening up to each other. We talked constantly, but it was always about the present, never about our past or our families. In hindsight, we both held back.

"I know." I sigh again, finally making eye contact with Graham. "It's not just that. It's something Chris said that's bothering me."

"What did he say?" Graham grabs the cardboard box the vases were in and breaks it down, waiting for me to answer.

I don't know what it is about him, but he's easy to talk to. Graham has such a calming presence. He's never judged me or looked at me in a way that made me feel like his friendship was anything but genuine.

Even though Graham wasn't supposed to be here, in a way I'm glad he is, but it's also got me freaking out. This is all Chris's fault, with his stupid comment about Mason being jealous of my date. I can't get the idea out of my head. What if he's right?

"Chris said that if Mason acts jealous because you're with me, then he's not over me and is probably still in love with me." I wince, noticing how ridiculous that sounds as soon as I say it.

"He's not wrong."

My jaw flops open, and my friend throws his head back and laughs, closing my mouth.

"Us men are simple creatures. There's a reason we are called cavemen."

"But—"

"But nothing. Chris is right. If Mason takes one look at me and wants to rip my head off, you've got your answer. If he's a smart man, he'll beg for forgiveness and come crawling back."

I jerk back at his remark. "I don't want him to come crawling back."

"You're cute when you lie, my friend."

Okay, fine. I might be lying a little. Just a smidge. Okay, a lot.

I miss Mason like crazy, but that doesn't mean I want him back. Right?

He hurt me when he walked away without talking to me, ghosting me for weeks, only to fuck me and tell me it meant nothing. He left me feeling used—a feeling I've felt all my life—and I'm through with being made to feel unloved. He walked away from me without a backward glance.

As much as I love him and possibly want to forgive him, losing him without a word was one of the hardest things I've ever had to endure. I don't want to go through that again.

Graham knowingly squeezes my shoulder, giving me a soft smile, empathetic to the emotional turmoil I'm wading through.

"It will work out, my friend. I have a good feeling about it." He walks away, leaving me with my thoughts.

Do I want Mason back? More importantly, does Mason want me back?

The butterflies in my stomach swirl again, and I'm not sure whether or not I want to puke. I guess I'll just have to wait and see how tonight plays out.

FORTY-ONE

Mason

ELI, CAMERON, AND I arrive at the restaurant a little late. Our flight from L.A. was delayed taking off, and we barely had enough time to check into the inn—a cute little place in the mountains, where they will get married—before hightailing it here for dinner.

As we enter the restaurant, the sound of clinking dishes, loud conversations, and the scent of Mexican food assault my senses. My stomach rumbles, and I don't know if it's from being hungry or nervous to see Emery. As it turns out, she helped Rylann with the wedding planning. I'm not surprised, that's the direction she wanted to move in with the company, and both Rylann and Scarlett agreed to support her.

I head straight to the bar. I need a fucking drink if I'm going to make it through tonight. I have been a mess, confused by Jace's comments at Thanksgiving. He wasn't wrong when he said I shouldn't worry about her. Emery and I aren't together. But hearing it out loud? Well, it didn't sit well with me. I've had this uneasy feeling since then.

I always knew it was the wrong move walking away from Emery, but lately it feels like more than that. It feels like I might have made the biggest mistake of my life. Since Thanksgiving, my dreams have morphed into what feels like a bad omen. Night after night, I dream that Emery and I are holding hands, walking through a crowd, when someone bumps into me and I lose my grip on her.

When I turn around to find her, people get in the way and she slips further out of my reach. I wake up in a cold sweat, with my heart beating a million miles an hour and a crippling pain in my chest.

The bartender approaches and I shake off my unease, ordering a gin and tonic. Cameron and Eli do the same, ordering beers, before we make a beeline for our parents.

They've been here since Christmas, and I have a sneaking suspicion they might relocate soon. They love being with their grandchildren as often as possible. My parents are now retired and have been traveling up here a lot, and with them growing closer to Rylann's parents, Rita and Ryan, it seems like their move is inevitable.

My stomach groans again when I think about Rita and her tamales. Damn, those are good. Okay, so maybe I'm hungrier than I thought.

I lean in and kiss my mom's cheek, greeting her, "Momma."

"You three are late," she scolds, giving each of us a hug and kiss on the cheek.

Cameron points at me and Eli. "It's their fault."

"The plane was delayed." Eli shoves Cameron's gigantic frame, barely budging him.

"Sorry, Ma. We had to check into the inn and change before coming here," I add.

I know she's just giving us grief, but it's funny how we—three grown-ass men—just resorted to blaming and pleading our case just as quickly.

"Fine. You're excused." She chuckles, shaking her head at our antics.

She loves giving us a hard time. It seems fair, seeing as we put her through hell with our constant bickering, the endless number of sports practices, and all the other stuff moms have to put up with raising four boys. She should get an award for all she's done to raise us.

My dad joins us as we all fall into easy conversation. Jace and Rylann join us, as does my main man, Rhys. He looks fucking adorable tonight, dressed in a black suit and gray shirt that matches Jace's.

I lift him up in my arms, not tired of holding him yet. He's seven going on eighteen, but he still loves getting doted on by his uncles, and we very much love to oblige.

"How are you doing tonight, buddy? Are you having fun?" I ask him.

"Totally. Mom said I can have three desserts today." He holds up his fingers, completely excited about his reward.

"That's awesome. How did you earn that?"

"I helped clean up Sariah's messy playroom, and I helped set up the flowers with Graham."

Who the fuck is Graham?

Cameron taps my shoulder and points behind me. I turn, and all the air is sucked from my lungs.

Standing across the room, wearing a sexy-as-fuck charcoal wide-legged pantsuit and a skin-tight black top that shows the tops of her full breasts, is Emery. She's stunning. Perfect.

"Who's that guy with Emery?" Cam whispers.

I slowly tear my eyes away, and notice a man with black hair and black eyes standing at her side. He says something to her, and she chuckles.

"That's Graham," Rhys interjects, oblivious to the fact that my heart just fell through my ass.

I lower Rhys to the ground and he runs off, no doubt in search of his *girlfriend*.

She brought a date? To my brother's wedding? I don't know if I'm more angry that she's moving on or that she had the audacity to bring a fucking date with her.

He places his hand on the small of her back, and it makes me want to walk over there and rip his fucking arm off.

Scarlett sidles up beside me. "I see you saw Graham. He's Emery's *friend* and new to town. He was kind enough to offer up his truck, and help us bring all the flowers and decorations for tonight. He's hot, right?"

Friend or *friend*?

"Short Stack," Levi growls at his wife.

She rolls her eyes. "Don't worry, babe, he's not as hot as you. You're the hottest."

"I know you're bullshitting me, but I'm going to take it anyway." Levi kisses her.

I turn away, sipping my drink. I knew I was going to have to see Emery, but a little warning about her bringing a date would have been nice.

I can't fucking take it anymore. I've been watching Emery like a creep all night, internally seething every time I've watched that douche-canoe lay a finger on her. Every molecule in my body is screaming, *Mine,* while simultaneously begging me to rush over there, throw her over my shoulder, and carry her away.

I place my drink on the bar and walk out of the private dining room Jace and Rylann have reserved for tonight's dinner, towards the bathroom. I need a breather and to get my fucking head straight. Gin, confusion, anger, hurt, and longing make for a dangerous mix.

As I approach the restrooms, I hear muffled moaning and the distinct sound of pounding coming from behind the door of the ladies' room.

"That's it, Sunshine, take my cock."

I freeze at the familiar voice.

What the fuck? No, it can't be. I edge a little closer towards the bathroom.

"That's a good girl. You like that?" I hear the voice say, confirming my suspicions, and quite honestly, my nightmares.

My brother and my soon-to-be sister-in-law are going at it in the bathroom during the middle of their rehearsal dinner.

"Yes, yes, right there. Don't stop, Ace."

"I can't wait to fuck you as my wife tomorrow," he grunts.

Oh hell. I groan. I feel like a fucking pervert standing out here, listening to this shit. I move away from the hall but block the path. I can't let anyone else hear this, especially not my nephew. That would scar him for life. Fuck, it's scarring me. I'm going to need therapy after this.

My aunt, Marie—Dad's sister—approaches the hall, and I rush over to block her path. "Hi, Aunt Marie. You're looking spectacular tonight." I lean in and give her a hug, just as a loud bang comes from the bathroom behind me, drawing her attention.

"What's going on, Mason?" Her head inclines toward the bathrooms behind me.

"Oh, just a little problem with the pipes. Clogged toilet. The plumbers are fixing it right up. I'll come get you when it's back in working order," I say loudly, trying to mask the sounds behind me.

"Thank you, dear. You're such a good boy." She pats my cheek and ambles her way back towards the private room as another crash echoes behind the closed door.

What the hell are they doing in there making all that goddamn noise?

Cameron struts his way over to me, and I let out another groan. Now, I'm going to have to block this nosy fucker. I should just let everyone hear what's going on.

Walk away.

My feet stay rooted to the floor. I can't move. As much as listening to the two of them go at it makes my ears burn, I can't let Jace get caught by our extended family.

"Fuck yes."

I roll my eyes and the muffled grunts. Apparently, my brother is a fucking animal. Who knew?

Okay, I get it. If I still had the woman I loved, I'd probably be doing everything I could to get inside her all the time too.

A vision of Em, bent over the sink while I slam into her tight body from behind as she screams my name pops into my head, and my dick perks up.

"Hey, Mase." Cameron tries to walk past me, but I step in his path. "I gotta piss. Move the fuck out of the way." He shoves me, but I don't budge. "Why are you blocking, bro?"

Just then, we both hear Rylann moan, "Jace. I'm about to—"

"Not yet, Sunshine. You come when I tell you." A resounding slap can be heard through the door.

"Yes, sir," Rylann pants.

My face burns, and I wish the floor would open up and swallow me so I didn't have to hear this.

Cameron looks at me, eyes wide in shock. He points behind me and stammers, "Is-Is that...?"

"Yup." I nod.

He lowers his voice. "And they're ..."

"Yup."

"Am I dreaming? Is this a nightmare?" He shakes his head in disbelief.

"Nope. Believe it, Cam. It's happening."

"Now, Sun. Now, you can come on my cock," Jace growls.

We hear a dainty groan and then silence.

Cam looks at me, stunned, before we both burst out laughing. This place really needs to get better soundproofing. The walls and doors are pretty much paper-thin.

"Holy shit." Cam tries to cover his laugh to prevent the naughty little expeditionists from hearing they got caught.

"I know," I agree.

Another few minutes pass before the door opens, and a very flushed and freshly fucked Rylann steps out of the bathroom. She freezes at the sight of us and almost gets bowled over by Jace.

"Uh, h-hey guys," she stammers.

"What the fuck are you doing out here, lurking outside the bathroom door like a couple of damn perverts?" Jace growls.

Fist to my mouth, hiding my smile, I say, "Just keeping your guests away while you defile your fiancée in the bathroom."

"Loudly," Cameron adds with a cackle.

"Ohgod, ohgod, please no." Rylann shakes her head like maybe if she does it hard enough, the last few minutes will have disappeared.

Sorry, Ry. It happened, and you're never going to live it down. I don't tell her that, though. She knows how us brothers are, especially Cameron.

Jace wraps his arms around her and tilts her chin up, looking her in the eyes. "Shh," he soothes her.

She visibly calms, her shoulders dropping as she regulates her breathing. It's a beautiful thing to watch, their connection. No wonder they can get through even the worst of shit. You can literally feel their bond in the air as they come together and the world around them falls away.

"You okay now?" She nods, and he kisses her cheek. "Good. Now go back inside, and I'll be there in a minute. I just need to beat the shit out of my brothers first."

"Okay," she whispers.

Rylann avoids eye contact with me and Cam, and turns around. Before she can take a step, Jace pinches her ass, and she spins on her heels. Her earlier embarrassment melts away as she glares at him—fire burning in her eyes— and slaps him in the chest.

"I told you messing around in the bathroom was a bad idea."

Jace plants a wet kiss on her, rendering her speechless. When he pulls back, she sways on her feet.

"Fucking my gorgeous fiancée is always a good idea."

"You're so bad. Why do I let you get away with this every time we're here?" She fluffs her hair, mumbling to herself as she walks away.

"I love you too, Sunshine," Jace calls after her.

Over her shoulder, she smiles and blows a kiss at him as she keeps on walking.

Cameron starts to slow-clap just as Eli appears in the hall.

"What's going on?" Eli asks, brows crunched.

"Oh, nothing. We just caught the end of Jay and Ry's live sex show, that's all," Cameron snickers.

Jace points a finger at him. "I'll kill you, kid"

"Seriously?" Eli asks, completely shocked.

"Yes!" Cam and I howl at the same time.

"Ry? The short little thing that wears yellow 24/7, sweet as pie, mother to your son and daughter lets you bang her in the bathroom at a Mexican restaurant?"

Jace visibly puffs with pride but tries to cover it with false irritation. "That's none of your fucking business."

That's a yes. And if Rylann's mumbles are to go by, I bet it's happened before and is most likely the reason the rehearsal dinner is being held here too.

"Damn. I'm jealous." Eli says.

Me too.

Jace growls.

"Not about listening, you idiot. That you have a girl who loves you and is willing to have sex with you in a public bathroom. You're a lucky fucking bastard."

"I am." Jace grins, preening like a peacock. The cocky asshole.

"I'm more impressed," Cameron pipes in. We all look at him, and he shrugs. "What? I am. Way to go, big bro. I didn't think you had it in you. You're the true stallion. Straight up animal. Fucking in public..." Cam shakes his head in proud disbelief as he pats Jace's chest with pride.

Now that Cameron mentions it, I'm impressed too. I used to visit them often enough to know how much they go at it. I just didn't know that it extended outside of the bedroom.

"Okay, enough of this. Thanks for the assist while I spent time with my woman. If you ever repeat this story to anyone and embarrass my wife..." He points at all of us. "No one will find your bodies. I will fucking bury you. All. Of. You. Understand?"

Cam, Eli, and I burst out laughing. No way are we going to let them live this down.

Jace ignores us and smooths down his dress shirt beneath his blazer as he walks away, leaving us laughing in his wake, more than a little shocked and awed at what just transpired in the bathroom.

"He's my hero," Cameron says, making his way to the bathroom.

God, he's ridiculous. But he's not wrong. Jace is a fucking hero. I want what he has with Rylann. I want to be so wrapped in the person I'm with that I can't keep my hands off of her.

Their relationship didn't come easy, my inner voice reminds me.

It's true, Jace and Rylann went years without each other before finding themselves back where it all had started, and they reconnected. Then, when everything came to a head, they still managed to find their way to be together.

Anything worth having is worth fighting for, right?

The old quote gives me pause. I had it, but I didn't fight for it. I ran away and fucked it all up. Maybe if I fought with Emery instead and listened to her version of the story, she wouldn't have slipped through my fingers. Now, the only woman I have ever loved is with another man.

"Don't look too sad, Mase. It doesn't look like Airport Girl is too serious about her date," Eli says, reading my thoughts.

"Don't call her that," I grouse.

"Fine. Emery doesn't look interested in her date."

"And you know that... how?"

He shrugs. "Call it a hunch."

Eli gives me a wink as Cameron walks out of the bathroom and takes his place.

"See you out there, Mase." Cameron leaves me standing alone in the hallway with my jumbled thoughts.

Pulling out my phone, I slide it open and bring up my contacts list. Scrolling to her name, I stare at her picture icon. It might be tiny, but I know the picture well. I have it memorized. I took it when she visited me in L.A. that first time and we took a drive along the coast. She was staring out at the sun setting behind the ocean, the light bathing her in soft oranges and reds.

I knew then that I loved her. The words were on the tip of my tongue, but I was just too scared to tell her. Her walls were still up, and I didn't want to freak her out and have her run away from me.

Irony at its finest when I'm the one who ended up running away in the end.

Now, her pictures are hidden away in a folder on my phone because I couldn't bear to hit delete. I've pulled them up to scroll through a few times when missing her felt unbearable. Sitting in an empty hotel room will do that to you. When memories of the woman you love haunt you.

I remember every moment. Every sound of her sweet laughter. Every twinkle of her eye as she smiled up at me. Every video call that would end with me wanting to be near her.

After listening to my brother in the bathroom with the love of his life and thinking about how far they have come, it has me wondering. Could that be me and Emery? Can we get past this?

It sure as fuck won't be easy.

In the end, I'm pretty sure my choice to walk away did more damage to her, to me, to us. We've left too much unsaid and unresolved. Even if what Eli said is right and she's not into her date, do I stand a chance at getting her back?

I royally fucked up.

But I can't keep going like this. I still love her, and if there's even the slightest hope, I need to take a chance and find out before it truly is too late for us.

Doing one of the many things I should have done months ago, I unblock her number. I wish I could see all the text messages she must have sent come in, but they don't load. A small part of me is glad I can't read them. Her missed messages would only dig the knife I buried in my chest deeper.

Pulling up my voicemail, I check under blocked messages, and sitting there—like she said—is one new voicemail.

Clicking heels on the tile floor have my attention, and I shove my phone in my pocket. My eyes catch on the black stilettos that will forever star in my dreams as they stride my way. I can't even tell you the number of times I've dreamt of those heels digging into my ass as strong thighs wrapped around my waist. How many times I've dreamt about the woman walking towards me.

Emery's lips are stained burgundy, and that juicy bottom lip of hers is trapped between her teeth. I wish I could wipe the look of apprehension that adorns her beautiful face as she approaches me.

"Hi." She gives me a soft smile that makes my heart pump faster.

"Hi." I shift nervously, rubbing the scruff on my chin. Fighting the urge to dig my hands in her hair and bring her lips to mine, I clench my fists at my sides.

We stand there, staring at each other as the temperature of the air turns up and hot sparks flicker to life. She breaks the connection first, and my chest aches.

She looks behind me at the door to the women's room. "I better hurry. It's almost time for dinner."

"Yeah, okay."

I move out of her way, but before I can stop myself, I grab her wrist—the fire in my stomach roaring to life at her touch—and yank her body to mine.

Her pulse strums against my thumb as she stares up at me. A million questions flicker in her eyes, questions I don't have the answers for yet, so instead, I crush my mouth to hers in a bruising kiss, catching her off guard.

Her lips part, and I don't waste time diving my tongue into her mouth. Her sweet taste explodes on my tongue as I lose myself in her.

I know it's a dick move—she's here with someone else—but fuck, I've missed her. The feel of her body against mine. The way her lips mold to mine like they were made for only me to kiss.

I deepen the kiss, twirling our tongues together, greedily taking full advantage of the way her body still responds to me. Her addicting vanilla and pear scent surrounds me, and my cock springs to life for her.

Sorry, no can do, buddy.

I just need a little taste because I know I only have a matter of seconds before she realizes that she's kissing me back or someone else sees us.

Breaking away from her, I release my hold on her head and step back. Her lips are puffy, and her lipstick is smeared from our kiss in the way I like. She looks absolutely dazed, and completely and utterly stunning.

Emery looks at me with wide eyes. "What was that?"

Everything. I love you. I'm mad at you. I miss you. You hurt me. I don't care if you're with someone else. You're mine. Always will be mine.

Instead I shrug, playing it off, because I honestly don't know what that was, only that I want to do it again, and a million other things to her body.

"You look gorgeous tonight, baby doll."

Her eyes flutter closed at the use of my nickname for her, and it brings a grin to my face. She still feels something for me, and it's not all hate and anger.

Hope flickers.

The last thing I want is for her to question that kiss, to regret it. Before she opens her eyes, I leave her standing outside the bathroom door. I don't have a lot of control over my emotions right now, and I don't want to do something stupid, like fuck her in the bathroom.

Fucking in the bathroom must be a Miller kink.

I chuckle to myself and make my way back to the dining room, replaying our kiss. The moment her lips touched mine, everything inside me clicked into place. A stolen moment never felt so right. The way her body instantly melted into mine, like butter over pancakes. It was exactly what I needed.

I know what I have to do—listen to her voicemail.

I think about Jace and Rylann, and the struggles they went through to get to where they are now. They are so happy and in love. You would never know their road was bumpy as fuck.

My thoughts swirl and clash as a storm of emotions rolls through me. I don't know what my next steps are beyond listening to her message, but it's the first step to getting there.

Because one thing is for sure: I'm still head over heels in love with Emery. Without her, a piece of me has been missing and I want it back.

I want *her* back.

And if I love her as much as I think I do, and if she loves me too, then we can get past anything.

AFTER MY LITTLE RUN in with Emery, I gave her space. I tried my best not to stare at her—or glare daggers at her date—for the rest of dinner. Not that I was successful.

My eyes can find her in a crowded room without trying. She's the beacon calling me home to shore, and I can spot her light from a mile away.

I know I'm hers too. The hairs on the back of my neck stood at attention under her watchful eyes throughout the night. But every time I tried to make eye contact, she'd look away. It took all of my willpower not to take her into my arms, sweep her off her feet, and take her away so we could be alone. To talk, of course.

As much as I want to run my hands and lips over every inch of her body, show her just how much I missed her, I need to figure some shit out. The state I left her in by the restrooms probably confused her more.

No doubt, she's feeling whiplashed by my behavior—or at least. I hope she is because I sure as hell am.

Our encounter at the bachelor party didn't end well. I lied through my teeth when I told her the sex was a mistake. I let my anger and frustration—my longing—cloud my vision. I implied we were a mistake, and that couldn't be further from the truth. Nothing about us or our relationship was a mistake.

Months of no contact with her have gotten me nowhere. My initial anger with her has dissipated and has been replaced with a deep yearning, and her absence has left a gaping hole in my life and my heart, and I'm the one that put it there.

I'm a fucking idiot for thinking I could walk away from her and feel nothing.

I unlock the door to my room and step inside, locking it behind me.

The inn Jace and Rylann booked for their wedding is pretty cool. It's nestled north of their hometown, an area that is up and coming, and teeming with vineyards. The property is the perfect reflection of them as a couple. The place itself has history and charm, and the interior has been completely modernized. It's the same inn they stayed in when they went on their babymoon, so there is a lot of sentimental meaning here.

Looking around the room, I'm reminded of the weekend Emery and I locked ourselves away in the hotel suite, too wrapped up in each other to leave.

I chuck my phone on the bed, strip off my clothes, and march into the bathroom to turn on the shower. When the water is warm, I slide under the hot water, letting it ease the tension in my back.

It's been a day, and I still have a lot to figure out before I see Emery tomorrow. My heart does a foreign leap in anticipation of seeing her beautiful face again. She looked breathtaking tonight in that sexy-as-fuck pantsuit.

The mere thought of her brings my dick to life. But after seeing her tonight, on the arm of another man, I can't bring myself to fuck my palm to visions of her like I usually do. I know I kissed her—and she kissed me back—and no matter how right it felt in the moment, it was wrong as fuck for me to put her in that position.

Ignoring my hardening cock, I wash up and hop out of the shower. After drying off, I rush to put on a pair of boxers, brush my teeth, and take a seat on the edge of the bed. The need to listen to the voicemail eclipses all else.

Grabbing my cell, I slide it open and tap on my messages. My heart pounds like a jackhammer in my chest, and I hesitate. Watching her with another man tonight fucking killed me.

That kiss? Fuck. I will go to the grave with that kiss on my mind and her taste on my mouth.

The phone in my hand weighs a hundred pounds. Everything hangs on what this voicemail says. Every word can either send me running to her, or from her.

Or does it?

Do I hate that she lied to me? Hell fucking yes. I'm angry and hurt, but that doesn't mean I stopped loving her. I've tried to push my feelings away by drowning myself in work. It's done fuck all to help me. I think about her every minute of every day. That is the crux of it all. She is all I think about. No matter how angry I am at her, I still want her. I still love her.

I hit play.

"Mase, it's me, Emery. I mean, of course you know that." She pauses and hiccups, which makes her chuckle to herself.

Is she drunk? That's not like her; she hates drinking more than a glass or two of wine.

"Anyway, I don't know if you're getting my messages or not, but I need to get this out. I-I need you to hear me when I say I am so sorry. You have no idea how sorry I am. I know I hurt you, and maybe you're right for walking away from me. You don't deserve to be lied to. It was never my intention to lie."

Her voice wavers, and I can picture her trying to hold back tears as she speaks.

"I told you from the beginning that I didn't want to get into a relationship with you. I tried to say it was about the distance. But that wasn't true. It was because I was trapped. For years, my parents used Chris's safety against me and tried to manipulate me into marrying someone I didn't love. You need to know that Lex—that's his name,

by the way—sure as hell didn't love me. We had a deal—pretend to accept the marriage terms, and eventually, we would get out of the arrangement. He'd go his way and I'd go mine.

"His parents are like mine—manipulating assholes that care more about the family business than their children. But of course, nothing ever goes my way, and Lex went rogue on me. He fucked everything up. I swear, I didn't know what he was doing behind my back. Anyway, it's a long story and not really mine to tell, except that he's in love with someone else too.

"Just like I am. I-I love you, Mason. With every fiber of my soul. I love you. I hate that you walked away. I hate that you won't talk to me. I hate that you're gone. I miss you so much, it's killing me." Her voice cracks, breaking my heart.

I close my eyes as tears cloud my vision. Her confession rips away at the narrative I created in my head about her so-called fiancé.

"I just... I was trying to get myself out of that situation on my own. I thought that if I could extricate myself from the agreement, my parents ... that life, everything would be fine. We could move on and be happy, and the past would be behind me. I had just finished calling off the whole farce with my parents when you showed up. I swear it was never real. The engagement with him was fake from the start. Even his girlfriend knew it was fake."

She sighs and her voice turns somber, pulling at the thick rope wrapped around my chest.

"There is only one man I love. You. You're the only man I've ever loved and will always love. I swear, everything I told you was the truth. Yes, I kept this secret from you, but I didn't do it to hurt you. It's the opposite, actually. I did it to protect you. To protect us. I didn't want to taint what we had. It was so real ... and beautiful. It was everything to me. You are everything to me. I didn't want you to know how horrible, controlling, and mean my parents truly are. They are the worst kind of people, and I know this is going to sound stupid, but I didn't want you to know I came from them.

"I am nothing like them. Nothing. All I ever wanted from you was the love you gifted me. You made me feel love for the first time in ... forever. You made me whole again. I felt it from the start but was too scared to admit it, and now it's too late. I've lost you."

She sniffles, no longer able to hide her tears on the other side of the line, pouring her heart out. My strong girl is breaking, and I did nothing to help. All I did was inflict more pain on her.

"I love you. I know that's not enough for you to forgive me. I accept that. I just... I guess I wanted you to know how I feel. I hope you find what you're looking for. I want you to be h-happy, even if it's not with m-me. I love you. Goodbye, Mason."

The message ends as Emery's watery voice evaporates into deafening silence.

Dropping the phone to the floor, I drop my chin to my chest. The way she sounded, so ... so vulnerable and broken, shatters me to my very soul.

Standing up, I pace the room, pulling at my hair, my cheeks wet from tears. Regret slices through me, and I double over in pain. Anger burns me from the inside out.

I was so stupid. I did this to her, to us. She might have lied, but I'm the one that broke us, and I hate myself for hurting her. For walking away without a word. For not letting her explain. I should have heard her out. Of course she wasn't fucking around behind my back. She would never.

She deserved to tell me the full story. I owed her that much, for her and myself. If I hadn't let my past dictate my future or had been so stubborn, we wouldn't have lost the last few months.

And now? Now, she's with someone else.

One look at her with another man, and I saw red. I wanted to smash his fucking teeth in for touching my woman.

"Fuck, fuck, fuck!"

What the fuck did I do?

Panic takes its chokehold on me as my heart rate spikes and my breathing gets choppy. I need to get the hell out of here and get a drink.

Throwing on a pair of sweatpants and a hoodie, I rush out the door, with a million questions running through my mind and the soul-crushing knowledge that I may have lost Emery forever.

How will she ever forgive me for abandoning her when she needed me?

How can I ever forgive myself for the way I've treated her?

My nose tingles from the cold, and the numbness starts to spread to the rest of my appendages. Eyes closed, I burrow into my hoodie, trying to find an ounce of warmth.

I've been sitting outside by the fire, drinking and thinking. A deadly combination, and it's resulted in me sitting here for hours, mentally beating myself up over my choices.

I knew Emery was a selfless person, but I never realized to what extent. The fact that she would sacrifice her happiness for her brother amazes me, and yet I get it. I would do anything for any one of my brothers, and they for me. So, of course, Emery did what she had to do to take care of Chris. He's her brother, her best friend, and her only family that loves her unconditionally.

The sound of gravel crunching underfoot has my ears perking, but I don't bother opening my eyes. I knew someone would find me eventually.

"Mason, what the fuck are you doing out here, man?" Eli calls out behind me, his voice breaking the silence I've buried myself in.

"Go away," I mumble, my words slightly slurred. I should open my eyes, but I don't want to. I'm tired as fuck.

"Shit, are you drunk?"

"Nah," I slur again.

Wait? Am I drunk? I slowly force my eyes open and regret it instantly. They are gritty and dry, and the morning light burns my retinas, blurring my vision.

Eli takes the seat next to me, the wood creaking under his weight as he scoops up the half empty bottle of gin by my feet.

I had a hard time trying to convince the guy at the front desk to put it on my room's tab. Maybe it was the promise of a tip or the deranged desperation in my eyes—could be either, at this point—that eventually had him handing it over.

Since I finished listening to Emery's message, I've been sitting out here, drowning myself in the juniper spirit, wishing like hell it could erase the last couple of months.

My heavy head rolls to the side as I take in my brother's appearance. He's in jeans and a sweater, freshly shaved, and ready for the day.

"Fuck, what time is it?" I mumble.

"Early. I was worried about you."

"I'm fine."

"Clearly." He rolls his eyes at me.

"How'd you know I was here?"

"I didn't. I banged on your door for twenty minutes before going to the front desk and asking the guy there if he saw you. He pointed me in this direction."

"Ah." Of course he did.

"Talk to me. What's going on?" Eli's phone buzzes. "Hold that thought. Yo." He pauses, Cameron's muffled voice coming through on the other end. "Yeah. I found him." My kid brother chatters on some more, and I know they are talking about me.

I couldn't care less. My life is ruined. I lost my girl and, as punishment, I have to watch her on the arm of another man.

"Yeah. Oh, and bring the hangover cure. Mase is gonna need some help this morning."

"Fuck off. I do not need help." I grumble like the surly bastard I am. I do need help, but not the kind he wants to give me. Right now, all I want to do is sulk.

Eli looks at me and shakes his head. He laughs at something Cameron jabbers on about. "I'll take that action," he says before ending the call and shoving his phone in his pocket. He holds up the bottle of booze. "This yours?"

I look at the mostly empty bottle and shrug.

"Did you drink this by yourself?" he asks, waiting for me to answer.

"It is, and yes," I confess. No use in lying. Closing my eyes, I turn my face to the sky.

Eli sits quietly beside me, a calming presence before the storm that is Cam arrives. I blindly reach out for the bottle, but he slaps my hand away, clicking his tongue at me in disappointment. No one is more disappointed than me.

I tuck my hands into my pocket and wait. More crunching gravel catches my attention, but I sit still.

"What the fuck are you guys doing out here?" Cameron huffs.

"I was enjoying the silence until you showed up," I groan.

"Fuck off, Mister I'm Too Quiet and Broody to Talk About My Man-feels." Ei chuckles at Cameron's taunts. "Newsflash, we're in this bromance together, so start talking, ass wipe."

I open my eyes for the second time to find Cameron sitting in the Adirondack chair on my other side, his arms crossed, waiting. It reminds me of the morning we went to Jace's place to help him get out of his funk and chase after the woman he loved.

Too bad you won't be getting your girl back, numb nuts.

"Let's see..." I hold up my fingers, ticking off my transgressions. "I'm an asshole, I lost the only woman I ever truly loved, and I'm an asshole."

"You said asshole twice." Cameron leans forward and places a red drink near my nose.

Nausea rolls through me as the smell of pickles and spice hits my nostrils.

"First, drink."

I push it away, but he forces my hand and makes me hold it. The concoction smells horrific.

"That's your punishment. Drink the hangover cure," he demands.

"I don't want to," I whine, holding the rancid drink away from my face.

"Tough shit. We aren't about to let you ruin Jace and Rylann's wedding day."

Fuck.

See? I'm an asshole, only thinking of myself and my own shit.

Cameron's right. I need to get my shit together and man the fuck up for my brother.

With a groan, I bring the nasty liquid to my lips and take it down in four big gulps. My stomach churns and grumbles, cramping, as the disgusting liquid slides down my throat and settles in my belly. It's some kind of miracle that I don't hurl.

"That is by far the worst thing I have ever tasted. What's in that? Rat poison and old boots?"

Cameron throws his head back and laughs. "It really is nasty, but Thompson gave me the recipe. He said the results are instant. You either feel alive again or..."

"Or what, Cam?"

He shrugs. "Or you barf your guts out."

My eyes bug out of my head. "Seriously?"

"Hey, we took a chance, and it paid off. You're fine, right?"

I take stock of my body. Even though my stomach bubbles from the disgusting drink, my eyes don't burn as much, my body is humming, and my head seems a little clearer. "Yeah, I guess so."

"Hair of the nuts. It always works," Cam jokes.

"It's the hair of the dog. Now pay up, Cam." Eli chuckles and puts his palm up, wiggling his fingers.

Cam sighs and hands him a twenty.

"Thank you very much."

"Betting on whether or not I'm going to puke is messed up, you fuckers," I grunt, lifting my hood over my head as they roar with laughter at my expense.

"So, what happened between dinner last night and this morning?" Eli asks. "Actually, hold that thought." He pulls out his phone again, his fingers flying across the screen. Putting his phone down, he twists the cap off the gin, takes a swig, and holds it out to Cam. "I have a feeling we might be needing this."

Cam grabs the bottle and takes a gulp. "Ugh, I fucking hate gin." He wipes his lips with the back of his hand. "I don't know how you drink this garbage. It's horrible."

"Like your face."

"Har har. Funny," Cameron deadpans as the sound of gravel crunching has me looking over my shoulder.

I should have known.

I shrink back into my seat as Jace approaches the warm hearth we are sitting at.

"I'm here. What's the emergency?" He points at the bottle in Cam's hand. "What the hell, guys? It's my wedding day. Why are you drinking at..." He looks at his phone. "7am?"

"I only took a sip. Your man over there drank all this by himself." Cam points at me and places the bottle on the ground.

I have half the mind to pick it up and take a swig, but my gut gurgles, so I shove that thought away real quick.

As Jace takes a seat in the chair across from me, Eli speaks up, "I was worried about Mase. He wasn't picking up his phone or answering his texts. When I knocked on his door, no one answered, so I came down to find him. The guy at the front desk told me I would find him out here. Apparently, he's been out here all night. Also, if he's not nursing a hangover already, the idiot is still drunk. I'm not sure yet."

"I'm not drunk," I slur.

Fuck. I run my hand over my face, trying to get some feeling back.

Jace pulls at his hair before leaning back in his chair. "This is about Emery, right?"

I nod. Of course it's about Emery. Why else would I be outside, drinking alone?

Although, I don't think my brothers have ever seen me less than put together and ready to get down to business. My last breakup didn't have me on my knees, feeling like my life was over. Then again, my feelings for my ex don't hold a candle to how I feel about Emery.

"Start from the beginning," Jace says, taking his big brother role seriously. Like the lawyer he is, he calmly begins his interrogation. "How did you two meet?"

"We met at the airport. Actually, the first time I saw her was the night you proposed to Ry. I saw her reflection in the mirror, but before I could talk to her, she was gone. The second time was in the airport café. We shared a flight to L.A.. I thought we hit it off, but she walked away. Third time I saw her was in January, at the airport again, waiting for a car. It was the weekend I was watching Rhys while you brought Ry here for your babymoon."

"So she's the girl you took to movie night at the museum?" he asks while Cam and Eli sit silently, letting Jace continue taking the lead.

"Yes."

"Then what happened?"

"Then we started seeing each other. It was a long-distance thing at first but got serious after Valentine's Day. We spent Valentine's weekend together in Portland."

"Of course it did," Cameron interjects. "Dude, never take a chick out on Valentine's Day. That shit screams committed relationship."

"Shut up, you idiot." Eli throws a pebble at Cam. "He wanted to be committed."

Jace rolls his eyes, waving his hand for me to continue.

"After that, she had me hooked. Every free moment I had, I spent on the phone with her. When we could make it work, we saw each other in person either here or in L.A., until I ended it in July."

"Is she the reason you left Chicago early?"

"Yes."

Jace looks at Eli. "You knew."

"Wasn't my story to tell," he says with a nod.

"So, why did you break up?" Jace queries.

Now, this is the hard part.

"So, I'm going to have to explain this in parts, and I need you to be understanding. I already know I fucked up, but hear me out." I look around the circle, making sure each one agrees before I continue, "I showed up to surprise her, only to be surprised myself. We were out on the boat deck, watching the fireworks, when this guy shows up, calling Emery his fiancée. She didn't deny it. I blew up, said some shit I didn't mean, and stormed off."

"Why do I feel like there is more to the story?" Cameron asks.

Eli narrows his eyes at me. "What did you do?"

"I—" I swallow the lump in my throat. They are going to kick my ass when I tell them. And I will deserve every punch. "I walked off the property, called a cab, and then... Fuck." My head starts to pound, and the acidic drink in my gut threatens to come up. "I blocked her number."

"You did what?" Eli shouts. He shakes his head in disbelief. "Please tell me you did not ghost this woman. The woman you told me you loved."

"I did. I was just so fucking angry. After months of dating, some guy shows up, claiming to be her fiancé, for fucks sake. What was I supposed to think?" I try to rationalize my behavior. "For half a year, she lied to me like some side fucking piece, all while she had a fiancé back east. How would you feel?"

"Mad, but I would have at least heard her out. Did you do that?" Eli asks.

"No," I admit.

"You are an asshole," he mutters.

"Damn, that's cold, bro. Even for you," Cam retorts, taking the cap off the gin and taking another swig before handing the bottle to Eli.

Jace's forehead crunches as he narrows his eyes on me, the disappointment obvious. His voice is steely. "What happened at the bachelor party?"

I can't stand their eyes on me. I throw my head back against the chair and cover my face with my arms. Shame washes over me. "I went after her and accused her of knowing who I was. She said she didn't know. Then I called her a bad person or some shit for lying about having a fiancé, to which she said there was more to the story and that I would know that if I had returned any of her text messages. She also mentioned leaving a voicemail, hoping I would listen to it. But I didn't want to hear it. So, instead of listening to her, I— Fuck. Please don't make me say it."

"Say it," Jace grits through his teeth.

"I fucked her in the bathroom and told her it was a mistake. Actually, I implied that we were a mistake."

Silence fills the air as the logs crackle in the pit, the fire burning warm. A stark contrast to the frosty looks no doubt directed my way. Sure enough, when I open my eyes, my brothers are staring at me with shock and disgust.

"That's not even the worst part," I confess.

"That's not the worst part?" Camerons asks, eyes bulging out of his head.

"The voice mail," Eli says. "What did she say on the voicemail? Wait. Where's your phone?"

"Why?"

"We need to hear this message. Assess how fucked you are. Because if you want this girl back—which I know you do, otherwise you wouldn't have gone all Jace and drank a bottle of gin alone—you're going to need our help."

"Hey," Jace grouses. "I take offense to that."

"You should." Eli stands and digs his hand into my pocket, grabbing the key to my room.

I don't bother stopping him. It's better if they know now, and besides, I'm too tired to fight.

"Don't let him out of your sight." Eli disappears into the inn as I reach over and grab the bottle of gin off Cameron's lap, and take a swig before he can stop me. It burns my throat, and I can't hide my revolution as my stomach flips and bile rises in my throat. *Bad idea.*

Cameron chuckles. "I bet that made you want to puke, didn't it? Serves you right. Go on, puke."

I force the vomit down. I will not give him any more ammunition.

Eli comes back with my phone in his hand. He sits on the chair's arm between Cam and Jace, and pushes play.

"Mase, it's me, Emery."

I close my eyes, trying to ignore the way my chest caves in and my heart shrivels up as I listen to Emery's voice again. The pain, the hurt, the regret. It's all there.

When it ends, Cameron breaks the silence. "Dude, you're an asshole."

"I know. I already said that."

"I just wanted to make sure you still knew."

"Thanks for the reminder."

"I don't think you're as fucked as you think you are," Eli states calmly. His words spark the hope I thought died to life, and I sit up, giving him my full attention. "She clearly loves you. Women don't just turn off their feelings."

"He's right," Jace adds. "Rylann and I never stopped loving each other. I think when you find the right person, the person you're meant to be with, those loving feelings remain. Question is... Do you still love her and want to fight for her?"

"I can't. She's moved on. She has Graham now. *Graham.*" I scoff. "What kind of fucking name is that anyway?" I sneer, making my three brothers chuckle at my childishness.

I stare into the fire, clenching my fists as I remember the way that douche stood next to Emery and placed his hand on her lower back, and how I wanted to rip his fucking hand off for touching her. Still do.

"Mason," Jace calls out my name, drawing my attention back to him. "They are not together."

"I saw them together. I'm not an idiot."

"Yes, you are. Listen. I didn't know the extent of what went down with Emery. Rylann only said her parents were horrible people. But now, everything makes sense, and why Ry's been so hard on you. She wants you to see that you made a mistake and for you to fix it."

"I can't fix it when she's dating another man. I lost her, Jace. I—" My voice cracks as tears tickle my nose.

"No, you didn't. They aren't dating. They are just friends," he cuts me off.

Some of the shame and guilt I'm holding for kissing her last night washes away. I still shouldn't have kissed her without knowing for sure.

"I knew it!" Eli barks out, pumping his fist. "I love being right."

"How'd you know?" Jace asks.

"I saw the way her eyes kept searching for Mason. When the dude placed his hand on her back, her body stiffened. Shit like that."

"Why were you watching her in the first place?" I growl.

He shrugs. "I was afraid you were going to cause a scene, so I was watching out for you. Plus, it's what I do. I have to constantly watch out for shady fuckers in my industry. Keep myself and my clients safe from schizoids, and let me tell you, there are a fuck-ton in Hollywood." Eli looks off into the distance, making me think there is more to what he's saying.

"So, what now?" I ask.

"Now, you get your girl back, duh."

I look at Cameron and lift a brow in question.

"What? Just because I don't want to be in a committed relationship doesn't mean I don't love love. I love receiving love, giving love, spreading love." He wiggles his eyebrows suggestively at me. "Besides, I liked you better when you were getting laid."

"What the kid is trying to say" — Jace throws his thumb at Cameron — "and failing terribly at is ... we want you to be happy. When you were with her, you were happy."

"What Jace really means is..." Cameron mocks. "You've been in an insufferable, grouchy dickhead the last couple of months, and we are all tired of it."

Eli laughs. "Cam's right. But seriously, though, you love Emery. You told me so. Now, do you want to fight for her or walk away again like a coward?"

My hackles rise at that apt description. I want to argue, but he's right. I'm a total chicken-shit for walking away.

"Mase," Jace injects. "It's a fake fiancé. If I can get past all the shit that happened with me and Rylann, you can get past this. Don't be stupid. Don't waste time that could be spent together."

Hearing Jace gloss over all that happened last year so nonchalantly brings tears to my eyes. When he found out the truth it broke him, and in some ways, me too. My big brother spent seven years without the love of his life, and during that time, he suffered a fuck-ton of heartache. I don't want to waste seven years, let alone seven hours.

Emery did lie, but what I did was worse. I walked away, abandoning her when she needed me to listen. To be there as her support system. To hear her out and be empathetic. To be her rock. Her shoulder to lean on.

She was young when her parents convinced her to marry someone as a business arrangement instead of for love. Who even asks that of their children in this day and age? Assholes. That's who.

I don't want to be just another asshole that lets Emery down.

"I want to fight for her. But where the hell do I start?"

Emery has always been cautious, and based on what I know and have ascertained with her confession, her parents have never given her the security she needs to know she's loved. They used her and held her to impossible expectations. It was hard enough to get her walls to crumble the first time. Now? I don't know if I stand a chance.

"Biden her," Cameron states.

"What?" I ask, confused by his outburst.

"I said, Biden her," he says again like I know what the fuck he means.

"Please explain because I have no idea what the President has to do with this."

"Don't judge, but I was bored and started watching reruns. There was this one episode where the guys tell the main character to 'Biden' the guy she wants to hook up with. It means just be there. Like the trusty fucking sidekick, you're always there at her side."

Eli snaps, "I've seen that episode. Fucking *New Girl*. Great show and fucking genius, Cam."

"I don't follow."

Eli explains this time. "You fucked up. Now, she doesn't know whether or not she can trust you or if you will run away again. She thinks you can't put her first, that she can't rely on you, so you have to *be there* for her. For everything, no matter what. Take her lunch at the office."

"Drop off dinner. Walk her dog," Jace adds. "But don't fuck her, you idiot. You have to prove to her that she's your number one priority, not just a fuck."

My fists clench at his callous comment, even though I'm to blame for it. I look at all my brothers. "Seriously? This will work?"

They shrug, but Jace answers honestly, "What have you got to lose at this point? It's either this or walk away."

"I don't want to walk away again."

"Good. Then it's settled. Get your girl. Then, once you have her and your ring is on her finger, you can fuck her in any restaurant bathroom you want. Just like big bro over there," Cameron says with a shit-eating grin.

Jace growls at him.

"You really make me proud, bro." Cam holds out his fist to Jace, who bumps it.

"Thanks. I think?"

Eli chuckles. "Cam, you're an idiot. But this time, I think you have the right idea. With the Biden thing, not the bathroom. While I am impressed, Jace, the bathroom is gross." Eli mock shivers.

Jace smirks. "Yeah, come see me when you find the girl that knocks you on your ass. Your tune will change when you can't keep your hands off of her." He turns to me, his voice taking a serious tone. "You want to fight for her, but I don't know if you've thought this all through. I need you to really think. Are you all in? Because her life is here, Mase. Her business is here, and while her brother is in California, she's made this place her home. I don't foresee Emery moving to L.A.. So are you willing to make the sacrifice and move here for her? Is that really something you can do, considering your job?"

Can I do that? I don't know. What I do know is that Emery is worth it. I would sacrifice it all to be with her.

With the company's self-imposed sabbatical, I don't have to figure that out until after the New Year. Besides, I know my colleagues—my friends. They will support me in any way they can. They're also tired of me being a grumpy dick.

"Yes." My answer is strong and steady, and feels right.

Jace's face splits into a grin. "Looks like another Miller will be moving to Oregon."

Eli and Cameron groan while Jace and I laugh.

Fuck, it feels good to laugh.

The hope I thought was dead and gone comes roaring back to life. Now, I just have to get the girl back—mind, heart, body, and soul.

Because I want it all.

FORTY-FOUR

Emery

FOREST MEETS PARADISE AT the Setting Sun Inn, and it is breath-taking. I take another satisfied look around the banquet room in awe. The onsite coordinator did an amazing job bringing my sketches to life. I hope it's the vision Rylann had in mind.

Fairy lights blanket the ceiling like a sheet of stars above white linen-covered tables. Candles surrounded by evergreen centerpieces—with white and yellow plumeria leis woven through—adorn each table, filling the room with a rustic pine and sweet flower scent.

It's been a long day helping decorate, but it's been the best part of it. I've been lost in the hands-on creative aspect of things, and it's triggered this passion for planning more events like this. I thought corporate events and conferences would be enough to quell my secret passion for event planning, but it's done the opposite. I've been wanting something bigger, and this wedding has been that.

Don't get me wrong, I love my job. I love working with Rylann and Scarlett. But this? This is the next level.

The decorations and small details are going to live on in every memory the happy couple and their family have of this day. It's a pretty freaking special feeling being a part of something so much bigger than me.

Maybe I can do this more on the side, for fun?

A glance at my watch tells me it's time to get ready. I make my way to the bridal suite, which is actually a single room on the first floor Rylann reserved, that houses my suitcase and dress. Rylann handed me the extra key in case I changed my mind about staying the night. It was really sweet of her, but I declined. I think it's best if I head home after the festivities.

Graham offered to drive me home after midnight, and I took him up on his offer. With Mason here and how weird things are between us, it seems wrong to stick around.

As I open the door, I take in the small quiet room. From the looks of it, Rylann and Scarlett aren't here yet, and I take that as a sign. I'm a little sweaty after working all afternoon, and with the ceremony being held at seven this evening, it's probably a good idea to take a quick shower.

Grabbing my clothes and toiletries bag from my suitcase, I proceed to the bathroom. Turning on the water to warm, I place my clean clothes on the counter and strip. My feet hit the cold tile floor, sparking memories.

Pushing them back, I open the shower door and slip into the steam, letting the hot water soak me. I can't stop the visions as the sleek white and gray motif of the shower transports me back to the first weekend Mason and I spent together in Portland.

With only one date under our belt before that weekend, we spent the entire month leading up to it talking on the phone, video calling, or texting. As soon as I saw his handsome face standing at the bar, my heart flipped and the butterflies in my belly soared. Dinner was all heated looks and slight touches, before we made our way upstairs and attacked each other, the simmering chemistry between us exploding. I can still feel the cold tiles stinging my back as Mason pushed me against the wall and fell to his knees in front of me as he buried his face in my pussy.

My nipples harden under the warm water, my skin tingling with energy, and my clit pulses with need. It's the same way my body reacted last night when Mason claimed my mouth with his. He caught me by surprise, but it didn't stop me from kissing him back. My body is defenseless to his touch.

That kiss.

My pelvic muscles clench air just thinking about his hot hand wrapped around my wrist as he pulled me close and crushed his soft lips to mine. My heart beats in my ears as his spicy ginger scent wraps around me, bathing me in heat and melting me like ice cream on a summer's day.

My soapy fingers graze my aching center as a door slams close by, sobering me up and dousing the heat between my legs. I carefully wash my face and body, then quickly rinse off, making sure my hair doesn't get wet. Turning off the water, I grab a towel and dry off.

Cool air hits my skin, pebbling my flesh, in no way similar to the flaming shivers my skin experiences when Mason touches me. He's a crackling fire that burns me to my core, fast and hot. I groan to myself as I finish drying. Guilt gnaws at me.

What was Mason thinking, kissing me like that? Like I'm his. I was with a date, for crying out loud.

But you aren't with Graham. He's your friend.

Yeah, well, Mason doesn't know that.

Shame burns my cheeks and guilt builds in my stomach, bubbling like a sickness, for letting Mason believe Graham is more to me than just a friend.

I lather lotion onto my skin before putting on my strapless bra and matching beige thong. I give my body a quick dry with the blow dryer—because who likes feeling sticky under their clothes—and then pull on a pair of leggings and a button-up shirt. Sniffing at the collar, hoping to catch a whiff of the spicy cologne that used to linger on the soft fabric, I come up empty, and my heart pinches like it normally does at the loss. Rolling up the sleeves, I walk out of the bathroom as Rylann and Scarlett enter.

"You're here!" Rylann squeals, rushing to me as she wraps her arms around my waist. Looking up at me with wide happy eyes, a grin spreads across her face.

She's four years older than me but I'm four inches taller, and it's a funny juxtaposition when I actually look up to her. She is everything I want to be when I grow up.

"I just walked through the banquet room, and it's amazing. You did such a wonderful job. It's even better than I imagined, Em. Thank you." Rylann hugs me again before letting me go.

"You're welcome. I'm just so glad you love it."

"Are you kidding? Your talents are wasted in marketing."

"Shut up, Ry. We don't want her leaving us."

"Scarlett's right. You did a horrible job. The absolute worst." Rylann's eyes sparkle, relaying the opposite of her words.

"Don't worry. You ladies are stuck with me." While I might want to plan a wedding here or there, I love working with these two women.

"I think it's the other way around." Scarlett grabs the garment bags from the closet and moves them, hanging them over the closet doors. "Alright, bridezilla. How do you want to get this party started? Virgin mimosas?"

I can't help the snort that slips out. "Isn't that just orange juice?"

"Yes, but it sounds a lot cooler than saying, 'Hey, want a glass of OJ?' Please let me live in my delusions."

Rylann giggles at Scarlett as I nod in agreement.

"You're right. My apologies, Boss Bitch."

Scarlett smirks, her blue eyes twinkling with mirth. "You're catching on, grasshopper."

💋

I twist side to side, smoothing my dress down as I watch the silky fabric sway in the mirror. I'm in love with the spaghetti-strapped gold dress. It's butter soft, falls to the floor in waves, and has a slit up my left thigh. It's sexy as hell while still being classy.

Rylann pressured me into wearing it—calling me her honorary bridesmaid—as it matches the one Scarlett is wearing.

Scarlett looks stunning in her maid-of-honor's dress. It has cap sleeves and wraps around her waist in a dramatic A-line before flowing to her ankles.

My friendship with Rylann and Scarlett has grown exponentially these past few months. Their kindness and acceptance have meant the world to me. I don't know how I would have managed these dark months without them. We have spent many lunches together since this summer, talking and getting to know each other. Rylann and Scarlett are a riot. They make me feel so welcome, like I've always been a part of their group.

I've also gotten to know Scarlett's sisters-in-law, Laci and Lexi, after meeting them at the bachelorette party. Turns out they are my age, and both are sweet and funny. I really like them, and we plan on meeting up the next time I'm in the L.A. area visiting Chris.

"You look beautiful, Em." Rylann gives my shoulder a squeeze.

My eyes well at her praise. "Thanks. But you're the one that looks stunning tonight."

Rylann blushes at the compliment. She shouldn't—she looks downright amazing in her wedding dress. It was made for her, molding to her every curve perfectly. The long-sleeved dress's neckline dips into a dramatic V, making her cleavage something to envy. The gold belt at her waist accentuates her hourglass figure, and the lace overlay of her dress is beaded in gold sequins and crystals. Her hair is curled in beach waves and pinned to the side. Her makeup is sun-kissed, and it highlights her cheekbones perfectly. Like a bronze statue all shimmery and sweet, Rylann is covered—head to toe—in gold sparkles and looks every bit the setting sun on a summer night—bold and beautiful. A shining light.

"Thank you. Do you think Jace will like it?" Her voice is timid.

"Are you kidding?" Scarlett steps behind her. "His tongue is going to roll out his mouth like one of those cartoon characters'. He's going to be dragging you to the bathroom in seconds."

"Scar." Rylann gasps, smacking her best friend on the shoulder.

Scarlett shrugs. "Whatever. You know I'm right. I bet that's where you two disappeared yesterday during the cocktail hour."

"How did you know?"

"Sex flush," Scarlett says.

My face burns. What does that mean?

"Oh god." Rylann groans. "Don't get me started. It was so hot..."

I bet. Memories of Mason and me in the bathroom at the bar have my body heating up for a completely different reason. I get the appeal. Jace is the older, slightly darker-haired version of Mason. There is something about those Miller men. They are fine as hell and completely irresistible.

"But?"

Rylann covers her face with her hands. "We got caught."

Scarlett cackles. "Of course you did. What about you, Em? Did you take a visit to the bathroom yesterday?" Her phone dings with a message. "Shit, that's Levi. The boys are fussy. Do you mind if I go check on them before the ceremony?"

"Of course not," Rylann assures her.

"Okay, I'll be back soon."

Scarlett slips out the door, and I take a deep breath. Sometimes, she can be a little much. She means well, but she has no filter whatsoever. According to Rylann, that happened after she met Levi.

"Ignore her. How are you doing?" Rylann asks.

"I should be asking you that. You're the bride," I deflect, hoping she takes the bait. I've been working hard to keep thoughts of Mason at bay.

"I am absolutely fantastic. I can't wait to marry Jace and officially become Mrs. Miller. But stop deflecting," she calls me out.

She's good at that. "It's okay to be nervous to see him. How was yesterday? Did he see Graham?"

If this dress wasn't silk, I'd sit on the bed and curl up into a ball. My anxiety is at an all-time high. I have no idea which Mason I'm going to see tonight—the loving sweet Mason that made me fall in love with him on our first date, or will he be the angry, mean jackass he was at the bachelorette party?

Last night, he was … different.

"Yes, Mason saw Graham. He kept his distance, but—" That damn kiss. My lips still tingle from his touch.

"But what?"

"Mason kissed me."

"He did?" She gasps in shock, hand on her heart. "When?"

"By the bathroom. I went to use the ladies' room before dinner, and he was just standing there staring at his phone. Before I knew it was happening, his lips were on mine."

"How was it?"

"Amazing." I sigh.

That kiss sent sparks crackling across my skin and through every nerve of my body, waking me like a jolt of adrenaline to my system. My knees wobble beneath me just thinking about it. I give up trying to stay wrinkle-free and sit on the edge of the bed.

"And that's a bad thing?" she prods.

See? This is where my head and my heart start to battle it out.

"Yes. No… I don't know, Ry. I'm so confused. One minute, he's that charming guy who opened his laptop to have a conversation with me on a plane, making me fall in love with him, and the next, he's a hostile broody jerk who walked away and broke my heart."

Rylann sighs. "Yeah, those Miller brothers do that to you. They put you through the wringer before they sweep you off your feet forever. Let's play a little game. Scarlett made me do this when I was struggling with my feelings the first time. I only needed one question then, but this round might need a few. Anyway, just answer my questions without thinking."

"I feel like I've heard about this game."

"You might have; it's a classic. It's called *The Phoebe*. Now, close your eyes and don't think," she says with a wink.

I close my eyes. "Okay."

"Take a deep breath." I do, and she clears her throat. "Do you miss Mason?"

"Yes." That was easy. Of course I miss him. I feel like I have a missing limb without him.

"Don't think... Do you still love him?"

"Yes." I don't think I ever stopped loving him.

"Can you forgive him?"

"Yes." I slap a hand over my mouth.

Oh.

Well, that's a new one. Doesn't mean I'm ready to let Mason back in. He hurt me to my core. But maybe ... in time?

"Can you walk away from him without regret?"

"No." The thought of walking away from him makes me sick to my stomach, and my chest feels hollowed out.

"When you picture your future, is it Mason standing at your side or someone else?"

I open my eyes and look at the blushing bride before me. She looks gorgeous, and my stomach twists with envy. I want what she has. I have always wanted a place to call home. A person to call home.

"I don't know," I tell her honestly.

She sits down beside me and places her hand on mine.

"It used to be him. I wanted it to be him so badly."

"It still can be. If you want. I know that Mason's a little quiet and can come off a touch grumpy. I don't think that's the case at all. I think he's actually... what's the word?" She nods back and forth. "Guarded. He has a hard time letting people in. Being vulnerable is hard for him. The two of you are very similar in that respect. One of you is going to have to step up and start the process. I have a feeling he's going to be groveling at your door pretty soon. But you have to keep an open mind and an open heart. You both deserve to find happiness with someone who will put you first, and just maybe, you're it for each other."

Scarlett bursts through the door. "It's time, Rice Cakes!"

Rylann and I stand up as Scarlett rushes into the room with Rylann's bouquet. While I might be an honorary bridesmaid, only Scarlett will stand at her side during the ceremony. Rylann explained the significance to me over lunch, and it is a beautiful story. Not only is Scarlett her best friend, but she's also her found sister. It doesn't hurt that Scarlett and her husband orchestrated Jace and Rylann finding each other again seven years after being separated by circumstance.

Rylann looks over at me and smiles. "Follow your heart, Em." Then she turns, with Scarlett on her heels, to join her father and son outside.

Follow my heart.

Her words strike a chord. If I listen to my heart, I could end up hurt again. But if I don't follow my heart, I might regret it even more.

FORTY-FIVE

Emery

I'VE BEEN TO A few weddings before, but none of them compare to watching Jace and Rylann promise to love and cherish each other. It was heartbreakingly beautiful to listen to how much they have endured to get to where they are now. Listening to them speak about their past struggles and finding each other again broke my heart, and mended it together at the same time. It's clear they were always meant to be.

I'm not ashamed to say they had me shedding a few tears and gave me hope for the same someday. I couldn't stop myself from fantasizing about Mason and me standing at the altar, making our own promises and vows.

I make my way to the bar, where Graham is waiting for me with a glass of wine. The ceremony ended a few minutes ago, and the bride and groom slipped away to take pictures with their family while the rest of their guests gathered in the banquet room, waiting for their return. I slide in beside Graham as he hands me a glass.

"Thank you. I need this." My nerves are jittery.

Lifting my glass up for him to clink, I see that he ordered me red, and while I don't hate it, it's not what I like, so I take a tentative sip and place it on the bar.

I turn to my friend, checking him out in his all-black suit. Very monochromatic, but he pulls it off. "You look good tonight."

"Thanks," he easily takes my compliment, grinning and popping his collar at me. "You look beautiful tonight as well."

"Thanks."

"No, thank you, for the invite."

"Oh no, that was all Jace and Rylann. You helped out, and as soon as they learned you had no family besides your grandmother, they insisted you be here to celebrate. Besides, who can decline a kickass New Year's Eve wedding designed by *moi*?"

"Ah, angling for compliments. I get you."

I gasp in mock horror. "I would never."

Graham chuckles, sipping his whiskey. "The place looks amazing. You did a fantastic job, Emery."

"You really think so?" I know Rylann said she loved it, but taking compliments for my work is still hard to accept. Years of being told your efforts aren't good enough will damage a girl's self-esteem.

"Absolutely."

"Thanks, I appreciate you saying that." I take another sip of my wine. Ugh.

"I saw that. What's wrong?" my friend asks.

"Honestly? I don't love red wine."

Graham throws his head back and laughs. "Of course you don't. Let me get you a new one." He calls the bartender over to take the red away as I ask to replace it with white.

The bartender, dressed in what I'd call a hipster tuxedo—black dress slack, a white long-sleeved dress shirt rolled to the elbows, and black suspenders—obliges with a healthy pour.

"So?" Graham probes.

"So, what?" I ask, taking a sip of my wine. The cold liquid hits my tongue with the perfect balance of tart and sweet. Perfect.

When I look up, Graham's eyebrow is arched at me.

"Nothing to report. I saw him at the ceremony, but he was sitting with his family. We haven't spoken."

The hair on the back of my neck prickles, and I know without looking that Mason has entered the room. My body is still tuned to his channel. I look over my shoulder, and sure enough, Mason is watching me with no trace of emotion, and it's a little unsettling. Is he happy to see me? Angry? I have no idea.

Ripping my eyes away from his, I take another sip of my wine.

"Oh, yeah. That guy definitely wants to rip my head off." Graham hides his smile with his glass.

"Oh, stop. He does not."

"He does. I don't blame him. You're a catch. It's a shame we've got no spark. But I think having you as my friend is even better. I haven't had one in a very long time."

My heart softens at his vulnerability. I hope the woman Graham falls for treats him right. He's one of the good ones.

It would have been easy if there was a spark between us, but there is only one man my body calls for, and it's the broody one glaring holes into the back of my head.

"Me too, Graham."

"So... What are you going to do about him?"

I groan. "Why does everyone keep asking me that?"

Not counting the rapid-fire questions Rylann threw at me earlier, I spent an hour on the phone with Chris last night, lying through my teeth about being over Mason. My brother did not believe one word of my bullshit. To be honest, neither did I.

"What do you think I should do?"

"Nope. Only you have the answer to that question."

"Why is this so hard?"

"Because it's love. Love is a complicated emotion. It's not easy to find or to hold onto. You have to work at that part, and all that hard work makes the love you find so much more special when it's with the person you're supposed to spend the rest of your life with."

"Thanks, old wise one." I playfully roll my eyes at him.

He's right, though. It is special when you find the right person.

"Funny," my friend huffs, self-consciously running a hand over the sprinkle of gray at his temple. "I'm going to give you some space."

"No, don't go."

"I'm not leaving. I'm just afraid your man will murder me before the night ends if I don't walk away now."

"What?"

Graham pops his chin, and I feel it. Goosebumps spread across my skin like wildfire as the air grows thicker and sparks crackle.

"That's my cue. Good luck. You're going to need it because that man is clearly still in love with you. Stop denying you're in love with him too. Talk to him. Figure your shit out." He taps the bar, grabs his drink, and disappears into the crowd.

Seconds pass before Mason presses his chest to my back and whispers in my ear, "Hey, baby doll."

"Mason." His name is my next breath, a prayer on my lips.

"One look at you in this dress, and you took my breath away. You're gorgeous, Emery. The most beautiful woman in the room." His fingertips skim over my shoulder, spreading flames of heat across the back of my neck.

The world dissolves around me as his spicy cologne envelops me. My heart stutters in my chest, and my knees wobble. His breath fans across my face as he places a soft kiss on the apple of my cheek. His large hands grip my shoulders as he turns me around, bringing us face to face.

Now, it's my turn for my breath to get taken away. Mason looks different tonight. Don't get me wrong, he's still hot as hell wearing a black tuxedo that fits perfectly to his broad shoulders and chest. His shaggy hair is swept back from his face but still manages to curl at the ends the way I like. His green eyes sparkle as his lips turn up at the edge, fighting a smirk.

The music changes, and the band's lead singer calls out for everyone to turn their attention to the door as the bride and groom make their way into the banquet room.

Everyone cheers as the two take the dance floor for their first dance. The opening chords of a slowed-down R&B version of Barry White's *I Can't Get Enough of Your Love, Babe* begin as Jace and Rylann sway back and forth. You can see the hearts in their eyes as they stare at each other. It's the most beautiful thing I've ever seen.

Mason wipes his thumb under my eye, catching the tear I didn't feel roll down my cheek.

"Take a walk with me?" He holds out his hand.

I glance at Rylann, her dress sparkling in the dim lights, and back at Mason. If I walk away, I'll regret it. The only way to know if there is something salvageable between us is to take a chance and find out.

"Okay." I place my hand in his and let him lead me to the side entrance that leads to the patio.

Mason never lets go as he guides me around to the dark side of the brightly burning fire pit. After dinner, it will be the surprise marshmallow station, set up specifically for Rylann's son, Rhys. Mason's nephew.

Even months later, that news still shocks me. Fate has a funny way of connecting people sometimes.

"Dance with me, please." The bossy tone behind his request peaks through and brings a smile to my lips as I fight the jolt of arousal that hits my core and my heart.

Yes sticks to my tongue like honey, so I nod.

He places his free hand on my back, bringing us flush. The heat of his chest seeps through the layers of fabric between us, keeping me warm in the chilly night air. Placing my hand on his shoulder, I follow his lead and sway to the soft sounds of music coming from inside. My speeding pulse starts to slow as we slow-dance under the stars. Emotion clogs my throat, stopping me from speaking.

Mason breaks the silence for us. "I've missed you, Em."

Me too.

Instead of answering, I lay my head on his shoulder, my cold nose grazing the warm skin of his neck. I breathe in his masculine scent, letting it soothe my nerves, as he places my other hand on his shoulder and wraps both his arms around me. His fingers brush dangerously close to the slope of my ass before he places them possessively on my back. My body ignites under his palm as we move against each other to the beat of the music.

"Emery," Mason whispers my name.

"Hmm." I close my eyes, not ready for this stolen moment to end.

His hands roam up my back, his fingers snaking through my hair. He gives the strands a soft tug, forcing me to tilt my chin to the sky and look into his eyes. Out here in the dark, the gold streaks in them glow in the firelight.

"I'm sorry, baby doll. For everything."

"I—"

He shakes his head, placing his thumb over my lips, shushing me. My lips tingle, and the temptation to lick it overwhelms me.

"No talking. Can you handle that for a minute?" he asks firmly, his eyes penetrating my soul, begging me to let him speak first.

"Yes," I mumble, my lips rubbing against the pad of his thick digit.

"Good girl." He presses a soft kiss to my forehead.

I preen under his praise, reminded of the way Mason makes me feel seen and cherished.

I shove those thoughts away and brace myself. I can't just let myself fall right back into him. He broke my heart when he walked away. When he shut me out without explanation.

"I need to get this out before midnight. I don't want to start the new year without saying what I need to say. I finally listened to your voicemail. I'm sorry it took me so long."

"Oh." My cheeks heat, and my eyes dart to his strong chest. I probably sounded like a blubbering idiot. That night—that call—is still blurry.

"None of that. Eyes on me, beautiful girl. I need you to look at me when I beg you for forgiveness."

"Oh," I stupidly say again, bringing my eyes back to his green ones.

His lips quirk, but he fights a smile. Gah, I sound like a lovesick idiot.

"I'm a fucking dumbass. I never should have walked out on you. I should have trusted you and listened to your side of the story. Of course, you did what you had to for your brother. You are the bravest woman I have ever met. To give up something so precious for someone you love is beyond selfless. I will never forgive myself for giving up on us the way I did. For ghosting you. I will understand if you never forgive me. What I did to you was unacceptable. It was the biggest mistake of my life."

Tears spring to my eyes at his sincere apology. I wish he would have said all this months ago. As much as I love him, I don't know where we go from here.

"You broke my heart, Mason. I—"

"I know, baby. I'm so sorry for breaking you like that. You deserve the world. You deserve someone who will put you first. Someone who will drop everything to be there for you and comfort you when you need it. To be there for you after a long day of work, to make you dinner and rub your feet. Someone to walk Henry when it's too cold and rainy out."

Everything he's saying is exactly what I want, but it doesn't sound like he's that person. Was everyone wrong? Was I wrong? Is this a goodbye?

A lead ball forms in my stomach as my nose tingles with unshed tears.

"I-I—" My voice cracks. Closing my eyes, I fight back my tears.

"Baby doll, look at me, please."

I shake my head. I don't want to see the look in his eyes when he says goodbye. When he walks away again.

Oh god, I'm going to be sick.

I suck in a deep breath, gathering my thoughts, and slowly peel my eyes open.

"It's okay, Mason. I understand. I lied. There's no coming back from that. I forgive you. Thank you for giving me closure to move on." I step back, removing myself from his arms. I don't want to break down in front of him, to let him know that he's breaking my heart all over again.

Spinning around on my heels, I race to the bathroom without a backward glance, praying he doesn't see me fall apart.

C LOSURE?

Emery takes advantage of my shock and slips out of my hold. In a stupefied state, I watch her back as she races around the side of the inn, her gold dress glimmering in the moonlight.

What the fuck just happened? How could she interpret my apology for a goodbye?

I don't know how long I stand outside—could be seconds or minutes—when I hear Cameron calling my name.

"Mason." He approaches, the fire crackling between us. "Dude, dinner is being served. What are you doing out here?"

My mouth opens and closes a few times, like a floundering fish, but words escape me.

"Bro, you okay?"

"No." I shake my head, shell-shocked. One second Emery is in my arms, and the next she's running away from me. "I'm not okay."

"What the hell happened?"

Rubbing my hands over my face, I shrug. "Fuck if I know. I-I'm really confused as to what just went down."

"Well, either spit it out or let's get back inside because dinner is about to start and everyone is already sitting at the table."

"Yeah, okay. Let's go inside."

As much as I want to chase after Emery, I can't. It's my brother's wedding and being here for him is important. Today, Rylann officially became a part of our family, and I don't want to miss a minute of that.

As I take my seat, I watch Emery slip back through the doors, finding her seat next to that fucking guy again. She avoids eye contact with everyone as she places her napkin on her lap.

He leans over and whispers something to her, and I wish I could read lips. What the fuck is he telling her? She nods her head and smiles, placating him, but I know better. That smile is fake. My girl is trying to be strong, hiding her emotions below the surface, masking her pain for the sake of everyone around her.

Clenching the fork in my hand, I do my best to ignore the pain searing in my chest at seeing the hurt on her face. She can hide from everyone else, but I know. I did that. Again.

Why the fuck would she think I was walking away from her? She is my world. The air I breathe. I'm nothing without her. I was seconds away from telling her I love her and falling to my knees to beg her for another chance.

Instead, she took my words as a farewell.

Servers take the plates away, refilling wine glasses as they go. I couldn't tell you what I'm eating or how it tastes, all of my focus is on the stunning woman in the gold dress sitting two tables too far away from me. Hell, two inches is too far from me. I need her by my side.

I stand, ready to shake some sense into my girl, as Levi takes the microphone to give his best-man speech, forcing me back into my seat.

"Good evening, everyone. On behalf of the bride and groom, I would like to thank you for being here tonight to finally celebrate these two getting married. To Jace and Rylann!"

Everyone cheers, lifting their glasses into the air to toast the happy couple.

"Even though both of them have yet to make it through one of my weddings..."

Jace punches Levi in the side as everyone chuckles. Aside from our immediate family, very few people know Jace and Rylann's full love story and how they both, at different times, missed their best friends' weddings.

"I'm kidding, folks. These two people here beside me mean the world to me and my wife. So, what I really am is grateful and honored. Grateful for having them in my life, and honored to stand beside my best friend as he married the love of his life tonight. I know the road to each other wasn't a straight line, but it doesn't matter how you get there, as long as you're here now. I have watched your relationship and family grow this past year, and I have never seen two people more in love. You fight for each other every day, with unwavering love and dedication. It is beautiful to watch, even though you gross us out sometimes. Right, Rhys?"

Rhys nods emphatically as the crowd erupts into laughter.

"With that being said, I wish you a lifetime of love and happiness. To the happy couple."

"To the happy couple!"

Unwavering love and dedication.

Levi's speech strikes a nerve. I can't go back into my relationship with Emery half-cocked. Thinking about moving and doing something about it are two separate things. Not only do I need to get my ducks in a row and have a solid plan in place, but I need to act on it. I need to make it real and provide Emery with proof that I'm in this forever.

I pull out my phone, type a short email to my partners, and hit send, making my transition official. For the plan to work—like Jace said—I have to be here, and that starts now.

Emery needs to be shown how much she means to me, and that means I need to start over from scratch. No sex, just getting to know her all over again, only amplified. I'm going to give her all the reasons she needs to trust me again.

And more.

My eyes never leave Emery as she dances with her friends and my nephew. I chuckle to myself as he holds her hands and jumps around. That little turd better keep up his end of the bargain, or I won't be paying him. Cost me forty bucks and three promised trips to the ice cream shop to convince him to dance with Emery all night, keeping that fucking Graham guy away from her.

I watch Emery slip away to the bathroom, creating the perfect opportunity for me to make my move. Like the stalker I am, I follow her. Not bothering to wait for her outside this time around, I stride right into the bathroom behind her.

"Mason, what are you doing in here?" She crosses her arms under her tits, lifting them in the air.

Fighting the urge to stare at their perfection, I check under the stalls to make sure we are alone before locking the door. "We need to talk," I all but growl at her.

Calm down, asshole. I take a deep breath.

"No, we don't. We said what we needed to say. Now, it's time for us to move on." She tries to walk around me, but I block her path.

I puff my chest, using the bossy tone I know turns her on. "No. That's not going to work for me."

I watch her lips part a fraction, no doubt still aroused by my gruff voice, as her body shivers before she stands tall, readying herself for a fight.

"Why is that?"

The pure sass and confidence in her tone make my dick twitch to life. She's fucking beautiful when she's angry.

"There is no moving on from you," I state.

I tried, or at least I think I did, but I don't think burying myself in work is really moving on. I was trying to forget, and there is no universe in which I am capable of forgetting Emery Rhodes.

She's without a doubt unforgettable.

Not only is she gorgeous, but she's smart, ambitious, resilient, kind-hearted, and generous to a fault. It's those qualities that got her mixed up with her parents in the first place.

"What?" she asks, dumbfounded.

"You heard me."

"I-I don't understand."

"I know. That's the problem, baby doll. You don't understand."

But I'm going to make you.

She places her hand on her popped hip and narrows her eyes at me. "I understand perfectly clear—"

"The fuck you do. You completely misunderstood what I was trying to tell you outside. You thought I was trying to give you closure or some shit. Closure, my ass. We will never be over, Emery."

"It's been months, Mason."

She crosses her arms again, and it takes everything in me to keep my eyes on her face and not stare at her chest as she arches her back, giving me the perfect view of her perky tits.

Focus.

"So?" I shrug, getting my thoughts back on track. "Look at Jace and Rylann. It took them years. Look how happy they are now."

I gesture toward the door. Toward the marriage that just took place. A marriage that might never have happened if it wasn't for a fuck-ton of hard work and forgiveness. All of which I am willing to do the lion's share of.

Walking away from Emery again is out of the question.

"That's different." She rolls her eyes at me.

It makes me want to bend her sassy ass over the sink and spank her cheeks raw, leaving my handprint on her skin before I fuck the brat right out of her.

Fuck, I need to cool it.

"How is that different?" I ask, bringing the conversation back to where I need it. "I made a mistake, but instead of it taking years to fix, I'm here now." I drop to my knees in front of her.

She gasps, gripping her chest. "What are you doing?"

"Showing you how serious I am. I will stay on my knees forever if I have to. You will have to drag my dead body away before I walk away from you again. Do you hear me?"

She nods, tentatively, so I continue.

"If you had let me finish, you'd know that I was two seconds away from doing this," I huff, pointing to the ground. "And begging you for another chance. I can't live without you. You're it for me. We are not done, nor will we ever be done. You are mine, and I am yours. I will prove it to you."

"But—"

"But nothing. I am going to show you every day that I am here to stay. That I choose you, no matter what. I let you down before, but I won't be making the same mistake twice." I run my hand over my jaw, debating my next words. "This is not how I wanted to tell you for the first time, but fuck it. I'm not wasting any more time. I love you, Emery. Without you, my life doesn't work. I need you more than the air I breathe. I love you, just the way you are, no conditions, no expectations. Just you." I grab her hips and pull her to me, resting my face on her stomach.

Her fingers twine through my hair as her knees give out. Only this time, I catch her. I will always catch her. She can guaran-fuck-ing-tee I'm going to be by her side, holding her up, supporting her from here on out.

My knees begin to ache from kneeling on the tile floor. One foot at a time, I pull myself up to a stand, never letting Emery go, keeping her body flush to mine in an embrace that rivals a straitjacket.

"I thought—" She sobs against my chest.

"I know. I'm sorry. I shouldn't have let you spend the night thinking we were over. I tried to tell you, but then dinner and time kept slipping away from me."

Her breaths pick up speed as her eyes flicker between mine, searching for the truth.

"You left me," she whimpers, her heartbreak clear.

Her words crack my ribcage wide open like an ax to a log. It doesn't escape my notice that she doesn't say "I love you" back. While it hurts, I understand. I need to earn those words. Down to my soul, I know she loves me. She's just afraid to let me in again.

"I know, baby. Fuck. I don't know what else to say, but I'm sorry. I'm so fucking sorry." I squeeze her tighter, breathing in her sweet scent as she cries into my chest. "I'm here, and I'm never letting you go again. I swear it. I love you so fucking much. I will never forgive myself for breaking your heart, but I promise I will make it up to you. Every day for the rest of our lives if you let me."

She looks up at me with those sad topaz eyes, almost destroying me with her next words. "I don't know if I can do it all again."

"I know." I release her, giving us space as I wipe the tears from under her eyes. "I've lost your trust. But if you let me, I want a chance to earn that trust back. You say the word. If you want me to leave you alone and never speak to you again, I'll do it. Even if it kills me. I will do whatever you want. Whatever you need, it's yours. Just tell me and be honest. Do I have a shot? Do we have a shot?"

Searching my face, her hands clutch the lapels of my jacket as her voice cracks. "I—"

She bites her bottom lip, and fuck if I don't want to suck it into my mouth instead. Last night's kiss wasn't nearly enough.

"There might be a chance," she whimpers.

"'Might be' like 'maybe someday'? Or 'might be' like 'you'll give me a chance at proving I can be the man you need, and we have a chance to turn this into forever'?" I hold my breath, waiting for her to answer.

"I must be crazy because it's the latter."

"You're going to give me another chance?"

She nods, her sparkling brown orbs twinkling.

My breath whooshes out of me in relief. She's giving me a chance.

I envelop her in my arms, squeezing her tight, afraid to let go only to find out I've been dreaming. "Say it again. Please."

"There's still a chance for us," she signs, closing her eyes. "You hurt me, Mason. I don't expect you to be perfect. We are going to have ups and downs, but you can't run away and shut me out when things get hard. I can't go through that again."

"Never, baby doll. If I had handcuffs, I'd use them right now to prove I'm here to stay."

She chuckles, and the fist clamped around my chest loosens. Her lingering hesitation burns, but all I need is an inch. I'm prepared to run miles for her.

Cupping her soft face in my palms like the precious treasure she is, I lean down, stopping an inch away from her mouth. "Before I kiss you, please tell me you are single and aren't dating that guy out there. I need to know."

"It didn't stop you last night."

"I know. But this is different. I stole that kiss. Now, I'm asking for all your kisses."

A soft smile graces her lips. "No. I'm not dating Graham."

I growl at the sound of his name on her tongue. Only my name should leave her mouth, or be screamed out in pleasure.

"Don't be like that. He's my friend. Things have changed since you left. I won't apologize for that. You either accept it, or there is no us. I like having friends, people to talk to."

"I'm your person," I grunt. She's right, even though I fucking hate it. "You have me."

"We'll see," she says, careful not to let all her walls strip away at my promises.

She needs action, not just the pretty words. Which I plan on giving her, from now until forever.

"We will," I vow. I won't squander this chance. I know what we have is special. It's the real deal, her and I. Which is why I say, "I will never stop you from having friends or doing something you want to do. Whatever it is you want to do, count me in. You're stuck with me now."

"We'll see," she repeats, her mouth twitching as she fights a smile on those big red lips of hers. The tension in my muscles wanes at the playful lilt of her words.

"You can count on it, baby doll." I lower my mouth to hers and plant a chaste kiss on her lips. My heart regulates, finally at ease, as I hold Emery in my arms. "Let's get back to the party."

I hold my hand out, and she easily places her hand in mine.

"Wait," she shouts, stopping me from unlocking the door.

"What's wrong? Did you change your mind?" *Please don't change your mind, baby.*

"No. I really need to use the bathroom." She hooks her thumb back at the stalls, and I can breathe again.

"Okay, I'll wait."

I lean against the sink, fully prepared to wait for her to use the toilet. Hell, I wasn't kidding when I said I would handcuff myself to her. I'll wait forever for her. My beautiful selfless girl.

Her eyes bug out of her head, and she vehemently shakes her head. "Nope. None of that. Out. I need to use the restroom. Alone."

"Fine. You have three minutes, or I'm coming back in here to drag you out."

"You're insane."

"Insane for you."

"Charmer." She smirks, and just like that, the little spark of hope I had for us becomes an inferno.

"Only for you," I assure her.

When she's done, I lead her to the patio, where everyone is gathered to begin the countdown. I try to stay close, but I don't want to push my luck. She might have said I have a chance, but I can still sense her skepticism.

I'm going to take the chance she's offering me and run with it. I'm going to—as Cameron would say—woo the fuck out of her.

I'm going to be right here, showing up every day, taking care of her, and proving that she's my number one priority.

Emery deserves a man that will be her biggest supporter, a man that will love her no matter what. To be there for her on her darkest of days, showing her how loved she is. That man is me. I let her down before, and I won't be making that mistake again.

The countdown begins.

Standing on the other side of the firepit, I watch Emery smile at my nephew as he dances around. She looks so fucking beautiful it hurts. I ache to be at her side, but now isn't the time. She must feel me watching because her eyes find mine.

That's right, baby doll. I'm right here watching, and I won't be walking away from you again.

The spark between us crackles like the fire dividing us.

I mouth, *Happy New Year.*

A smile splits across her gorgeous face, filling the hole in my chest that existed without her.

FORTY-SEVEN

Emery

"Five, four, three, two, one. Happy New Year!"

The crowd cheers as the clock strikes midnight. The band starts to play *Auld Lang Syne* as the entire party of guests fills the patio and surrounds the fire pit, waiting for the surprise Jace and Rylann have planned.

I watch as my little dance partner blows his paper horn and jumps around celebrating, before taking off to find his dad. I shake my head at the adorable display of him jumping into Jace's arms.

I haven't been able to shake Rhys all night, and weirdly enough, I love having him at my side. He's made me laugh and dance, eat about a hundred s'mores, and forget all about my conflicting feelings. He's been the perfect little distraction I've needed. His sweet little face makes me melt. He's the spitting image of his daddy and his uncle. The man that, for the past few months, has been the source of my chagrin.

The hair on the back of my neck stands at attention, and I know he's watching me again. He hasn't kept his eyes off of me all night.

I lift my gaze to his and my stomach flips, anxiety and lust swirling in my belly. His eyes smolder with desire, heating me to my core, as he mouths *Happy New Year* from the other side of the fire pit.

I can't look away or stop the smile that creeps across my face. I give him a finger wave and his smile matches mine.

In the past few hours I went from the lowest of lows to the highest of highs. I still can't believe he followed me to the bathroom and fell to his knees, begging me to forgive him. Even though I vehemently denied it to everyone, I dreamed of Mason coming back to me since the day he walked away.

When we danced by the fire, I was certain he was telling me it was over for good. It shocked me to my core to see Mason, who is a stubbornly proud man, on his knees in the bathroom, professing his love for me as he wrapped his arms around my legs, clinging to me like I was his lifeline. The paper-thin walls I built back around my heart shook loose with every one of his heartfelt and genuine words.

He sounds certain that this—us—is what he wants, and while his confession of love and apologies glued slivers of my heart back together, I need him to show me he loves me. I need action. I won't let myself fall completely back into him without being sure of us. I made mistakes, but he hurt me too deeply by cutting me out of his life so quickly. His actions spoke more loudly than his words of love. I've been let down so many times by the people that claim to love me that I've lost my faith.

Forgiveness isn't the only hurdle we face. I don't want to go back to only spending a few days here and there together. I want more. I want him to want more. What we had before was amazing, but it's no longer enough for me. I want a better version of us to rise from the ashes because, let's face it, he burnt us down to the ground. It's been months since we've spoken, and our last union didn't end on the best of terms, so it's hard for me to wrap my head around his proposal to try again.

Mason's eyes stay locked on mine as I point up. He follows my directive, tilting his chin up as fireworks light the night sky. Memories of him walking away on the Fourth of July hit me as the explosive display shoots off overhead. Red light floods the patio as our gazes return to each other.

My breath catches in my lungs at the sight of him grinning, the gold streaks in his eyes glimmering in the firelight. His previously growly expression has softened, and he looks like the Mason I fell in love with at the beginning of last year. Butterflies erupt into a frenzy in my belly, bringing with it a wave of heat that rolls through me, settling in my chest. I wish I knew what was going on in that head of his.

As if he knows what I'm thinking, he crooks his finger at me.

"Happy New Year, Em!" Scarlett yells, pulling me into a hug, breaking my connection with Mason.

Oh, thank heavens. I might have done something stupid, like go to him and let him kiss me senseless in front of everyone.

"Happy New Year, Scarlett." I return her hug.

"I have a feeling someone's New Year's wish is going to come true," she says, releasing me.

"How do you know what I wished for?"

"Not you. Him." Scarlett inclines her head in Mason's direction.

He's still watching me, a smile on his lips.

Looking back at Scarlett, she stops me. "Nuh-uh. Open mind and open heart."

My mouth falls open at Rylann's echoed words. "How—"

"What? Do you really think you're the only one she's used that line on?" she asks.

I shrug. There is still so much I need to learn about these two.

"She told me the same thing when I met Levi all those years ago and I was unsure of starting something with a man I met on vacation. Turns out, it was the best advice I could have received. So maybe you should do the same. But—and I'm serious when I say this—don't go easy on him. Make him work for it." She wiggles her brows at me, and I can't help but laugh. "I'll see you later, and if you change your mind about the room, let me know."

"I will. Thank you, Scarlett."

"Always, Em." Scarlett heads off in Levi's direction as Mason approaches and the firework show ends.

"Happy New Year, beautiful."

"Happy New Year."

He leans down, placing his lips a fraction of an inch away from my ear and whispers, "It's definitely going to be a good year."

Shivers wrack my body as he pushes a strand of my hair behind my ear, lighting my body on fire.

Mason steps back, putting distance between us, taking his woodsy ginger scent with him. "Are you staying here tonight?"

His eyes track my tongue as I lick my suddenly parched lips.

"No. I was planning on going home. I can't leave Henry alone all night. But..." I glance around, searching the faces of party guests bundled up outside. Where the hell did Graham disappear to? "I seem to have misplaced my ride home."

"I can drive you," he says, scraping his hand across his jaw.

My thighs clench, recalling the way his scruff chaffed my skin as he buried his head...

I'm so screwed. I can't be trapped in a car alone with him. He's dangerous.

"Oh, no. You don't have to. It's late, and we've been celebrating."

"I haven't had a drop to drink tonight, and I have the keys to the rental. Please. Let me drive you home. Besides, you'll be doing me a favor."

"How will driving me home be doing you a favor?" My house is, at the least, a forty-five minute drive.

"I'll be able to rest easy tonight knowing you're home safe and sound. And alone."

"Mason," I warn, ignoring the way his jealousy makes my stomach dip and my clit pulse with desire.

He bites his lip, hiding a smirk, like he knows what I'm thinking. "Sorry, not sorry, baby doll."

"Well, you better get used to it. Graham is my friend, and it's none of your damn business who I hang out with," I huff.

I will not let him boss me around. I might like him to take charge in the bedroom, but that's where I draw the line. Not that I'm going to be letting him boss me around in bed.

Yet.

The thought hits me like a bolt of lust just thinking about Mason and his magical cock. Oh god. What is wrong with me? Now is not the time to be thinking about sex. *Mind-blowing sex.*

"Oh, Em. That's where you're wrong, love. You are my business."

"You're the worst."

He chuckles, offering me the crook of his arm. "Only for you. Now, come on, let's get you home."

I slide my hand through the crook of his arm and rest it on his thick bicep, letting him lead us away from the party.

Mason opens the door for me, and I slide into the passenger seat. He closes the door, and I watch as he walks around the car and slips into the driver's seat.

"Are you sure you're up for the drive?" I ask.

It took me longer than expected to say goodnight to my friends and gather my stuff from the bridal suite. It's almost one in the morning, and the last thing I want is for him to get into a wreck because he's too tired to drive back.

"I'm fine. Don't worry about me." He reaches across my body, grabbing the seatbelt and bucking me in. "I'll get you home to Henry in no time."

His hand grazes my jacket, searing my skin as if there weren't layers of fabric between us. He puts on his seatbelt and then pulls up my favorite playlist on his phone before putting it on low and backing out of the parking spot. Out of the corner of my eye, I watch as he navigates the dark highway, heading south towards my home.

Mason's brow is furrowed in concentration as the dashboard illuminates his face, highlighting his angular jaw and straight nose. He's as devastatingly handsome as ever. He's lost his bow tie and undone the top two buttons of his shirt, leaving the dip of his chest uncovered. Biting my bottom lip, I stifle the groan building in my chest at the sight of him.

Mason glances in my direction, caching me off guard. His eyes dip to my mouth before returning to the road ahead of him as a slight grin pulls at the corner of his lips while he continues to drive.

The temperature in the car ratchets up to an unbearable degree as the tension between us builds. My breaths become choppy as his cologne suffocates and turns me on at the same time.

"I have a confession to make," he says, breaking the silence, dousing the flames licking at me from the inside out.

I swear I'm going to be sick if he says he's been dating.

"Okay," I hedge, breathing through my rising anxiety.

"A couple of months ago, I saw Chris at an event Eli made me go to, and I snuck out before he could see me."

I throw my head back and laugh, listening to him confirm my brother's story. I was sure he was exaggerating. "I know."

"You do? How?"

"Chris saw you."

Mason groans. "Fuck, that's embarrassing."

"It's fine. Chris thought it was hilarious. He ragged on you for, like, an hour." He didn't really, but letting Mason wriggle on the hook for a bit is good punishment.

"I deserve that," he says with a chuckle.

"How has work been?" I ask.

I know how much he loves his job and how passionate he is about the work he's doing to protect the everyday person from getting their identity stolen. I love that in his own way, he's trying to help the little guy by using his talents. Mason has a bigger heart that he lets on, letting very few people close enough to see that.

I guess Rylann is right—we are more similar than I thought.

"Work is work." His hands grip the steering wheel, his knuckles turning white from strain.

It's been months since I've been with Mason, but I can still read him. Something is clearly bothering him as his jaw and grip tighten.

"What are you not telling me?" I blurt.

He turns to me with a furrow in his brow, and the look sends a wave of humiliation washing over me. I'm the one that set this whole thing in motion by lying to him, and here I am, asking him to lay all his cards on the table.

"I shouldn't have said that. I—"

Mason places his hand on mine, electrocuting me with his touch. "It's okay. It's not what you think. I understand why you kept your..." His jaw ticks as his brain works to communicate while mine shorts out. "Arrangement a secret. Why you did what you did. If we stand a chance, we have to both be honest with each other from here on out."

I nod as tears sting my eyes. "I'm sorry. I wanted to tell you. I just... I didn't want you to change your opinion of me. When I was with you, I was the real me. The me that wasn't hindered by being scrutinized under a microscope every day of her life. With you, I felt free."

He twines our fingers together and brings my hand to his lips, kissing my knuckles. "I felt the same way, baby. I still do. We will get there again."

For the rest of the ride home, Mason keeps my hand grasped tightly in his, driving us towards my place in comfortable silence, our conversation about his work long forgotten.

Nostalgia washes over me as I remember sitting next to him as he drove down the coast along the Pacific Ocean. It was one of the best days we spent together.

Mason pulls into the driveway and cuts off the engine. "Stay right here."

I watch as he opens his door, climbs out, and walks around the car. He opens my door and offers me his hand. I place my palm in his, basking in his warmth.

The piece of my heart that doesn't want the night to end twinges in my chest as he walks me to my door. Henry yips from his kennel as my feet hit the porch steps, bringing a smile to my face.

Mason cups my face, tilting my chin up as he runs his thumb over the apple of my cheek. My body tenses with anticipation, waiting for him to kiss me, but the kiss never comes.

"Go on inside, and I'll bring in your bags."

"Okay," I whisper as both relief and disappointment wash over me.

My body is at war with itself when it comes to Mason. I want to throw myself at him, and at the same time, keep him at arm's length.

Unlocking my door, I step inside and make my way to my tiny pup. His little Yorkie tail waggles with such force that his whole body twists with the movement. I open his cage, letting him out before cleaning up the training mat. I'm washing my hands in the kitchen sink when Mason walks through the door, carrying my bags.

Henry races toward him, barking a hello, as Mason places my bags on the floor. He squats down to pick the little furball up, and the sight of Mason's big-muscled body cuddling the tiny pup nearly does me in. Why is it so hot seeing big burly men with little dogs?

"Hey there, Henry. Have you been taking care of your mom for me?"

Henry barks.

"Good job. You make sure to chase all the guys away from her, and I'll spoil you with some of those doggie cookies. Do you remember those?"

Mason scratches behind Henry's ear, and my traitorous dog practically rolls onto his back mid-air for Mason to rub his belly.

The man who stole my dog's loyalty looks over at me and smiles. "He missed me."

"Yeah, I guess he did."

"Was he the only one?"

"Fishing, are you?" I lean against the counter.

"Maybe." Mason places Henry on his paws. "Does it help if I say I missed you?"

"Doubtful," I quip.

He frowns at my response. "You doubt I missed you?"

Baiting him, I shrug.

With hooded eyes, Mason closes the distance between us, caging me in with his arms as he towers over me, bringing us chest to chest. My breath hitches, and my heart races behind my ribcage at the heat of his body pressed flush to mine.

"It appears that I have my work cut out for me." He dips his head, brushing his mouth over mine.

My lips tingle at the slight yet sensual touch.

"I missed you. Every second, of every minute, of every day. Even when I didn't want to, I missed you. These past months, I have thrown myself into work trying to drown the pain of your loss. I have wasted too much time, too many precious moments, that we could have had together, by walking away from you. I will do anything and everything I can to rebuild your faith in me. In us. You're it for me, baby doll." He presses a kiss to my cheek and steps back, taking his heat with him.

"O—" I croak out. Clearing my dry-as-the-Sahara throat, I jerk my head up and down like a bobble head. "Okay, then."

He blasts me with a devastatingly wide grin, soaking my panties. My thighs clench, desperate for friction.

"I need to head back to the inn."

"You're leaving?"

"For now. But I'll see you tomorrow."

"You will?"

"I will. I suggest you get some rest. You're going to need it for what I have planned."

My blood turns to lava in my veins with all the possibilities. "Why? Are you going to try getting into my pants?" I tease.

Mason throws his head back and barks a laugh. The gruff sound is like a straight shot of whiskey to my heart, warming me from the inside out. My eyes land on his exposed neck as his Adam's apple bobs, beckoning me to lick it.

His eyes collide with mine as he flashes me a knowing smile, and I don't know if I want to smack him for being charming or kiss the heck out of him because I missed him terribly.

He steps close to me, his heat enveloping me, suffocating me in the most delicious way. "To answer your question, no. At least, not tonight, baby. Maybe one day, when I deserve to be back in your bed. One step at a time. I'm in this with you for the long haul. Understand?"

"Yes."

"Besides, you're not ready yet."

"Ready for what?"

"For me. Because when I do finally get to bury my cock inside your tight pussy again and ruin you for all other men—because I will ruin you—I want you to be sure that my cock is the only one you want to be riding for the rest of your life."

Done.

He ruined me ages ago, and tonight is yet another reminder of how badly he's done so. The way he wraps his sweet declaration in pure sex is like a bolt of liquid lust to my center. He's got me hypnotized, and my mind is conjuring up images of all the ways he can wreck my body. If I were a lesser woman, I would drag him into my room and ride him until dawn.

I won't, though. He's right, I'm not ready. I need to be confident in us before I let him back into my heart, let alone my bed, no matter what my slutty vagina wants.

My brain is broken because all I can do is stare at his back as he strolls to the front door.

Opening the door, he turns to face me. "Lock up, beautiful. I can't drive off until I know you're safe."

My feet move before my brain kicks in, grasping onto the tether Mason has on my heart, leading me straight to him. "Good night, Mason."

"Good night, baby doll. Happy New Year."

Mason slips out the door into the night, and as ordered, I turn the lock. Spinning around, I rest my back against the door, listening to his footsteps fade, his car start, and drive away.

I suck in a deep breath and hope—with every fiber of my being—that opening my heart again to Mason doesn't backfire.

JANUARY

I POUR MYSELF A cup of coffee and yawn. I gave up trying to sleep about an hour ago. Instead, I lay in bed, going over yesterday's every detail.

Ambling over the fridge, I grab the vanilla creamer from inside. It's definitely a treat-myself kind of day. As I take a sip of my sweet creamy coffee, I hear a soft knock on my door.

Who in the world would be knocking on my door at—I glance at the microwave—*nine* in the morning?

I groan as another knock hits the door. I know Mason said he was stopping by, but he had even less sleep than I did. It can't be him.

"Just a second," I shout, wrapping my robe around my waist and tying the sash into a knot. Leaving my coffee on the counter, I make my way toward the uninvited guest. I pull open the door to find a little blue marshmallow standing on my porch.

"Hi, Miss Emery." Rhys beams up at me. He's bundled up in a puffy coat, matching blue pants, a beanie, and gloves.

"Hi, sweetie. What are you doing here so early?" I ask, squatting down.

Mason steps behind him from the side, wearing a black puffy coat and a smile, nearly knocking the breath out of me. He looks just as sexy as he did on our second date, which was a hike on the mountain trails close by.

My hand flies to my hair, and I try to smooth it out to no avail as I stand.

Mason roams his eyes over my body, eating me up as if I were wearing scantily clad lingerie before him and not a red fleece robe and matching pajamas.

"We came to take you on a hike," Rhys says, breaking up the eye-fucking his uncle and I were just lost in. "Are you ready to go?"

I glance down at my jams again and chuckle. "No. I just woke up, but if you give me a minute, I can go change. Is that okay with you?"

"Okay. Can I play with Henry, please?" He clasps his hands under his chin as he bounces excitedly on his toes. He has been obsessed with my pup since he dog-sat for me on Valentine's weekend. The same weekend I completely fell for his uncle.

"Of course. Come on in. It's cold out." I open the door wider, gesturing for him and the silent Mason to come inside.

Today is your typical winter day in the Pacific Northwest. Gray, cold, cloudy, and—let's not forget—wet. But I love it. It totally beats the freezing temperatures and snow I lived through growing up back east.

Rhys runs straight for Henry, who is sleeping on the couch, no doubt tired from all my tossing and turning.

I spin around, coming face to face with Mason. His warm spicy scent hits me, making my mouth water, and my knees wobble like a baby lamb's as I breathe in his intoxicatingly deliciousness.

"Good morning, baby doll." He leans down and kisses the corner of my mouth, making my brain glitch.

My inner devil is on her knees, begging for him to press those soft lips to mine and give me a proper kiss. When my brain switches back on, I step back and take a breath while fiddling with my sash.

"Bringing your very cute nephew so I can't say no is pretty low."

"I have to do whatever I can to sway you," he says with a sexy smirk.

"Is that right? So I should expect to be ambushed again?" I cross my arms over my chest.

Mason tries not to stare at my boobs as they plump up. He licks his lips. "Ambushed?" He quirks a brow at me. "I told you I'd see you today."

"I didn't think you were serious. You didn't even say when, so..." I let the sentence dangle, biting my lip.

If I'm being real, I didn't think he'd actually show up today—his brother got married yesterday, and Mason has to have work or something. I did not expect a knock on my door at nine in the morning.

"Hmm." He grunts, running his hand over his jaw.

Sorry sits at the tip of my tongue, but I swallow it down.

"I deserve that. I guess I'm going to have to work harder at getting you to believe me."

"Mason..."

"No. I was serious last night. This is where I want to be. I want to be with you, and I am going to earn your trust back."

"But—"

"No," he snaps. "We are done talking about this. Now, go change." I narrow my eyes at him before he adds, "Please."

"You can't—"

"Miss Emery?" Rhys calls from the couch, stopping me from snapping back at his uncle's bossy tone.

"Yes, sweetie?"

"Can we please take Henry with us?" he pleads, giving me puppy dog eyes that brim with hope.

I can't help smiling at all his sweetness. Oh hell, I bet that cute look on his face works on everyone. I glance back at Mason, whose face matches his nephew's, and I freaking melt.

Damn these Miller boys and their handsome faces.

"That's a great idea. I bet Henry would love that. I do have to warn you, his little legs get tired fast."

"That's okay. I can carry him," Rhys says matter-of-factly, petting Henry's head.

"Em."

I return my gaze to Mason's burning hazel orbs that singe my skin and make my center pulse with desire.

"Go change."

Uncontrollable shivers race up my back at his bossy tone. He doesn't miss my body's reaction and flashes me a smug smirk. He knows exactly what he's doing to me.

"Fine. I'll get dressed." I point at him, biting back a smile. "But only for Rhys."

"I'll take it," he grumbles, muttering, "For now," under his breath.

Hiding my smile, I turn on my heels and race to my room as I feel his eyes track my every move. As quickly as I can, I tie my hair into a messy bun on top of my head, wash my face, rub on some moisturizer, and throw on a pair of black fleece workout leggings, a matching thermal, and a pair of socks.

When I return to the living room, Mason is sitting on the couch with Rhys, Henry lying between them with his tongue hanging out, getting his tummy scratched. I lean against the wall, watching them laugh and fawn over my dog.

Mason is so sweet and attentive with Rhys, and I can picture him being the same way with his own son. Their shaggy brown hair flopping around as they'd laugh and joke around. I'd be sitting next to them with Mason's arms around me, holding me tight. The idea of having a family of my own grows stronger watching them.

"Are you ready?" a gruff voice asks, ripping me out of my Daddy Mason daydreams.

"Do you want kids?" I blurt out. Slapping a hand over my mouth, I can feel my face burn red.

Why the hell would I ask that?

Mason chuckles, the sound vibrating deep in his chest. Eyes locked on mine, he stands from the couch and strides towards me until we are toe to toe, leaving Rhys out of earshot with my happily spoiled dog.

Cupping my cheeks, he whispers, "Ask me again."

My eyes bounce between his green- and gold-streaked gaze, searching for the answer. His cheek twitches as my teeth find my bottom lip and dig in, too afraid to ask again. He nods his head, giving me the confidence I need.

"Do you want kids?"

"Only with you," he confesses.

The butterflies in my stomach flutter at his answer, reminding me again why I fell for him in the first place.

Biting back a smile, I nod back like a happy idiot. "Charmer."

"Only for you." Mason winks at me. He fucking winks.

In all the months I've known him, I have never seen him wink. Sure, he's playful, but there has always been a seriousness about him. But this? It's unexpected. It's hot. It makes my damn knees wobble.

If he keeps pumping up the charm, there is no doubt in my mind Mason will have me falling all over again. Maybe even deeper this time around.

We need to have a serious talk about what happens next. I can't go back to what we had before. I want more. If we are going to try making this work, he needs to know that, before I or both of us get hurt.

He holds out his hand and I take it, once again letting him lead me out the door and into the unknown.

"Rhys, don't go too far ahead," Mason shouts as his nephew.

"Okay, Uncle Mills." Rhys continues to hop along ahead of us, with the leash in hand and a happy Henry at his side.

"Uncle Mills," I repeat, shaking my head. "I still can't believe I didn't catch it sooner."

Mason squeezes my hand. He hasn't let go since we left the house, tightly twining his fingers through mine as if he's afraid I might disappear if he lets go. I wouldn't have it any other way. I'm afraid if he lets go, I'll wake up from this wonderful dream.

He pulls me to a stop, softly rubbing his thumb over my knuckles, sending a surge of heat through me.

"It's all my fault. I should have spoken about my family more. You weren't the only one holding back. I'm sorry, baby doll."

He's right. We did hold back parts of ourselves. I did it to protect my brother, and he did it to protect himself. I knew about his ex and how other women have used him to get closer to his brothers. I hate those women for hurting him, for making him think he's not worthy of love and attention. Mason is perfect just as he is.

"Me too," I rasp, emotion clogging my throat. I want to throw my arms around him and hug him like nothing has changed, but the fear of losing him again holds me back.

Mason glances ahead and my gaze follows, watching Rhys's back as he continues walking without a care in the world.

"We better catch up."

Picking up our pace, we close the widening gap between us and Rhys, Henry still happily trotting along.

Is this how a future with Mason would be? He said he wanted children with me, but there is a lot I need from him before I fully let him back in.

"Penny for your thoughts." He bumps his shoulder against mine, pulling a smile out of me.

"You'd be poor."

Mason chuckles and shrugs. "I'd hand over every cent in my bank account." He lifts my hand to his lips as he presses a kiss to my knuckles, sending my heart racing. "I'd give you everything right now if I thought it would help erase my mistakes and make you mine again."

At his admission, my insides twist and dip like I'm on the roller-coaster ride of my life. Adrenaline and excitement course through my veins as my hold on his hand tightens, and I stop on the trail in disbelief.

"You can't say things like that," I squeak out, licking my suddenly dry lips.

He watches the movement like a hawk. "Why?" His voice is gruff, thick with lust as he stares at my mouth. "It's the truth. I love you. I'll do anything for you."

"Please, stop." My heart thuds in my chest.

"Never. Get used to it, baby doll. I'll never go another day without you. You'll never go another day not knowing you mean everything to me." He stares into my eyes so intently there is no doubt in my mind that he's telling the truth.

He leans forward, and I close my eyes, waiting for another kiss that never comes. He runs his nose up my neck and jaw, breathing me in before placing a soft kiss on my temple. I snap my eyes open when he tugs at the hand he's still holding.

My feet find a way to keep moving with him as I attempt to wrap my head around this new Mason. A Mason who tells me how he feels. Everything about him and us feels the same, and yet it's also so very different, like we are finally opening all the parts of ourselves we held back before.

"Aside from work, how have you been?" he asks after a few feet of silence.

"Umm. Fine, I guess." I shrug. What does he want me to say? The truth?

I was sad and lonely. I spent countless nights crying myself to sleep, dreaming about you, wondering where you were, who you were with.

A growly hum rumbles in his chest as his shoulder brushes mine.

"What's that sound for?"

"Nothing."

I glare at him, and he laughs. Like, really laughs. Where the hell has this carefree Mason been?

"We all know 'fine' means 'not fine'. Which is fine. I deserve that answer."

The leaves and dirt crunch beneath our feet as we continue walking for another few beats.

"I wasn't fine," he says nonchalantly.

Oh.

"You weren't?"

"Hell no. I was miserable. You can ask Kenzo. He called me an insufferable asshole. He and the others..."

"Hurry up, guys!" Rhys shouts, popping our bubble. "I haven't got all day, you know." He leans down and picks up Henry.

"Where do you need to be, dude? You're supposed to be hanging out with me today."

"I know," Rhys says, rolling his eyes. He lifts a finger and points at the views. "But you also owe me ice cream before Mom finds out."

Mason chuckles. "What happens if your mom finds out?"

"She won't let me eat leftover wedding cake," he says, the *duh* implied in his tone.

"Little shit," Mason mumbles with affection as we step up beside Rhys at the top of the trailhead.

I step up to the wood fence and look out over the small town. The valley below is green and littered with trees. Scattered homes surround the main drag of buildings that make up small downtown Pine Hills.

"Beautiful," I breathe out, staring at the only place that has ever felt like home.

"You're beautiful," Mason whispers in my ear, stealing my attention. His hot breath fans across my ear, pebbling my skin and sending scorching chills down my spine.

Without thinking, I turn into him, bringing us chest to chest. He cups my face with his free hand, tilting my chin up. Our breaths mingle as Mason stares at me, giving me the opportunity to stop him.

I don't. I want him to kiss me.

"Gross. Are you guys going to kiss like my mom and dad?" Rhys groans, making me laugh.

I drop my forehead to Mason's chest, shaking my head. "He's a riot."

"More like a little cockblocker," Mason grouses.

"Oh stop, he's funny." I step away, giving us space, but Mason clings to my hand, refusing to let me go.

I like that he feels the need to keep us connected. I missed this. I missed him.

"I guess we're going to have ice cream. Interested in joining?" he asks.

"Sure. I love vanilla ice cream." I smirk at him while I let my eyes roam up and down his body.

"Vanilla? I'll give you vanilla." Mason throws his arm over my shoulders, tugs me to his side, and whispers, "With whip cream and sprinkles on top as I lick it off of you."

Heat swirls low in my stomach as my thighs clench at his innuendo. Thoughts of being covered in dessert as Mason devours me flood my brain.

Hmm. Maybe someday?

Someday soon, I hope.

FORTY-NINE

Mason & Emery

TEXT CHAIN

JANUARY 1

Mason: Thank you for going on a hike with me and Rhys.

Emery: I had a great time.

Mason: I forgot to tell you that I need to head to L.A. for work. But I'll be back soon.

Emery: OK.

Mason: Emery?

Emery: Mason?

Mason: I'll be back.

Emery: I know.

Mason: I love you.

Emery: Charmer.

Mason: Only for you.

Emery: We'll see.

Mason: Good night, baby doll.

Emery: Good night, Mason.

FIFTY

Bro-tally Awesome

TEXT CHAIN

MASON: HEADED TO L.A. tonight. Gotta tie up some loose ends.

Cam: What flight? Eli and I are too.

Mason: 9pm.

Eli: Same. See you at the airport, brother.

Cam: Oh shit! Did you hear?

Mase: Hear what?

Cam: That guy Graham hooked up with Lexi.

Jace: What?!

Cam: Yup. Saw him sneaking out of her room this morning.

Eli: How do you know it wasn't Laci?

Jace: Does it matter?

Mase: As long as it's not my girl, that guy can fuck who ever he likes.

Cam: **Crying Laughing Emoji** Believe me, it was Lexi.

Eli: Think Levi knows?

Jace: No. And you better not say a damn thing.

Cam: I thought you liked him?

Jace: I do. But he's older than me. I don't think Lee would like Lexi dating an older guy.

Cam: Who said anything about dating? **Eggplant Emoji** **Cat Emoji** **Water Emoji**

Mase: See you at the airport. Jace, I'll see you when you get back from your honeymoon.

FIFTY-ONE

Mason & Emery

TEXT CHAIN

JANUARY 2

Mason: Good morning.

Emery: Morning.

Mason: How did you sleep?

Emery: Good. I think it was the hike. You?

Mason: Like shit.

Emery: Why?

Mason: I hate sleeping without you.

Emery: **Eye Roll Emoji** It's been months since we've shared a bed.

Mason: And I've slept like shit every night.

Emery: What are you doing to me?

Mason: Hopefully, getting you to fall in love with me. Is it working yet?

Emery: **Zipper Mouth Emoji**

Mason: I guess I need to step up my game. Have a good day, baby doll.

Emery: You too.

Emery: Thank you for dinner. **Red Heart Emoji**

Mason: You're welcome. Did you like it?

Emery: It's thin-crust pizza. Why wouldn't I like it?

Mason: Just making sure.

Mason: Good night, baby doll.

Emery: Good night, Mr. Bossy

💋

January 3

Mason: Good morning.

Emery: Good morning.

Mason: Are you headed back to work today?

Emery: I am. I'm going to miss Rylann, though. She keeps Scarlett in line. What about you?

Mason: I bet she does. Yeah, I'm headed to work. I have a lot of meetings today. I'm making my team work, even though they don't want to.

Emery: Why not? You guys love what you do.

Mason: They do. But I told you I was an insufferable asshole and they banded against me.

Emery: You, insufferable? Yes. Asshole? I don't believe it.

Mason: Believe it, baby doll. Without you, I was a wreck.

Emery: ...

Mason: I gotta go, but I'll be home in a few days.

Emery: What do you mean, home?

Emery: Mason?

Mason: How was dinner?

Emery: Delicious. It reminded me of our drive up PCH. How on earth did you find clam chowder in a bread bowl?

Mason: I have my ways.

Emery: Hmm. So cryptic.

Mason: I'm not cryptic. I'm romantic.

Emery: Oh no. Are you with Cam?

Mason: No, why?

Emery: Sounds like a line he would use.

Mason: You're going to pay for that comment.

Emery: **Eye Roll Emoji**

Mason: Emery...

Emery: Mason...

Mason: You're such a brat.

Emery: But you like it.

Mason: Wrong.

Mason: I love it.

Emery: BTW, you never answered my question earlier.

Mason: If that's how it's gonna be...

Mason: What question?

Emery: Ugh, never mind.

Mason: **Winky Face Emoji**

Emery: **Eye Roll Emoji**

Mason: I love you.

Emery: ...

Mason: Good night, Em.

Emery: Good night, Mase.

◆

January 4

Mason: Good morning.

Emery: Morning.

Mason: How's your day?

Emery: Busy. Yours?

Mason: Same. I just ate a pear, and it made me think of you.

Emery: **Blushing Emoji**

Mason: Fuck, I didn't mean for that to sound so dirty.

Emery: Sure you didn't.

Mason: Now I am thinking about it, and it's not the best time to have a hard-on.

Emery: **Laughing Emoji** Are you working?

Mason: No, I'm with my mom. She's helping me with something. I doubt she wants to see her son's boner.

Emery: Have fun with that.

Emery: **picture of Emery blowing the camera a kiss**

Mason: You're not helping.

Emery: Tell your mom I said hi. It was lovely meeting her at the wedding.

Mason: She says hello.

Emery: Did she know who I was?

Mason: No, but she does now, and she's very excited to meet you as my girlfriend next time.

Emery: Girlfriend?

Mason: Yeah, babe. Girlfriend.

Emery: ...

Mason: Emery?

Emery: Yeah?

Mason: Don't freak out.

Emery: I'm not. At least, not completely. How will this even work, Mason?

Mason: We can talk when I get home. I gotta go.

Emery: There's that word again.

Mason: Good night, babe.

Emery: Good night.

Mason: Dream of me.

Emery: ...

Emery: I always do.

Mason: I fucking love you.

💋

January 5

Mason: Rise and shine, baby doll.

Emery: Why are you texting so early?

Mason: I thought you would be up. Don't you have kickboxing this morning?

Emery: I was going to skip. I'm exhausted. But since I'm up...

Mason: Sorry. I'll make it up to you.

Emery: You better.

Mason: From now until forever. Your wish is my command.

Emery: It's too early for this.

Mason: Grouch.

Emery: Says the broody brother.

Mason: That's two.

Emery: Two what?

Mason: ...

Emery: Mason? Two what?

Mason: Go check by your front door.

Emery: Don't think I don't see what you're doing.

Mason: I'm not doing anything.

Emery: **picture of box**

Emery: What is it?

Mason: Open it.

Emery: You bought me new boxing gloves.

Mason: Do you like them?

Emery: Love them. How did you know I needed a new pair?

Mason: I figured you might have worn out the last pair picturing my face while you beat the punching bag

Emery: Cute.

Emery: Thank you.

Mason: You're welcome. I'll be home soon. Love you.

Emery: Home?

FIFTY-TWO

Mason

I PURPOSEFULLY IGNORE EMERY'S last text about home, dropping my phone on the bed with a smile. It's going to drive her crazy, but I need to finish packing the two suitcases I'm taking with me to Portland.

Everything else is packed and ready to be shipped. My mom—the saint of a woman she is—helped me pack up my house yesterday. Everything I will need is ready to be shipped north when the sale of my Pine Hills house goes through.

Yep. I bought a house two blocks from Jace and Rylann. It's still pending, but I couldn't pass it up. I made an offer on the place after my hike with Emery. I was driving Rhys back home when I saw the *For Sale* sign on the front yard of a cute little white ranch. I called the realtor, who surprisingly answered on New Year's Day, and immediately set up a viewing. I made an offer, and the owners accepted.

The four-bedroom, three-bathroom home is a fixer-upper but has great bones. It's the perfect size to raise a family. If Emery prefers to stay at her place, I'm good with that too. She holds all the cards. I want her to be happy, and she deserves the freedom to choose.

But the family? That's non-negotiable. I haven't been able to stop thinking about it since Emery asked if I wanted to have kids. I almost proposed to her on the spot, but I could tell she freaked herself out. Since then, I've imagined her belly swollen with our babies growing inside her. Little girls that look like her, with caramel-brown hair and topaz-colored eyes.

Cameron honks the horn just as I zip my case. I grab my bags, lock up my house, throw my bags in the trunk, and slide into Cam's Mercedes G-Class. He's my ride to the airport since I opted to sell my car back to the dealership yesterday.

"Sup, bro? Are you all set?"

"Yup. I'm ready."

"Have you told her yet?"

"No. I was waiting until our first date."

"Smooth."

I rest my head back against the seat, second-guessing my decision to keep the house a surprise. "Should I have told her? Do you think she's going to be pissed I didn't tell her sooner?"

"Nah. You're good. It's a panty-melting grand gesture. She's going to love it. Just don't ask her to move in right away. You don't want to come off as a desperate, needy simp."

I groan. "Fuck. Am I really that pathetic?"

Cameron chuckles. "A little. But when it's for love, you can't go wrong. Look at Jace. He's the biggest simp I know, and he's happy as fuck. Plus, he has a fucking hot wife, so being a simp can't be that bad, can it?"

I bark a laugh. "If Jace were here, he'd kick your ass for calling Rylann hot."

"But he's not." Cameron turns up the radio and takes the freeway to L.A. International Airport.

❦

I knock on Emery's door, making Henry bark.

My girl doesn't know I got back into town today. I wanted to surprise her myself with dinner tonight—tacos from Blue Cantina, which I've been craving since the rehearsal dinner. Bonus, Mexican food is Emery's favorite.

For the last few days, I have had dinner delivered to her. She's been busy covering for Rylann, who left on her honeymoon with Jace, and I wanted to make sure she didn't have to think about anything after a long day of work—my way of taking care of her while I'm away.

So far, every meal has been a reminder of meals we've shared or talked about. Reminders of us. I'm trying to recreate all the special moments we've shared together, molding them into new memories. Memories untainted by our mistakes.

She swings open the door, knocking the breath from my lungs. I caught her at the perfect time. Her face is free of makeup, her hair is tied into a side braid, and she's changed from her work clothes into her favorite old UNY flannel pants and an eerily familiar gray dress shirt. A shirt I have been missing and couldn't remember where I left it.

I love knowing that she's had it all this time. A piece of me was still with her, even when I wasn't. I hope she wore it and missed me as much as I missed her. I did some pretty unconscionable things to sate my need to know how she was doing.

"Hello, baby doll." My face splits into a grin.

She looks motherfucking gorgeous in my clothes. Like mine.

"Mason, what are you doing here?" She tugs at the shirt's collar.

"I'm here to deliver your dinner." I hold up the white paper takeout bag in my hand.

She takes it from me and peeks inside the bag that contains chicken tacos, rice and beans, and a side of guacamole and chips. I may have left my burrito in the bag in hopes of a dinner invitation. She closes the bag and looks up at me with a wide smile that makes my heart grow two sizes as it beats wildly in my chest.

She so fucking pretty.

"You didn't have to, but thank you."

"I wanted to. I want to take care of you."

Emery surprises me by wrapping her arms around my waist. Her sweet scent invades my nose as I hug her back, pulling her tight to my chest. Her nearness soothes the jagged pieces inside me that have longed for her to be in my arms again.

"I missed you so fucking much, baby doll."

I've hated being away from her these last few days. Texting wasn't near enough. Hell, it wasn't enough before everything turned to shit, but I can't dive back in head first.

At least, she can't. She needs to ease back into the waters, so to speak. I don't want to scare her off, but I'm ready for more of her, being with her, by her side, in her bed. I'd chain myself to her if it wasn't considered crazy.

But I am crazy. Crazy for Emery. It feels fantastic having my girl back in my arms.

She releases me first and pulls me inside her home. It's warm and smells just like her, sweet and fruity. I stand by the door and watch her ass sway as she walks to the kitchen, and then places the bag of food on the counter.

I almost miss her, "I missed you too," because I'm staring at the way her body moves.

My eyes snap to hers. "Say it again."

She shakes her head, fighting a smile. She knows I was ogling her like a pervert.

"Come on, say it," I urge her, shooting her a wink. It's an odd thing for me, but I can't find it in me to stop.

Cameron's right—Jace is rubbing off on me. I'm becoming a simp. Fuck if I care.

"Fine. I missed you. Happy?" She crosses her arms under her chest, lifting her perfect tits up, and boy do they look edible in my shirt. The opened buttons give me the right amount of cleavage to admire.

"Incredibly happy," I admit.

Her cheeks flush, and damn if it doesn't remind me of the way she looks as she comes all over my cock. My dick thickens behind my zipper. Stuffing my hands in my pockets, I step back.

"Can I walk Henry for you?" I need something to do, and a bit of fresh air will definitely kill my growing hard-on.

"You don't have to. I—"

"I'd like to do it. I checked the weather, and it's supposed to rain soon. Let me help you. You go and eat, decompress. Do whatever you need to do, and I'll take him for a few minutes."

"Are you sure?"

"Absolutely."

She lifts Henry from his spot on the couch while I grab his leash from the hook. After clipping the leash to his collar, I take the little Yorkie around the block and let him do his business.

When I return, I find Emery sitting at her small table, with two place settings and the bag of food in the middle of it. Music I've never heard is quietly playing in the background, and she's on her phone, texting.

Henry runs to her, taking me by surprise and the leash along with him.

"There's my boy. Did you have a good walk?"

Henry yips, his tongue dangling to the side.

She scratches behind his ear, and for a moment, I'm jealous of a fucking tiny-ass dog that's getting all the attention of the girl I like.

She looks up at me and smiles, and I swear my heart skips a beat. Her brown eyes shine as she watches me watch her.

"Are you going to stand by the door and stare at me all night, or are you going to come over here and eat dinner with me?"

Both.

"Are you sure? I can grab my burrito and head out."

She raises a brow at me. "Mason?"

"Yeah?"

"Please come sit down and eat with me." She pats the table.

My feet automatically move in her direction.

She removes the to-go containers from the bag, spreading them out, and places the burrito on the plate beside her as I take my seat.

"What did you get?" she asks, dipping a tortilla chip in guac.

I watch her mouth open wide as she places the triangle on her tongue, and her lips wrap around her finger as she licks the creamy avocado dip off. Images of her on her knees with her mouth open wide hit me like a ton of bricks, and my cock springs to life.

Holy fuck. I'm screwed. I don't think I'm going to make it. She doesn't even realize how gorgeous and sexy she is when ... when she does anything. That's how unassumingly stunning she is.

"Mason."

My eyes find hers, giving her my full attention.

"What kind of burrito did you order?" she asks again.

"Ch—" My throat constricts, so I clear it. "Chicken."

What the fuck, man? Get your shit together.

Biting her thick bottom lip, she fights a smile. Thankfully, she overlooks my bumbling and continues with the small talk. "Their chicken is good."

With her help, I pull my head out of my ass.

Ass? Okay, fine. The gutter.

"Yeah. I was impressed by the food at Jace and Rylann's rehearsal dinner."

"It's Rylann's favorite spot. She introduced me to it when I first moved here, but over the summer, I went with her and Scarlett for lunch and I fell in love with it too. The owners are the nicest people. Did you know we designed their logo and website? Rylann loves going around town and getting businesses to change their graphics—"

"What about you? What do you like to do?" I interrupt.

She would talk about work all night if I let her. She loves her job and working with my sister-in-law.

"Well, you know, I liked doing corporate events, but..."

"But what?"

"Promise not to judge?"

"Why would I judge?"

She glares at me, and it's adorable. I want to kiss that sassy look right off her face.

Instead, I throw my hands up in surrender. "I promise."

"Well, helping Rylann plan the wedding was really fun. Growing up, my mother always threw these fancy parties and I always wondered what I would do differently. So maybe... I don't know. I was thinking planning another wedding could be fun. You know, in my spare time, obviously," she rambles.

She's so fucking cute when she gets nervous.

"Then that's what you should do."

I unwrap my burrito and take a huge bite. The flavor hits my tongue, and I hum. It's spicy and savory, and while it's delicious, nothing tastes better than the woman next to me. The woman that consumes my every thought.

"Really?"

I shrug, wiping my mouth. "You should do whatever makes you happy. If that means planning weddings, do it. If it includes what you do now, great. If not, well, you can cross that bridge when you get to it."

"Thank you," she whispers, her eyes glassy.

"For what?"

"For listening and not judging me. For letting me figure it out on my own without pushing me towards something you think would be better."

Her words hit me in the gut like a punch. That little bit of information says so much about her relationship with her parents. How they pushed her to be what they wanted her to be, instead of who she wants to be.

"Baby doll, you can do anything and everything you want, and I will stand by your side, supporting you. As long as you are happy—that's all that matters to me. So if you want to start another business, run a marathon, or climb Mount Everest, I will be there right beside you."

She scrunches her nose. "I think I'll pass on the marathon and the death-defying mountain climbing for now."

She cups my jaw in her soft palm, and like the addict I am, needing more of her, I lean into her touch.

"Thank you. I appreciate your support. And who knows, maybe someday ... I'll get back to you on the second business idea."

"Rylann's going to kill me," I groan.

She drops her hand and throws her head back as she barks a laugh. "I'd be more afraid of Scarlett."

"True."

She props her cheek on my shoulder, and I kiss the top of her head, sinking into and absorbing the comfortable intimacy of our dinner. Of us.

I had hoped she'd ask me to stay and eat dinner with her, but this is better than I ever expected. I run my fingers over her braid, and she shivers at my touch.

"Eat your dinner, Em."

"Yes, Mr. Bossy."

I growl and she laughs, diving into her tacos without a care that she just made my cock harder than steel with that response.

Fuck, I missed her—this—so much.

I smile to myself as I come up with ways to make her pay for it later.

FIFTY-THREE

Emery

AFTER DINNER, I CONVINCED Mason to hang around to watch an episode of our favorite show. Not like that was hard. It was cute watching him try playing it cool.

The episode ends, and we continue to sit side by side on the couch. We are snuggled up, with his arm around me and my head on his shoulder. Another episode starts to play, and I can't bring myself to hit stop.

I want him to stay. I missed him so much these last few months. In the days since he's apologized and confessed his love, he has managed to heal a considerable amount of the damage he caused to my heart by walking away. Every time he texts, calls, and sends me a small gift or dinner, he's showing me he's here for me. He tells me he loves me constantly.

I want to say it back, but I'm scared, and the words end up getting caught on the tip of my tongue. I do love him. With all my heart. I'll tell him when the time feels right, and it will for sure be in person. I want to see the look on his face when he hears the words back for the first time.

His fingers glide over my shoulder, searing me through the fabric of his shirt—the one I wear almost every night. I could tell by the huge grin on his face that he recognized it when I opened the door. He likes me in his clothes.

I splay my hand over his chest, feeling his steady heart beat beneath, running my fingers over his shirt in mindless circles. My core throbs, begging for him to touch me. I shift, letting my hand brush over the noticeable bulge in his jeans. My body hums as the energy between us grows hot, crackling and licking at my skin.

Mason adjusts himself beside me, drawing my eyes to his.

With his free hand, he tilts my chin up. "Em?"

"Hmm."

"I need to head out." His voice is gruff and sultry.

I can't stop myself from pouting at his attempt at leaving. I'm not ready for him to go, even though he probably should.

He presses my bottom lip down with his thumb. "Don't give me that face."

"What face?" I won't admit it to him, but I'm annoyed. He can't leave; he hasn't even kissed me yet.

Mason chuckles and presses a chaste kiss to my mouth that makes my lips tingle and the throb between my legs intensify.

"You're cute. Now, up you go. Time to walk me to the door." He scoops me up in his arms, bridal style, and strides to my front door.

Henry barks from the couch, pissed at being jostled awake.

Mason places my feet on the floor and brings our bodies flush against each other, his grip firm on my waist. I place my hands on his chest, relishing the feel of his hard body beneath me.

"Do you have any plans for Saturday?" he asks, brushing a stray hair behind my ear.

"Depends." I internally cross my fingers, hoping this is when he asks me out on a date. While I love all the delivered meals and texts, I want to spend more time with him like this.

"Brat." He kisses my forehead. "Would you like to go out on a date with me?"

I fight the urge to squeal. "I'd like that very much. Where are we going?"

"It's a surprise." He boops my nose and sweetly kisses me, making my insides melt like ice cream in the desert.

"Where are you staying?" It just occurred to me that I have no idea where Mason has been staying, nor do I know how long he plans to stick around.

"With Rhys," he whispers, pecking at my lips.

Figures that's where he'd be, especially since Rylann is off on her honeymoon for the next week. A small, teeny tiny part of me thought he might stay at the hotel we stayed in.

"Will I see you tomorrow?"

"Baby, you couldn't get rid of me if you tried." Mason covers my mouth with his in a soul-searing kiss.

My eyes flutter closed as his tongue delves past my lips, sensually exploring my mouth, stealing my breath. His fingers glide up my spine and into my hair, setting my body on fire. I moan into his mouth, arching my body into his, getting as close to him as I can. Wrapping my arms around his shoulders, I dig my fingers into his soft hair as our kiss turns hungry and desperate.

Mason breaks away, pressing his forehead to mine, his eyes squeezed tight as his rapid breaths mingle with mine in short puffs. "What are you doing to me?"

"I could ask you the same question."

"I have to go before I do something dangerous."

"Like me?" I meant the question to be a tease, not the sultry, sexy, innuendo it was.

"Yes. Fuck." Mason groans. He releases my hair and takes a step back, widening the gap between us. "Being alone with you, here in this space where your scent alone is driving me fucking wild, is dangerous."

"Dangerous? Why?"

"Because I want you so fucking badly, and I'm afraid fucking you into next week will ruin any chance I have at proving to you that you can trust me. I want more than your forgiveness, Emery."

"What do you want?"

"Everything. I want everything with you."

Everything.

My heart does a triple axel in my chest. Does this mean he wants a future with me? A real future, like one where he comes home to me every night and we don't have to waste time at airports, or worry about our time together running out?

The questions dance on the tip of my tongue, but I hold back. We can talk more this weekend when he takes me out on a date.

"Me too."

"Really?"

Is he kidding? I've wanted everything with Mason since the first moment he came crashing into my conversation with Chris.

"Really."

"Fuck yeah." Mason smashes his mouth to mine in a short, hard kiss, leaving me in a daze. He opens the door and steps through. "Lock the door as soon as I close it."

"You got it, Mr. Bossy," I sass with a salute.

"Oh, baby, I love it when you're a brat." He winks at me, and my pussy pulses.

"I know." My face splits into a cheeky grin. I know it turns him on, and then he likes to take it out on my body.

I love how easily we have fallen into us. Are we healed? No. But we'll get there.

"Good night, baby doll."

"Good night, Mason."

He closes the door and I turn the lock like he demanded, listening to his footsteps disappear into the night.

Saturday can't come soon enough.

The sound of my cell phone beeping pulls me from my sexy dreams of Mason. Last night's kiss left me aching. I tried using Bog to relieve the throb and ended up making it worse. There's only one thing—or person—that will be able to help me with my problem.

Grabbing my phone, I peel open my eyes and smile.

Mason: Good morning, baby doll

Mason's declaration pops up in my head again as I read his message. *Everything.* The word makes my stomach flip with excitement.

Emery: Good morning, Mr. Bossy.

Placing my phone on the bedside table, I throw my legs over the side of the mattress and stretch. I might as well get a head start and catch the early kickboxing class at the gym.

A knock on the door stops me in my tracks. A smile curls at my lips as I grab my robe and tie it around my waist. When I swing open the door, Mason is standing on the other side, looking delicious in jeans and boots. His jacket is open, giving me a view of his sweater at work as it stretches across his broad chest.

"Good morning, baby doll."

His gravelly voice hits me right in the center. Hearing his greeting in person is better than any text message.

He quickly kisses the corner of my mouth.

"Morning. What are you doing here?" I almost pinch myself to make sure it's really him standing at my door.

"I was up early for a call and thought I'd bring you breakfast." He lifts up a to-go cup of coffee and white paper bag stamped with the cute pastry shop in downtown Pine Hills.

"Work call?" I open the door, letting him inside.

I follow him as he saunters towards the kitchen and answers me over his shoulder, "Kind of."

Kind of? What does that mean?

"Are you going to go to your class this morning?"

"I was thinking about it. But since you're here, would you like to have breakfast with me instead?"

"More than anything." Opening the bag, Mason pulls out four foil-wrapped packages. "I didn't know what you'd like from here, so I got a couple of different options."

"Thank you." I take a seat at the counter, and opt for the veggie omelet with bacon and cheese bagel sandwich, and take a bite.

"You're welcome. So, I was thinking—"

I groan as the salty taste of bacon hits my tongue. Using my thumb, I shove a piece of the stringy, melty cheese into my mouth. Swallowing my bite, I turn to Mason. "You didn't finish your sentence."

His throat bobs as he lifts his gaze from my mouth to my eyes. "I can't think when you moan like that."

My cheeks heat. "That's so embarrassing. I'm sorry."

"Don't apologize. Ever. I love hearing you moan like that. It's a reminder of how you sound when you're coming on my cock."

My thighs clench, and I can't stop the whimper that escapes me. "You can't say things like that."

"Why?" he croons, pushing my hair behind my ear. He leans close, his lips a hair's breadth away. "Does it turn you on?" His minty breath fans across my face.

He's so close that if I move even an inch, our lips will be touching.

"Does it remind you of riding my cock until you come?"

Shivers wrack my spine at the seductively low timber in his voice and the way his gaze bores into mine.

Sucking in a ragged breath, I whisper, "Yes."

His pupils dilate as he shifts in his seat, adjusting himself. My eyes drop to his lap, and the noticeable bulge in his jeans has electricity humming in my veins, shooting straight to my center.

"Good." He kisses my nose, and sits back in his seat with a grin as he lifts his sandwich and takes a bite.

If I didn't want to kiss him and climb into his lap to ride him, I'd smack him for teasing me. But touching him right now is risky.

I shift in my seat, seeking a little friction to ease the steady drumming of my clit, and shake my head at him. "You did that on purpose."

He grins and shrugs, taking another bite of food. We sit in silence for a beat, eating our breakfast, and I make a conscious effort not to moan over my sandwich. Mason rolls his foil wrapper into a ball and gets up to throw it in the trash. I check the time—a little over an hour until I have to be at the office.

"I have some calls I need to take, but what are you doing for lunch?"

I try not to pout at his abrupt departure. "Um, nothing." Not with Rylann out and Graham incommunicado.

Dang, I'm a bad friend. I've been so wrapped up in Mason that I've forgotten about him. It doesn't help that he's been radio-silent since the wedding. I hope his grandmother is okay.

"Would you like to have lunch with me? Say, one o'clock?"

The giddy school girl in me abandons all other thoughts, focusing solely on her crush. "I'd like that very much."

"Then it's a date."

"I thought our first date was tomorrow night?" I ask, letting the tease in my tone shine through.

He sees right through me, moving to stand in front of me, and pulls me to my feet, bringing us chest to chest. "Every time we're together, it's a date." He kisses my cheek. "Like breakfast dates. Lunch dates." He kisses my forehead. "Dinner dates. Movie dates. Snuggle dates." He kisses the corner of my mouth. "Kissing dates."

"Hmm."

I moan as he places my hands on his chest. The hasty strum of his heartbeat matches mine as we stare at each other. The vivid gold in his eyes flickers like the yellow flames of a fire, warming me from the inside out. The blistering tension that exists between us builds, curling its fingers around us, pulling us closer together. Or maybe it's his large hands that grip my hips, squeezing.

Mason's phone starts ringing, shattering the intense moment between us. I have to bite my lips from screaming, *Why?*

He reaches into this pocket and pulls out his phone, looking at the screen. "Fuck. I have to take this." He gives me a soft peck on my lips and rushes out of the kitchen, but stops at the door and turns around. "I will be at your office at one. Absolutely nothing will stop me from being there. Bye, baby doll." He's out the door before I can utter a word.

What the hell just happened?

Doubt starts to creep in, taking my good mood with it. What started as a wonderful day is now clouded with uncertainty.

Can we really make this work when his life isn't here?

My palms sweat, and my gut churns as I turn down Emery's street.

I fucked up. Emery's shut down on me. She was quiet at lunch, and it left our conversation stunted. I know it's because of my abrupt departure after breakfast yesterday. I so badly wanted to tell her why I had to leave, and I would have if not for the elaborate plan I have in place for tonight.

We were in the middle of having a heated moment, where I was so close to kissing the hell out of her. I would fucking curse the real estate agent for calling at the absolute worst time if I didn't appreciate all her help. She has been invaluable in getting the escrow paperwork done and processed, as well as working with the sellers to agree on letting me onto the property immediately. They want to divest the house as quickly as I want to acquire it.

Thank fuck.

I spent most of yesterday meeting with contractors, finalizing the paperwork with the bank for the Pine Hills house, and putting my house in Venice on the market. I doubt it will sit empty for very long. It's in a highly desired neighborhood.

I pull into Emery's driveway and kill the engine. The lights are on in the window, but the lack of movement behind the curtains sends my heart racing. With a deep breath, I grab the blood-red roses I ordered for my girl—because I couldn't get the burgundy dahlias like last time—and the little white paper bag next to it, then walk to her door.

Henry barks at my knock seconds before Emery opens the door, taking my breath away.

Holy fucking shit.

I'm speechless. My mouth dries like I just ate a stack of saltines, and I almost choke on my tongue.

"Hi." She smiles, and even though it's tentative, it's genuine. She's still happy to see me.

"You're a goddamn vision," is all I can get out. I think she broke my brain.

"Thank you." Emery laughs.

The tinkling sound warms my chest and kickstarts the neurons in my cerebrum, allowing it to work again. I hand her the bouquet and the little white bag.

She sniffs the flowers, then peeks inside the bag.

"It's some doggy treats for Henry. I promised the little furball that I would bring him some more."

She chuckles again, and the warmth in my chest expands, spreading to the rest of my body. *Okay, maybe I haven't completely fucked everything up.*

"Would you like to come in for a minute?" she asks.

Her soft, sultry voice is like a shot of blood to my already thickening dick. My eyes drag and gawk down her curvy body. She's wearing a black pinstripe jumpsuit that makes her legs—even while completely covered—look a mile long. The heart-shaped top accentuates her perky tits, making my mouth water, and the belt cinched around her waist emphasizes her curves in all the right ways.

A minute would be too much time because I might say *fuck it*, attack her pouty mouth, and rip that sexy fucking thing off of her body.

"No, baby, we have a reservation we need to get to."

"Will we be home after the date?"

Home. I doubt she even realizes she said it like this is our home. She is my home.

"We will."

Her bottom lip pops out, but she recovers quickly.

"You can go and put your flowers in a vase and Henry in his pen. I'll wait here."

She looks at me, quizzically, probably wondering what the hell is wrong with me. "Are you sure?"

I give her the short answer. "Yes."

The truth is, I don't trust myself. There's a chance that if I go inside, I might maul her face off and fuck her into oblivion. Then the perfectly planned date I have for us would be ruined.

"Okay. Be right back."

She slips inside while I stand on her porch, taking deep gulping breaths, trying to calm my nerves—and my cock—down. When she opens the door again, she's wearing a wool coat that flawlessly matches her lips. A vision of her on her knees with those pretty thick lips wrapped around my thick cock ravages my already fraying control. Tonight is going to be torture.

"Where are we headed to?" She tilts her head, trying to get a read on me. She's cute.

I lead her to the car as a devious smile pulls at my mouth. Now, it's my turn to torture her. "That's a surprise."

I open the car door for her and watch her slide into the passenger seat. Her coat is open, giving me the perfect view of her cleavage as I slam the door shut. I slip into the driver's seat and turn to face her, reaching across her chest to grab the seatbelt. I buckle her in, and her breath hitches as my fingers graze her chest and thigh in the process.

Emery turns her head, bringing us nose to nose, the urge to kiss her coursing through me.

Not yet, baby doll.

"For this next part, I'm going to need you to trust me. Do you think you can do that?"

She stares into my eyes, and I'm tempted to turn my request into an order, using the bossy tone I know drives her wild.

I don't have to when she gives me a slight nod, agreeing.

The nervous tension in my shoulders is replaced with elation at her willingness to put her faith in me. Reaching into the back seat, I grab the silk tie and hold it up for her. "I'm going to need you to wear this over your eyes for the next twenty minutes."

"Mason—"

"I know it's a big ask, but I promise it will be worth it."

She bites her lip, considering her options.

I get it. I'm not sure I'd be so willing myself, but I want—no, need—her to choose this.

"Please," I beg.

"Okay. I'll do it. I trust you."

"You won't regret it."

"I know."

As promised, twenty minutes later, I lead Emery into the dimly lit room I have reserved for tonight. I also paid an extra fee to have it set up with our dinner and a bottle of wine.

"Can I take this off now?" Emery asks, bouncing on her toes, her fingers brushing the soft fabric covering her eyes.

"Let me." I stand behind her, pressing my chest to her back, and carefully undo my tie at the back of her head so as not to pull her hair.

The blindfold falls, and I watch as she blinks, adjusting to the light. My anxiety gets the best of me as she silently takes in the room.

"I know it's not exactly where we had our first date, but I wanted to recreate a part of it. Do you like it?"

I tried to get us tickets to Reel Eats again, but it didn't work out this time around. Instead, I came up with the next best thing and rented out the theater's small screening room, where they hold birthday parties. It's small and the perfect size for an intimate date.

A slow smile spreads across her face. "I love it."

"Really?"

She nods, throwing her arms around me. "Yes. It's perfect." Twining her finger through mine, she leads me to the table where the food is set up. "Tell me what you have picked out."

Her giddiness soothes the ache in my stomach that has been building up since she shut down yesterday. I feared she wouldn't be receptive to coming out with me after how we left things. But her clear excitement at what I have planned has me puffing out my chest like a damn ape.

"Tonight's delectable menu starts off with some deliciously buttery popcorn and candy of your choice." I wave my hand around the table, and she giggles. *I finally did something right.* "Followed by pepperoni pizza and nachos that will be served with a glass of your favorite sauvignon blanc."

"I didn't know they let you have wine here."

"They don't. I had to slip the manager sixty bucks under the table for him to agree, and a promise that we'd take the evidence when we leave."

"Oh, he's good."

"Tell me about it," I grumble. That fucker had me by my proverbial balls. He knew I was going to pony up the cash. Honestly, I would have paid more, so the joke's on him. "And last but not least, we will finish off with a special dessert for the lady." I point to the pink baker's box.

She glimpses at the pastry container and back at me.

I nudge her forward. "Open it. I had them specially made for you."

She reaches for the box and flips the lid with a gasp. "Are these..."

"White Russian cupcakes? Yep," I confirm.

Six specially made vanilla cupcakes with Kaluha frosting and chocolate shavings sit in the box just for her. The owner of the little bakery in town was more than happy to whip these up for me. Probably because I have eaten there every day for breakfast since I arrived.

"Oh my god, Mason. You remembered? How?"

She looks up at me in wonder, and my damn knees almost give out. Does she really not know?

"Baby doll, I remember everything you've ever told me. Every word has been ingrained in my head" — I tap my head, then place my finger on my chest — "and my heart. From the very beginning, it's all been right here."

Her eyes turn glassy, but the soft smile on her lips encourages me to lay it all out there.

"I love you, Emery. The real you. The you that loves your brother more than anything. The you that loves country music, Keanu's action movies, Geralt of Rivia, the color burgundy, New York-style pizza, and so much more. I know you hate being cold but love the rain. I know you would rather stay home in your ratty college pajamas than get dressed and go out for dinner. I know you work hard and care so much about everyone around you that you put yourself last, and I know I let you down, Em. I was so fucking stupid to walk away without letting you explain. You don't know how sorry I am. I will never forgive myself for that, but I promise I will never walk away again. I—"

Emery jumps into my arms, surprising me. I grip her under her ass, and she throws her arms around my neck and slams her mouth to mine in a hard kiss that ends too quickly for my liking.

"Stop. I forgive you. This ..." She waves her hand around the room. "It's too much and everything all at once."

"Yeah?" I assumed she had forgiven me, but hearing is better. It's the confirmation my heart needed.

Emery cups my jaw in her warm palms and nods.

Without a second to waste, I close the distance and kiss her like my life depends on it. Like she's the very air I breathe. Because she is.

I'm an idiot for walking away. I squandered too much being angry and miserable without her. But no more. I'm holding onto this woman for the rest of my life.

Emery tangles her tongue around mine, and the sweet taste of mint hits me like a Category 5 storm. My blood boils over as the heat in my veins travels south, right to my cock.

Fuck, she tastes so good.

Taking control of her mouth, I pull her closer, deepening the kiss, twirling my tongue around hers while she moans in my mouth. It feels so good to have her back in my arms.

As if she knows what I'm thinking, she wraps her legs around my waist and pulls on the strands of my hair, gripping me as tightly as possible, like I might disappear if she doesn't.

Never gonna happen. She can bet on it.

I cup the firm globes of her ass in my palms and hold her up. She rolls her hips, grinding herself on my hardening shaft, and the heat of her pussy seeps through the fabric between us, eroding the last remaining pieces of my control.

There is so much more I need to tell her. After.

I have a plan.

Before I snap and screw up my plans by fucking her right here in the movie theater, I break the kiss. "You're killing me, Em."

She giggles, and the sultry sound is like a straight shot of blood to my dick. Unlocking her legs from around my hips, she slowly drops them to the floor and glides her heat over my painfully hard cock, eliciting a groan from deep in my chest.

"Fuck," I grind out.

She rubs the lipstick from around my mouth with her thumb, and I can't help myself from biting it, making her throw her head back and laugh. The sound pushes me closer to blowing my load in my jeans.

"Go sit down," I demand.

She narrows her eyes at me, but instead of fighting back, she walks up the stairs with an exaggerated sway in her hips. When she looks over her shoulder at me and bats her lashes, I almost fall to my knees and crawl to her. It's the look in her eyes that gets me.

She's happy. Her flirty smile reaches her eyes, and the earthy topaz of her irises sparkles with love. I take an extra second to memorize this look. It's one I hope to earn every day for the rest of our lives.

Then the sexy brat bites her thick bottom lip, snapping me out of my daydream, and I all but growl as I chase after her. She's in her seat before I can scoop her up and place her on my lap, which is probably for the best. Taking the seat next to her, I adjust my body, so that I am facing her, thankful that this theater has fancy stadium seats and the armrests and tray tables are out of the way, making it feel like we are sitting on the couch instead of an uncomfortable chair.

"What are we watching?" she asks, pretending like she didn't just wave a red flag in my face.

"You're a brat."

She smirks at me. "You like it."

I do.

"I should have asked if you wanted anything to eat before we sat down."

"Oh, good call. I'm hungry."

I stop her as she stands, pulling her down to sit.

"Stay. I got this. Tonight is all about you. What do you want?"

She visibly swallows, and I know she's thinking about wanting more than just food. "A little of everything?"

With a lascivious grin, I stand. "Oh, baby Doll. I hope you're ready for a lot more of everything."

FIFTY-FIVE

Emery

I WATCH AS MASON fixes two plates of food for us to eat. I can't believe he did all this for me. He's trying to recreate our first date, and while I love it, this time it means so much more.

We mean so much more.

Even though yesterday felt like a setback and I still want to know what had him rushing out of my house so quickly, we are heading in the right direction tonight. He has more than earned my forgiveness, not only with words but with actions.

Carrying one of those cardboard food trays, he makes his way up the stairs. "Here's your food, my lady." He hands me the box that has a small container of popcorn, a slice of pizza, some nachos, and of course, a cupcake.

I almost melted on the spot when I opened the pastry box. One whiff of the coffee-infused frosting, and I knew they were like the ones I mentioned serving if we were screening *The Big Lebowski*.

"Thank you, kind sir." I giggle. Freaking giggle. I'm definitely drunk on the sexy man serving me.

"Please don't call me 'sir'," he grumbles.

I raise an eyebrow, waiting for him to continue.

"I don't want to talk about it, but let's just say I heard Jace get called 'sir', and now it makes my dick shrivel up."

"Wait, that means..."

"Yup. She said it, and I heard it."

I throw my head back and laugh. "Wow, I'm impressed. I didn't realize Rylann was so adventurous."

"If you only knew," he mumbles under his breath. I know he didn't mean for me to hear it, but the comment sparks my curiosity.

Another time. Tonight is for us.

I take a few bites of pizza and wash it down with a sip of wine, which helps take the edge off my nerves. Before I can ask him about the duration of his stay in Pine Hills, the lights flicker.

"I forgot to mention that I wasn't able to get them to play your movie. The manager was pretty adamant about only showing what was available here, even though I offered to buy the film. The asshole."

I place my hand on his. "I don't care about the movie, Mason. This is perfect."

He leans forward and places a chaste kiss on my lips. "I'm glad you like it. I have more surprises for you after the movie."

"Really?"

He nods at me with a wink, and poof, my panties disintegrate. His lips turn up in a smug, sexy grin, and I'm powerless to keep from kissing him. So I do.

Sparks shock me as I press my lips to his in a soft kiss. It starts off slow but quickly turns rough and deep, like we can't get enough of each other. The movie starts, but we stay lip-locked, making out like a couple of teenagers, our hands roaming each other's bodies. His hands are everywhere—in my hair, tugging, groping my breasts, digging into my hips. It's glorious.

I have no idea what movie is playing, nor do I care. My focus is on the way Mason's scruff scratches my chin as he sucks on my tongue, my lips, my neck. The way my body aches for him to be inside me and my clit pulses with the need to come. The fire that simmers low in my stomach travels between my legs, making me desperate for his touch.

"Mason," I moan, his name a plea and a prayer on my lips.

He sucks the spot below my ear, no doubt marking my sensitive skin as I grab and tug at his shirt.

"I need you."

"Not yet." He covers my mouth with his as he swallows my needy moans. His tongue slides against mine, reminding me just how talented he is with it.

A flood of arousal soaks my core and I can't take it anymore. I need more. Throwing my leg over his lap, I straddle his firm thighs. His hands fly to my ass and hold me still as my lips find his neck, and I take my turn nipping at his throat.

"Baby, I need you to slow down." He gently nudges me back, forcing inches between.

"Why? No one is here. I missed you." Batting my lashes, I twirl his hair through my fingers.

"Fuck, I missed you too. But not like this. I refuse to let a dirty movie theater be the first place I fuck you after all these months. Not after—"

The bathroom.

He pushes a strand of hair behind my ear, and my breath hitches at the look in his eyes, begging me to let him make the next time we come together be special. To erase the past.

"I want that too."

Mason flashes me a smile that reaches his eyes. The tension and worry in them has dissipated, leaving him looking happy. It's hard to imagine him as the sweet and silent, albeit slightly broody man he was when we first started dating. He's opened himself up to me in ways never expected.

"Want to get out of here?" he asks.

I glance behind me at the screen and back at the man whose lap I'm on. No contest. "Definitely."

"Thank fuck. You're killing me. I also promised you more surprises, and I'd like to deliver."

"Good ones?" I hedge, curious about what else he has up his sleeve.

"I fucking hope so."

Mason stands, still holding me in his arms, and my stomach grumbles. Mason scowls as I muffle a laugh at the timing.

"I'm already doing a shit job at taking care of you. You need to eat, Em."

"I'm fine, Mr. Bossy. We can pack up the food to go. I'm ready to get out of here."

He growls but concedes after I agree to eat some popcorn on the way. I make a vain attempt at helping Mason clean up, knowing my charmingly growly man will refuse it. So, I just stand back and watch his strong arms move as he packs our meal into canvas bags. He's pulled his sweater to his elbows, giving me the perfect view of Mason's forearm porn.

Feeling my stare, he looks up and winks at me ogling him. My thighs clench at his sexy smolder. I'm glad my friends talked me into a special shopping trip before my date. Tonight has been perfect. Better than I imagined.

What could Mason possibly surprise me with next?

The butterflies in my stomach flutter at the possibilities. He really has gone all out. Good thing I have something up my sleeve too.

💋

Mason makes his way down the streets of Pine Hills. Instead of turning towards my neighborhood, he turns in the opposite direction and pulls the car into a bumpy driveway, cutting the engine.

The house that sits to the right is an older ranch. It's cute and looks spacious, though it obviously needs work. The front yard is small, but the large two-car garage more than makes up for it. The home reminds me of the ones Rylann and Scarlett live in. I look around, trying to figure out where we're at.

Twisting in my seat, I face Mason. "Whose house is this?"

"About that. I need to talk to you about something." He rubs his jaw.

The scratching sounds that usually makes my panties wet, sounds ominous. My stomach flips, and not in the good way like when he holds my hand or kisses me. This is a lead ball of fear and anxiety. It's never good when someone says, *I need to talk to you about something,* right?

"Should I be worried?" I swallow the lump in my throat. Dropping my eyes to my coat, I pick at the non-existent lent in the dark car, too afraid to look at him.

"Emery, please look at me."

Dragging my eyes up his torso, I watch his rapid pulse beat in the vein of his neck and his Adam's apple bob as he swallows, before bringing my eyes to his.

"Yesterday, when I got that call and had to leave, it wasn't because of work. I want you to know my career will never come before you. I know it was a mistake to leave, but I wanted this to be a surprise in case it didn't work out."

"In case what didn't work out?" I whisper.

He brushes his thumb over my bottom lip and up my cheek bone. "The house, baby doll. I bought it. It's mine."

"Wait..." My brain short-circuits, and I don't know what to say. His house? But he lives in...

"Your house?" I mull over the words, tasting them on my tongue. "Your. House."

"You can say it again if it helps. This is my house. I'm moving here. I put the house in Venice on the market and bought this one. That's why I left last week. I saw this place and knew I had to buy it. I went back to Los Angeles to pack my belongings. This house is why I had to rush out yesterday. The real estate agent called, asking me to meet her and finalize the paperwork. Then, I met with the contractors and—"

"Wait! You—" I point at him. "You're moving here? T-to Pine Hills?" I stutter, tripping over my words as my heart races and my brain tries to play catch-up.

"Where the hell else am I going to live? You live here, right?"

I nod, stupidly, as my nose tickles with unshed tears as I squeak out, "Are you serious?"

"Dead fucking serious. Do I need to remind you that you're it for me? When I was on my knees, I swore to you. I'm here, and I'm never letting you go again."

"But what about your work?"

"Fuck my work," he snaps.

"Mason—"

"No, baby doll." He curls his palm around my neck, digs his fingers into my nape, and squeezes, boring his determined eyes into mine. "I have been miserable without you. My best friends hate me. My entire team is over my grumpy attitude. I love my career, my company, but what's the point? None of it matters if I don't have you."

I grab his jacket, shaking him. "You can't quit. What you do is too important. I won't let you."

Mason throws his head back and laughs, covering my hand with his big warm palms. "Relax, Emery. I'm moving, not quitting. I'm not an idiot."

"What does all this mean?"

"First, thank you for understanding how important my work and career are to me. Second, it means I work from home. I still have to travel, but when I'm not, I'll be here. With you."

"And Kenzo is okay with this?" I bite my lip. Is this really happening?

"He is. He's happy for me. Everyone is, actually. Maybe a little too happy."

I can't help the high-pitched laugh that comes out of me. He must have been a really grouchy asshole these past few months.

"So, what do you think?"

"I think I can't believe it."

He gave up his home for me. He moved here so we could make *us* work. He's really all in.

Mason releases my neck as the car gets eerily quiet. "Shit." Mason closes his eyes, resting his head against his seat. "I fucked up, didn't I?"

While my insides and my brain have been throwing a parade, I forgot to let my man know just how excited I am to have him here. Every day.

I climb over the center console and crawl into his lap, cradling his face in my hands, staring into his warm hazel eyes. "You have made me the happiest girl on the planet. You didn't fuck up at all. You made everything better. I've been too afraid to tell you that I want more this time around. When you left after breakfast, I was worried nothing had changed and I didn't want to get my hopes up." The happy tears that I've been holding back slide down my cheeks. My heart is beyond full. It's overflowing with love for this man.

"Don't cry, Em. Shh. I'm here now." He runs his thumbs under my eyes, wiping away my tears. "I'll take care of you."

Mason hurt me by walking away without a word, but he's not alone when it comes to making mistakes. I broke his heart and his trust too. I could have told him the truth long before he found out I was "engaged" the way he did. I hurt him just as badly.

And yet ... here we are. Trying to dig ourselves out of the hurt. Together.

He's here because he wants to be here. Because he wants me, and I never felt more loved than I do now. He's offering me ... everything.

"I love you, Mason. I-I'm sorry I didn't say it before. But, I do. I love you. I never stopped loving you," I confess between sobs.

"Shh, it's okay, baby. Don't cry."

"No, it's not okay. I let my fear win. No one has ever put me first until now. No one has ever loved me like you. You show up here with your dinners, dog biscuits, and specialty cupcakes, and tell me you love me and that you're selling your beautiful home in Los Angeles to move here to be closer to me. I love you, you beautiful man." I pepper his face in kisses.

"I would have waited forever for you to say it. But please, I need to hear it again."

"Hear what?" I tease, pulling back to look him in the eye.

"You know what I want to hear," he grunts, digging his hands into my hair.

"Hmm. Let me see. You want me to say there is no one else but you. You're it for me. I'm yours forever and a day, or..."

Mason growls, sending me into a fit of giggles.

"I love you, Mason Miller."

I barely get the words out before he's on me, kissing me like there is no end in sight. In a way, there isn't. He can spend every day and the rest of forever kissing me, and I'd be happy.

We stay lip-locked on for minutes, maybe even hours—who knows—while we whisper I-love-yous between kisses. When we finally break apart, the car windows are foggy, and the ache between my legs is at a fever pitch. I need him so badly. But before I rip his clothes off, I need to see the house.

"Can we go inside?" I flick my head to the house.

Excitement bubbles up in my belly at the thought of him being so close by and maybe, someday, us moving in together. I'm high on all the possibilities.

Mason frowns.

Oh no.

I glance at the house and back at the frowning man, whose lap I'm still straddling. "What's wrong?"

"Nothing is wrong, per se, but the house is outdated. It has good bones, and the contractor I hired already started working on it this morning. So..." He lets his sentence linger.

"So, it's a real fixer-upper?" I ask.

"You can definitely call it that." He grins at me, and my chest flutters. His eyes are bright, the gold electricity in them sparking, warming me from the inside out.

"I love you. Now, show me your new house." I climb back into the passenger seat and wait for Mason to open my door—at his bossy directive, of course—before hopping out.

I won't tell him yet, but I missed the commanding tone he likes to use on me to get his way in and out of the bedroom. It's so freaking hot how he has my body trained to respond to his gritty voice. I'll tell him later, when I feel like being his brat.

"Tell me about the place."

Mason sighs and places his hand on the small of my back, leading me up the path to the front door.

"It's four bedrooms, two bathrooms. The master bedroom has a great walk-in closet but no ensuite, so the contractor is creating plans to add that, as well as a laundry room and a lanai that leads to a new deck."

"That sounds like a lot of work."

He pulls the keys from his pocket and unlocks the door. "It will be, but I'm paying extra for a shorter timeline."

The door swings open, and I let Mason lead. He turns on the light, and my jaw hits the floor.

"Mason," I murmur, shocked.

"It's fine. It will only be for a couple of months."

I look around, and the rising anxiety in my chest makes my stomach ache.

The living room has been stripped to the studs, as have the floors. In the middle of the room is a half-demolished wall with exposed electrical hanging free, and rubble sitting in wheelbarrows and on the floor. If I look carefully through the half wall, I can see it leads to the kitchen. No doubt, this place will be beautiful when it's done, but ...

"This is a disaster." I shake my head.

Mason chuckles. "It's not so bad. My stuff will be out of the way in the master bedroom while they work on the living room and dining room first. Then the bathrooms, extra bedrooms, and finish with the master bedroom and bath," he says like it's fine for him to be living in a home with no way to store food, let alone have constant running water and heat.

"You're not staying here."

"I can't stay with Jace and Rylann forever, baby doll. You have no idea the horrors that take place in that home. I don't even know if it's safe to sit anywhere," he says with a mock shiver.

I involuntarily bark a laugh at his ridiculousness. He might be making light of this, but I'm not. There is no way in hell I am letting him stay here. It's a tetanus shot waiting to happen. I guess our timeline just moved up because more is happening now.

"I've had enough. Let's go home." I grab his wrist and pull him out the door.

I know he said he was paying extra for a shorter timeline, but there are so many variables when it comes to remodeling your home. How on earth does he think he can work here while construction chaos surrounds him?

"And don't bother moving your stuff in here when Jace and Rylann return home. If you think for one second I am going to let you live here while the house is getting remodeled, you're out of your mind. You're moving in with me."

Mason freezes. "Emery."

I swing around and hold up my finger to him. "No. Just no. Now, let's go."

Mason covers his mouth with his fist, trying to hide his smile, and for once in our entire relationship, he doesn't say a word—bossy or otherwise. He flicks off the lights and locks the front door while I wait on the porch. I march to the car, throw open the door, slide into my seat, and slam it shut. I can hear Mason laughing as he makes his way to the driver's side and slips into his seat.

The drive back to my place is tense. Sensing I'm in a mood, Mason stays silent.

Good. Let him think I'm mad. It's probably for the best that he thinks I'm upset about the house, and while I am—a little—I'm ready to move onto the next part of our date. I've had enough surprises for the night.

Now, I want to show this sexy, sweet, thoughtful man, just how happy he has made me and how much I love him. By riding him until tomorrow.

FIFTY-SIX

Mason

EMERY IS STEWING IN the passenger seat like a sexy little angry kitten while I drive back to her house.

I wish I knew what was going on in her head. She was adamant about me staying with her and not in the new house. *Our* house. At least, I hope it will be someday. My plan is to sneakily get her input and make sure the contractor takes it all into account. I want this to be her dream home. Our dream home, where we will raise our family together.

I should have shown her the place before I let the contractor's crew get a head start on the demolition, but I got really excited to start construction. Things are progressing quickly with Emery, and the prospect of moving into the new home with her, sooner rather than later, triggered my need to get the ball rolling as quickly as possible.

I was also honest when I told her that I cannot stay with Jace and Rylann when they return from their honeymoon. I need my own space for work, and I need to be as far away from their bedroom as possible. I've heard enough of them to last a lifetime.

When she looked around at the destruction and then demanded I stay with her, I wanted to whoop and holler. I want nothing more than to live with her. But is she really ready? I'm afraid that if we move too fast, it will ruin our progress or she'll regret it, and all my effort to win back her trust will be for nothing. I don't want to lose her again, and going slow is the right move. Now, I need to break my decision to her.

I pull my car in behind Emery's silver BMW X5 and kill the engine. She turns to face me, her teeth sunk into her plump bottom lip. Fuck, she's so pretty my chest aches every time I look at her.

Neither of us says anything for a minute as we stare at each other. The air shifts, the tension between us reaching a fever pitch. Her stomach grumbles, bringing me back to reality.

"You still need to eat."

"I'm fine." She waves me off like her well-being isn't important. If she thought I was bossy before, she has no idea what she has in store.

I shake my head at her. "Nice try. Now, let's go finish our dinner."

I push open the door before she can argue and climb out of the car. She groans but follows me as I grab the canvas bags that contain our food.

Henry barks as we enter the dimly lit living room, and I head straight for the kitchen island, dropping our bags on top.

"What are you doing?" A wave of protectiveness washes over me as I watch Emery attach the leash to her tiny dog.

"Taking Henry out for a short walk. He's been cooped up all day. It rained this morning and I've been gone, so he needs to work out his stumpy legs."

"It's dark out," I state the obvious.

She smiles, rolling her eyes at me. I cross my arms and narrow my eyes at her. She can't be serious.

"I walk him all the time. To the stop sign and back. That's, like, five houses. I'll be fine."

Fuck, she is serious. Thoughts of something happening to her hit me like a punch in the gut. It's dark out and people drive for shit. Anything could happen to her. It doesn't matter that she's on the sidewalk. Henry could get away from her, and she could chase after him without looking. I can't let anything happen to her. I just got her back.

I shut down the dark thoughts pinching my chest, making me panic. "Of course you will be. I'm coming with you."

"Okay, Mr. Bossy." She giggles as the Yorkie happily yips, his tongue hanging out of his mouth.

Emery ushers him down the porch and leads him to the sidewalk. I stalk after her, fuming that she walks him in the dark, late at night. From now on—I look at my watch and check the time—I'll be here at eleven on the dot to walk him for her.

"Don't be so grumpy. Let's talk about something else to take your mind off whatever you're thinking."

"I'm thinking you will never walk the damn dog by yourself late at night again. It's my job now, and when I'm not here, I'll hire someone to walk him for you."

"You're crazy."

Henry stops to sniff the grass and I take advantage, pulling Emery into my arms. "Crazy for you."

"Such a charmer," she whispers.

"Only for you, baby doll."

She sighs as I cover her mouth in a kiss that's too short for my liking because the damn dog yaps, breaking us apart. *Little fucker.*

After another five minutes, the dog does his business, and we head inside to wash up for a dinner of cold pizza and nachos. We spend our dinner talking about her family and the events that led up the fake engagement to her childhood friend. If I had known what was going on when I was outside her father's office, I would have walked right up and punched him in the face. The idea of any parent forcing their child to do something against their will—through manipulation or otherwise—is abhorrent. They should have put her happiness, not their business, above all else and loved her for the wonderfully kind and giving person she is.

Fucking assholes.

They don't matter anymore. Emery doesn't need them in her life. I'm here, and I plan on taking care of her for the rest of our lives. She doesn't need to worry about family; she'll have mine. My mom is already chomping at the bit to meet her as my girl-friend—which I hope isn't for too long—and it doesn't hurt that Rylann already adores her.

A vision of Emery in white, walking down the aisle towards me hits me like a bolt of electricity. A thought that used to scare me fills me with joy. Yeah, I'm definitely going to make this woman officially mine.

Soon.

Emery laughs as I regale her with the story of my oldest brother's bathroom dalliance as we sit on the couch, her legs draped over my lap.

"That's rich, Mase." She pokes me in the side with her toe.

"What is?"

"That you're on his case for doing something that we did not so long ago."

"That was different."

"How?" she deadpans, but the playful smile on her lips has me chuckling along with her.

I think back to our tryst in the bathroom, and shame washes over me. I never meant to be so rough with her. I was angry. I missed her. I was completely out of control. There is no doubt we were loud, and based on the looks I received after, everyone knew what went down while we were gone.

"Fine, I see your point."

"Besides, I think it's hot."

What the fuck? I arch a brow at her.

"Are you jealous because I said it's hot?" she asks.

I growl at her, sending her into a fit of giggles.

"Oh my god. You are, aren't you? You're jealous of your brother?"

Hell no. My brother is a taken man and very much in love with his wife. I've never been the "look at her, and I'll rip your eyes out" type, but with Emery I am. She brings out the caveman in me, and that neanderthal does not share.

I get fucking jealous at the thought of her thinking *any* other man is hot. I don't want her thinking about anyone but me. Full stop.

Sorry, Superman. You're out too.

It's ridiculous, but here I am, a green-eyed motherfucker over this girl.

I grab her sides and tickle her. The sweet sound of her laughter settles deep in my bones like a soothing balm. Pushing her onto her back, I lay between her legs and rest most of my body weight on my elbows so I don't crush her.

"Fine, I was jealous," I admit. I brush a stray lock of her hair behind her ear.

She pops her head up and pecks my lips. "You're cute when you're jealous. But what I meant was, I think it's hot that they can't keep their hands off of each other. It's sweet." She bites her lip in the way that makes my dick stir, and I know she's wondering if that's us.

It is. There is no way I will be able to keep my hands off of her. It's taken a Herculean effort to keep from taking her since I kissed her on New Year's Eve.

I run my hand up her thigh and squeeze, letting my touch do the talking. If I could live inside this insanely beautiful and smart woman for the rest of my life, I would, and I'd die a happy man doing it. Just not yet.

"Stay," she whispers like she knows what I'm thinking.

I shake my head, even though my heart—and my dick—are screaming at me to do as she commands. She pouts, and I can't stop from sucking that pillowy soft bottom lip in my mouth. She hums, and the sexy noise is like a beacon to my cock, calling it to attention.

"Is it because you're helping with your niece and nephew?" she asks, fishing for answers.

"No." I smile. I see what she's doing. "They are with Rylann's parents."

"Then stay," she says again. She locks her ankles behind my back, pressing us closer together.

My dick jumps in my jeans at the proximity of her hot center. I gulp back the groan building in my throat. "You're killing me ... and my plan." I cradle her face, brushing my thumb over the apple of her soft cheek.

"Fine," she pouts, hiding a devious smile, but the glint in her eyes gives her away.

I'm in so much fucking trouble.

I quickly sit up, bringing her with me. I need to get out of here before my plan goes to shit and I start thinking with my dick.

"I'll be back bright and early tomorrow morning." With Emery in my arms, bridal style, I stand.

She giggles, and my heart twists happily behind my ribs. I want to hear that sound every day for the rest of my life. I place her on her feet and lean in for a kiss.

She presses her hand to my chest, stopping me. "Wait, I have something for you."

Before I can stop her, she takes off toward her bedroom.

"If it's my shirt, I don't want it back!" I shout at her retreating form.

She scoffs at me, throwing over her shoulder, "You'll never get that back. Finders, keepers, Miller."

With a smile on my face, I watch as her bedroom light flicks on, illuminating the hallway. I look between the door and her room. The invisible ropes that bind me to Emery tug, begging me to go after her. It takes everything in me not to follow and give her space.

I train my ear on her movements, but aside from some rustling, I can't figure out what she's doing. "What's taking so long, Em?"

"Be right there," she hollers back.

Shoving my hands in my pocket, I stare up at the ceiling, attempting to get a hold of myself. The suspense is killing me.

Just go after her, dumbass. You know you want to.

Oh, I want to, but I don't trust myself not to lay her out on her bed and devour every fucking inch of her body. I should put my shoes on and get the fuck out of here. Keep to the plan.

"Mason." Emery's voice closer is than before.

My eyes snap to hers, and I think I've died and gone to heaven.

Holy fuck.

My cock throbs in my jeans at the sight of her in the sexiest fucking scrap of lingerie I have ever seen as she leans against the door frame. She's wearing a high-cut burgundy lace one-piece—who the fuck knows what it's called—that's so sheer it leaves nothing to the imagination. Her pointy, hard caramel nipples and her perfectly plump pussy tempt me through the sheer material. She's stunning.

So much fucking trouble.

I groan when I bring my eyes back to her face. She's reapplied the fucking burgundy lipstick that I like on her lips. The lipstick that makes my cock harder than stone.

"Do you like what I got you?" She bites her finger, putting on a seductive show for me.

I watch, entranced, as she slides her finger down the center of her body. She's fucking flawless. Every single inch of her.

I find my voice, but when it comes out, it's gruff and thick with lust. "You're not going to make this easy on me, are you?"

She shakes her head. "Nope. I told you to stay. I also told you, you weren't staying in that disaster of a house while construction goes on. But you didn't want to listen, so here I am, pulling out the big guns."

Emery is finding her voice, and her confidence and it's hot as fuck. It drives me wild when she's a little bratty and wants her way.

"I can see that." My feet stay planted on the ground as I fight the urge to charge her.

"It's my turn."

"For what?" I grit out.

Emery sashays her sexy ass toward me, taking her time. She places her hands on my chest and stares up at me with her heavy-lidded topaz eyes that spear me to my soul.

"This." She falls to her knees in front of me, gripping my thighs for leverage. "I don't want to wait anymore. I don't want to go slow. I don't want you to recreate our memories. I love our story, Mason. Just as it is. I don't need you to change it. I need you to stay. To love me, no matter what. I'm sorry too. You're not the only one that made mistakes; we both did. But that's in the past. Now, it's time to move forward towards our future."

She finally says the words I've been dying to hear, and the sight of her on her knees, declaring them so confidently, brings me to mine. I kneel before her, wrapping my arms around her, feeling her soft body beneath my hands.

Fuck, this woman. She's everything.

"Em, I—" I tumble over my words.

How did I get so lucky?

"No," she declares, using the same tone I've used on her to get my way or make her listen, and I can't help but grin at her as she continues, "We are done with this conversation. You live here now. With me. Now, pick me up off this floor, carry me to our bedroom, and have your way with me already."

The carefully constructed control I have falls away like it was held together by tape. This woman owns me. Whatever she asks for, it's hers. So if she wants to ruin my plans... Fuck it. Fuck it all to hell.

She's just going to have to settle for it being on my terms first.

"I love you," I promise. More than she will ever know, but I will show her every day just how much I do.

"I love you, too." Hearing those words fall from her lips is like a healing balm to my sore spots. I will never tire of hearing them.

I run my palm up over her ass and lower back before cupping her neck in a tight hold. She moans at the pressure, and her eyelids flutter.

"Do you want to get fucked, baby doll?"

"Oh god, yes." She arches her pert tits into my chest, begging for my touch.

"Uh-uh. You only cry out my name." I trace a path down the valley of her breasts with my other hand, in the same way she did herself. "Now, tell me. What's my name?"

"Mason."

"Who do you want to fuck you?"

"You, Mason. Only you," she whines, wiggling her needy body against me.

"Damn straight. Only my cock will ever be inside you." I cup her hot pussy. "Isn't that right?"

"Yes. Only you."

Her eyes close as I roughly grind my hand over her clit, using the fabric to increase the friction she so desperately needs.

"Hmm," I purr, running my nose up her neck, settling my lips at her ear.

"Mason," she whispers my name again, and my cock grows harder at her raspy prayer.

Don't worry, baby, I'll answer every one of them.

I run my thumb over her bottom lip, smearing her lipstick, dirtying her up. "Did you put this on for me?"

"You know I did," she sasses back.

I smile against her neck as I rain kisses down the length of it. "Brat," I mumble against her sweet vanilla skin.

Her flesh pebbles at my hot breath.

"You like it."

Wrong.

"I fucking love it, baby doll," I profess. I want her to know what she does to me. That she can ask for anything, and I will gladly give it to her.

My hands roam her body, getting reacquainted with every inch of skin on the woman I love.

"Take me to bed, Mason."

I smack her ass cheek with my palm before groping it. Emery's eyes fly open as she lets out a squeaky moan, grabbing my shirt in her fists.

"Please," she amends.

My cock weeps in my boxers at her needy plea. I cup her pussy again, feeling her arousal soaking through the fabric. I trace the seam of her pussy with my fingertips as my mouth waters, dying for a taste.

"Is this pretty little cunt wet for me?"

"Yes," she hisses, lifting her hips to meet my hand as she grinds against it.

As much as I love toying with her, it's time to move this to the bedroom. Sitting back on my heels, I shift my weight and stand. Emery grabs the top of my pockets, holding me in place. With her eyes on mine, she undoes the button and zipper of my jeans, and lets her fingers graze the stiff bulge in my pants. She bats her lashes, waiting for me to make a move. For me to give her permission to do as she pleases with me.

"Is this what you want?" I ask, slightly jerking my hips at her.

She licks her lips and nods. "Yes."

My dick peeks out the top of my boxers, a drop of precum beading at the tip. Emery's eyes light up at the sight. She wipes the bead away with her thumb before bringing it to mouth and sucking it clean, moaning around her finger.

"Fuck." I groan.

My girl smiles, that devilish gleam in her eyes again.

Fine. She wants to play. I'm here for it.

"Take my cock out and put it in your mouth, Emery."

Without hesitation, she does my bidding, and shoves my boxers and jeans around my thighs, flattening her tongue at the base of my shaft, licking a line up my hard length like I was a damn ice cream cone, teasing me. I push her hair back from her face, wrapping it around my fist for a better view, watching as she wraps her dark red lips around my cock and sucks. Inhuman growls rumble in my chest as she works my dick in and out of her mouth, taking more with each pass until my tip hits the back of her throat with a gag.

"Look at you on your knees for me, with my cock in your mouth. I've never seen a prettier sight."

Emery hums around my cock at the praise, swallowing me deeper.

"Yes. Just like that. You suck me so good."

The suction, her hot wet mouth, her squeezing hands on my ass, it all feels too fucking good. When her small hand cups my balls, rolling them between her fingers, my knees almost buckle.

"Fuck, you're too good. You're going to make me come."

She hums again, sucking me faster. Harder. My spine starts to tingle, and if I'm not careful, she's gonna have me coming down her pretty throat instead of in her tight pussy. I can't let that happen. Not before she comes.

I pull my cock out of her mouth with a pop, admiring the red stains covering my thick shaft.

Hers.

The sight turns me feral. I pull her to a stand, squat down, and dig my shoulder into her stomach, throwing her over my shoulder.

"Your playtime is over. Now, it's my turn." I nip her ass cheek with my teeth, and with my pants around my thighs, I miraculously make it to her bedroom without falling over. I toss Emery on the bed and watch as her tits bounce with the movement.

"You're fucking gorgeous. You know that?"

Her cheeks pink at the compliment.

My girl, so humble. So fucking sexy.

"Is this new?"

She nods.

"Do you like it?" I ask, debating my next move.

"Yes." She smirks at me, wondering where I'm going.

"Then you better take it the fuck off before I rip it off."

Emery moans, rubbing her thighs together. "Okay."

I damn near choke on my spit as she spreads her legs wide for me to see the small silver snapping between her pussy lips. Her cunt glistens on either side of the thin fabric, begging for my mouth to taste it.

"Oh, this is going to be fun." I yank the shirt I'm wearing over my head, push my pants and boxers off the rest of the way, and kick them to the side. Crawling up Emery's body, I settle between her legs, hovering over her chest so I don't crush her. "I missed you so much, baby."

Her eyes glass over, and I hope those are happy tears. I cup her cheek, cherishing this moment for a second longer. She's finally back in my arms. For good.

"I missed you too. So much," she whispers against my lips, running her hands up my sides.

My body shivers at her touch.

"I love you."

"I love you. Only you," I promise before covering her mouth with mine. I kiss her with everything I have, every ounce of love, devotion, and adoration I have for her.

Her hands fist my hair as I lavish her neck with attention, nipping and sucking at her soft skin, trailing kisses over the tops of her breasts. Over the delicate material, I cup her tits, lifting them to my mouth as I take her nipple between my lips and suck. She moans her approval, her body bowing at the contact. Releasing with a pop, I give her other nipple the same attention until she's a squirming, needy mess.

"I need you," Emery keens.

"Shh. I know, baby."

I make my way down her stomach, situating myself between her legs, with her pussy in my face. I place her legs over my shoulders, spreading her wide for me to get a better view. Her hips lift as I blow a stream of air over her aching center. I unsnap the fabric between her legs and run my finger through her slit, admiring the way her wet pussy glistens.

"Is all this for me?"

She moans, "Yes."

I slowly use my finger to spread her arousal over her swollen clit, rubbing tight circles around the sensitive bud.

"I-I need more, please," she whines, chasing my touch.

Breathing her in, my mouth waters, begging for a taste. I'm going to savor every last drop of her. I'm going to drive her wild, slowly bringing her over the edge.

"Look at this pretty pussy. So needy for me. Do you know why?"

She shakes her head.

"Because I own this cunt. I know what it needs. Only I know how to work this pussy until it explodes in pleasure so good that your cum pours over my tongue, down my chin, and all over my cock."

Without wasting another second, I flatten my tongue on the skin above her cute little rosebud and lick up to the top in one slow wipe, swirling my tongue around her clit. The tangy taste of her explodes on my tongue, sending me into a lust filled tailspin.

Like everything else about tonight, my plans burn up in flames. Going slow is no longer an option. Without easing her body into it, I dive in, eating at her with a feral hunger. I'm like a starving man finally served a plate of food. I can't stop myself from feasting on her sweet nectar.

Her body bucks off the bed as I close my lips around her clit and suck, flicking my tongue over the sensitive nerves. She's already close. Her thighs tense, shaking. I slide two fingers into her tight hole, curling them forward, stroking the spot I know makes her explode.

"Let go. Come for me. I need you to come right now."

I bury my face in Emery's pussy, spearing her with my fingers as I rub my face in her cream, lapping at her clit. I flick and suck at her swollen nerves until I feel her cunt pulse under my tongue as it clenches around my thick digits.

"Yes, yes, yes," Emery chants as she chases her orgasm.

Her muscles spasm and flutter as a gush of warm liquid pours down my hand. Pulling my finger out, I lap at her center, gathering as much of her juices on my tongue as I can, drinking her down. Fuck, I love when she squirts for me.

She's lost in bliss as I sit on my heels, stroking my painfully hard cock, watching her chest rise and fall. Her lips are parted, her cheeks are flushed pink, and her sexy lingerie is bunched around her waist. She's never looked more gorgeous. More *mine*.

I give my dick another squeeze, loving the red color covering my thick length. Grabbing under her knees, I pull her down to me and grab her ass, lifting her hips and notching my cock at her entrance.

"Look at me, beautiful," I command.

Emery's eyes pop open to meet mine, and it pierces me right through the heart. She looks up at me with awe and so much love it takes my breath away. *How did I get so damn lucky?*

"I love you."

"I love you," she says.

I slam into her, straight to the hilt in one swift thrust. We groan in unison as she wraps her tight, soaking-wet heat around me.

"Fuck," I grunt. Stilling my hips, I wait, letting her get used to my girth. Her pussy's vise grip on my cock is too much. "You feel too good, Em. I'm not going to last."

"I don't care. I need you to move. I need you to fuck me, Mason. Please, fuck me," she whines.

My fingers dig into the globes of her ass as I do what she asks. Pulling out, one inch at a time, I stare at the way our bodies are connected. "Look at your pussy take my cock."

Emery lifts onto her elbows and watches my cock slide in and out of her as her red lipstick shines coated in her cum. The salacious sound of our sex coming together fills the room. My short thrusts turn longer, harder, as I work my cock deep inside her cunt as I can, rutting into her like a savage.

Keeping us connected, I release her legs, lay over her, and quickly roll onto my back, flipping our position so that she's on top. I tug at the lacy material still covering her body. She helps me by pulling it the rest of the way off and throwing it across the room like it offends her.

"You're so fucking beautiful." My eyes skim over her perky tits, her hard nipples begging for my attention.

Sitting up, I take one into my mouth, swirling my tongue over the hardened peak. I release the pebbled bud, scraping it with my teeth, and she whimpers, shifting her hips, driving my cock deeper into her tight cunt.

"Ride me, Emery. Show me how much you like to fuck my cock."

I grope her ass as she stares down at me, her hair a curtain around her face. Placing her hands on my chest, she leans down and kisses me, pushing her tongue into my mouth as she sensually rubs it against mine. She moans, tasting her cum on my tongue. My dick pulses inside her as she rocks her hips.

Breaking our kiss, she gives me a mischievous smile. "I don't like riding your dick, Mr. Bossy." She puts her lips to my ear and whispers, "I love it."

She squeezes my dick with her pelvic muscles, and my eyes roll to the back of my head. She lifts her hips, and I open my eyes in time to watch her impale herself on my cock, her tits bouncing.

"You feel so good," Emery moans. Her nails dig into my chest as she uses my body, riding me fast and hard, grinding her clit on the base of my cock.

With one hand, I reach up and roll her nipple between my fingers, pinching and tugging. Her cries grow louder as her pussy flutters around me, her orgasm close to boiling over.

"Yes. Again."

Emery picks up her pace, and my balls start to tingle. I'm not going to last. I pinch her nipple again and grab a fistful of her hair, pulling her down harder as I thrust up into her.

"That's it, baby doll. You look so beautiful riding me. Go ahead. Come on my cock like a good girl."

My words of praise do their job and take Emery over the edge. She throws her head back with a scream and my name on her lips as she comes around me.

Gripping her hair tighter, I tug. Three more thrusts, and I follow her as the tension in my groin explodes in a burst of white-hot heat. I coat her womb in thick ropes of my cum. Marking her as mine. Forever.

Emery collapses on my chest, my dick still pulsing inside her, gasping for breath. "That was…"

"Amazing," I finish her sentence.

Wrapping my arms around her body, I crush her to my chest. Her heart beats wildly in time with mine, and I've never been more content. This is exactly where I am supposed to be. Why am I scared to move forward?

"You're right."

Emery rests her cheek in the crook of my neck, kissing my jaw. "About?"

"Going slow."

She hums her agreement, basking in the afterglow as I run my fingers through her hair, inhaling the sweet vanilla pear scent. I never want this to end. Falling asleep with her in my arms every night and waking up with her in my arms every morning. This is where I'm supposed to be.

"Marry me," I blurt, and she freezes.

Did I really just ask Emery to marry me after sex while my dick is still inside her? I'm a fucking idiot. She said she didn't want to go slow, not fucking light speed.

My heart races, and anxiety blooms in my chest at her silence. I'm a little scared for her to say yes, but it's mixed with excitement and I know my future is her. What scares the fuck out of me more is her saying no.

Until she whispers, "Yes. I'll marry you."

Wait. What?

A grin spread across my face as I roll her onto her back, my cock slipping from its home as I settle between her legs. She's biting that sexy lip, staring up at me with confidence and so much fucking love.

"Yes?" I ask again. I can't have heard her correctly, right?

"Yes," she says louder, and it's like music to my ears. "Yes. I'll marry you. I love you. I want to start our life together. Now. I don't want to wait. I—"

Before she can finish, I cover her mouth with mine, kissing away any doubt she's ever had and replacing it with certainty. She's it for me.

"Fuck, Em. You just made me the happiest man alive." I pepper her face in kisses as she giggles.

"Really? You weren't just blurting it out because we just had amazing sex?"

"One, it was mind-blowing sex. And two, fuck yes. I want to marry you. I want to call you my wife. I want you to help me design the new house, so when we're ready, we can watch our kids grow up there." I kiss her again, stealing her breath.

Her hips twist, and I let her roll me onto my back as she sits up and straddles my hips, my cum leaking out of her and onto my stomach. My dick perks up at the sight. I want to shove my cum back inside her, but she stops me before I can.

"I have a crazy idea. You can say no if you want to." She looks away nervously.

Finger under her chin, I turn her face back to mine. "I'm listening."

"What do you think about getting married on Valentine's weekend?" she asks, worrying her top teeth over her lip.

I hope she means this Valentine's Day. Pulling her lip free, I ask, "Like, next month?"

She shrugs. "Well, yeah, it will sort of be the anniversary of ... you know, our first weekend together."

She's so cute. *Our first weekend together.* As in, our first fuck-a-thon. One of many I plan to have from now until the day I can't get my cock up anymore.

I grin at her. "I say hell fucking yes."

"Really?"

I cup her cheek in my palm. "Really. You're it for me, baby doll."

Her shoulders fall, and she melts into my palm.

"We can get married tomorrow or a year from now. As long as you become my wife, I don't care when it happens. Just as long as it does. But I like sooner rather than later."

Emery's eyes shine with unshed tears. "I love you."

"I love you more, beautiful."

"You know, you're it for me too, Mr. Bossy. Or should I say, fiancé?"

"I like the sound of that ... fiancée." I grab her ass and punch my hips up.

She giggles, leaning down and sealing her mouth over mine. Our kisses turn hungry with every stroke of our tongues. Emery glides her pussy over my thickening cock, moaning as my tip bumps her clit. I break the kiss and flip us again so she's on her back, her legs spread wide.

Emery places a hand on my chest and pushes me back. "Wait."

I stop at her command.

"When we tell people about your proposal, can we lie and say we were fully clothed while you dropped to one knee and asked me to marry you?"

She's right. I don't think I will ever live it down if my brothers know I asked Emery to marry after sex. They'll think I was sex-drunk, when in reality this is the most sober I have ever been. I'm pretty sure my parents would kill me, especially since I don't have a ring. I'm going to need to rectify that situation tomorrow.

I chuckle. "Sure, baby. It will be our little secret that I proposed while being balls deep inside you."

"You're as charming as ever, Mason Miller."

"Only for you, Emery soon-to-be Miller."

Fuck, I love the sound of that, and by the look on her face, so does my fiancée.

She pulls my head down and kisses me. We spend the rest of the night wrapped up in each other, talking, fucking, laughing, making love, and planning our future.

Everything.

I can't wait to spend the rest of my life with Emery. Pulling my head out of my ass and finding my way back to her was the best thing I have ever done. Being here, with her in my arms, is the only place I want to be.

Making her happy and showing her how much I love her will be my life's mission. From here on out, every moment of my life will be dedicated to making sure every moment of hers is happy.

FEBRUARY

I KNOCK ROUGHLY ON the door of the hotel room accommodating Emery and her friends today. The muffled voices of the women in my life go quiet, and I smile, shaking my head at the door.

My quiet self-induced solitary fiancée is no longer alone. She has people by her side. People who love her and value the kind-hearted and hard-working person she is. Turns out the bachelorette weekend may not have been our best moment, but it was for Emery.

In the last months, Emery has grown even closer to Scarlett and Rylann—who, in less than an hour, will become her sister—as well as Levi's sisters. The group of them are behind this door, laughing and having a good time. A fraction of my anxiety eases, knowing she has them.

"Who is it?" Scarlett sings, and the throng of women erupts into giggles.

My chest does that warm swelling thing it's been doing since Emery agreed to marry me.

"It's me," I answer, my voice cracking a little.

Fuck. I sound nervous. I wipe my sweaty palms over my slacks and take a deep breath to calm my racing heart.

"Just a second," Rylann shouts.

I can't make out their hushed conversation, so I wait. I'd wait forever for Emery if I had to, but I don't. Today is our wedding day and the happiest day of my life. I get to watch the love of my life walk down the aisle to me—the guy who completely fucked up and almost lost her for being a stubborn ass. Somehow, she still loves me, just as I am.

I'm the luckiest man in the world. She chose me, and I get to pledge my unconditional love to her in front of our friends and family, binding her to me for life. I get to place my ring on her finger for every man to see she's mine.

My stomach drops. *Ring.*

One reason I'm nervous. Emery has been adamant that she didn't want an engagement ring. It's been a point of contention for us. We agree on everything: the new house's renovation, the new design, our future, our careers, dinner. Everything.

Except the ring.

I wanted to buy her the biggest diamond I could find, but she shot me down every time. I know it's because of her past and her family. Not wanting to waste my time fighting with her—or dredging up the past—I dropped the issue and came up with a plan to surprise her with one instead.

But that's not why I'm standing outside her door, begging to hear her voice. The last thing I want is for Emery to think I'm nervous about getting married. I'm not. At all. The last month has been a whirlwind, but I wouldn't have it any other way. She was right—going slow was pointless. When you know you know.

But right now, I need to know she's okay. That she's happy.

As expected, Emery's parents have cut all communication. It breaks my heart that the only person in her family attending our wedding will be her brother, Chris, who has the honor of giving her away. He more than makes up for their loss in his own way, but I know Emery puts on a brave face. She had hoped they would change their minds when they learned she was happy. I couldn't care less about those assholes.

My family has stepped up, bringing her into the fold with ease. My parents adore her, especially my mom, who is beyond thrilled to have two daughters around her all-boy clan.

Rylann cracks the door open. "Can I help you?"

"I came by to check on, Em."

I peek over her head, but my sister-in-law—the guard dog—pushes me back. "You know you can't see her before the ceremony," she tuts.

I'd be annoyed with her blocking me if it wasn't for the fact that she's been a huge supporter of my girl from the beginning. Even when I was being an idiot, Rylann was there for Emery, coaxing her out of her shell, being her shoulder to cry on, and loving her like a sister.

"I know. I just need to hear her voice. Please," I plead. I need to hear for myself that she's happy, that she's okay.

"Mason Miller, you softy." Rylann glances between me and the door. "I have an idea. Wait one second."

"I'll be right here."

She nods and slips inside the room, closing the door.

The seconds stretch to minutes and my patience grows thin. I haven't seen Emery since this morning, and I miss the fuck out of her. We've been inseparable since I moved in with her last month. I've become the simp Cameron said I'd become, and I couldn't give a single fuck. I'd do anything for that woman. Since the moment I saw her reflection in the mirror at the airport, she has flipped my world upside down.

In all the best ways.

For years, I was convinced I'd never find someone to share my life with. Someone who understood all the parts of me—the bossy grump, the workaholic, the silent observer—and accepted them. I had all but given up.

Until her.

She sees me, the real me, and loves me in spite of my flaws. I've never been happier, and it's all because of her. It's cheesy as fuck, but it's the truth. Emery completes me. She is the other half of my soul. I love her so much I'm not sure I'd survive without her a second time.

The door creaks open, and Rylann returns with a robe sash in her hand and holds it up to me. "Cover your eyes with this, or no dice."

"Really?"

Rylann pops her hip, waiting for me to do as I'm told. I squash my smile as I grunt. I'd agree to anything right now, and she knows it.

"Fine." I take the silk fabric and tie it behind my head, shrouding my view in darkness.

"Can you see anything?" Air fans my face as Rylann tests my handiwork. "How many fingers am I holding up?"

I chuckle, knowing her. "A fist, but if you were Scarlett, I'd say the middle finger."

Rylann bursts out laughing. "You got that right. Okay, let me lead you in. We will give you five minutes of alone time, but under no circumstances are you allowed to take off the blindfold."

"Yes, ma'am."

She takes hold of my arms and leads me into the room.

I can smell her before I see her—well, in this case, hear her. My girl's sweet fruity vanilla scent permeates the room, invading my nose, and easing my stressed nerves.

"Someone's looking for a quickie," Scarlett jokes.

The ladies all cheer and make kissy noises, and if I could see, I'd find Emery with flaming pink cheeks.

"Enough, you guys," Emery's voice catches my attention.

"Five minutes," Rylann says, herding the rest of the women out the door.

"Thank you," Emery calls after them as the door closes with a click.

I can't stop my hands from reaching for her. She takes my hands in hers, squeezing.

"Is everything alright?" The apprehension in her voice is clear; I've worried her.

"No, baby doll. Everything is perfect."

"Then why are you here?"

"I needed to see you."

"Charmer."

I can see her biting that sexy lip in my head.

"Only for you."

Her hands glide up my arms, encircling my shoulders, her fingers threading through the hair at the back of my neck as my hands find her lower back.

Hmm, backless. Looks like she's been holding out on me.

"I love you. Now, tell me why you're really here?" I can hear the smile on her face.

"Full transparency?" I run my thumb over her silky skin, reveling in the shivers that wrack her body at my touch.

"Always," she whispers.

"First, I wanted to make sure you were happy. I know things didn't work out the way you wanted with your family. I hate that you had to go through all that. If there was a way to fix it, I would do it for you. I'd do anything for you."

"You sweet, sexy man. I love you." She kisses my cheek. "Yes, I was disappointed, but I knew they weren't going to be here. I don't need them here to know I have people in my life who care about me. Marrying you, becoming your wife, that's all I want to focus on. I'm so happy."

She kisses my other cheek, and all the anxiety I had been holding onto falls away.

"The other reason?"

"Second, I fucking missed you. You left without saying goodbye this morning. I didn't like it. I never like it when I can't start my day buried between your legs."

She hums a non-answer, driving me crazy.

"Tell me you missed me too. I know how much you like when I wake you up with my mouth on your pussy," I tease, gliding my hands over the globes of her ass, squeezing.

"You're cute when you get all needy," she purrs.

I growl. I move my hands to the place I know tickles her, and she laughs, placating me.

"I'm kidding. I'm sorry I left without waking you up. Next time, I'll make sure to wake you up with your cock in my mouth. How does that sound?" She tugs on the sash covering my eyes.

"Fuck," I growl. My cock stiffens in my pants as I picture her beneath the sheets, stroking me awake, her pouty mouth wrapped around my tip, sucking.

Nope. Don't go there. There isn't time.

"You're a brat."

She giggles, laying her head on my chest and as I pull her close, she sighs, melting into me.

"I love you, baby doll. Thank you for humoring me. I wish I could see you right now. I have no doubt you look fucking stunning in this dress."

"You don't look so bad yourself."

"Have you put your lipstick on yet?"

"No."

A smidge of disappointment hits me at the missed opportunity to smudge her pretty lips, but... I slide my hands up her body, grip her neck, and cup her cheek.

"Good," I grunt as I crush my mouth to hers, capturing her startled moan with my lips.

She parts her lips, and I slip my tongue in her mouth, slowly sliding it against hers in a seductive game of twister. She tastes like orange juice, champagne, and quintessential Emery. She tastes like mine.

I could kiss her all fucking day, and it wouldn't be enough. I deepen the kiss, my hunger and longing for her taking over. My blood rushes south as the heat in my veins spreads like wildfire throughout my body, begging for her touch to douse the flames.

I hear the faint sound of the door opening over the rushing, pulsating blood pounding in my ears, but I ignore it, pulling Emery closer, swallowing her moans and greedily keeping her attention on me.

"Alright, break it up, you two."

Emery and I pull apart at the sound of Rylann's chiding voice. My head feels dizzy, and I wish I could rip this fucking blindfold off.

Emery rubs her palms over my pecs, soothing the horny beast inside my chest clawing to be set free. "Mason?"

"Yes, baby doll?"

"As much as I don't want you to go, I need to finish getting ready. I'll meet you at the altar?"

"I'll be counting down the minutes. I love you."

"Time's up."

Without warning, a third hand grabs my arm and hauls me back. I release my hold on Emery and stumble back, allowing my sister-in-law to shove me out of the room and slam the door in my face.

I yank the tie from around my eyes and grin at the piece of wood separating me from my bride. I check my watch.

I can hold out for another forty minutes.

Cameron bumps his shoulder against mine. "Are you sure you're ready, brother?"

"More than ready." My answer is firm, oozing confidence. I have no doubts that Emery is the one for me.

We're standing at the altar under an arch of white and deep red flowers, waiting for the ceremony to start. We took a chance and looked into booking the hotel where Emery and I spent our first weekend together. Fate was on our side, and the banquet room was open and available for us to use the day before Valentine's Day.

"Of course he's ready." Jace slaps my back, a wide smile on his face. He's officiating the ceremony while Cameron and Eli stand at my side. "When you know, you know."

"Don't get me wrong, Emery is a cool chick—and hot as fuck—but it's been, like, a minute, and now they are getting married? Am I really the only one concerned?"

"Yes," Jace and Eli answer at the same time, making me chuckle.

To someone on the outside, Emery and me getting married does look too fast. But we have been a year in the making.

"Don't listen to the pretty boy." Eli slaps my back. "I'm proud of you for going after what you want."

"Last chance," Cameron taunts, a smile tilting his lips. He's not serious, just messing around. He knows damn well I'm certain and has been nothing but supportive. I look forward to seeing him get knocked on his ass when the right girl shows up.

"I'm good."

"I know. I just like fucking with you."

See.

"You're such a douche." Eli shakes his head, hiding his laugh.

"Whatever. I keep things fun around here. Sip?" Cameron pulls out a small flask, offering it to Eli.

"Fuck it." Eli takes the flask and takes a swig, his face pinching. "Woo. That's strong. Mase?"

"Nah, I'm good." Adjusting my tie, I smooth down my shirt. I want to get on with this. I'm starting to get fidgety without Emery at my side.

"Rylann texted they are on their way," Jace announces.

Finally.

The music changes, and the doors swing open. Two blonde heads emerge as Lily and Sadie—Scarlett's twin girls—make their way down the white aisle, scattering rose petals.

Rhys appears next, wearing a huge grin, and struts his way to the altar in his matching black tuxedo, where he stands between Eli and Cameron. He looks up at me and pats his pocket, letting me know the rings are safe. Cameron ruffles Rhys's hair while Eli fist-bumps him. Our man.

Rylann makes her way down next, carrying our Miller princess, Riah, followed by Scarlett, Laci, and Lexi. All of them are wearing Emery's favorite shade of deep red, but my eyes skip over them, waiting for the woman who owns my heart to emerge.

The Wedding March begins and everyone rises, but my eyes stay rooted on the door. Without even seeing her, I know she's going to look stunning.

Emery appears, and her eyes lock on mine as she comes into view. She doesn't disappoint.

My bride looks classic and elegant in a skin-tight long-sleeved lace dress—that I now know is backless—with a slit that shows off her mile-long leg.

Absolutely breathtaking.

Emery walks towards me with a sparkle in her eye and a grin on her face. Her honey hair falls over her shoulders in waves, and a red flower is pinned by her ear. To top it all off, she's got her signature burgundy lipstick coating her mouth.

She has the prettiest fucking red lips. Lips designed to bring me to my knees and ruin me. I wouldn't have it any other way.

Chris leads Emery down the aisle, and I wish they would hurry the fuck up. I'm dying for her to be in my arms.

My feet move as Cameron grabs me, keeping me in place. "Give her a second, Mase."

Emery chuckles, mouthing, *Breathe.*

I do as she asks, and the happiness that's been simmering below the surface all day bubbles up. Tears cloud my eyes as Emery makes her way to me. When she reaches the end, Chris gives her a kiss on the cheek and places her small hand in mine.

"She's all yours, Mr. Smooth. Take care of her for me."

Eyes still on my bride, I answer, "Nothing else I'd rather do."

Chris slaps my arm and takes his place left of the altar as Jace begins the ceremony.

Emery wanted to do classic vows, and since I'd give her anything she wants, I agreed. A tear slips down her cheek as she recites her vows as practiced at last night's rehearsal. She places a thick platinum band on my ring finger, promising to love, honor, and cherish me, in sickness and health, for richer or poorer for as long as we both shall live.

"Mason, you're up."

Rhys steps up and pulls the two rings out of his pocket, placing them in the palm of my hand.

"Thanks, buddy. You're the best ring bearer a groom could ask for."

"You're welcome, Uncle Mills." He grins, his little chest puffed up proudly, and steps back in line with his other uncles.

Lifting her hand, I slide the platinum pavé diamond encrusted band down her ring finger as Jace leads me through our vows.

Jace stops, waiting for me to continue with my surprise.

"Baby doll, I know this wasn't part of the plan, but I promise I won't take too long."

Emery cocks her brow in question, and I wink at her. I'm going off-script now.

"My beautiful stubborn girl," I start, holding up the matching engagement ring I had made for her between my fingers. The band itself looks like her wedding band, but the stone in the middle is deep red.

She gasps, eyes wide, at the three-carat square garnet diamond. "What did you do?"

Our friends and family chuckle as more tears roll down her cheeks.

"I couldn't let you walk around with just that simple ring. I needed you to look down at your hand and be reminded of my undying love for you. You are the piece of me I never knew I needed and can't live without. I love you, Emery. I will always love you." I slide the ring down her finger, kissing the stone as a symbol of my devotion to her. To us.

"I love you so much, Mason. You and your love have made me whole. Something I never thought I'd have. Thank you for charming your way into my life."

Emery sniffles as I wipe the tears off her face with a stupidly happy grin on my face.

"Only for you, baby doll. Only ever for you."

"Since there isn't a dry eye in the room, I think it's time. Mason. Emery. With the power vested in me by the state of Oregon, I now pronounce you husband and wife. You may kiss your bride," Jace announces.

I wrap my arms around Emery and crush my lips to hers, dipping her back as I not-so-chastely kiss the hell out of my wife, easily making this the happiest moment of my life.

THE END

Stay connected

Website lawritesromance.com
Instagram @leslieann.author
Tiktok @leslieann.author
Facebook @Leslie Ann
Pinterest @Leslie Ann Author
Amazon @lawritesromance
BookBub @LeslieAnnAuthor

Scan the QR Code to visit my website, sign up for my newsletter and gain access to extras like Mason and Emery's spicy bonus scene.

About the author

LESLIE ANN RESIDES IN Westchester, NY with her husband, three sons, and wildly friendly dog, Pepper.

This pink-haired, sneaker-wearing Cali girl is, and always will be, an avid reader of all things romance. She loves tea, summer, cooking, arts & crafts, and chilling at home with a glass of wine. When she's not reading or writing, she's watching her boys play soccer or watching their favorite team play.

You can bet her stories will be steamy and have that happily ever after you crave.

Every. Time.

Back of the book stuff

First, THANK YOU, my lovely reader, for taking a chance on me and reading my story. As a romance reader myself, I aim to give you all the feels and HEAs I love when reading.

To my wonderful ARC Team. Thank you so much for reading, reviewing, and posting about Mason's story. Your time and energy is beyond appreciated. I am forever grateful for your love and support.

Lakshmi, thanks a million for your help with the Beta read. Your notes and comments were not only helpful, they cracked me up. You rock!

To my editor, Nina, thank you so much for your encouraging notes and editing expertise. As usual, you put your shine on my words and took my story to the next level.

Echo, thank you for creating the perfect cover for Mason and Emery. I don't think I will ever stop squealing when I see it.

C, thank you for your never-ending questions about the quiet brother. Without you, there wouldn't be a Miller Brothers series. NEVER stop picking my brain. Enjoy your lover.

Mommy—aka my number one fan—thank you for ... everything. I'd be nothing without you.

To the men in my life, thank you so much for your support. I know it's not easy when I am in the thick of it, but you hang in there and for that, I can't tell you I LOVE YOU enough.

Printed by Amazon Italia Logistica S.r.l.
Torrazza Piemonte (TO), Italy

59550250R00256